"Oh, cruel angel."

"*W*hy do you call me that? Is that a name you give many of your London ladies?" said Lucy.

"No, only you." He touched a fingertip—only a fingertip—to her cheek. Her skin was warm, even in the night air, and soft, so soft.

Then she stepped away. "I don't believe you."

Did she sound breathless? He grinned like a demon in the dark, but didn't answer. God, he wished he could simply pull her into his arms, open her sweet lips beneath his, feel her breath in his mouth, and her breasts against his chest. He stood and ventured a step toward her, until they almost touched and she had to turn her pale face up to his.

A lock of her hair bridged the scant inches between them and caressed his throat. She reached her hand out, hesitated, then touched his cheek lightly with one fingertip. He felt the contact sizzle throughout his body down to his very toes.

The Serpent Prince

"4½ Stars! TOP PICK! Fantastic... magically blends fairy tale, reality, and romance in a delicious, sensual feast."
—*RT Book Reviews*

"Exquisite romance... mesmerizing storytelling... incredibly vivid lead characters, earthy writing, and an intense love story." —*Publishers Weekly*

Praise for
The Legend of the Four Soldiers Series

To Taste Temptation

"Hoyt... is firmly in control of her craft with engaging characters, gripping plot, and clever dialogue."
—*Publishers Weekly*

"4½ Stars! Hoyt's new series... begins with destruction and ends with glorious love. She begins each chapter with a snippet of a legend that beautifully dovetails with the plot and creates a distinct love story that will thrill readers." —*RT Book Reviews*

To Seduce a Sinner

"4½ Stars! TOP PICK! Hoyt's magical fairy-tale romances have won the hearts of readers who adore sizzling sensuality perfectly merged with poignancy. Her latest showcases her talent for creating remarkable characters and cherished stories that make us believe in the miracle of love." —*RT Book Reviews*

"Hoyt expertly sifts a generous measure of danger into the latest intriguing addition to her Four Soldiers, Georgian-era series. Her ability to fuse wicked wittiness with sinfully sensual romance is stunning."　　　　　—*Booklist*

To Beguile a Beast

"Hoyt works her own brand of literary magic...in the exquisitely romantic, superbly sensual third addition to her extraordinary Georgian-set Legend of the Four Soldiers series."　　　　　—*Booklist*

"4½ Stars! TOP PICK! A magical love story that reads like a mystical fable and a very real and highly passionate romance. Hoyt has found a unique niche that highlights both her storytelling abilities and her considerable talents for depth of character and emotion."

—*RT Book Reviews*

To Desire a Devil

"Rich with dangerous intrigue, suffused with desire, and spiked with wit, *To Desire a Devil* is nothing less than brilliant."　　　　　—*Booklist* (starred review)

"4½ Stars! TOP PICK! The kind of powerfully emotional, sensual romance, tinged with fairy tale, that readers have come to expect from this gifted storyteller."

—*RT Book Reviews*

ELIZABETH HOYT

THE SERPENT PRINCE

GC

GRAND CENTRAL
PUBLISHING

NEW YORK BOSTON

Copyright © 2007 by Nancy M. Finney
Excerpt from *To Taste Temptation* copyright © 2008 by Nancy M. Finney
Excerpt from *Thief of Shadows* copyright © 2011 by Nancy M. Finney

Grand Central Publishing
Hachette Book Group
237 Park Avenue
New York, NY 10017
www.HachetteBookGroup.com

Grand Central Publishing is a division of Hachette Book Group, Inc.
The Grand Central Publishing name and logo is a trademark of Hachette Book Group, Inc.

The publisher is not responsible for websites (or their content) that are not owned by the publisher.

Printed in the United States of America

First printing: September 2007
Reissued: August 2010
First limited edition printing: April 2012

10 9 8 7 6 5 4 3 2 1

For JADE LEE, the critique partner who has it all: coffee, chocolate, and wisdom...not necessarily in that order.

Acknowledgments

Thank you to MELANIE MURRAY, a wise and wonderful editor, and to my agent, SUSANNAH TAYLOR, for always watching out for the details.

Chapter One

The dead man at Lucinda Craddock-Hayes's feet looked like a fallen god. Apollo, or more likely Mars, the bringer of war, having taken human form and struck down from the heavens to be found by a maiden on her way home. Except that gods rarely bled.

Or died, for that matter.

"Mr. Hedge," Lucy called over her shoulder.

She glanced around the lonely lane leading from the town of Maiden Hill to the Craddock-Hayes house. It appeared the same as it had been before she'd made her find: deserted, except for herself; her manservant, puffing a ways behind her; and the corpse lying in the ditch. The sky hung low and wintry gray. The light had already begun to leak away, though it was not yet five o'clock. Leafless trees lined the road, silent and chill.

Lucy shivered and drew her wrap more closely about her shoulders. The dead man sprawled, naked, battered, and facedown. The long lines of his back were marred by a mass of blood on his right shoulder. Below were lean hips; muscular, hairy legs; and curiously elegant, bony feet. She blinked and returned her gaze to his face. Even in death he was handsome. His head, turned to the side, revealed a patrician profile: long nose, high bony cheeks, and a wide mouth. An eyebrow, winging over his closed eye, was bisected by a scar. Closely cropped pale hair grew flat to his skull, except where it was matted by blood. His left hand was flung above his head, and on the index finger was the impression where a ring should have been. His killers must've stolen it along with everything else. Around the body the mud was scuffed, the imprint of a boot heel stamped deep beside the dead man's hip. Other than that, there was no sign of whoever had dumped him here like so much offal.

Lucy felt silly tears prick at her eyes. Something about the way that he'd been left, naked and degraded by his murderers, seemed a terrible insult to the man. It was so unbearably sad. *Ninny,* she chided herself. She became conscious of a muttering, drawing steadily closer. Hastily, she swiped at the moisture on her cheeks.

"First she visits the Joneses and all the little Joneses, snotty-nosed buggers. Then we march up the hill to Old Woman Hardy—nasty biddy, don't know why she hasn't been put to bed with a shovel yet. And is that all? No, that's not all by half. Then, *then* she must needs call round the vicarage. And me carting great jars of jelly all the while."

Lucy suppressed the urge to roll her eyes. Hedge, her man, wore a greasy tricorne smashed down over a shock of gray hair. His dusty coat and waistcoat were equally disreputable, and he'd chosen to highlight his bowlegs with scarlet-clocked stockings, no doubt Papa's castoffs.

He halted beside her. "Oh, gah, not a deader!"

In his surprise, the little man had forgotten to stoop, but when she turned to him, his wiry body decayed before her eyes. His back curved, the shoulder bearing the awful weight of her now-empty basket fell, and his head hung to the side listlessly. As the pièce de résistance, Hedge took out a checkered cloth and laboriously wiped his forehead.

Lucy ignored all this. She'd seen the act hundreds, if not thousands, of times in her life. "I don't know that I would have described him as a *deader*, but he is indeed a corpse."

"Well, best not stand here gawping. Let the dead rest in peace, I always say." Hedge made to sidle past her.

She placed herself in his path. "We can't just leave him here."

"Why not? He was here before you trotted past. Wouldn't never have seen him, neither, if we'd've taken the shortcut through the common like I said."

"Nevertheless, we did find him. Can you help me carry him?"

Hedge staggered back in patent disbelief. "Carry him? A great big bloke like that? Not unless you want me crippled for sure. My back's bad as it is, has been for twenty years. I don't complain, but still."

"Very well," Lucy conceded. "We'll have to get a cart."

"Why don't we just leave him be?" the little man protested. "Someone'll find him in a bit."

"Mr. Hedge . . ."

"He's stabbed through the shoulder and all over bloody. It's not nice, that." Hedge screwed up his face until it resembled a rotted pumpkin.

"I'm sure he didn't mean to be stabbed, through the shoulder or not, so I don't think we can hold that against him," Lucy chided.

"But he's begun to go off!" Hedge waved the handkerchief in front of his nose.

Lucy didn't mention that there hadn't been any smell until he'd arrived. "I'll wait while you go fetch Bob Smith and his cart."

The manservant's bushy gray eyebrows drew together in imminent opposition.

"Unless you would prefer to stay here with the body?"

Hedge's brow cleared. "No, mum. You knows best, I'm sure. I'll just trot on over to the smithy—"

The corpse groaned.

Lucy looked down in surprise.

Beside her, Hedge jumped back and stated the obvious for both of them. "Jaysus Almighty Christ! That man ain't dead!"

Dear Lord. And she'd been standing here all this while, bickering with Hedge. Lucy swept off her wrap and threw it across the man's back. "Hand me your coat."

"But—"

"Now!" Lucy didn't bother giving Hedge a look. She rarely used a sharp tone of voice, making it all the more effective when she did employ it.

"Awww," the manservant moaned, but he tossed the coat to her.

"Go fetch Doctor Fremont. Tell him it's urgent, and he must come at once." Lucy gazed sternly into her manservant's beady eyes. "And, Mr. Hedge?"

"Yes'm?"

"Please run."

Hedge dropped the basket and took off, moving surprisingly fast, his bad back forgotten.

Lucy bent and tucked Hedge's coat around the man's buttocks and legs. She held her hand under his nose and waited, barely breathing, until she felt the faint brush of air. He was indeed alive. She sat back on her heels and contemplated the situation. The man lay on the half-frozen mud and weeds of the ditch—both cold and hard. That couldn't be good for him, considering his wounds. But as Hedge had noted, he was a big man, and she wasn't sure she could move him by herself. She peeled back a corner of the wrap covering his back. The slit in his shoulder was crusted with dried gore, the bleeding already stopped to her admittedly inexperienced eyes. Bruises bloomed across his back and side. Lord only knew what the front of him looked like.

And then there was the head wound.

She shook her head. He lay so still and white. No wonder she'd mistaken him for dead. But all the same, Hedge could've already been on his way to Doctor Fremont in the time they'd taken to argue over the poor man.

Lucy checked again that he was breathing, her palm hovering above his lips. His breath was light but even. She smoothed the back of her hand over his cold cheek. Almost invisible stubble caught at her fingers. Who was he? Maiden Hill was not so big that a stranger could pass through it without notice. Yet she had heard no gossip about visitors on her rounds this afternoon. Somehow he'd appeared here in the lane without anyone noticing. Then, too, the man had been obviously beaten and robbed. Why? Was he merely a victim, or had he somehow brought this fate upon himself?

Lucy hugged herself on the last thought and prayed Hedge would hurry. The light was fading fast and with it what little warmth the day had held. A wounded man lying exposed to the elements for Lord knows how long . . . She bit her lip.

If Hedge didn't return soon, there would be no need of a doctor.

"HE'S DEAD."

The harsh words, spoken at Sir Rupert Fletcher's side, were much too loud in the crowded ballroom. He glanced around to see who stood near enough to overhear, then stepped closer to the speaker, Quincy James.

Sir Rupert gripped the ebony cane in his right hand, trying not to let his irritation show. Or his surprise. "What do you mean?"

"Just what I said." James smirked. "He's dead."

"You've killed him?"

"Not me. I sent my men to do it."

Sir Rupert frowned, trying to comprehend this information. James had settled on a course of action by himself, and it had succeeded? "How many?" he abruptly asked. "Your men."

The younger man shrugged. "Three. More than enough."

"When?"

"Early this morning. I had a report just before I left." James flashed a cocky grin that gave him boyish dimples. Seeing his light blue eyes, regular English features, and athletic form, most would think him a pleasant, even attractive, young man.

Most would be wrong.

"I trust the matter cannot be traced back to you." Despite his efforts, an edge must've crept into Sir Rupert's voice.

James lost the smile. "Dead men can't tell tales."

"Humph." *What an idiot.* "Where did they do it?"

"Outside his town house."

Sir Rupert swore softly. To waylay a peer of the realm outside his own home in broad daylight was the work of a half-wit. His bad leg was giving him the very devil tonight and now this nonsense from James. He leaned more heavily on the ebony cane as he tried to think.

"Don't get worked up." James smiled nervously. "N-n-no one saw them."

The elder man arched an eyebrow. Lord save him from aristocrats who decided to think—let alone act—on their own. There'd been too many generations of leisure for the typical lordling to easily find his own prick to piss with, never mind something more complicated like planning an assassination.

James was blithely unaware of Sir Rupert's thoughts. "Besides, they stripped the body and dumped it half a day's ride outside London. Nobody'll know him there. By the time it's found, there won't be much to recognize, will there? P-p-perfectly safe." The younger man's hand crawled up to poke a finger into his golden-yellow hair. He wore it unpowdered, probably as a vanity.

Sir Rupert took a sip of Madeira as he contemplated this latest development. The ballroom was a stifling crush, redolent of burning wax, heavy perfume, and body odor. The French doors leading into the garden had been thrown open to let in the cool night air, but they had little effect on the room's heat. The punch had given out a half hour before, and there were several hours yet before the midnight buffet. Sir Rupert grimaced. He didn't hold out much hope for the refreshments. Lord Harrington, his host, was notoriously stingy, even when entertaining the cream of society—and a few upstarts such as Sir Rupert.

A narrow space had been cleared in the middle of the room for the dancers. They swirled in a rainbow of colors. Lasses in embroidered gowns and powdered hair. Gentlemen turned out in wigs and their uncomfortable best. He didn't envy the young people the pretty movements. They must be dripping sweat under their silks and lace. Lord Harrington would be gratified at the massive turnout so early in the season—or rather, Lady Harrington would. That lady had five unmarried daughters, and she marshaled her forces like an experienced campaigner readying for battle. Four of her daughters were on the floor, each on the arm of an eligible gentleman.

Not that he could stand in judgment with three daughters under the age of four and twenty himself. All of them out of the schoolroom, all of them in need of suitable husbands. In fact . . . Matilda caught his eye from some twenty paces away where she stood with Sarah. She arched a brow and looked meaningfully at young Quincy James, who was still standing beside him.

Sir Rupert shook his head slightly—he'd rather let one of his daughters marry a rabid dog. Their communication was well developed after nearly three decades of marriage. His lady wife turned smoothly away to chat animatedly with another matron without ever revealing that she had exchanged information with her husband. Later tonight she might quiz him about James and ask why the young man wasn't up to snuff, but she wouldn't dream of badgering her husband right now.

If only his other partners were so circumspect.

"I don't know why you're worried." James apparently couldn't stand the silence anymore. "He never knew about you. Nobody knew about you."

"And I prefer to keep it that way," Sir Rupert said mildly. "For all of our sakes."

"I wager you would. You left m-m-me and Walker and the other two for him to hunt in your stead."

"He would've found you and the others in any case."

"There's s-s-some who would still like to know about you." James scratched at his scalp so violently he nearly dislodged his queue.

"But it would not be in your best interest to betray me," Sir Rupert said flatly. He bowed to a passing acquaintance.

"I'm not saying I would let it out."

"Good. You profited as much as I from the business."

"Yes, but—"

"Then all's well that ends well."

"Easy for y-y-you to s-s-say." James's stutter was growing more frequent, a sign the man was agitated. "You didn't see Hartwell's body. He was skewered through the throat. Must've bled to death. His seconds said the duel lasted only two minutes—two minutes, mind you. A-a-awful."

"You're a better swordsman than Hartwell ever was," Sir Rupert said.

He smiled as his eldest, Julia, started a minuet. She was wearing a gown in a becoming shade of blue. Had he seen it before? He thought not. It must be new. Hopefully it hadn't beggared him. Her partner was an earl past his for-tieth year. A mite old, but still, an earl . . .

"P-p-peller was an excellent swordsman, too, and he was k-k-killed first." James's hysterical voice interrupted Sir Rupert's thoughts.

He was too loud. Sir Rupert tried to calm him. "James—"

"Challenged at night and d-d-dead before breakfast the next morn!"

"I don't think—"

"He lost three f-f-fingers trying to defend himself after the s-s-sword was wrenched from his hand. I had to search the g-g-grass for them afterward. G-g-god!"

Nearby heads swiveled their way. The younger man's tone was growing louder.

Time to part.

"It's over." Sir Rupert turned his head to meet James's gaze, holding and quelling him.

There was a tic under the other man's right eye. He in-haled to begin speaking.

Sir Rupert got there first, his voice mild. "He's dead. You've just told me."

"B-b-but—"

"Therefore, we have nothing further to worry about." Sir Rupert bowed and limped away. He badly needed an-other glass of Madeira.

"I'LL NOT HAVE HIM IN MY HOUSE," Captain Craddock-Hayes pronounced, arms crossed over his barrel chest, feet braced as if on a rolling deck. His bewigged head was held high, sea-blue eyes pinned on a distant horizon.

He stood in the entrance hall to Craddock-Hayes house.

Usually the hall was quite large enough for their needs. Right now, though, the hall seemed to have shrunk in proportion to the amount of people it held, Lucy thought ruefully, and the captain was right in the center of it.

"Yes, Papa." She dodged around him and waved the men carrying her stranger farther in. "Upstairs in my brother's bedroom, I think. Don't you agree, Mrs. Brodie?"

"Of course, miss." The Craddock-Hayes housekeeper nodded. The frill of her mobcap, framing red cheeks, bobbed in time with the movement. "The bed's already made, and I can have the fire started in a tick."

"Good." Lucy smiled in approval. "Thank you, Mrs. Brodie."

The housekeeper hurried up the stairs, her ample bottom swaying with each step.

"Don't even know who the blighter is," her father continued. "Might be some tramp or murderer. Hedge said he was stabbed in the back. I ask you, what sort of a chap gets himself stabbed? Eh? Eh?"

"I don't know, I'm sure," Lucy answered automatically. "Would you mind moving to the side so the men can carry him past?"

Papa shuffled obediently nearer the wall.

The laborers panted as they wrestled the wounded stranger inside. He lay so terribly still, his face pale as death. Lucy bit her lip and tried not to let her anxiety show. She didn't know him, didn't even know the color of his eyes; and yet it was vitally important that he live. He'd been placed on a door to make it easier to carry him, but it was obvious that his weight and height still made the maneuver difficult. One of the men swore.

"Won't have such language in my house." The captain glared at the offender.

The man flushed and mumbled an apology.

Papa nodded. "What kind of a father would I be if I allowed any sort of gypsy or layabout into my home? With an unmarried gel in residence? Eh? A damned rotten one, that's what."

"Yes, Papa." Lucy held her breath as the men negotiated the stairs.

"That's why the blighter must be taken somewhere else—Fremont's house. He's the doctor. Or the poorhouse. Maybe the vicarage—Penweeble can have a chance to show some Christian kindness. Ha."

"You're quite right, but he's already here," Lucy said soothingly. "It would be a shame to have to move him again."

One of the men on the stairs gave her a wild-eyed look.

Lucy smiled back reassuringly.

"Probably won't live long in any case." Papa scowled. "No point ruining good sheets."

"I'll make sure the sheets survive." Lucy started up the stairs.

"And what about my supper?" her father grumbled behind her. "Eh? Is anyone seeing to that while they rush about making room for scoundrels?"

Lucy leaned over the rail. "We'll have supper on the table just as soon as I can see him settled."

Papa grunted. "Fine thing when the master of the house waits on the comfort of ruffians."

"You're being most understanding." Lucy smiled at her father.

"Humph."

She turned to go up the stairs.

"Poppet?"

Lucy stuck her head back over the rail.

Her father was frowning up at her, bushy white eyebrows drawn together over the bridge of his bulbous red nose. "Be careful with that fellow."

"Yes, Papa."

"Humph," her father muttered again behind her.

But Lucy hurried up the stairs and into the blue bedroom. The men had already transferred the stranger to the bed. They tramped back out of the room as Lucy entered, leaving a trail of mud.

"You shouldn't be in here, Miss Lucy." Mrs. Brodie gasped and pulled the sheet over the man's chest. "Not with him like this."

"I saw him in far less just an hour ago, Mrs. Brodie, I assure you. At least now he's bandaged."

Mrs. Brodie snorted. "Not the important parts."

"Well, maybe not," Lucy conceded. "But I hardly think he poses any risk, the condition he's in."

"Aye, poor gentleman." Mrs. Brodie patted the sheet covering the man's chest. "He's lucky that you found him when you did. He'd've been frozen by morn for sure, left out there on the road. Who could've done such a wicked thing?"

"I don't know."

"Nobody from Maiden Hill, I'm thinking." The housekeeper shook her head. "Must be riffraff down from London."

Lucy didn't point out that riffraff could be found even in

Maiden Hill. "Doctor Fremont said he'd be around again in the morning to check his bandages."

"Aye." Mrs. Brodie looked doubtfully at the patient, as if assessing his odds of living to the next day.

Lucy took a deep breath. "Until then, I suppose we can only make him comfortable. We'll leave the door ajar in case he wakes."

"I'd best be seeing to the captain's supper. You know how he gets if it's late. As soon as it's on the table, I'll send Betsy up to watch him."

Lucy nodded. They only had the one maid, Betsy, but between the three women, they should be able to nurse the stranger. "You go. I'll be down in a minute."

"Very well, miss." Mrs. Brodie gave her an old-fashioned look. "But don't be too long. Your father will be wanting to talk to you."

Lucy wrinkled her nose and nodded. Mrs. Brodie smiled in sympathy and left.

Lucy looked down at the stranger in her brother, David's, bed and wondered again, who was he? He was so motionless that she had to concentrate to see the slight rise and fall of his chest. The bandages about his head only emphasized his infirmity and highlighted the bruising on his brow. He looked so terribly alone. Was anyone worried about him, perhaps anxiously awaiting his return?

One of his arms lay outside the covers. She touched it.

His hand flashed up and struck at her wrist, capturing and holding it. Lucy was so startled she only had time for a frightened squeak. Then she was staring into the palest eyes she'd ever seen. They were the color of ice.

"I'm going to kill you," he said distinctly.

For a moment, she thought the grim words were for her, and her heart seemed to stop in her breast.

His gaze shifted past her. "Ethan?" The man frowned as if puzzled, and then he shut his weird eyes. Within a minute, the grip on her wrist grew slack and his arm fell back to the bed.

Lucy drew a breath. Judging from the ache in her chest, it was the first breath she'd taken since the man had seized her. She stepped back from the bed and rubbed her tender wrist. The man's hand had been brutal; she'd have bruises in the morning.

Whom had he spoken to?

Lucy shuddered. Whoever it was, she did not envy him. The man's voice held not a trace of indecision. In his own mind, there was no doubt that he would kill his enemy. She glanced again at the bed. The stranger was breathing slowly and deeply now. He looked like he was slumbering peacefully. If not for the pain in her wrist, she might have thought the whole incident a dream.

"Lucy!" The bellow from below could only be her father.

Gathering her skirts, she left the room and ran down the stairs.

Papa was already seated at the head of the dinner table, a cloth tucked in at his neck. "Don't like a late supper. Puts my digestion off. Can't sleep half the night because of the gurgling. Is it too much to ask for dinner to be on time in my own home? Is it? Eh?"

"No, of course not." Lucy sat in her chair at the right of her father. "I'm sorry."

Mrs. Brodie brought in a steaming roast beef crowded with potatoes, leeks, and turnips.

"Ha. That's what a man likes to see on his dinner table." Papa positively beamed as he picked up his knife and fork in preparation for carving. "A good English beef. Smells most delicious."

"Thank you, sir." The housekeeper winked at Lucy as she turned back to the kitchen.

Lucy smiled back. Thank goodness for Mrs. Brodie.

"Now, then, have a bite of that." Papa handed her a plate heaped with food. "Mrs. Brodie knows how to make a fine roast beef."

"Thank you."

"Tastiest in the county. Need a bit of sustenance after gallivantin' all over the place this afternoon. Eh?"

"How have your memoirs gone today?" Lucy sipped her wine, trying not to think of the man lying upstairs.

"Excellent. Excellent." Papa sawed enthusiastically at the roast beef. "Put down a scandalous tale from thirty years ago. About Captain Feather—he's an admiral now, damn him—and three native island women. D'you know these native gels don't wear any—*Ahurmph!*" He suddenly coughed and looked at her in what seemed like embarrassment.

"Yes?" Lucy popped a forkful of potato into her mouth.

"Never mind. Never mind." Papa finished filling his plate and pulled it to where his belly met the table. "Let's just say it'll light a fire under the old boy after all this time. Ha!"

"How delightful." Lucy smiled. If Papa ever did finish his memoirs and publish them, there would be a score of apoplectic fits in His Majesty's navy.

"Quite. Quite." Papa swallowed and took a sip of wine.

"Now, then. I don't want you worrying over this scoundrel you've brought home."

Lucy's gaze dropped to the fork she held. It trembled slightly, and she hoped her father wouldn't notice the movement. "No, Papa."

"You've done a good deed, Samaritan and all that. Just as your mother used to teach you from the Bible. She'd approve. But remember"—he forked up a turnip—"I've seen head wounds before. Some live. Some don't. And there's not a blessed thing you can do about it either way."

She felt her heart sink in her chest. "You don't think he'll live?"

"Don't know," Papa barked impatiently. "That's what I'm saying. He might. He might not."

"I see." Lucy poked at a turnip and tried not to let the tears start.

Her father slammed the flat of his hand down on the table. "This is just what I'm warning you about. Don't get attached to the tramp."

A corner of Lucy's mouth twitched up. "But you can't keep me from feeling," she said gently. "I'll do it no matter if I want to or not."

Papa frowned ferociously. "Don't want you to be sad if he pops off in the night."

"I'll do my very best not to be sad, Papa," Lucy promised. But she knew it was too late for that. If the man died tonight, she would weep on the morrow, promises or no.

"Humph." Her father returned to his plate. "Good enough for now. If he survives, though, mark my words." He looked up and pinned her with his azure eyes. "He even thinks about hurting one hair on your head, and out he goes on his arse."

Chapter Two

The angel was sitting by his bed when Simon Iddesleigh, sixth Viscount Iddesleigh, opened his eyes.

He would've thought it a terrible dream, one of an endless succession that haunted him nightly—or worse, that he'd not survived the beating and had made that final infinite plunge out of this world and into the flaming next. But he was almost certain hell did not smell of lavender and starch, did not feel like worn linen and down pillows, did not sound with the chirping of sparrows and the rustle of gauze curtains.

And, of course, there were no angels in hell.

Simon watched her. His angel was all in gray, as befit a religious woman. She wrote in a great book, eyes intent, level black brows knit. Her dark hair was pulled straight back from a high forehead and gathered in a knot at the nape of her neck. Her lips pursed slightly as her hand moved across the page. Probably noting his sins. The scratch of the pen on the page was what had woken him.

When men spoke of angels, especially in the context of the female sex, usually they were employing a flowery

fillip of speech. They thought of fair-haired creatures with
pink cheeks—both kinds—and red, wet lips. Insipid Italian
putti with vacant blue eyes and billowy, soft flesh came to
mind. That was not the type of angel Simon contemplated.
No, his angel was the biblical kind—Old Testament, not
New. The not-quite-human, stern-and-judgmental kind.
The type that was more apt to hurl men into eternal damnation with a flick of a dispassionate finger than to float
on feathery pigeon wings. She wasn't likely to overlook
a few flaws here and there in a fellow's character. Simon
sighed.

He had more than just a few flaws.

The angel must have heard his sigh. She turned her un-
earthly topaz eyes on him. "Are you awake?"

He felt her gaze as palpably as if she'd laid a hand on
his shoulder, and frankly the feeling bothered him.

Not that he let his unease show. "That depends on one's
definition of *awake*," he replied in a croak. Even the little
movement of speaking made his face hurt. In fact, his entire body seemed aflame. "I am not sleeping, yet I have
been more alert. I don't suppose you have such a thing as
coffee to hasten the awakening process?" He shifted to sit
up, finding it more difficult than it should be. The coverlet
slipped to his abdomen.

The angel's gaze followed the coverlet down, and
she frowned at his bare torso. Already he was in her bad
graces.

"I'm afraid we don't have any coffee," she murmured to
his navel, "but there is tea."

"Naturally. There always is," Simon said. "Could I
trouble you to help me sit up? One finds oneself at a distressing disadvantage flat on one's back, not to mention

the position makes it very hard to drink tea without spilling it into the ears."

She looked at him doubtfully. "Perhaps I should get Hedge or my father."

"I promise not to bite, truly." Simon placed a hand over his heart. "And I hardly ever spit."

Her lips twitched.

Simon stilled. "You're not really an angel after all, are you?"

One ebony brow arched ever so slightly. Such a disdainful look for a country miss; her expression would've fit a duchess. "My name is Lucinda Craddock-Hayes. What is yours?"

"Simon Matthew Raphael Iddesleigh, viscount of, I'm afraid." He sketched a bow, which came off rather well in his opinion, considering he was prostrate.

The lady was unimpressed. "You're the Viscount Iddesleigh?"

"Sadly."

"You're not from around here."

"Here would be . . . ?"

"The town of Maiden Hill in Kent."

"Ah." Kent? Why Kent? Simon craned his neck to try and see out the window, but the gauzy white curtain obscured it.

She followed his gaze. "You're in my brother's bedroom."

"Kind of him," Simon muttered. Turning his head had made him realize something was wrapped about it. He felt with one hand, and his fingers encountered a bandage. Probably made him look a right fool. "No, I can't say I've ever been to the lovely town of Maiden Hill; although

I'm sure it's quite scenic and the church a famous touring highlight."

Her full, red lips twitched again bewitchingly. "How did you know?"

"They always are in the nicest towns." He looked down—ostensibly to adjust the coverlet, in reality to avoid the strange temptation of those lips. *Coward.* "I spend most of my wasted time in London. My own neglected estate lies to the north in Northumberland. Ever been to Northumberland?"

She shook her head. Her lovely topaz eyes watched him with a disconcertingly level stare—almost like a man. Except Simon had never felt stirred by a man's glance.

He tsked. "Very rural. Hence the appellative *neglected.* One wonders what one's ancestors were thinking, precisely, when they built the old pile of masonry so far out of the way of anything. Nothing but mist and sheep nearby. Still, been in the family for ages; might as well keep it."

"How good of you," the lady murmured. "But it does make me wonder why we found you only a half mile from here if you've never been in the area before?"

Quick, wasn't she? And not at all sidetracked by his blather. Intelligent women were such a bother. Which was why he should not be so fascinated by this one.

"Haven't the foggiest." Simon opened his eyes wide. "Perhaps I had the good fortune to be attacked by industrious thieves. Not content to leave me lie where I fell, they spirited me off here so I might see more of the world."

"Humph. I doubt they meant for you to see anything ever again," she said quellingly.

"Mmm. And wouldn't that've been a shame?" he asked in false innocence. "For then I wouldn't have met you."

The lady raised a brow and opened her mouth again, no doubt to practice her inquisition skills on him, but Simon beat her to it. "You did say there was tea about? I know I spoke of it disparagingly before, but really, I wouldn't mind a drop or two."

His angel actually flushed, a pale rose wash coloring her white cheeks. Ah, a weakness. "I'm sorry. Here, let me help you sit up."

She placed cool little hands on his arms—an unsettlingly erotic touch—and between them they managed to get him upright; although, by the time they did so, Simon was panting, and not just from her. His shoulder felt like little devils, or maybe saints in his case, were poking red-hot irons into it. He closed his eyes for a second, and when he opened them again, there was a cup of tea under his nose. He reached for it, then stopped and stared at his bare right hand. His signet ring was missing. They'd stolen his ring.

She mistook the reason for his hesitation. "The tea is fresh, I assure you."

"Most kind." His voice was embarrassingly weak. His hand shook as he grasped the cup, the familiar clink of his ring against the porcelain absent. He hadn't taken it off since Ethan's death. *"Damn."*

"Don't worry. I'll hold it for you." Her tone was soft, low and intimate, though she probably didn't know it. He could rest on that voice, float away on it and let his cares cease.

Dangerous woman.

Simon swallowed the lukewarm tea. "Would you mind terribly writing a letter for me?"

"Of course not." She set the cup down and withdrew safely to her chair. "To whom would you like to write?"

"My valet, I think. Bound to be teased if I alert any of my acquaintances."

"And we certainly wouldn't want that." There was laughter in her voice.

He looked at her sharply, but her eyes were wide and innocent. "I'm glad you understand the problem," he said dryly. Actually, he was more worried that his enemies would learn that he was still alive. "My valet can bring down miscellaneous things like clean clothes, a horse, and money."

She laid aside her still-open book. "His name?"

Simon tilted his head, but he couldn't see the book's page from this angle. "Henry. At 207 Cross Road, London. What were you writing before?"

"I beg your pardon?" She didn't look up.

Irritating. "In your book. What were you writing?"

She hesitated, the pencil immobile on the letter, her head still bent down.

Simon kept his expression light, though he grew infinitely more interested.

There was a silence as she finished scratching out the address; then she laid it aside and looked up at him. "I was sketching, actually." She reached for the open book and placed it on his lap.

Drawings or cartoons covered the left page, some big, some small. A little bent man carrying a basket. A leafless tree. A gate with one hinge broken. On the right was a single sketch of a man asleep. Himself. And not looking his best, what with the bandage and all. It was an odd feeling, knowing she had watched him sleep.

"I hope you don't mind," she said.

"Not at all. Glad to be of some use." Simon turned back a page. Here, some of the drawings had been embellished by a watercolor wash. "These are quite good."

"Thank you."

Simon felt his lips curve at her sure reply. Most ladies feigned modesty when complimented on an accomplishment. Miss Craddock-Hayes was certain of her talent. He turned another page.

"What's this?" The sketches on this page were of a tree changing with the seasons: winter, spring, summer, and fall.

The rose tinted her cheeks again. "They're practice sketches. For a small book of prayers I want to give Mrs. Hardy in the village. It's to be a present on her birthday."

"Do you do this often?" He turned another page, fascinated. These weren't the pallid drawings of a bored lady. Her sketches had a kind of robust life to them. "Illustrate books, that is?" His mind was furiously working.

She shrugged. "No, not often. I only do it for friends and such."

"Then maybe I can commission a work." He looked up in time to see her open her mouth. He continued before she could point out that he didn't fall under the heading *friends*. "A book for my niece."

She closed her mouth and raised her eyebrows, waiting silently for him to continue.

"If you don't mind humoring a wounded man, of course." Shameless. For some reason it was important that he engage her.

"What kind of a book?"

"Oh, a fairy tale, I think. Don't you?"

She took back her book and settled it on her lap, slowly turning to a blank page. "Yes?"

Oh, Christ, now he was on the spot, but at the same time he felt like laughing aloud. He hadn't felt this lighthearted in ages. Simon glanced hurriedly around the little room and caught sight of a small, framed map on the opposite wall. Sea serpents frolicked around the edges of the print. He smiled into her eyes. "The tale of the Serpent Prince."

Her gaze dropped to his lips and then hastily up again. His smile grew wider. Ah, even an angel could be tempted.

But she only arched a brow at him. "I've never heard it."

"I'm surprised," he lied easily. "It was quite a favorite of my youth. Brings back fond memories, that, of bouncing on my old nurse's knee by the fire while she thrilled us with the tale." In for a penny, in for a pound.

She gave him a patently skeptical look.

"Now let me see." Simon stifled a yawn. The pain in his shoulder had died to a dull throb, but his headache had increased as if to make up for it. "Once upon a time—that's the prescribed way to begin, isn't it?"

The lady didn't help. She merely sat back in her chair and waited for him to make a fool of himself.

"There lived a poor lass who made a meager living tending the king's goats. She was orphaned and quite alone in the world, except, of course, for the goats, who were rather smelly."

"Goats?"

"Goats. The king was fond of goat cheese. Now hush, child, if you want to hear this." Simon tilted his head back.

It was aching terribly. "I believe her name was Angelica, if that's of any interest—the goat girl, that is."

She merely nodded this time. She'd picked up a pencil and had begun sketching in her book, although he couldn't see the page, so he didn't know if she was illustrating his story or not.

"Angelica toiled every day, from the first light of dawn until the sun had long set, and all she had for company were the goats. The king's castle was built on top of a cliff, and the goat girl lived at the foot of the cliff in a little stick hut. If she looked far, far up, past the sheer rocks, past the shining white stone of the castle walls to the very turrets, sometimes she could just catch a glimpse of the castle folk in their jewels and fine robes. And once in a very great while, she would see the prince."

"The Serpent Prince?"

"No."

She cocked her head, her eyes still on her drawing. "Then why is the fairy tale called *The Serpent Prince* if he isn't the Serpent Prince?"

"He comes later. Are you always this impatient?" he asked sternly.

She glanced up at him then as her lips slowly curved into a smile. Simon was struck dumb, all thought having fled from his mind. Her fine, jeweled eyes crinkled at the corners, and a single dimple appeared on the smooth surface of her left cheek. She positively glowed. Miss Craddock-Hayes really was an angel. Simon felt a strong, almost violent, urge to thumb away that dimple. To lift her face and taste her smile.

He closed his eyes. He didn't want this.

"I'm sorry," he heard her say. "I won't interrupt again."

"No, that's all right. I'm afraid my head hurts. No doubt from having it bashed in the other day." Simon stopped babbling as something occurred to him. "When, exactly, was I found?"

"Two days ago." She rose and gathered her book and pens. "I'll leave you to rest. I can write the letter to your valet in the meantime and post it. Unless you would like to read it first?"

"No, I'm sure you'll do fine." Simon sank into the pillows, his ringless hand lax on the coverlet. He kept his voice casual. "Where are my clothes?"

She paused, halfway out, and shot him an enigmatic look over her shoulder. "You didn't have any when I found you." She closed the door quietly.

Simon blinked. Usually he didn't lose his clothes until at least the second meeting with a lady.

"THE VICAR'S HERE TO SEE YOU, MISS." Mrs. Brodie poked her head into the sitting room the next morning.

Lucy sat on the blue damask settee, darning one of Papa's socks. She sighed and glanced at the ceiling, wondering if the viscount had heard her visitor below his window. She didn't even know if he was awake yet; she hadn't seen him this morning. Something about his amused gray eyes, so alert and alive, had flustered her yesterday. She was unaccustomed to being flustered, and the experience wasn't pleasant. Hence her cowardly avoidance of the wounded man since leaving him to write his letter.

She laid aside her mending now. "Thank you, Mrs. Brodie."

The housekeeper gave her a wink before hurrying back

to the kitchen, and Lucy rose to greet Eustace. "Good morning."

Eustace Penweeble, the vicar of Maiden Hill's little church, nodded his head at her as he had every Tuesday, barring holidays and bad weather, for the past three years. He smiled shyly, running his big, square hands around the brim of the tricorne he was holding. "It's a beautiful day. Would you care to come with me as I make my rounds?"

"That sounds lovely."

"Good. Good," he replied.

A lock of brown hair escaped from his queue and fell over his forehead, making him look like an immense little boy. He must have forgotten the powdered, bobbed wig of his station again. Just as well. Lucy privately thought he looked better without it. She smiled at him fondly, gathered her waiting wrap, and preceded Eustace out the door.

The day was indeed beautiful. The sun was so bright it nearly blinded her as she stood on the granite front step. The ancient orange brick of Craddock-Hayes House looked mellow, the light reflecting off the mullioned windows in front. Old oak trees lined the gravel drive. They'd already lost their leaves, but their crooked branches made interesting shapes against the crisp, blue sky. Eustace's trap waited near the door, Hedge at the horse's head.

"May I assist you in?" Eustace asked politely as if she might actually turn him down.

Lucy placed her hand in his.

Hedge rolled his eyes and muttered under his breath, "Every blamed Tuesday. Why not a Thursday or Friday, for Jaysus' sake?"

Eustace frowned.

"Thank you." Lucy's voice overrode the manservant's,

drawing Eustace's eyes away from him. She made a production out of settling herself.

The vicar got in next to her and took the reins. Hedge retreated to the house, shaking his head.

"I thought we'd drive around to the church, if that meets with your approval." Eustace chirruped to the horse. "The sexton has alerted me that there may be a leak in the roof over the vestry. You can give me your opinion."

Lucy just refrained from murmuring an automatic *how delightful*. She smiled instead. They bowled out of the Craddock-Hayes drive and into the lane where she'd found the viscount. The road looked innocent enough in the light of day, the empty trees no longer menacing. They topped a rise. Dry stone walls rolled over the chalk hills in the distance.

Eustace cleared his throat. "You visited Mistress Hardy recently, I understand?"

"Yes." Lucy turned to him politely. "I brought her some calf's foot jelly."

"And how did you find her? Has her ankle healed from the tumble she took?"

"She still had it up, but she was feisty enough to complain that the jelly was not as tasty as hers."

"Ah, good. She must be getting better if she can complain."

"That's what I thought myself."

Eustace smiled at her, coffee-brown eyes crinkling at the corners. "You're a wonderful help to me, keeping track of the villagers."

Lucy nodded and tilted her face into the wind. Eustace frequently made similar comments. In the past they'd been comforting, if dull. Today, though, she found his complacency slightly irritating.

But Eustace was still talking. "I wish some of the other ladies of the village would be so charitable."

"Who do you mean?"

A wash of red stained his cheekbones. "Your friend Miss McCullough, for one. She spends most of her time gossiping, I think."

Lucy raised her eyebrows. "Patricia does like a good gossip, but she's really quite kind underneath."

He looked skeptical. "I will accept your word on the matter."

A herd of cows crowded the road, milling stupidly. Eustace slowed the trap and waited while the cowherd followed his charges off the thoroughfare and into a field.

He shook the reins to start the horse again and waved to the man as they passed. "I've heard you had an adventure the other day."

Lucy was unsurprised. Probably the whole town had news of her find within minutes of Hedge summoning Doctor Fremont. "Indeed. We discovered the man right over there." She pointed and felt a shudder run up her spine as she saw the spot where she'd found the viscount so close to death.

Eustace dutifully looked at the ditch. "You should be more careful in the future. The fellow might've been up to no good."

"He was unconscious," Lucy said mildly.

"Still. It's best not to wander about by yourself." He smiled at her. "Wouldn't do to lose you."

Did Eustace think her a complete wigeon? She tried not to let annoyance show. "I was with Mr. Hedge."

"Of course. Of course. But Hedge is a small man and getting on in years."

Lucy looked at him.

"Right. Just to keep in mind for the future." He cleared his throat again. "Do you have any idea who the fellow you found is?"

"He woke yesterday," Lucy said carefully. "He says his name is Simon Iddesleigh. He's a viscount."

Eustace twitched the reins. The horse, an aging gray, shook its head. "A viscount? Really? I suppose he's a gouty old boy."

She remembered the quick eyes and quicker tongue. And the expanse of bare chest she'd seen when the coverlet had slipped. The viscount's skin had been smooth and taut, long muscles running underneath. The dark brown of his nipples had contrasted quite explicitly with the pale surrounding skin. Really, she shouldn't have noticed such a thing.

Lucy cleared her throat and turned her gaze to the road. "I don't think he's much over thirty."

She felt Eustace shoot a glance at her. "Thirty. Still. A viscount. A bit rich for Maiden Hill blood, don't you think?"

What a depressing thought! "Perhaps."

"I wonder what he was doing here anyway."

They had reached Maiden Hill proper now, and Lucy nodded to two elderly ladies haggling with the baker. "I'm sure I don't know."

Both ladies smiled and waved at them. As they drove past, the gray heads bent together.

"Hmm. Well, here we are." Eustace pulled the trap alongside the little Norman church and jumped down. He crossed around and carefully helped her descend. "Now, then. The sexton said the leak was in the nave. . . ." He strode to the back of the church, commenting on its general shape and the needed repairs.

Lucy had heard all of this before. In the three years they'd been courting, Eustace had often brought her by the church, perhaps because that was where he felt most in command. She listened with half an ear and strolled behind him. She couldn't imagine the sardonic viscount going on and on about a roof, especially a church roof. In fact, she winced to think what he would say about the matter—something sharp, no doubt. Not that the viscount's probable reaction made church roofs unimportant. Someone had to look out for the details that kept life running, and in a small village, the matter of a church roof leaking was rather large.

The viscount most likely spent his days—and nights— in the company of ladies like himself. Frivolous and witty, their only care the trimming on their gown and the style of their hair. Such people had very little use in her world. Still . . . the viscount's banter was amusing. She'd suddenly felt more awake, more alive when he'd started bamming her, as if her mind had caught a spark and was lit.

"Let's go look inside. I want to make sure the leak hasn't worsened the mold on the walls." Eustace turned and entered the church, then popped his head back out. "That is, if you don't mind?"

"No, of course not," Lucy said.

Eustace grinned. "Good girl." He disappeared back inside.

Lucy followed slowly, trailing her hands over the weathered tombstones in the churchyard. The Maiden Hill church had stood here since shortly after the Conqueror had landed. Her ancestors hadn't been here that long, but many Craddock-Hayes bones graced their small mausoleum in the corner of the cemetery. As a girl, she'd played here after church on Sundays. Her parents had met and married in Maiden Hill and spent their entire life here, or at least Mama had. Papa had been a sea captain and had sailed around the world, as he liked to tell anyone who would listen. David was a sailor as well. He was on the ocean at this very moment, perhaps nearing an exotic port of call. For a moment Lucy felt a stab of envy. How wonderful it would be to choose one's own destiny, to decide to become a doctor or artist or sailor on the open seas. She had a fancy that she wouldn't be half bad as a sailor. She'd stand on the poop deck, the wind in her hair, the sails creaking overhead, and—

Eustace looked round the church door. "Coming?"

Lucy blinked and conjured a smile. "Of course."

SIMON EXTENDED HIS RIGHT ARM at shoulder height and very carefully lifted it. Flames of pain pulsed across his shoulder and down the arm. *Damn.* It was the day after he'd woken to find Miss Craddock-Hayes sitting beside him—and he hadn't seen her since. A fact that irritated him. Was she avoiding him? Or worse—did she just not feel inclined to visit him again? Maybe he'd bored her.

He winced at that depressing thought. His head was better, and they'd removed the ridiculous bandages, but his back still felt like it was on fire. Simon lowered the arm and breathed deeply while the pain subsided to a dull ache. He looked down at his arm. His shirtsleeve ended six inches short of his wrist. This was because the shirt he was wearing belonged to David, the absent brother of the angel. Judging from the length of the garment, which made rising from the bed embarrassing, the brother was a midget.

Simon sighed and glanced around the little room. The one window had begun to darken with night. The room was large enough to hold the bed—which was rather narrow for his taste—a wardrobe and dresser, a single table by the bed, and two chairs. That was all. Spartan by his standards, but not a bad place to convalesce in, especially since there was no other choice. At the moment, the fire was dying, making the room chill. But the cold was the least of his worries. He needed his right arm to hold a sword. Not just to hold it, but to parry, riposte, and repel. And to kill.

Always to kill.

His enemies may not have murdered him, but they'd certainly disabled his right arm, at least for a while—maybe permanently. Not that it would stop him in his duty. They'd killed his brother after all. Nothing but death could stop him in his pursuit of vengeance. Nevertheless, he must be able to defend himself when next they attacked. He gritted his teeth against the pain and raised the arm again. He'd dreamed last night of fingers again. Fingers blooming like bloody buttercups in the green grass at Peller's feet. In his dream, Peller had tried to pick up his severed digits, horribly scrabbling in the grass with his mutilated hands. . . .

The door opened and the angel entered, carrying a tray. Simon turned to her gratefully, glad to push aside the madness in his mind. Like the last time he'd seen her, she was dressed in nun gray with her dark hair pulled into a simple knot at the back of her neck. Probably she had no idea how erotic a woman's nape could be when exposed. He could see little wisps of hair curling there and the beginning of the delicate slope of her white shoulders. Her skin would be soft, vulnerable, and if he ran his lips along that angle where shoulder met neck, she would shiver. He couldn't help but smile at the thought, like a half-wit given a cherry pie.

She frowned austerely at him. "Should you be doing that?"

Most likely she was referring to his exercise, not the fatuous expression on his face. "Undoubtedly not." He lowered his arm. This time it felt like only a thousand bees were stinging it.

"Then I suggest you stop and have some supper." She put the tray down on the table by his bed and went to the hearth to stir the fire, returning with a taper to light the candles.

He raised his arm. "Ah. What delectable dishes do you have there? Pap in warm milk? A cup of beef tea?" Such had been the menu for the last two days. Hard, dry bread was beginning to sound downright delicious.

"No. A slice of Mrs. Brodie's beef and kidney pie."

He lowered the arm too fast and had to bite back a groan. "Really?"

"Yes. Now stop that."

He inclined his head in a teasing half-bow. "As my lady commands."

She arched her eyebrow at him but didn't comment. Simon watched her remove the dish cover. Praise whatever saints would listen, the lady did not lie. A thick slab of meat pie reposed on the plate.

"Blessed, blessed lady." He broke off a piece of crust

with his fingers and almost wept when it touched his tongue. "Like the ambrosia of the gods. You must tell the cook that I am overwhelmed with devotion and will die if she won't run away with me at once."

"I'll tell her that you thought the pie very good." She placed a slice of pie on a plate and handed it to him.

He settled the plate on his lap. "You refuse to convey my offer of marriage?"

"You didn't mention marriage the first time. You only offered to disgrace poor Mrs. Brodie."

"The love of my life is named Mrs. Brodie?"

"Yes, that's because she's married to *Mr.* Brodie, who is away at sea at present." She sat in the chair by his bedside and looked at him. "You might be interested to know that he is considered the strongest man in Maiden Hill."

"Is he? And by that remark, I suppose you wish to cast aspersions on my strength?"

Her gaze wandered over his form, and his breath quickened.

"You are lying in bed recovering from a near-fatal beating," she murmured.

"A mere technicality," he said airily.

"But a decisive one."

"Hmm." He forked up some of the pie. "I don't suppose there is red wine as well?"

She gave him a chiding look. "Water for now."

"Too much to hope for, I agree." He swallowed a meat-filled bite. "Yet the wise men do counsel us to be content with what we have and so I shall."

"You're very welcome," she said dryly. "Is there a reason you're torturing yourself by exercising your arm?"

He avoided her topaz eyes. "Boredom, simple boredom, I'm afraid."

"Indeed?"

He'd forgotten how quick she was. He smiled charmingly. "I didn't get very far with my fairy tale last night."

"Do you really have a niece?"

"Of course I do. Would I lie to you?"

"I think, yes. And you don't seem the kind of man who would be a doting uncle."

"Ah. What kind of man do I seem to you?" he asked without thinking.

She cocked her head. "One who tries too hard to hide his soul."

Good God. For the life of him he didn't know how to reply to that.

Her lips twitched in that bewitching way she had. "My lord?"

He cleared his throat. "Yes, now as to my fairy tale, where was I?" What a spineless ass he was! Next he would be fleeing toddlers with sticks. "Poor Angelica, the goat maid, the tall, white castle, and—"

"The prince who wasn't the Serpent Prince." She conceded defeat and picked up a charcoal stick. She'd brought a different book this time—one bound in sapphire blue—and she opened it now, presumably to draw his story.

A great feeling of relief came over him that she wouldn't pursue her questions, wouldn't find him out—at least not yet. Maybe never, if he was lucky.

He tucked into the pie, speaking between bites. "Quite. The prince who wasn't the Serpent Prince. Need I mention that this prince was a fine, handsome fellow with golden curling hair and sky-blue eyes? In fact, he was almost as beautiful as Angelica herself, who rivaled the sparkle of the stars with her midnight tresses and eyes the color of treacle."

"Treacle." Her voice had a disbelieving, flat tone, but her mouth pursed as if she fought back a smile.

How he wanted to make her smile. "Mmm, treacle," he said softly. "Ever noticed how pretty treacle is when light shines through it?"

"I've only noticed how very sticky it is."

He ignored that. "Now, although poor Angelica was as beautiful as a celestial orb, there was no one about to notice. She had only the goats to keep her company. So imagine her thrill when she did catch a glimpse of the prince. He was a person far, far above her, both literally and figuratively, and she longed to meet him. To gaze into his eyes and watch the expressions on his face. Merely that, for she dared not hope to even speak to him."

"Why not?" Miss Craddock-Hayes murmured the question.

"To be frank, it was the goats," he said solemnly. "Angelica was rather conscious of the odor she'd picked up from them."

"Of course." Her lips twitched, reluctantly forming a curving smile.

And a strange thing happened. His cock twitched as well, although what it formed was definitely not a curve—or a smile, for that matter. Good Lord, how gauche to become blue-veined over a girl's smile. Simon coughed.

"Are you all right?" She'd lost the smile—thank God—but now she was looking at him with concern, which was not an emotion he usually elicited in the fairer sex.

His pride would never recover from this low. "I'm fine."

He took a drink of water. "Where was I? Ah, yes, so it seemed that Angelica would spend the rest of her days mooning about for the golden-haired prince, doomed to never even be on the same level as he. But one day something happened."

"I should hope so; otherwise, this would be a terribly short fairy tale," Miss Craddock-Hayes said. She'd turned back to her sketchbook.

He chose to disregard her interruption. "Late one evening, Angelica went to herd her goats home, and as she did every night, she counted them. But on this night the count was one short. The smallest of her goats, a black nanny with one white foot, was missing. Just then she heard a very faint bleat that seemed to come from the cliff on which the castle was built. She looked but saw nothing. Again the bleat came. So Angelica climbed as close as she could to the cliff, always following the bleating, and imagine her surprise when she discovered a crack in the rock."

He paused to take a sip of water. She didn't glance up. Her face looked so serene in the firelight, and even though her hand moved swiftly over the page, she seemed to have a stillness within her. Simon realized that he felt comfortable with this woman he hardly knew at all.

He blinked and began his story again. "There seemed to be a flickering light coming from the crack. The space was narrow, but Angelica found that if she turned sideways, she could just slip in, and when she did, she saw an astonishing thing. A very strange man—or at least he seemed to be a man. He was tall and lean and had long silver hair, and he was quite, quite nude. He stood in the light of a small, blue-flamed fire that was burning in a brazier."

Her brows arched.

"But what was strangest of all, was that as Angelica watched, he seemed to vanish. When she went to look where he had stood, there lay a giant silver snake, coiled around the base of the brazier." He absently rubbed his index finger, running his thumb against the place his ring should be. Suddenly he was very tired.

"Ah, at last we come to the infamous Serpent Prince." She looked up and must have caught the weariness in his expression. Her own face sobered. "How does your back feel?"

Like hell. "Plucky, just plucky. I think the knife wound may've actually improved it."

She watched him for a moment. And for the life of him, even with all his years of studying women, he'd not a clue as to what she thought.

"Are you ever serious?" she asked.

"No," he said. "Not ever."

"I thought not." Her eyes were intent on him. "Why?"

He looked away. He could not sustain that intense, too-perceptive regard. "I don't know. Does it matter?"

"I think you do know," she said softly. "As to whether or not it matters . . . Well, that isn't for me to say."

"Isn't it?" It was his turn to stare at her, pressuring her to admit . . . what? He wasn't sure.

"No," she whispered.

He opened his mouth to argue further, but some belated sense of self-preservation stopped him.

She inhaled. "You should rest, and I've been keeping you up." His angel shut her book and rose. "I sent the letter to your valet yesterday. He should receive it soon."

He let his head fall back against the pillows and watched

her as she gathered the empty dishes. "Thank you, beautiful lady."

She paused by the door and looked back at him. The candlelight flickered over her face, turning it into a Renaissance painting, most fitting for an angel. "Are you safe here?"

Her voice was soft, and he had begun to drift into dreams, so he wasn't sure of the words—hers or his.

"I don't know."

Chapter Three

"Iddesleigh. Iddesleigh." Papa frowned as he chewed his gammon steak, his chin jerking up and down. "Knew an Iddesleigh in the navy when I sailed *The Islander* five and twenty years ago. Midshipman. Used to get terribly seasick right out of port. Always hanging over the middeck rail looking green and heaving up his accounts. Any relation?"

Lucy suppressed a sigh. Papa had been twitting the viscount all through supper. Normally, her father enjoyed entertaining new guests. They were a fresh audience for his hoary sea stories, retold countless times to his children, neighbors, servants, and anyone else who would hold still long enough to listen. But something about Lord Iddesleigh had gotten her father's back up. This was the first meal the poor man had been able to come down for after spending the last four days bedridden. The viscount sat at the table appearing urbane and at ease. One had to look closely to notice he still favored his right arm.

She wouldn't blame him if he hid in his room after tonight. And that would disappoint her terribly. Even though she knew, deep in her soul, that she should stay away from the viscount, she couldn't stop herself from thinking about him. All the time. It was really rather irritating. Perhaps it was merely the novelty of a new person in her narrow circle of acquaintances. After all, she'd known the people she saw every day since infancy. On the other hand, maybe it was the man himself, and wasn't that an uncomfortable thought?

"No, I don't believe so." Lord Iddesleigh answered her father's question as he helped himself to more boiled potatoes. "As a rule, the members of my family avoid anything resembling work. Much too taxing, and it has an unfortunate tendency to lead to sweat. We much prefer to idle our days away eating cream cakes and discussing the latest gossip."

Then again, Lucy reflected, the younger man did seem to be holding his own with her father. Papa's eyes narrowed ominously.

She picked up a basket and waved it under her parent's nose. "More bread? Mrs. Brodie baked it fresh this morning."

He ignored her ploy. "Old landed gentry, are they?" Papa sawed vigorously at his meat while he spoke. "Let others toil on their land, eh? Spend all their time in the sinful fleshpots of London instead?"

Oh, for goodness' sake! Lucy gave up and set the bread basket down. She would enjoy the meal even if no one else did. Their dining room was hopelessly out of date, but it was cozy for all that. She tried to focus on her surroundings rather than on the distressing conversation. She turned to her left, noting in approval the cheerfully burning fire.

"Why, yes, I quite like a fleshpot now and then," Lord Iddesleigh said, smiling benignly. "That is, when I can find the energy to get myself out of bed. Have since I was but a tiny lad in leading strings accompanied by my nurse."

"Really—" she began, only to be cut off as Papa snorted. She sighed and looked to the other end of the room where a single door led into the hall and then the kitchen. It was so nice that the room wasn't cursed by a draft.

"Although," the viscount continued, "I must confess I'm a bit hazy on what exactly constitutes a fleshpot."

Lucy's gaze dropped to the table—the only safe thing to look at in the room at the moment. The old walnut dining table wasn't long, but that made meals all the more intimate. Mama had chosen the striped burgundy and cream wallpaper before Lucy'd been born, and Papa's collection of sailing ship prints graced the walls—

"I mean, flesh and pot, how did the two come together?" Lord Iddesleigh mused. "I trust we are not discussing chamber pots—"

Dangerous territory! Lucy smiled determinedly and interrupted the awful man. "Mrs. Hardy told me the other day that someone let Farmer Hope's pigs out. They scattered for half a mile, and it took Farmer Hope and his boys a whole day to get them back."

No one paid attention.

"Ha. From the Bible, fleshpot is." Papa leaned forward, apparently having scored a point. "Exodus. Have read the Bible, haven't you?"

Oh, dear. "Everyone thought it might be the Jones boys that let them out," Lucy said loudly. "The pigs, I mean. You know how the Joneses are always up to mischief. But when Farmer Hope went round to the Jones place, what do you think? Both boys were in bed with fever."

The men never took their gaze from each other.

"Not recently, I confess." The viscount's icy silver eyes sparkled innocently. "Too busy idling my life away, don't you know. And fleshpot means . . . ?"

"Harrumph. Fleshpot." Papa waved his fork, nearly spearing Mrs. Brodie as she brought in more potatoes. "Everyone knows what fleshpot means. Means fleshpot."

Mrs. Brodie rolled her eyes and set the potatoes down hard at Papa's elbow. Lord Iddesleigh's lips twitched. He raised his glass to his mouth and watched Lucy over the rim as he drank.

She could feel her face warm. Must he look at her like that? It made her uncomfortable, and she was sure it couldn't be polite. She grew even more warm when he set the glass down and licked his lips, his eyes still holding hers. Wretch!

Lucy looked away determinedly. "Papa, didn't you once tell us an amusing story about a pig on your ship? How it got out and ran around the deck and none of the men could catch it?"

Her father was staring grimly at the viscount. "Aye, I've got a story to tell. Might be educational for some. About a frog and a snake."

"But—"

"How interesting," Lord Iddesleigh drawled. "Do tell us." He leaned back in his chair, his hand still fiddling with the glass stem.

He wore David's old clothes, none of which fit him, her brother being shorter and broader in the torso. The scarlet coat's sleeves let his bony wrists stick out and at the same time the coat hung about his neck. He had gained some color in his face in the last days to replace the awful dead white he'd sported when she'd first found him, although his face seemed to be naturally pale. He should have looked ridiculous, yet he did not.

"Once there was a little frog and a great big snake," Papa began. "The snake wanted to cross a stream. But snakes can't swim."

"Are you sure?" the viscount murmured. "Don't some types of vipers take to the water to catch their prey?"

"*This* snake couldn't swim," Papa amended. "So he asked the frog, 'Can you take me across?'"

Lucy had stopped even pretending to eat. She switched her gaze back and forth between the men. They were engaged in a conflict with multiple layers that she was powerless to influence. Her father leaned forward, red-faced under his white wig, obviously intent. The viscount was bare-headed, pale hair glinting in the candlelight. On the surface he was relaxed and at ease, maybe even a little bored, but below that surface she knew he was just as focused as the older man.

"And the frog says, 'I'm not a fool. Snakes eat frogs. You'll gobble me down, sure as I'm sitting here.'" Papa paused to take a drink.

The room was silent, save for the snap of the fire.

He set down his glass. "But that snake, he was a sly one, he was. He said to the little frog, 'Never fear, I'd drown if I ate you crossing that big stream.' So the frog thinks things over and decides the snake is right; he's safe while he's in the water."

Lord Iddesleigh sipped his wine, his eyes watchful and amused. Betsy began clearing the dishes, her fat, red hands quick and light.

"The snake creeps on the little frog's back, and they

start into the stream, and halfway across, do you know what happens?" Papa glared at their guest.

The viscount slowly shook his head.

"That snake sinks his fangs into the frog." Papa slapped the table to emphasize his point. "And the frog, with his last breath, calls, 'Why did you do that? We'll both die now.' And the snake says—"

"Because it's the nature of snakes to eat frogs." Lord Iddesleigh's voice mingled with her father's.

Both men stared at each other for a moment. Every muscle in Lucy's body tightened.

The viscount broke the tension. "Sorry. That story made the rounds several years ago. I just couldn't resist." He drained his glass and set it carefully by his plate. "Perhaps it's in my nature to spoil another man's tale."

Lucy let out a breath she didn't know she'd been holding. "Well. I know Mrs. Brodie has made apple tart for dessert, and she has a lovely cheddar cheese to go with it. Would you care for some, Lord Iddesleigh?"

He looked at her and smiled, his wide mouth curving sensuously. "You tempt me, Miss Craddock-Hayes."

Papa slammed his fist on the table, rattling the dishes.

Lucy jumped.

"But as a lad, I was warned many times against temptation," the viscount said. "And although, sadly, I've spent a lifetime disregarding the warnings, tonight I think I shall be prudent. If you will excuse me, Miss Craddock-Hayes. Captain Craddock-Hayes." He bowed and left the room before Lucy could speak.

"Impudent young bounder," Papa growled, pushing his chair back from the table suddenly. "Did you see the insolent look he gave me as he left? Damn his eyes. And fleshpots. Ha, London fleshpots. I don't like that man, poppet, viscount or no viscount."

"I know that, Papa." Lucy closed her eyes and wearily laid her head in her hands. She felt the beginnings of a migraine.

"The entire *house* knows that," Mrs. Brodie proclaimed, banging back into the room.

CAPTAIN CRADDOCK-HAYES HAD IT RIGHT, the old bombastic bore, Simon reflected later that evening. Any man— especially a shrewd, eagle-eyed father—would do well to guard an angel as fine as Miss Lucinda Craddock-Hayes against the devils in the world.

Such as himself.

Simon leaned against the window frame in his borrowed bedroom, watching the night outside. She was in the dark garden, apparently strolling in the cold after that delicious but socially disastrous supper. He followed her movements by the pale oval of her face, the rest of her lost to the shadows. It was hard to tell why she fascinated him so, this rural maiden. Perhaps it was simply the draw of dark to light, the devil wanting to despoil the angel, but he thought not. There was something about her, something grave and intelligent and harrowing to his soul. She tempted him with the perfume of heaven, with the hope of redemption, impossible as that hope was. He should leave her alone, his angel entombed in the country. She slumbered innocently, doing good works and managing with a steady hand her father's house. No doubt she had a suitable gentleman who called upon her; he'd seen the trap and horse pull away the other day. Someone who would respect her position and not test the iron that he sensed lay underneath her facade. A gentleman entirely unlike himself.

Simon sighed and pushed away from the window frame. He'd never dealt very well with the *shoulds* and *shouldn'ts* of his life. He left his temporary room and stole down the stairs, moving with ridiculous care. Best not to alert the protective papa. An angle on the dark landing caught him on the shoulder and he swore. He was using his right arm as much as possible, trying to exercise it, but the damn thing still felt like the very devil. The housekeeper and maid were working in the kitchen when he passed through. He smiled and walked swiftly.

He was already through the back door when he heard Mrs. Brodie's voice. "Sir—"

He gently shut the door.

Miss Craddock-Hayes must have heard it. Gravel crunched beneath her feet as she turned. "It's cold out here." She was only a pale shape in the dark, but her words floated toward him on the night breeze.

The garden was perhaps a quarter acre. What he'd seen of it in daylight from his window was very neat. A low-walled kitchen garden, a small lawn with fruit trees, and beyond, a flower garden. Gravel walks connected the different parts, all of them properly put to bed for the winter, no doubt the work of her hands as well.

By the light of the dim sickle moon, though, it was hard to get his bearings. He'd lost her again in the dark, and it bothered him inordinately. "Do you think it cold? I hadn't noticed, really. Merely brisk." He shoved his hands in his coat pockets. It was bloody freezing in the garden.

"You shouldn't be out so soon after being ill."

He ignored that. "What are you doing here on a chilly winter night?"

"Looking at the stars." Her voice trailed back to him as if she were walking away. "They're never so bright as they are in winter."

"Yes?" They all looked the same to him, whatever the season.

"Mmm. Do you see Orion over there? He glows tonight." Her voice dropped. "But you should go in, it's too cold."

"I can do with the exercise—as I'm sure your father would point out—and winter air is good for a decrepit fellow like myself."

She was silent.

He thought he moved in her direction, but he was no longer sure. Shouldn't have mentioned the father.

"I'm sorry about Papa at supper."

Ah, farther to the right. "Why? I thought his story quite clever. A trifle long, of course, but really—"

"He's not usually so stern."

She was so close he could smell her scent, starch and roses, curiously homey and yet arousing at the same time. What an ass he was. The crack to his head must have addled his wits.

"Ah, that. Yes, I did notice the old boy was a bit testy, but I put it down to the fact that I'm sleeping in his house, wearing his son's clothes, and eating his very fine food without a proper invitation."

He saw her face turn, ghostly in the moonlight. "No, it's something about you." He could almost feel her breath brushing against his cheek. "Although you could have been nicer, too."

He chuckled. It was that or weep. "I don't think so." He shook his head, though she couldn't see it. "No, I'm certain. I definitely can't be any nicer. It's simply not in me. I'm like that snake in your father's story, striking when I shouldn't. Although in my case, it's more that I quip when I shouldn't."

The treetops moved in the wind, raking arthritic fingers against the night sky.

"Is that how you ended up nearly dead in the ditch outside Maiden Hill?" She'd crept closer. Lured by his studied frankness? "Did you insult someone?"

Simon caught his breath. "Now why do you think the attack was any fault of mine?"

"I don't know. Was it?"

He settled his rump against the kitchen garden wall, where it promptly started freezing, and crossed his arms. "You be my judge, fair lady. I shall set my case before you, and you may pronounce sentence."

"I'm not qualified to judge anyone."

Did she frown? "Oh, yes, you are, sweet angel."

"I don't—"

"Hush. Listen. I got up that morning at a horribly unfashionable hour, dressed, after a small argument with my valet over the advisability of red-heeled pumps, which he won—Henry absolutely terrorizes me—"

"Somehow I very much doubt that."

Simon placed a hand over his heart, even though the movement was wasted in the dark. "I do assure you. Then I descended my front steps, magnificently arrayed in a dashing blue velvet coat, curled and powdered wig, and the aforementioned red-heeled pumps—"

She snorted.

"Strolled down the street less than a quarter mile and was there set upon by three ruffians."

She caught her breath. "Three?"

Gratifying.

"Three." He made his voice light. "Two I might have bested. One, assuredly. But three proved to be my downfall. They relieved me of everything I had on, including the pumps, which put me in the embarrassing position of having to meet you for the first time both in the nude and—even more shockingly—unconscious. I don't know if our relationship will ever recover from the initial trauma."

She declined the bait. "You didn't know your attackers?"

Simon started to spread wide his arms, then winced and lowered them. "On my honor. Now, unless you consider red-heeled pumps to be an unbearable temptation to London robbers—in which case I was certainly asking for a drubbing going out in broad daylight wearing them—I think you will have to pardon me."

"And if I don't?" So soft, the wind nearly bore the words away.

Such a cautious flirt. Yet even this little hint of laughter caused his loins to tighten. "Then, lady, best call my name no more. For Simon Iddesleigh will be naught but a wisp, an exhalation. I will expire and disappear utterly, were you to denounce me."

Silence. Perhaps the *exhalation* bit was overdone.

Then she laughed. A loud, joyful sound that made something in his breast leap in reply.

"Do you feed the ladies in London this poppycock?" She was literally gasping for breath. "If you do, I think they would all go about with grimaces on their powdered faces to keep from giggling."

He felt unaccountably put out. "I'll have you know, I am considered quite a wit in London society." Good Lord, he sounded like a pompous ass. "The great hostesses vie to have me on their invitation lists."

"Really?"

Imp!

"Yes, really." He couldn't help it; the words came out sounding disgruntled. Oh, that would impress her. "A dinner party can be proclaimed a success when I attend. Last year a duchess fainted dead away when she heard I couldn't make it."

"Poor, poor London ladies. How sad they must be at the moment!"

He winced. *Touché.* "Actually—"

"And yet they survive without you." The laughter still lurked. "Or perhaps not. Perhaps your absence has caused a rash of hostess faintings."

"Oh, cruel angel."

"Why do you call me that? Is that a name you give many of your London ladies?"

"What, *angel*?"

"Yes." And suddenly he realized that she was closer than he'd thought. Within reach, in fact.

"No, only you." He touched a fingertip to her cheek. Her skin was warm, even in the night air, and soft, so soft.

Then she stepped away.

"I don't believe you."

Did she sound breathless? He grinned like a demon in the dark but didn't answer. God, he wished he could simply pull her into his arms, open her sweet lips beneath his, feel her breath in his mouth and her breasts against his chest.

"Why *angel*?" she asked. "I'm not particularly angelic."

"Ah, there you are wrong. Your eyebrows are most stern, your mouth curved like a Renaissance saint. Your eyes are wondrous to look upon. And your mind . . ." He stood and ventured a step toward her, until they almost touched, and she had to turn her pale face up to his.

"My mind?"

He thought he felt the warm puff of her breath. "Your mind is an iron bell that rings beautiful, terrible, and true." His voice was husky, even to his own ears, and he knew he'd revealed too much.

A lock of her hair bridged the scant inches between them and caressed his throat. His cock came painfully erect, its beat echoing the one in his heart.

"I have no idea what that means," she whispered.

"Perhaps that's just as well."

She reached her hand out, hesitated, then touched his cheek lightly with one fingertip. He felt the contact sizzle throughout his body down to his very toes.

"Sometimes I think I know you," she murmured so low he almost didn't catch the words. "Sometimes I think that I've always known you, from the very first moment you opened your eyes, and that, deep inside your soul, you know me, too. But then you make a joke, play the fool or the rake, and turn aside. Why do you do that?"

He opened his mouth to shout his fear or say something else entirely, but the kitchen door opened, spilling an arc of light into the garden. "Poppet?"

The guardian father.

She turned so that her face was silhouetted against the

light from the kitchen. "I must go in. Good night." She withdrew her hand, and it brushed across his lips as she retreated.

He had to steady his voice before he could speak. "Good night."

She walked toward the kitchen door, emerging into the light. Her father took her elbow and searched the shadows of the garden over her head before closing the door behind her. Simon watched her go, choosing to stay in the dark rather than confront Captain Craddock-Hayes. His shoulder ached, his head pounded, and his toes were frozen.

And he played a game he could not possibly win.

"I D-D-DON'T BELIEVE YOU." Quincy James paced to Sir Rupert's study window and back, his strides quick and jerky. "They t-t-told me he was bleeding from the head. They stabbed him in the b-b-back and left him in the freezing cold, naked. How c-c-could a man survive that?"

Sir Rupert sighed and poured himself a second whiskey. "I don't know how he survived, but he did. My information is impeccable."

The third man in the room, Lord Gavin Walker, stirred in his armchair by the fire. Walker was built like a navvy, big and broad, his hands the size of hams, his features course. If not for the costly clothes and wig he wore, one would never guess he was an aristocrat. In fact, his family line dated back to the Normans. Walker withdrew a jeweled snuffbox from his coat pocket, deposited a pinch of snuff on the back of his hand, and inhaled it. There was a pause; then he sneezed explosively and employed a handkerchief.

Sir Rupert winced and looked away. Filthy habit, snuff.

"I don't understand, James," Walker said. "First you say Iddesleigh is dead and we have no further worries, and then he resurrects himself. Are you sure your men got the right gentleman?"

Sir Rupert leaned back in his desk chair and looked at the ceiling as he waited for the inevitable outburst from James. His study walls were a masculine deep brown, broken at waist height by a cream chair rail. A thick black and crimson carpet lay underfoot, and old-gold velvet curtains muffled the street noise from without. A collection of botanical engravings hung on the walls. He'd started the collection with a small study of a *Chrysanthemum parthenium*—feverfew—that he'd found in a bookshop over thirty years ago now. The print was not a good one. It had a water stain in the corner, and the engraved Latin name of the plant was smudged, but the composition was pleasant, and he'd bought it at a time when it meant going without proper tea for a month. It hung between two much larger, more expensive prints. A *Morus nigra*—mulberry—and a rather elegant *Cynara cardunculus*. Cardoon.

His wife, children, and servants knew never to disturb him in his study unless it was the most dire of emergencies. Which made it all the more galling to give up his personal domain to James and Lord Walker and the troubles they brought with them.

"Sure? Of c-c-course I'm sure." James whirled and tossed something to Walker. It glittered as it flew through the air. "They brought that back to me."

Walker, usually a slow, lumbering fellow, could move quickly when he wanted to. He caught the object and examined it, and his eyebrows rose. "Iddesleigh's signet ring."

The hairs on the back of Sir Rupert's neck stood up. "Dammit, James, what the hell did you keep that for?" He was working with dangerous idiots.

"Didn't matter, d-d-did it, with Iddesleigh d-d-dead." James looked petulant.

"Except that he's not dead anymore, is he? Thanks to the incompetence of your men." Sir Rupert tossed back a healthy swallow of his whiskey. "Give it to me. I'll get rid of it."

"S-s-see here—"

"He's right," Walker interrupted. "It's evidence we don't want." He crossed the room and set the ring on Sir Rupert's desk.

Sir Rupert stared at the ring. The Iddesleigh crest was shallow, the gold eroded with age. How many generations of aristocrats had worn this ring? He covered it with his hand and palmed it, transferring it to his waistcoat pocket.

Covertly, he massaged his right leg under the table. His father had been an import merchant in the city. As a boy, Sir Rupert had worked in the great storehouse his father had maintained, carrying sacks of grain and heavy crates of merchandise. He didn't remember the accident that had crushed his leg—not entirely, at least. Only the smell of the cod packed in salt that had spilled from the broken barrel. And the pain of the smashed bone. Even now, the smell of salted fish was enough to turn his stomach.

Sir Rupert looked at his partners and wondered if they'd ever worked a day in their lives.

"What do you know?" James was facing the bigger man

now. "You haven't done anything to help so far. I was the one who seconded Peller."

"And more fool you. Should never have put Peller up to killing Ethan Iddesleigh. I advised against it." Walker took out his snuffbox again.

James looked close to weeping. "You d-d-did not!"

The big man was unperturbed as he ritually measured out the snuff on his hand. "Did. Thought we should do it more covertly."

"You liked the plan from the beginning, damn your eyes!"

"No." Walker sneezed. He shook his head slowly as he again withdrew his handkerchief from a waistcoat pocket. "Thought it foolish. Too bad you didn't listen to me."

"You ass!" James lunged at Walker.

The bigger man stepped aside, and James stumbled past comically. His face reddened, and he turned to Walker again.

"Gentlemen!" Sir Rupert rapped his cane against the desk to draw their attention. "Please. We are wandering from the point. What do we do with Iddesleigh?"

"Are we certain he is alive?" Walker insisted. The man was slow but dogged.

"Yes." Sir Rupert continued rubbing his aching leg. He would have to put it up after this conference, and it would be no good to him for the remainder of the day. "He's in Maiden Hill, a small village in Kent."

James frowned. "How do you know this?"

"That doesn't matter." He didn't want them looking too closely there. "What's important is that Iddesleigh is well enough to send for his valet. Once he's recovered sufficiently, no doubt he'll return to London. And we all know what he'll do then."

Sir Rupert looked from James, who was scratching at his scalp so hard that he must be drawing blood underneath the sunny blond hair, to Walker, who was staring thoughtfully back.

It was the bigger man who stated the obvious conclusion. "Then we had best make sure Iddesleigh doesn't return, hadn't we?"

Chapter Four

Sometimes I think I know you. The words seemed engraved
on Simon's brain. Simple words. Frank words. Words that
scared the hell out of him. Simon shifted in his armchair.
He was in his room, resting before a small fire in the grate
and wondering where Miss Craddock-Hayes was. She'd
not been at luncheon, and the captain had spoken—when
he'd spoken—only in monosyllables. Damn her. Didn't
she know such simplicity was embarrassingly gauche?
Didn't she know she was supposed to bat her eyelashes
and say meaningless things to a gentleman? To flirt and
banter and always, always hide her true thoughts? Not say
aloud words that had the potential to rip at a man's soul.

Sometimes I think I know you. What an appalling
thought, if she could truly know him. He was a man who
had spent the last months ruthlessly hunting Ethan's killers.
He sought them out one by one, challenged them to duels,
and then slaughtered them with a sword. What would an
angel make of such a man? She would cringe in horror if
she really knew him, back away and flee screaming.

Pray she never truly saw into his soul.

He became aware of some type of commotion going on downstairs. He could hear Captain Craddock-Hayes's rumbling voice, Mrs. Brodie's higher tones, and underneath, the constant mutter of that odd manservant Hedge. Simon levered himself out of his armchair and limped to the stairs. He was paying for his foray into the cold garden last night in pursuit of the angel. The muscles in his back had rebelled at being used too soon and had stiffened overnight. As a result, he moved like an old man—a recently beaten and stabbed old man.

Simon neared the first floor, and the voices became distinct.

". . . carriage half the size of a whaler. Ostentatious, that's what it is, plain ostentation."

The captain's baritone.

"Will they be wanting tea do you think, sir? I'll need to see to my scones. I've made just enough to go around."

Mrs. Brodie.

And finally, ". . . have a bad back, I do. Four horses, and great big beasts they are, too. I'm not getting any younger. May just kill me, it might. And does anyone care? No, 'course they don't care. Just another pair of arms, I am to them."

Hedge, naturally.

Simon smiled as he finished descending the stairs and walked to the front door where the others were gathered. Funny how the rhythm and tone of this house had so easily seeped into his bones.

"Good afternoon, Captain," he said. "What's all the fuss about?"

"Fuss? Ha. Great big vehicle. Wonder it could turn into

the drive at all. Why anyone has need of such a thing, I don't know. When I was a young man . . ."

Simon caught sight of the carriage out the open front door, and the captain's complaint faded. It was his traveling coach, all right, with the Iddesleigh coat of arms in gilt on the doors. But instead of Henry, his valet of five years, another, younger man climbed down from inside, folding himself nearly double to clear the carriage door frame. He was old enough to have reached his full height—thank God, otherwise he would have ended a giant—but his body had not yet filled the impressive frame it had produced. Thus, his hands were overlarge, and raw-knuckled to boot; his feet like a puppy's, too big for the thin shanks above; and his shoulders wide but bony.

Christian straightened, his orangey-red hair blazing in the afternoon sun, and grinned when he caught sight of Simon. "Rumor has it you're either close to death or dead already."

"Rumor, as always, manages to exaggerate the matter." Simon sauntered down the steps. "Have you come to attend my funeral or were you merely passing by?"

"I thought it only right to see if you really were dead. After all, you might've left me your sword and scabbard."

"Unlikely." Simon grinned. "I believe my will has you down for an enamel piss-pot. I'm told it's an antique."

Henry emerged from behind the young aristocrat. In an exquisite white wig with two tails, violet and silver coat, and silver-clocked black stockings, Henry was far and away better dressed than Christian, who wore dull brown. But then Henry always was more superbly turned out than almost any other man near him, servant or aristocrat. Simon sometimes found himself hard-pressed to not fall in the shadow of his own valet. Add to that the fact that Henry had the face of a dissolute Eros—all golden hair and full, red lips—and the man became an absolute menace where the fairer sex was concerned. It was a wonder, really, why Simon kept him around.

"Then I'm most glad in this case that rumor was exaggerated." Christian took Simon's hand in both of his, almost embracing him, watching his face with concern. "You really are well?"

Simon felt unaccountably embarrassed. He wasn't used to others worrying over his welfare. "Well enough."

"And who is this, may I ask?" The captain had caught up to him.

Simon half turned to the older man. "May I introduce Christian Fletcher, sir? A friend and fencing partner. Christian, this is my host, Captain Craddock-Hayes. He has shown me every hospitality, selflessly turning over his son's unused bedroom, his housekeeper's excellent food, and his daughter's exquisite company."

"Captain. An honor to meet you, sir." Christian bowed.

The captain, who had been eyeing Simon as if there might be a double meaning to *company,* switched his gimlet gaze to Christian. "I suppose you'll be wanting a room as well, young man."

Christian looked startled. He glanced at Simon as if for help before replying, "No, not at all. I was thinking of staying at the inn we passed in town." Christian gestured vaguely over his shoulder, presumably in the direction of the inn.

"Ha." The captain was momentarily stymied. Then he rounded on Simon. "But your servants, Lord Iddesleigh, they'll be staying at my house, whether we have the room or not?"

"Of course, Captain Craddock-Hayes," Simon said cheerfully. "I had thought of putting them up at the inn as well, but I knew your fine sense of hospitality would be insulted at the idea. So, rather than engage in one of those awkward tugs-of-war over propriety, I conceded the battle before it was ever fought and had my men come here." He ended this blatant pack of lies with a little bow.

For a moment the captain was speechless. He frowned thunderously, but Simon knew when he had scored a point.

"Ha. Well. Ha." The older gentleman rocked back on his heels and glanced at the coach. "Just what I'd expect from city toffs. Ha. Have to tell Mrs. Brodie, then."

He turned in time to nearly collide with Hedge. The manservant had come outside and was stopped dead in his tracks, gaping at Simon's liveried coachman and footmen.

"Gor. Would you look at that," Hedge said with the first hint of reverence Simon had ever heard in his voice. "Now that's the way a man oughter be dressed, silver braid and purple coats. 'Course, gold braid would be even better. But still, it's a lot finer than *some* dress their staff."

"Staff?" The captain looked outraged. "You're not staff. You're the odd-jobs man. Now help them with the boxes. Good God, *staff.*" And with that he stomped into the house, still muttering.

Hedge headed in the opposite direction, also muttering.

"I don't think he likes me," Christian whispered.

"The captain?" Simon started to the house with the

younger man. "No, no. The man positively adores you. That's just his way, really. Did you see the puckish twinkle in his eye?"

Christian half smiled, as if uncertain whether to take Simon's words at face value or not. Simon felt a momentary pang. To be so young in the world, like a new-hatched chick, its feathers still wet from the shell, surrounded by larger, less benign fowl and the threat of the foxes lurking just out of sight.

But then Simon frowned at a thought. "Where did you hear these rumors of my imminent demise?"

"There was talk about it at the Harrington's ball the other evening and again the next afternoon at my coffeehouse. But I didn't take it very seriously until I heard it at Angelo's." Christian shrugged. "And, of course, you didn't show for our regular match."

Simon nodded. Dominico Angelo Malevolti Tremamondo—known simply as Angelo to his patrons—was the fashionable fencing master of the moment. Many aristocratic gentlemen attended the Italian's lessons or came to his school of arms in Soho simply to practice and exercise. Simon had actually met Christian at the master's establishment several months ago. The younger man had openly admired Simon's technique. Somehow the admiration had turned into a weekly fencing match with Simon giving his acolyte pointers on form.

"What did happen to you?" They entered the hall, dark after the sun outside. Christian's strides were long and quick as he talked, and it was an effort for Simon to pace him without showing weakness. "Henry didn't seem to know."

"Stabbed." The captain was already in the sitting room

and must have overheard the question as they entered. "The viscount was stabbed in the back. Hit the shoulder blade. Farther to the left and the knife would've pierced a lung."

"Then I guess he was lucky." Christian stood as if uncertain how to proceed.

"Damn right, he was lucky." The captain made no move to welcome the other men. "Ever see a man die from a lung wound? Eh? Can't breathe. Suffocates in his own blood. Nasty way to end."

Simon sat down on a settee and leisurely crossed his legs, ignoring the pain in his back. "Your description fascinates me strangely, Captain."

"Ha." The captain settled in an armchair, a grim smile on his face. "What fascinates me is why you were attacked in the first place. Eh? Jealous husband? Insulted someone?"

Christian, left standing by himself, looked around and found a wooden chair by the settee. He lowered himself, only to freeze as the chair creaked ominously.

"I've insulted many, many men over the course of my lifetime, I'm sure." Simon smiled back at the captain. He mustn't underestimate the older man's perception. "As for jealous husbands, well, discretion forbids I say anything."

"Ha! Discretion—"

But the captain was interrupted by the entrance of his daughter, followed by Mrs. Brodie carrying a tea tray.

Simon and Christian stood. The captain made it to his legs and almost immediately sat back down again.

"My dearest lady," Simon said, bending over her hand. "I am overwhelmed by the radiance of your presence." He straightened and tried to tell if she'd been avoiding him today, but her eyes were veiled, and he could not discern her thoughts. He felt a surge of frustration.

The angel's lips curved. "You had better be careful, Lord Iddesleigh. One day my head may be quite turned by your flowery compliments."

Simon clapped his hand to his chest and staggered back. "A hit. A direct hit."

She smiled then at his antics but turned her golden eyes to Christian. "Who is your guest?"

"He is but the poor son of a baronet and red-haired to boot. Hardly worth your divine notice."

"For shame." She sent him a chiding glance—oddly effective—and held out her hand to Christian. "I like ginger hair. And what is your name, poor son of a baronet?"

"Christian Fletcher, Miss . . . ?" The younger man smiled charmingly and bowed.

"Craddock-Hayes." She curtsied. "I see you've already met my father."

"Indeed." Christian raised her hand to his lips, and Simon was forced to resist the urge to throttle him.

"You're a friend of Lord Iddesleigh?" she asked.

"I—"

But Simon had had enough of her attention elsewhere. "Christian is everything I hold dear in a fellow man." For once he didn't know if he spoke the truth or lied.

"Really?" Her face was solemn again.

Damn her for taking him so seriously; no one else did, not even himself.

She sat gracefully on the settee and began to pour the tea. "Have you known Lord Iddesleigh long, Mr. Fletcher?"

The younger man smiled as he accepted his teacup. "Only a few months."

"Then you do not know why he was attacked?"

"I'm afraid not, ma'am."

"Ah." Her eyes met Simon's as she proffered his tea.

Simon smiled and deliberately stroked a finger across her hand as he accepted the cup. She blinked but didn't drop her gaze. Brave little angel. "I wish I could assuage your curiosity, Miss Craddock-Hayes."

"Harrumph!" The captain exploded on the settee beside his daughter.

Christian selected a scone from the tray and sat back. "Well, whoever attacked Simon must've known him."

Simon stilled. "Why do you say that?"

The younger man shrugged. "It was three men, wasn't it? That's what I heard."

"Yes?"

"So they knew you were—are—a master swordsman." Christian sat back and munched on his scone, his face as open and innocent as it'd ever been.

"A master swordsman?" Miss Craddock-Hayes looked between Simon and Christian. "I had no idea." Her eyes seemed to search his.

Damn. Simon smiled, hoping he gave nothing away. "Christian overstates—"

"Oh, come! I have never known you to be modest, Iddesleigh." The younger man was all but laughing in his face. "I assure you, ma'am, bigger men quake in their boots when he walks by and none dare call him out. Why, only this fall—"

Good God. "Surely that tale isn't for a lady's ears," Simon hissed.

Christian flushed, his eyes widening. "I only—"

"But I enjoy hearing things not meant for my delicate

ears," Miss Craddock-Hayes said softly. Her gaze challenged him until he could almost hear her seductive siren's call: *Tell me. Tell me. Tell me who you truly are.* "Will you not let Mr. Fletcher continue?"

But the protective papa stirred, saving him from further folly. "I think not, poppet. Leave the poor fellow be."

His angel flushed, but her gaze did not waver, and Simon knew if he stayed here much longer, he would drown in those topaz eyes and bless the gods for his fortune even as he went down for the third time.

"NUDE? *ALTOGETHER* NUDE?" Patricia McCullough leaned forward on the ancient settee, nearly upsetting the plate of lemon biscuits on her lap.

Her round face with its peaches-and-cream complexion, plump ruby lips, and golden curls gave her the look of a vapid shepherdess in a painting. A look that actually was at odds with her personality, which was more like that of a housewife intent on bargaining down the local butcher.

"Quite." Lucy popped a biscuit into her mouth and smiled serenely at her childhood friend.

They sat in the little room at the back of the Craddock-Hayes house. The walls were a cheerful rose color with apple-green trim, invoking a flower garden in summer. The room wasn't as big or as well furnished as the sitting room, but it'd been Mama's favorite and was cozy for entertaining a dear friend like Patricia. And the windows overlooked the back garden, giving them a nice view of the gentlemen outside.

Patricia sat back now and knit her brows as she studied the viscount and his friend out the window. The younger man was in his shirtsleeves, despite the November chill.

He held a sword in his hand and was lunging about with it, no doubt practicing fencing in a serious way, although the steps looked rather silly to Lucy. Lord Iddesleigh sat nearby, either giving helpful encouragement or, more likely, searing his friend with his criticism.

What was the story that Mr. Fletcher had so nearly blurted out yesterday? And why had the viscount been so determined that she not hear it? The obvious answer was some kind of scandalous love affair. That was the sort of thing usually deemed too sordid for a maiden's ears. And yet, Lucy had the feeling that Lord Iddesleigh wouldn't mind overmuch shocking her—and her father—with his bedroom exploits. This was something worse. Something he was ashamed of.

"Nothing like that ever happens to me," Patricia said, bringing her back to the present.

"What?"

"Finding naked gentlemen beside the road whilst walking home." She pensively bit into a biscuit. "I'm more likely to find one of the Joneses drunk in the ditch. Fully clothed."

Lucy shuddered. "I should think it would be better that way."

"Undoubtedly. Still, it does give one something to tell the grandchildren on a cold winter's night."

"This was the first time it happened to me."

"Mmm. Was he facing up or down?"

"Down."

"Pity."

Both ladies turned back to the window. The viscount lounged on the stone bench under one of the apple trees, long legs stretched before him, shorn hair glinting in the sun. He grinned at something Mr. Fletcher said, his wide mouth curving. He looked like a blond Pan; all he needed was the hooves and horns.

Pity.

"What do you suppose he was doing in Maiden Hill?" Patricia asked. "He's as out of place here as a gilded lily on a dung heap."

Lucy frowned. "I wouldn't call Maiden Hill a dung heap."

Patricia was unmoved. "I would."

"He says he was attacked and left here."

"In Maiden Hill?" Patricia's eyes widened in exaggerated disbelief.

"Yes."

"I can't imagine why. Unless he was attacked by particularly backward robbers."

"Mmm." Privately, of course, Lucy had been wondering the same thing. "Mr. Fletcher seems a nice enough gentleman."

"Yes. Makes you wonder how he became friends with Lord Iddesleigh. They go together like crushed velvet and burlap."

Lucy tried to repress a snort and wasn't entirely successful.

"And red hair is never entirely satisfactory on a man, is it?" Patricia scrunched her freckle-covered nose, making herself look even more adorable than usual.

"You're being mean."

"*You're* being overly kind."

Mr. Fletcher made a particularly showy slash.

Patricia eyed him. "Although I have to admit he is tall."

"Tall? That's the only nice thing you have to say about him?" Lucy poured her more tea.

"Thank you." Patricia took her cup. "You shouldn't disparage height."

"You're shorter than I, and I am no Amazon."

Patricia waved a biscuit, nearly entangling it in her gold curls. "I know. It's sad, but there it is. I'm strangely drawn to men who tower over me."

"If that is your criteria, Mr. Fletcher is about the tallest man you're likely to find."

"True."

"Perhaps I should invite you to dine with us so that you may get to know Mr. Fletcher better."

"You should, you know. After all, you've already taken the only eligible bachelor in Maiden Hill who isn't a Jones or hopelessly simple." Patricia paused to sip her tea. "Speaking of which—"

"I should ring for more hot water," Lucy cut in hastily.

"*Speaking* of which." Patricia trundled right on over her. "I saw you out driving with Eustace yesterday. Well?"

"Well what?"

"Don't play stupid with me," Patricia said, looking like an irate marmalade kitten. "Has he said anything?"

"Of course he said something." Lucy sighed. "He discussed at length the repairs to the church roof, Mrs. Hardy's ankle, and whether or not it might snow."

Patricia narrowed her eyes.

She gave in. "But nothing about marriage."

"I take back what I said."

Lucy raised her eyebrows.

"I think we shall have to place Eustace into the hopelessly simple category."

"Now, Patricia—"

"Three years!" Her friend thumped a settee cushion. "*Three years* he's been driving you up and down and all around Maiden Hill. His horse can find the way in its sleep by now. He's made actual ruts in the roads he takes."

"Yes, but—"

"And has he proposed?"

Lucy grimaced.

"No, he has not," Patricia answered herself. "And why not?"

"I don't know." Lucy shrugged. It honestly was a mystery to her as well.

"The man needs a fire lit under his feet." Patricia jumped up and started trotting back and forth in front of her. "Vicar or no vicar, you're going to be gray-haired by the time he brings himself to the point. And what's the good of that, I ask you? You won't be able to bear children."

"Maybe I don't want to."

She thought she'd spoken too quietly to be heard over her friend's diatribe, but Patricia stopped short and stared. "You don't want to have children?"

"No," Lucy said slowly, "I'm not sure I want to marry Eustace anymore."

And she realized it was true. What just days ago had seemed inevitable and good in a predictable way, now seemed old and stale and nearly impossible. Could she spend the rest of her life having settled for the best of what Maiden Hill had to offer? Wasn't there so much more in the wider world? Almost involuntarily, her eyes were drawn to the window again.

"But that leaves only Jones men and the truly . . ." Patricia turned to follow her gaze. "Oh, my dear."

Her friend sat back down.

Lucy felt a flush start. She quickly drew her eyes away. "I'm sorry, I know you like Eustace, despite—"

"No." Patricia shook her head, curls bouncing. "This isn't about Eustace, and you know it. It's about *him*."

Outside, the viscount got up to demonstrate a move, his arm outstretched, one elegant hand on a hip.

Lucy sighed.

"What are you thinking?" Patricia's voice cut in. "I know he's handsome, and those gray eyes are enough to make the average virgin faint, not to mention that form, which apparently you got to see nude."

"I—"

"But he's a London gentleman. I'm sure he's like one of those crocodile creatures they have in Africa that waits until some unfortunate person gets too close to the water and then eats them up. Snip! Snap!"

"He's not going to eat me up." Lucy reached for her teacup again. "He's not interested in me—"

"How—"

"And I'm not interested in him."

Patricia raised an eyebrow, patently dubious.

Lucy did her best to ignore her. "And besides, he's out of my sphere. He's one of those worldly gentlemen who live in London and have affairs with stylish ladies and I'm . . ." She shrugged helplessly. "I'm a country mouse."

Patricia patted her knee. "It wouldn't work, dear."

"I know." Lucy chose another lemon biscuit. "And someday Eustace will propose to me and I'll accept him." She said it firmly, a smile fixed on her face, but somewhere inside her, she felt a building pressure.

And her eyes still strayed to the window.

*   *   *

"I HOPE I'M NOT DISTURBING YOU?" Simon asked later that evening.

He had prowled into the little room at the back of the house where Miss Craddock-Hayes hid herself. He was curiously restless. Christian had retired to his inn, Captain Craddock-Hayes had disappeared on some errand, Henry was fussily arranging his clothes, and he should probably be in bed, continuing his recovery. But he wasn't. Instead, after grabbing one of his own coats and dodging Henry—who'd wanted to put him through a full toilet—Simon had tracked down his angel.

"Not at all." She looked at him warily. "Please, have a seat. I had begun to think you were avoiding me."

Simon winced. He had. But at the same time, he couldn't stay away from her. Truth be told, he felt well enough to travel, even if he wasn't fully recovered. He should pack up and quit this house gracefully.

"What are you sketching?" He sat beside her, too close. He caught a whiff of starch.

She mutely turned her enormous book so he could see. A charcoal Christian danced across the page, lunging and feinting at an imaginary foe.

"It's very good." Immediately he felt a fool for so pedestrian a compliment, but she smiled, which had its now-predictable effect on him. He leaned back and flicked the skirt of his coat over his groin, then stretched out his legs. Carefully.

She frowned, her straight eyebrows drawing together terribly. "You've strained your back."

"You aren't supposed to notice a gentleman's infirmity. Our manly pride may become irreparably damaged."

"Silly." She got up and brought a pillow to him. "Lean forward."

He complied. "Also, you shouldn't call us silly."

"Even if you are?"

"Especially if we are." She positioned the pillow behind his back. "Absolutely devastating to the manly pride." God, that felt better.

"Humph." Her hand trailed lightly across his shoulder; then she went to the door and called for the housekeeper.

He watched her move to the fireplace and stir the embers into flame. "What are you doing?"

"I thought we'd have supper in here, if that agrees with you."

"Whatever agrees with you, agrees with me, fairest lady."

She wrinkled her nose at him. "I'll take that as a yes."

The housekeeper appeared, and they conferred before Mrs. Brodie bustled out again.

"Papa is dining with Dr. Fremont tonight," his angel said. "They like to argue politics together."

"Indeed? Is that the same doctor who saw to my wound?" The good doctor must be a formidable debater to take on the captain. He had Simon's best wishes.

"Mmm."

Mrs. Brodie and the one maid returned with laden trays. They took some time setting up the meal on the side table and then left.

"Papa used to have wonderful discussions with David." Miss Craddock-Hayes sliced a game pie. "I think he misses him." She handed the plate to him.

Simon had an awful thought. "Are you bereaved?"

She stared at him blankly for a second, her hand hovering over the pie; then she laughed. "Oh, no. David is away at sea. He's a sailor like Papa. A lieutenant on the *New Hope.*"

"Forgive me," Simon said. "I suddenly realized that I didn't know anything of your brother, despite using his room."

She looked down as she selected an apple for herself. "David's two and twenty, two years younger than I. He's been away at sea eleven months now. He writes often, although we get his letters in clumps. He can only post them when they make port." She settled the plate on her lap and glanced up. "Father reads them all at once when we get a packet, but I like to save the letters and read one or two a week. It makes them last longer." She smiled almost guiltily.

Simon had an urgent wish to find this David and make him write a hundred letters more to his sister. Letters Simon could give her so he could sit at her feet and watch that smile on her lips. More fool, he.

"Have you a brother or sister?" she asked innocently.

He looked down at his pie. This was what came of being beguiled by dark, level brows and a serious mouth. One let one's guard down. "I am deficient in sisters, alas." He cut into the friable crust. "I always thought it would be nice to have a little sister to tease, although they have a tendency to grow up and tease back, I hear."

"And brothers?"

"One brother." He picked up his fork and was surprised to find his fingers trembling, damn them. He willed the shaking to stop. "Dead."

"I'm sorry." Her voice was nearly a whisper.

"Just as well." Simon reached for his wineglass. "He

was the elder, so I would never have attained the title had he not seen fit to shuffle off this mortal coil." He took an overlarge sip of the red wine. It burned all the way down his throat. He set the glass down and rubbed at his right index finger.

She was silent, watching him from too-intense topaz eyes.

"Besides," he continued, "he was rather an ass, Ethan was. Always worried about the right thing and whether I was living up to the family name, which of course I never was. He'd call me down once or twice a year to the family estate and look at me with lugubrious eyes as he enumerated my many sins and the size of my tailor's bill." He stopped because he was babbling.

He glanced at her to see if he'd finally shocked her into sending him away. She merely gazed back, compassion in her face. Dreadful, dreadful angel.

He transferred his gaze to the pie, although his appetite had fled. "I don't believe I finished my fairy tale the other day. About poor Angelica and the Serpent Prince."

Thankfully, she nodded. "You'd got as far as the magical cave and the silver snake."

"Right." He breathed deeply, trying to rid himself of the tightness in his chest. He took another swallow of the wine and marshaled his thoughts. "The silver snake was much larger than any Angelica had seen before; its head alone was as big as her forearm. As she watched, the serpent uncoiled itself and swallowed her poor little goat whole. Then it slowly slithered away into the darkness."

Miss Craddock-Hayes shuddered. "It sounds awful."

"It was." He paused to take a bite of pie. "Angelica crept from the crack in the rock as quietly as she could and returned to her small stick shack to think things over, for she was quite frightened. What if the giant serpent continued to eat her goats? What if it decided to try a more tender meat and eat *her*?"

"How thoroughly disgusting," she murmured.

"Yes."

"What did she do?"

"Nothing. What could she do, after all, against a giant snake?"

"Well, surely she—"

He cocked a stern eyebrow at her. "Are you going to keep interrupting me?"

She pressed her lips together as if to quell a smile and started peeling her apple. He felt warmth spread through him. This was so comfortable, sitting here with her and bantering. A man could relax to the point that he forgot all his cares, all his sins, all the butchery he had yet to do.

He took a breath and shook the thoughts away. "Angelica's flock of goats began disappearing one by one, and she was at her wit's end. True, she lived alone, but sooner or later the king's steward would come to take count of the goats, and then how would she explain their depleted numbers?" He paused to take a sip of wine.

Her straight, solemn brows were drawn together as she concentrated on peeling the apple with a small knife and fork. He could tell by the pinch of her brow that she wanted to object to Angelica's lack of fortitude.

He hid a smile behind the wineglass. "Then late one night, a poor peddler woman came knocking at the stick shack's door. She displayed her wares: some ribbons, a bit of lace, and a faded scarf. Angelica took pity on the woman. 'I haven't a coin to my name,' she told her, 'but will you take this pitcher of goat's milk in trade for a ribbon?' Well, the old woman was glad enough to make the bargain, and she said to Angelica, 'Since you have a kind heart, I'll give you a bit of advice: If you capture the skin of a snake, you'll have power over the creature. You'll hold his very life in your hands.' And with that, the old peddler hobbled away before Angelica could ask her more."

The lady had stopped peeling her apple and was looking at him skeptically. Simon raised his eyebrows, sipped the wine, and waited.

She broke. "The old peddler woman just appeared out of the blue?"

"Yes."

"Just like that?"

"Why not?"

"Sometimes I have the feeling this story is being fashioned as you tell it." She sighed and shook her head. "Go on."

"You're sure?" he enquired gravely.

She gave him a look from under terrifying brows.

He cleared his throat to cover a laugh. "That very night, Angelica crept to the cave. She watched as the giant serpent slithered from the dark recesses at the back of the cavern. It circled the blue-flamed fire slowly, and then there appeared the nude silver-haired man. Angelica crawled closer and saw that a great snakeskin lay at the man's feet. Before her courage could leave her, she leaped forward and snatched the skin in her arms." Simon ate a bite of the pie, chewing slowly to savor the flavor.

He looked up to see Miss Craddock-Hayes staring incredulously at him. *"Well?"*

He blinked innocently. "Well what?"

"Stop teasing me," she enunciated distinctly. "What happened?"

His cock jumped on the word *teasing,* and an image formed in his demonic brain of Miss Craddock-Hayes stretched nude upon a bed, his tongue *teasing* her nipples. Christ.

Simon blinked and pasted a smile on his face. "Angelica had the Serpent Prince in her power, of course. She ran to the fire in the brazier, intending to throw the snakeskin into the blaze and thus destroy the creature, but his words stopped her. 'Please, fair maiden. Please, spare me my life.' And she noticed for the first time that he wore a chain—"

She snorted.

"With a small, sapphire crown hanging from it," he finished in a rush. "What?"

"He was a snake before," she said with exaggerated patience. "With no shoulders. How could he have worn a necklace?"

"A chain. Males don't wear necklaces."

She merely stared at him in patent disbelief.

"He was enchanted," he stated. "It stayed on."

She started to roll her eyes, but then caught herself. "And did Angelica spare his life?"

"Of course." Simon smiled sadly. "Celestial beings always do, whether the creature deserves it or not."

She carefully set aside what remained of her apple and wiped her hands. "But why wouldn't the snake be deserving of salvation?"

"Because he was a snake. A thing of darkness and evil."

"I don't believe that," she said simply.

He barked a laugh—too sharp and too loud. "Come, Miss Craddock-Hayes, I'm sure you read your Bible and know of the snake that deceived Adam and Eve?"

"Come, my lord." She tilted her head mockingly. "I'm sure you know that the world isn't that simple."

He arched an eyebrow. "You surprise me."

"Why?" Now, inexplicably, she was irritated at him. "Because I live in the country? Because my circle of friends doesn't contain the titled and sophisticated? Do you think only those who live in London are intellectual enough to explore beyond the obvious in our world?"

How had this argument happened? "I—"

She leaned forward and said fiercely, "I think you are the provincial one, to judge me without knowing me at all. Or rather, you *think* you know me, when in reality, you do not."

She stared a moment longer at his dumbfounded face and then got up and hurried from the room.

Leaving him with a painfully aching erection.

Chapter Five

"He's late!" Papa said the following night. He glared at the clock on the mantelpiece and then turned his glare on the rest of the room. "Can't tell time in London, eh? Just wander about, showing up whenever a body wants?"

Eustace tsked and shook his head in sympathy with Lucy's father—a rather hypocritical gesture since he was known to forget the time on occasion himself.

Lucy sighed and rolled her eyes. They were all assembled in the front sitting room, waiting for Lord Iddesleigh so they could go into supper. Actually, she wasn't all that anxious to see the viscount again anyway. She'd made a fool of herself the evening before. She still wasn't quite sure why her anger had suddenly boiled over; it had been so sudden. But it had been real. She was so much more than daughter and nursemaid; she knew that deep within herself. Yet, in tiny Maiden Hill, she could never become who she wanted to be. She was only dimly aware of who she might become, but stuck here, she knew she'd never discover herself.

"I'm sure he'll be down presently, sir," Mr. Fletcher said.

Unfortunately, Lord Iddesleigh's friend didn't sound sure at all. He cleared his throat. "Perhaps I ought to go—"

"What an exquisite company." Lord Iddesleigh's voice came from the doorway.

Everyone swung around, and Lucy almost let her mouth hang open. The viscount was magnificent. That was the only word for it. *Magnificent.* He wore a silver brocade coat embroidered in silver and black on the turned-back sleeves, skirts, and all down the front. Underneath was a sapphire waistcoat with vining leaves and multicolored flowers lavishly embroidered all over. His shirt had falls of lace at the wrists and throat, and he wore a snow-white wig on his head.

The viscount strolled into the sitting room. "Never say you have all been waiting for me."

"Late!" Papa exploded. "Late for my supper! Sit down promptly at seven o'clock in this household, sir, and if you cannot . . ." Papa trailed off and stared fixedly down at the viscount's feet.

Lucy followed his gaze. The viscount wore elegant pumps with—

"Red heels!" Papa shouted. "Good God, sirrah, think you this is a bordello?"

The viscount had made Lucy's side by this time, and he languidly lifted her hand to his lips as her father sputtered. He looked up at her, his head still bowed, and she saw that his eyes were only a few shades darker than his snowy wig. He winked as she stared, mesmerized, and she felt the wet warmth of his tongue insinuate itself between her fingers.

Lucy inhaled sharply, but the viscount let go of her hand

and whirled to face her father as if nothing had happened. She hid her hand in her skirt as he spoke.

"A bordello, sir? No, I confess that I never mistook your home for a bordello. Now, had you decorated the walls with a few paintings depicting—"

"Shall we go in to supper?" Lucy squeaked.

She didn't wait for an assent; the way the conversation was progressing, there would be all-out warfare before supper was ever begun. Instead she seized the viscount's arm and marched him into the dining room. Of course, she would never be able to physically force Lord Iddesleigh to go where he did not wish to go. Fortunately, he seemed content to let her lead him.

He bent his head close to hers as they entered the dining room. "Had I known, sweeting, that you desired my company so devoutly"—he pulled out a chair for her—"I would've damned Henry and come down in my smallclothes."

"Ass," Lucy muttered to him as she sat.

His smile widened into a grin. "My angel."

Then he was forced to round the table and sit across from her. As everyone else found their places, Lucy let out a small sigh. Maybe now they could be civil.

"I've often wanted to visit Westminster Abbey in London," Eustace said rather pompously as Betsy began ladling out potato and leek soup. "To see the graves of the poets and great men of letters, you understand. But I'm afraid I've never had the time on the occasions I've traveled to our wonderful capital. Always busy with church matters, you know. Perhaps you could give us your impressions of that magnificent abbey, Lord Iddesleigh?"

All heads at the dinner table swiveled in the viscount's direction.

The lines around his silver eyes deepened as he fingered his wineglass. "Sorry. Never had a reason to enter the dusty old mausoleum. It's not my cup of tea, really. Probably a terrible moral failing on my part."

Lucy could practically hear Papa and Eustace agreeing in their minds. Mr. Fletcher coughed and buried his face in his wineglass.

She sighed. When her father had invited Eustace to sup with them, Lucy had welcomed the diversion another guest would provide. Mr. Fletcher, although pleasant, had not been able to stand up to Papa's grilling and had looked quite wan by the end of the noon meal on the previous day. And the viscount, while he could withstand her father's obvious nettling, did it only too well. He drove her father into red-faced incoherence. She'd hoped Eustace would provide a buffer. Obviously, this was not to be the case. To make matters worse, she felt an absolute drab in her dark gray gown. It was well cut but so plain as to be nearly a rag next to the viscount's finery. Of course, no one she knew dressed so ostentatiously in the country, and Lord Iddesleigh really ought to feel self-conscious to be so out of place.

On that thought, Lucy raised her glass of wine defiantly and stared at the viscount sitting across from her. A puzzled look flashed across his face before his habitual expression of ennui resettled.

"I could give you a colorful description of the pleasure gardens at Vaux Hall," Lord Iddesleigh mused, continuing the topic Eustace had brought up. "Been there on too many nights to recall, with too many people I'd rather not recall, doing too many things . . . well, you get the picture. But I don't know that it's a description quite fit for mixed company."

"Ha. Then I suggest you not give it," Papa rumbled. "Not that interested in the sights of London anyway. Good English countryside is the best place in the world. I should know. Been around the world in my day."

"I quite agree, Captain," Eustace said. "Nothing is so fine as the English rural landscape."

"Ha. So there." Papa leaned forward and fixed a gimlet eye on his guest. "Feeling better tonight, Iddesleigh?"

Lucy nearly groaned. Papa's hints that the viscount should leave were growing more and more explicit.

"Thank you, sir, for inquiring." Lord Iddesleigh poured more wine for himself. "Except for the stabbing pain in my back, the unfortunate loss of sensation in my right arm, and a sort of nauseous dizziness when I stand, I'm as fit as a fiddle."

"Good. You look well enough. Suppose you'll be leaving us soon, eh?" Her father glowered from beneath his furry white brows. "Maybe tomorrow?"

"Papa!" Lucy cut in before her father had their guest out the door tonight. "Lord Iddesleigh just said he's not fully recovered."

Mrs. Brodie and Betsy came in to remove the soup dishes and serve the next course. The housekeeper took a look around at the uncomfortable faces and sighed. She met Lucy's eyes and shook her head in sympathy before she left. Everyone started on the roast chicken and peas.

"I once went in Westminster Abbey," Mr. Fletcher said.

"Were you lost?" Lord Iddesleigh inquired politely.

"Not at all. Mother and the sisters were on an architectural binge."

"I didn't know you had any sisters."

"I do. Three."

"Good God. Excuse me, Vicar."

"Two elder," Mr. Fletcher said chattily, "one younger."

"My felicitations."

"Thanks. Anyway, we toured the Abbey about ten years ago now, in between St. Paul's and the Tower."

"And you but a young and impressionable lad." The viscount shook his head sorrowfully. "It's so sad when one hears about this type of debauchery at the hands of one's elders. Makes one wonder what England is coming to."

Papa made an explosive sound beside Lucy, and Lord Iddesleigh winked across the table at her. She tried to frown at him as she raised her wineglass, but however awfully he behaved, she found it hard to censor him.

Next to the viscount's magnificence, Eustace was a dusty sparrow in his usual brown broadcloth coat, breeches, and waistcoat. Of course, Eustace looked quite well in brown, and one didn't expect a country vicar to go about in silver brocade. It would be improper, and he'd probably seem merely silly in such splendor. Which made one wonder why the viscount, instead of looking silly, appeared downright dangerous in his finery.

"Did you know if you stand in the middle of the Westminster nave and whistle, there is quite a nice echo?" Mr. Fletcher said, looking around the table.

"Absolutely fascinating," the viscount said. "I'll keep that in mind should I ever have occasion to visit the place and feel an urge to whistle."

"Yes, well, try not to do it within sight of a female relative. Got my ears boxed." Mr. Fletcher rubbed the side of his head, remembering.

"Ah, the ladies do keep us in line." Eustace elevated his glass and looked at Lucy. "I don't know what we would do without their guiding hands."

She raised her eyebrows. She wasn't certain that she'd ever guided Eustace, but that seemed beside the point.

Lord Iddesleigh toasted her as well. "Here, here. My dearest wish is but to lie prostrate and humble beneath my lady's iron thumb. Her stern frown makes me tremble; her elusive smile causes me to stiffen and shake in ecstasy."

Lucy's eyes widened even as her nipples tightened. The wretch!

Mr. Fletcher started coughing again.

Papa and Eustace scowled, but it was the younger man who got in the first word. "I say, that's a bit bold."

"It's quite all right—" Lucy attempted, but the men weren't listening to her, despite their flowery words.

"Bold?" The viscount lowered his glass. "In what way?"

"Well, *stiffen.*" The vicar blushed.

Oh, for goodness' sake! Lucy opened her mouth but was interrupted before she could get a word out.

"Stiffen? Stiffen? Stiffen?" Lord Iddesleigh repeated, sounding uncommonly silly. "A perfectly nice English word. Descriptive and plain. Used in all the best houses. I've heard the king himself employ it. In fact, it describes exactly what you are doing now, Mr. Penweeble."

Mr. Fletcher was bent double, his hands covering his reddened face. Lucy hoped he wouldn't choke to death in his amusement.

Eustace flushed an alarming shade of puce. "What about *ecstasy*, then? I'd like to see you defend that, sir."

The viscount drew himself up and looked down his rather long nose. "I would think that you of all people, Vicar, a soldier in the army of His Majesty's church, a man of learning and exquisite reasoning, a soul seeking the divine salvation only available through Christ our Lord, would understand that *ecstasy* is a most righteous and religious term." Lord Iddesleigh paused to eat a bite of chicken. "What else did you think it meant?"

For a moment, the gentlemen around the table goggled at the viscount. Lucy looked from one to another, exasperated. Really, this nightly war of words was getting tiresome.

Then Papa spoke. "Believe that may be blasphemy." And he started chuckling.

Mr. Fletcher stopped choking and joined in the laughter. Eustace grimaced and then he, too, laughed softly, although he still looked uncomfortable.

Lord Iddesleigh smiled, raised his glass, and watched Lucy over the rim with his silver eyes.

He'd been both blasphemous and improper—and Lucy didn't care. Her lips were trembling, and she felt short of breath just looking at him.

She smiled back helplessly.

"WAIT!" SIMON SCRAMBLED DOWN the front steps the next morning, ignoring the pain in his back. Miss Craddock-Hayes's trap was almost out of sight down the drive. "Oy, wait!" He had to stop running, as his back was burning. He bent over, propping his hands on his knees, and panted, head hung down. A week ago he wouldn't have even been winded.

Behind him, Hedge was muttering near the entrance to the Craddock-Hayes house. "Young fool, lord or no. Fool to get stabbed and fool to run after a wench. Even one like Miss Lucy."

Simon heartily agreed. His urgency was ridiculous. When had he ever run after a woman? But he had an awful need to talk to her, to explain his ungentlemanly conduct of the night before. Or perhaps that was an excuse. Perhaps the need was simply to be with her. He was conscious that the sands of time were running swiftly through his fingers. Soon he would run out of excuses to stay in tranquil Maiden Hill. Soon he would see his angel no more.

Thankfully, Miss Craddock-Hayes had heard his shout. She halted the horse just before the drive disappeared into a copse and turned in her seat to look back at him. Then she pulled the horse's head around.

"What are you doing, running after me?" she asked when the cart had drawn alongside him. She sounded not at all impressed. "You'll reopen your wound."

He straightened, trying not to look like a decrepit wreck. "A small price to pay for a moment of your sweet time, oh fair lady."

Hedge snorted loudly and banged the front door shut behind him. But she smiled at him.

"Are you going into town?" he asked.

"Yes." She cocked her head. "The village is small. I can't think what you could find there to interest you."

"Oh, you'd be surprised. The ironmonger's, the cross in the center of the square, the ancient church—all are items of excitement." He vaulted into the cart beside her, making it rock. "Would you like me to drive?"

"No. I can manage Kate." She chirruped to the sturdy little horse—presumably Kate—and they lurched forward.

"Have I thanked you for your charity in rescuing me from a ditch?"

"I believe you have." She darted a glance at him, then turned again to the road so that he couldn't see her face around the brim of her hat. "Did I tell you we thought you dead when I first saw you?"

"No. I am sorry for your distress."

"I'm glad you weren't dead."

He wished he could see her face. "As am I."

"I thought . . ." Her words trailed away; then she started again. "It was so strange finding you. My day had been very ordinary, and then I looked down and saw you. At first I didn't believe my eyes. You were so out of place in my world."

I still am. But he didn't speak the thought aloud.

"Like discovering a magical being," she said softly.

"Then your disappointment must've been severe."

"In what way?"

"To discover me to be a man of earthen clay and not magical at all."

"Aha! I shall have to note this day in my diary."

He rocked against her as they bumped over a rut in the road. "Why?"

"December the second," she intoned in a grave voice. "Just after luncheon. The Viscount of Iddesleigh makes a humble statement regarding himself."

He grinned at her like an idiot. "Touché."

She didn't turn her head, but he saw the smile curve

her cheek. He had a sudden urge to pull the reins from her hands, guide the horse to the side of the road, and take his angel into his clayish arms. Perhaps she had the spell that could turn the misshapen monster into something human.

Ah, but that would involve degrading the angel.

So instead Simon lifted his face to the winter sun, thin though it was. It was good to be outdoors, even in the chill wind. Good to be sitting beside her. The ache in his shoulder had subsided to a dull throb. He'd been lucky and not reopened the wound, after all. He watched his angel. She sat with her back upright and managed the reins competently with very little show, quite unlike the ladies of his acquaintance who were apt to become dramatic actresses when driving a gentleman. Her hat was a plain straw one, tied underneath her left ear. She wore a gray cloak over her lighter gray gown, and it suddenly occurred to him that he'd never seen her in any other color.

"Is there a reason you always wear gray?" he asked.

"What?"

"Your dress." He indicated her apparel with his hand. "You're always in gray. Rather like a pretty little dove. If you aren't in mourning, why do you wear it?"

She frowned. "I didn't think it was proper for a gentleman to comment on a lady's attire. Are the social conventions different in London?"

Ouch. His angel was in fine fettle this morning.

He leaned against the seat, propping his elbow behind her back. He was so close he could feel her warmth at his chest. "Yes, actually they are. For instance, it is considered de rigueur for a lady driving a gentleman in a trap to flirt with him outrageously."

She pursed her lips, still refusing to look at him.

That served only to egg him on. "Ladies not following this convention are frowned upon severely. Very often you will see the elder members of the *ton* shaking their heads over these poor, lost souls."

"You are terrible."

"I'm afraid so," he sighed. "But I'll give you leave to disregard the rule since we are in the benighted country."

"Benighted?" She slapped the reins, and Kate rattled her bridle.

"I insist on benighted."

She gave him a look.

He stroked one finger down her ramrod-straight spine. She stiffened even more but didn't comment. He remembered the taste of her fingers on his tongue the night before, and another less polite part of his anatomy stiffened as well. Her acceptance of his touch was as erotic as a blatant display in another woman. "You can hardly blame me, since, were we in the city, you would be compelled to say suggestive things to me in my blushing ear."

She sighed. "I can't remember what you asked me before all this nonsense."

He grinned even though it was gauche. He couldn't recall when he'd last had this much fun. "Why do you wear only gray? Not that I have anything against gray, and it does lend you an intriguing ecclesiastical air."

"I look like a nun?" Her terrifying brows drew together.

The trap bumped over another rut in the road and jostled his shoulder against hers.

"No, dear girl. I am saying, admittedly in a roundabout and rather obscure way, that you are an angel sent from heaven to judge me for my sins."

"I wear gray because it is a color that doesn't show dirt." She glanced at him. "What kind of sins have you committed?"

He leaned close, as if about to impart a confidence, and caught a whiff of roses. "I contest the word *color* used in reference to gray and submit that gray is not a color at all, but rather a lack thereof."

Her eyes narrowed ominously.

He drew back and sighed. "As to my sins, my dear lady, they are not the sort that may be spoken of in the presence of an angel."

"Then how am I to judge them? And gray is so a color."

He laughed. He felt like throwing wide his arms and perhaps breaking into song. It must be the country air. "Lady, I concede to the power of your well-thought-out argument, which, I think, would have brought even Sophocles to his knees. Gray, therefore, is a color."

She harrumphed. "And your sins?"

"My sins are numerous and irredeemable." The image flashed through his mind of Peller desperately flinging out his hand and his own sword slicing through it, blood and fingers spangling the air. Simon blinked and painted a smile across his lips. "All who have knowledge of my sins," he said lightly, "shrink in horror from the sight of me as if I were a leper revealed, my nose falling off, my ears rotting."

She regarded him, so grave and so innocent. Brave little angel, untouched by the stink of men. He couldn't help stroking her back again, cautiously, furtively. Her eyes widened.

"And so they should," he continued. "For instance, I have been known to leave my house without a hat."

She frowned. He wasn't wearing a hat at the moment.

"In *London*," he clarified.

But she wasn't worried about hats. "Why do you think that you're irredeemable? All men can find grace if they repent of their sins."

"So speaketh the angel of the Lord." He leaned close to her, under her flat straw hat, and smelled again the scent of roses in her hair. His cock twitched. "But what if I am a devil from hell itself and not of your world at all, angel?"

"I'm not an angel." She tilted her face up.

"Oh, yes, you are," he breathed. His lips brushed her hair, and for a wild moment he thought he might kiss her, might debauch this lady with his foul mouth. But the cart shook as they rounded a curve, and her head turned to mind the horse, and the moment passed.

"How independent you are," he murmured.

"Country ladies need to be, if we are to get anywhere," she said somewhat tartly. "Did you think I sit at home doing the mending all day?"

Ah, this was dangerous ground. They'd been in this territory when she'd grown angry with him two nights before. "No. I am aware of your many duties and talents, not least of which is to help the less fortunate of the village. I have no doubt you would make an admirable Lady Mayor of London, but that would involve quitting this lovely hamlet, and I am sure that the inhabitants would not survive without you."

"Are you?"

"Yes," he said sincerely. "Aren't you?"

"I think everyone would survive quite well without me,"

she said rather dispassionately. "Some other lady would soon fill my shoes, I am sure."

He knit his eyebrows. "Do you value yourself so lightly?"

"It's not that. It's simply that the charities I perform here could be done by anyone."

"Hmm." He considered her beautiful profile. "And were you to abandon all who depend on you here in Maiden Hill, what would you do?"

Her lips parted as she considered his question. He leaned closer. Oh, how he wished to tempt this innocent! "Would you dance upon the stages of London in purple slippers? Sail to far-off Araby in a boat with silken sails? Become a society lady famous for her wit and beauty?"

"I'd become myself."

He blinked. "You already are yourself, beautiful and stern."

"Am I? No one else notices but you."

He stared then into her serious topaz eyes, and he wanted to say something. It was on the tip of his tongue, yet unaccountably he could not speak.

She glanced away. "We're almost to Maiden Hill. See the church tower over there?" She pointed.

He dutifully looked, trying to regain some calm. It was past time he left. If he stayed, he would only be further tempted to seduce this maiden, and as he had proved his entire life, he was not capable of withstanding temptation. Hell, sometimes he ran toward it. But not this time. Not with this woman. He watched her now, her brow furrowed as she maneuvered her little trap into town. A lock of dark hair had come undone and caressed her cheek like a lover's hand. With this woman, if he gave in to temptation, he would destroy something honest and good. Something he had never found anywhere else on this wretched earth.

And he did not think he would survive the devastation.

LUCY SIGHED AND SANK into the warm water of her bath. Of course, she couldn't sink very far—it was only a hip bath—but it felt like pure luxury all the same. She was in the little room at the back of the house, her mother's room. Hedge complained enough as it was, hauling water for her "unnatural" bath, without making him go up the stairs as well. The room was only a few steps away from the kitchen, which made it quite convenient for her ablutions. The water would have to be hauled away again after she was done, but Lucy had told Hedge and Betsy that the chore could wait until morning. They could go to sleep, and she could wallow in the warm water without servants hovering impatiently.

She rested her neck on the high back of the tub and looked up at the ceiling. The fire cast flickering shadows over the old walls, making her feel quite cozy. Papa had dined with Doctor Fremont tonight and was probably still arguing politics and history. Lord Iddesleigh had gone to see Mr. Fletcher at his inn. She had the house to herself, save for the servants, who had retired for the night.

The scent of roses and lavender drifted around her. She lifted a hand and watched the water drip from her fingertips. How strange this last week had been, since she had found Lord Iddesleigh. She'd spent more time in the previous days thinking about how she lived her life and what she would eventually do with it than she had in all her prior years. It had never occurred to her before that there might be more to her existence than keeping Papa's house, doing charitable works here and there, and being courted by Eustace. Why had she not thought beyond being a vicar's wife? She'd never even realized she yearned for more. It was almost like waking from a dream. Suddenly there was this flamboyant man, like none other she'd ever met. Almost effete, with his airs and pretty clothes, yet so very masculine in his movements and in the way he watched her.

He poked and prodded her. He demanded more than simple acquiescence. He wanted her reaction. He made her feel alive in a way that she'd never before thought possible. As if she'd merely sleepwalked through everything else in her life prior to his arrival. She woke in the morning wanting to talk to him, wanting to hear his deep voice spilling nonsense that made her smile or made her angry. She wanted to find out about him, what made his silver eyes so sad at times, what he hid behind his blather, how to make him laugh.

And there was more. She wanted his touch. At night in her narrow bed when she was in that state that is almost but not quite sleep, she would dream he touched her, that his long fingers traced her cheeks. That his wide mouth covered hers.

She inhaled a shuddering breath. She shouldn't, she knew that, but she couldn't help herself. She closed her eyes and imagined what it would feel like if he was here now. Lord Iddesleigh.

Simon.

She drew her wet hands from the water, drops splashing softly into the tub, and trailed them across her collarbone, pretending her hands were his. She shivered. Goose bumps chased across her throat. Her nipples, rising just above the warm water, peaked. Her fingers skimmed lower, and she felt how soft her skin was, cool and damp from the water. She circled just the tips of her middle fingers underneath her breasts, which were full and heavy, then brought them up around to the small bumps of her areola.

She sighed and moved her legs restlessly. If Simon was watching her now, he would see her arousal, the damp prickles on her skin. He would see her nude breasts and erect nipples. The mere thought of being exposed to his eyes made her bite her lip. Slowly, she flicked her fingernails over her nipples, and the sensation made her clench her thighs. If he watched . . . She brought her thumbs and forefingers on either side of her nipples and pinched. Lucy moaned.

And suddenly she knew. She froze for an eternal second and then slowly opened her eyes.

He was in the doorway, his gaze locked with hers—hot, hungry, and very, very male. Then he let his eyes drop and deliberately perused her. From her flushed cheeks to her naked breasts, still encircled in her hands like an offering, down to what the water barely hid. She could almost feel his gaze on her naked skin. His nostrils flared and his cheekbones went ruddy. He looked up again and met her eyes, and she saw in his look both salvation and damnation. At that moment she didn't care. She wanted him.

He turned and left the room.

SIMON RAN UP THE STAIRS three at a time, his heart pounding, his breath coming hard and fast and his cock achingly erect. God! He hadn't felt this primed since he'd been a lad sneaking peeks at a footman groping the giggling downstairs maid. Fourteen, and so full of lust it was all he thought of morning, noon, and night: pussy and how, exactly, he could get it.

He slammed into his room and shut the door behind him. He leaned his head against the wood and tried to catch his breath as his chest heaved. Absently, he rubbed his shoulder. Since that long-ago day, he'd bedded many women, both high and low, some of them a quick tumble, some longer affairs. He'd learned when a woman's eyes signaled that she was available. He'd become something of a connoisseur of female flesh. Or so he'd thought. Right now, he felt like that fourteen-year-old boy again, equally excited and afraid.

He closed his eyes and remembered. He'd come back from sharing a nearly inedible dinner with Christian to find the house quiet. He'd presumed everyone was in bed. Not even Hedge had waited up to greet him; although, knowing Hedge, that hadn't been a surprise. His foot had actually been on the first tread of the stairs when he'd hesitated. He didn't know what had drawn him back to the little room. Maybe some male animal sense that knew what he would find there, what he would see. But all the same, he'd been dumbfounded. Turned like Lot's wife into a pillar of salt.

Or in his case, a pillar of pure lust.

Lucy in her bath, the steam dewing her pale skin, curling the wisps of hair at her temples. Her head thrown back, her lips wet and parted . . .

Simon groaned and unbuttoned the flap of his breeches without opening his eyes.

Her neck had been arched, and he'd thought he could see the pulse beating at her throat, so white and soft. A drop of water lay pooled like a pearl in an oyster's shell in the hollow between her collarbones.

He wrapped his hand around the hard meat between his legs and fisted up, the skin bunching before his fingers.

Her glorious, naked breasts, white and bell-shaped, and held, *held* in her small hands . . .

A faster downstroke, his hand wet with his leaking seed.

Her fingers encircling red, pointed nipples, as if she had been playing with them, arousing herself in her lonely bath.

He took his balls in his left hand and rolled them as he fisted rapidly with his right.

And as he had watched, she'd pinched her nipples between her fingers, squeezing and pulling those poor, sweet nubs until—

"Ahhh, *God!*" He jerked, his hips pumping mindlessly.

She'd moaned in pleasure.

Simon sighed and rolled his head against the wood. Once again he tried to catch his breath. Slowly, he drew out a handkerchief and wiped his hand, trying not to let self-loathing drown his soul. Then he walked to the tiny dresser and splashed water into the basin there. He doused his face and neck and hung his head, dripping, over the basin.

He was losing control.

A laugh burst from his lips, loud in the quiet room. He'd already lost control. God knew what he'd say to her on the morrow, his angel whom he'd ogled in her bath and whose privacy he'd stolen. Simon straightened painfully, dried his face, and lay down on the bed without bothering to undress.

It was past time to leave.

Chapter Six

Lucy pulled her gray woolen cloak more firmly about her shoulders. The wind was sharp this morning. It drove icy fingers under her skirt to wrap around her bones. Normally, she wouldn't have ventured forth, especially on foot, but she needed time to think alone, and the house was full of men. True, there was only Papa, Hedge, and Simon, but she didn't want to talk to two of them, and Hedge was irritating even in the best of circumstances. Hence a country ramble seemed in order.

Lucy kicked a pebble in the lane. How did one go about meeting a gentleman across the luncheon table when he'd last seen one nude and caressing one's own breasts? If she wasn't so embarrassed, she'd ask Patricia. Her friend would be sure to have some type of answer, even if it wasn't the right one. And maybe Patricia would get her past this ghastly self-consciousness. It had been so horrible, last night when he'd seen her. Horrible, but also wonderful, in a secret, wicked way. She'd liked him looking at her. If she was honest with herself, she'd admit that she wished he'd stayed. Stayed and—

Footfalls, rapid and heavy, came from behind her.

Lucy suddenly realized she was alone in the road, no cottage in sight. Maiden Hill was usually a sleepy hamlet, but still . . . She whirled to confront whoever was about to overtake her.

It wasn't a footpad.

No, much worse. It was Simon. She almost turned away again.

"Wait." His voice was subdued. He opened his mouth again but shut it abruptly as if he didn't know what else to say.

That unusual dumbness made her feel a little better. Could he possibly be as embarrassed as she? He'd stopped several paces away. He was bareheaded, without either a hat or a wig, and he stared at her mutely, his gray eyes yearning. Almost as if he needed something from her.

Tentatively, Lucy said, "I'm going for a walk over to the chalk downs. Would you like to accompany me?"

"Yes, please, most forgiving of angels."

And suddenly it was all right. She set off once again, and he measured his stride to hers.

"In the spring, these woods are full of bluebells." She gestured to the surrounding trees. "It's really too bad you've come this time of year when everything is so bleak."

"I shall try to be set upon in summer on the next occasion," he murmured.

"Spring, actually."

He glanced at her.

She smiled wryly. "That's when the bluebells bloom."

"Ah."

"When I was young, Mama used to bring David and me here for picnics in the spring after we'd been cooped up inside all winter. Papa was away at sea most of the time, naturally. David and I would pick as many bluebells as our arms could hold and dump them into her lap."

"She sounds a patient mother."

"She was."

"When did she die?" His words were soft, intimate.

Lucy remembered again that this man had seen her at her most vulnerable. She gazed straight ahead. "Eleven years ago now. I was thirteen."

"A hard age to lose a parent."

She looked at him. The only family he'd mentioned was his brother. He seemed more intent on finding out her meager history than revealing his own. "Is your mother alive?" Obviously, his father must already be dead for him to have inherited the title.

"No. She died a few years ago, before . . ." He stopped.

"Before?"

"Before Ethan, my brother, died. Thank God." He tilted his head back and seemed to stare at the leafless branches overhead, although perhaps he looked at something entirely different. "Ethan was the shining apple of her eye. Her one greatest accomplishment, the person she loved most in the world. He knew how to charm—both the young and the old—and he could lead men. The local farmers came to him with their squabbles. He never met a soul who didn't like him."

Lucy watched him. His voice was expressionless as he described his brother, but his hands twisted slowly at his waist. She wondered if he was even aware of their movement. "You make him sound like a paragon."

"He was. But he was also more. Much more. Ethan knew

right from wrong without having to think about it, without any doubts. Very few people can do that." He looked down and seemed to notice that he was pulling at his right index finger. He clasped his hands behind his back.

She must've made a sound.

Simon glanced at her. "My elder brother was the most moral person I've ever known."

Lucy frowned, thinking about this perfect, dead brother. "Did he look like you?"

He seemed startled.

She raised her brows and waited.

"Actually, he did a little." He half smiled. "Ethan was a bit shorter than I—no more than an inch or so—but he was broader and heavier."

"What about his hair?" She looked at his nearly color-less locks. "Was he fair as well?"

"Mmm." He ran his palm over his head. "But more a golden color with curls. He left it long and didn't wear wigs or powder. I think he was a bit vain about it." He smiled at her mischievously.

She smiled back. She liked him like this, teasing and carefree, and suddenly realized that despite Simon's care-less manner, he was very rarely at ease.

"His eyes were a clear blue," he continued. "Mother used to say they were her favorite color."

"I think I prefer gray."

He bowed with a flourish. "My lady honors me."

She curtsied in reply, but then sobered before asking, "How did Ethan die?"

He stopped, forcing her to a halt as well. She looked up into his face.

He seemed to be struggling; his brows were pulled together over those beautiful ice-gray eyes. "I—"

An insect buzzed past her head, followed by a loud shot. Simon grabbed her roughly and pushed her into the ditch. Lucy landed on her hip, pain and astonishment streaking through her, and then Simon landed on her, squashing her into the mud and dead leaves. Lucy turned her head, trying to draw a full breath. It felt like a horse was sitting on her back.

"Don't move, goddamnit." He placed his hand over her head and pushed it back down. "Somebody's shooting at us."

She spat out a leaf. "I know that."

Oddly, he chuckled in her ear. "Wonderful angel." His breath smelled of tea and mint.

Another shot. The leaves exploded a few feet from her shoulder.

He swore rather colorfully. "He's reloading."

"Can you tell where he is?" she whispered.

"Across the road somewhere. I can't pinpoint the exact location. Hush."

Lucy became aware that aside from the problem with breathing and the fact that she might die violently at any second, it was rather nice having Simon lying on her. He was wonderfully warm. And he smelled quite nice, not of tobacco like most men, but of some exotic scent. Maybe sandalwood? His arms, bracketing her body, felt comforting.

"Listen." Simon placed his mouth next to her ear, his lips caressing her with each word. "At the next shot, we run. He has only the one rifle, and he has to reload. When he—"

A ball burrowed into the ground inches from her face. "Now!"

Simon pulled her to her feet and ran before she had time to even register his command. Lucy panted to keep up, expecting any minute to feel the next shot between her shoulder blades. How long did it take to reload a gun? Only minutes, surely. Her breath rasped painfully in her chest.

Then Simon was shoving her ahead of him. "Go! Into the woods. Keep running!"

He wanted her to leave him? *Dear God, he would die.* "But—"

"He's after me." He glared fiercely into her eyes. "I cannot defend myself with you here. Go now!"

His last word coincided with the blast of yet another shot. Lucy turned and ran, not daring to look behind her, not daring to stop. She sobbed once and then the woods enveloped her in cool darkness. She ran as best she could, stumbling through the undergrowth, the branches catching on her cloak, tears of fear and anguish streaming down her face. Simon was back there, unarmed, confronting a man with a gun. Oh, God! She wanted to go back, but she couldn't—with her out of the way, he at least had a chance against their attacker.

Footsteps sounded heavily behind her.

Lucy's heart pounded right into her throat. She turned to face her attacker, her fists raised in puny defiance.

"Hush, it's me." Simon clasped her to his heaving chest, his breath panting across her face. "Shh, it's all right. You are so brave, my lady."

She laid her head against his chest and heard the pounding of his heart. She clutched the fabric of his coat with both hands. "You're alive."

"Yes, of course. I fear men like me never—"

He stopped because she couldn't keep back a choked sob.

"I'm sorry," he whispered in a more grave voice. He tilted her face away from his chest and wiped her tears with the palm of his hand. He looked concerned and weary and uncertain. "Don't cry, sweeting. I'm not worth it, really I'm not."

Lucy frowned and tried to blink away the tears that kept coming. "Why do you always say that?"

"Because it's true."

She shook her head. "You are very, very important to me, and I'll cry for you if I want."

The corner of his mouth curved up tenderly, but he didn't mock her silly speech. "I am humbled by your tears."

Lucy looked away; she couldn't bear to hold his gaze. "The shooter, is he . . . ?"

"He's gone, I think," Simon murmured. "A rather rickety farmer's cart came along the road, drawn by a sway-backed gray. The cart was filled with laborers, and it must've scared the shooter off."

Lucy puffed out a laugh. "The Jones boys. They've been useful for once in their lives." Then a sudden thought struck and she leaned back to look at him. "Are you hurt?"

"No." He smiled at her, but she could tell by his eyes that his thoughts were elsewhere. "We'd better get you home and then . . ."

She waited, but he'd trailed off again, thinking.

"Then what?" she prompted.

He turned his head so his lips brushed across her cheek, and she almost missed his words. "Then I need to leave this place. To protect you."

*   *   *

"SHOT AT!" CAPTAIN CRADDOCK-HAYES roared an hour later.

All at once, Simon could see the iron hand that had commanded a ship and men for thirty years. He half expected the diamond segments in the windowpanes to rattle right out of their lead frames. They were in the formal sitting room of the Craddock-Hayes house. It was prettily decorated—puce-and-cream-striped curtains, similarly colored settees scattered here and there, and a rather nice china clock on the mantel—but he preferred Lucy's little sitting room at the back of the house.

Not that he'd been given a choice.

"My daughter, a flower of womanhood, a meek and dutiful gel." The captain paced the length of the room, arm batting the air for emphasis, bandy legs stomping. "Innocent of the ways of the world, sheltered all her life, accosted not half a mile from her childhood home. Ha! Haven't had a murder in Maiden Hill in a quarter century. Five and twenty years! And then you show up."

The captain halted in midpace between the mantel and a table set with naval bric-a-brac. He drew an enormous breath. "Scoundrel!" he blasted, nearly taking Simon's eyebrows off. "Ruffian! Cad! Vile endangerer of English, ah, er . . ." His lips moved as he searched for the word.

"Wenches," Hedge supplied.

The manservant had brought in the tea earlier, instead of Betsy or Mrs. Brodie, apparently to deny Simon the succor of female sympathy. Hedge still lurked, fiddling with the silverware as an excuse, listening eagerly.

The captain glared. "*Ladies.*" He transferred his glower

to Simon. "Never have I heard of such villainy, sirrah! What do you have to say for yourself? Eh? Eh?"

"I say you're quite right, Captain." Simon leaned back wearily on the settee. "Except for the 'meek and dutiful' part. With all due respect, sir, I've not noticed Miss Craddock-Hayes to be either."

"You dare, sir, after nearly causing my daughter's death!" The older man shook a fist in his direction, his face purpling. "Ha. Have you packed off from this house before the hour's gone, I will. I'll not stand for it. Lucy's the very heart and soul of this community. Many people, not just me, hold her dear. I'll see you run out of town on a rail, tarred and feathered, if I have to!"

"Cor!" Hedge interjected, his emotions obviously stirred by the captain's speech; although, it was hard to tell whether from fondness for Lucy or the prospect of seeing a member of the nobility on a rail.

Simon sighed. His head was beginning to hurt. This morning he'd experienced the most bone-chilling fear he had ever felt, wondering if a bullet would kill the precious creature beneath him, knowing he would go mad if it did, terrified he would be unable to save her. He never wanted to feel that helpless dread for another's life again. Of course, he hadn't had much actual contact with the ground since Lucy's soft limbs interposed themselves between his body and the earth. And hadn't that been wonderful in a heart-stoppingly god-awful way? To feel what he'd vowed he never would—her face next to his, her rump snug against his groin. Even in the midst of his horror that this was all his fault, that his very presence had put her life in danger, even with layer upon layer of good English cloth between them, even then he'd responded to her. But Simon knew now that his angel could get a rise out of him if he were ten days dead, and it certainly wouldn't be of the religious variety.

"I apologize most profusely for putting Miss Craddock-Hayes in danger, Captain," he said now. "I assure you, though I know it does little good at this late date, that had I any inkling she would be imperiled, I would've slit my own wrists rather than see her harmed."

"Fffsst." Hedge made a derisive sound, oddly effective despite its wordlessness.

The captain merely stared at him for a very long minute. "Ha," he finally said. "Pretty words, but I think you mean them."

Hedge looked as startled as Simon felt.

"Still want you out of this house," the captain grunted.

Simon inclined his head. "I already have Henry packing my things, and I've sent word to Mr. Fletcher at his inn. We will be out within the hour."

"Good." The captain took a seat and contemplated him.

Hedge hurried over with a cup of tea.

The older man waved him away. "Not that bilge water. Get the brandy, man."

Hedge reverently opened a cupboard and brought out a cut-glass decanter half-full with a rich amber liquid. He poured two glasses and brought them over, then stood looking wistfully at the decanter.

"Oh, go ahead," the captain said.

Hedge poured himself a scant inch and held the glass, waiting.

"To the fairer sex," Simon proposed.

"Ha," the older man grumbled, but he drank.

Hedge tossed back his brandy in one gulp, then closed his eyes and shuddered. "Wonnerful stuff, that."

"Indeed. Know a smuggler on the coast," the captain muttered. "Will she still be in danger once you leave?"

"No." Simon tilted his head against the back of the settee. The brandy was fine, but it merely made his head worse. "They're after me, and like the jackals they are, they'll follow the scent away from here once I leave."

"You admit you know these murderers?"

Simon nodded, eyes closed.

"Same ones as left you for dead?"

"Or their hired thugs."

"What's all this about, eh?" the captain growled. "Tell me."

"Revenge." Simon opened his eyes.

The old man didn't blink. "Yours or theirs?"

"Mine."

"Why?"

Simon looked into his glass, swirling the liquid, watching it paint the interior. "They killed my brother."

"Ha." The older man drank to that. "Then I wish you luck. Elsewhere."

"I thank you." Simon drained his glass and stood.

"'Course, you know what they say about revenge."

Simon turned and asked the question, because it was expected and because the old man had been more lenient than he had any right to hope for. "What?"

"Be careful with revenge." The captain grinned like an evil old troll. "Sometimes it twists around and bites you on the arse."

*　　*　　*

LUCY STOOD AT HER NARROW BEDROOM window overlooking the drive and watched Mr. Hedge and Simon's valet load the imposing black carriage. They appeared to be arguing over how to stack the luggage. Mr. Hedge was gesticulating wildly, the valet had a sneer on his uncommonly handsome lips, and the footman actually holding the box in question was staggering. They didn't look like they would have the project done anytime soon, but the fact remained—Simon was leaving. Although she'd known this day would come, she somehow still hadn't been expecting it, and now that it was here, she felt . . . what?

Someone knocked at her door, interrupting her confused thoughts.

"Come." She let the gauzy curtain drop and turned.

Simon opened the door but remained in the hall. "May I have a word with you? Please."

She nodded mutely.

He hesitated. "I thought we could take a turn around your garden?"

"Of course." It wouldn't be proper for her to talk to him alone here. She caught up a woolen shawl and preceded him down the stairs.

He held the kitchen door for her, and Lucy stepped into the cold sunshine. Mrs. Brodie's vegetable garden was in a sad state this time of year. The hard earth was crusted with a thin layer of killing frost. Skeleton stalks of kale leaned in a drunken row. Beside them, some thin onion leaves were frozen to the ground, black and brittle. A few shrunken apples, missed at picking time, clung to the bare branches of the pruned trees. Winter overlaid the garden in a sleep that mimicked death.

Lucy folded her arms about herself and took a steadying breath. "You're leaving."

He nodded. "I can't remain and put you and your family at further risk. This morning was too close, too deadly. If the assassin hadn't missed his first shot . . ." He grimaced. "It was my own selfish vanity that let me stay so long as it is. I never should have lingered this past week, knowing what lengths they would go to."

"So you will return to London." She couldn't look at him and remain impassive, so she kept her gaze on the rattling tree branches. "Won't they find you there?"

He laughed, a harsh sound. "My angel, it is more a matter of me finding them, I fear."

She did glance at him then. His face was bitter. And lonely.

"Why do you say that?" she asked.

He hesitated, appeared to debate, then finally shook his head. "There is so much you do not know about me, will never know about me. Very few do, and in your case, I prefer it that way."

He wasn't going to tell her, and she felt an unreasoning spurt of rage. Did he still think she was a glass figurine to wrap in gauze? Or did he simply not respect her enough to confide in her?

"Do you really prefer I don't know you?" She turned to face him. "Or do you say that to every naive woman you meet so they'll think you sophisticated?"

"Think?" His lips quirked. "You cut me to the bone."

"You're fobbing me off with blather."

He blinked, his head rearing back as if she'd slapped him. "Blather—"

"Yes, blather." Her voice trembled with anger, but she

couldn't seem to steady it. "You play the fool so you won't have to tell the truth."

"I've only said it to you." Now he sounded irritated.

Well, good. So was she. "Is that how you want to live? All alone? Never letting anyone in?" She shouldn't push, she knew, as this was the last time they would see each other.

"It's less a matter of wanting as it is . . ." He shrugged. "Some things can't be changed. And it suits me."

"It sounds a very solitary existence, and a not entirely satisfactory one," Lucy said slowly, choosing her words carefully, lining them up like soldiers to do battle. "To go through life without a true confidant. Someone to whom you can reveal yourself without fear. Someone who knows your faults and weaknesses and who cares for you nonetheless. Someone for whom you don't have to play a role."

"You frighten me more than I can say at times." His silver eyes gleamed as he whispered the words, and she wished she could read them. "Do not tempt a man so long without the bread of companionship."

"If you stayed . . ." She had to stop and catch her breath; her chest felt tight. She gambled so much on these few seconds, and she needed to speak eloquently. "If you stayed, perhaps we could learn more about each other. Perhaps I could become that confidant for you. That companion."

"I will not put you at further risk." But she thought she saw hesitation in his eyes.

"I—"

"And that which you ask for"—he looked away—"I do not think I have it in me to give."

"I see." Lucy stared down at her hands. So this was defeat.

"If anyone—"

But she interrupted, talking quickly and loudly, not wanting to hear his pity. "You are from the fast city, and I am only a simple gentlewoman living in the country. I understand that—"

"No." He turned back and took a step toward her so they stood only a hand's width apart. "Don't reduce what is between us to a conflict of rural and urban mores and ways."

The wind blew against her and Lucy shivered.

He shifted so his body shielded hers from the breeze. "In the past week and a half, I have felt more than I ever have before in my life. You stir something in me. I . . ." He gazed over her head at the cloudy sky.

She waited.

"I don't know how to express myself. What I feel." He looked down at her and smiled faintly. "And that is very unusual for me, as you know by now. I can only say that I am glad that I've met you, Lucy Craddock-Hayes."

Tears pricked at the corners of her eyes. "And I, you."

He took her hand and gently uncurled her fingers so that her palm lay cupped between his own like a flower nestled among leaves. "I will remember you all the days of my life," he murmured so low she almost didn't hear. "And I am not sure whether that is a blessing or a curse." He bent over their hands, and she felt the warm brush of his lips against her cold palm.

She looked down at the back of his head, and one of her tears fell to his hair.

He straightened. Without looking at her, he said, "Goodbye." And walked away.

Lucy sobbed once and then she had herself contained.

She remained in the garden until she could no longer hear the departing carriage wheels.

SIMON CLIMBED INTO HIS CARRIAGE and settled into the red leather squabs. He rapped on the roof, then leaned back so he could watch the Craddock-Hayes house recede out the window. He couldn't see Lucy—she'd remained in the garden, still as an alabaster statue when he left—but the house could be her surrogate. They jolted forward.

"I can't believe you stayed in this country village as long as you did." Christian sighed across from him. "I would've thought you'd've found it terribly boring. What did you do all day? Read?"

John Coachman whipped the horses to a trot down the drive. The carriage swayed. Henry, sharing the seat with Christian, cleared his throat and cast his gaze to the ceiling.

Christian glanced at him uneasily. "'Course, the Craddock-Hayeses were very hospitable and all that. Good people. Miss Craddock-Hayes was nicely solicitous of me during those ghastly dinners. I fancy she thought she was protecting me from her father, the old blowhard. Very kind. She'll make a good vicar's wife when she marries that fellow Penweeble."

Simon almost winced, but he caught himself in time. Or thought he did. Henry cleared his throat so loudly that Simon feared he'd dislodge some vital organ.

"What's the matter with you, man?" Christian frowned at the valet. "Have you got some kind of catarrh? You sound like my father in one of his more disapproving moods."

The house was a toy now, a small, bucolic spot surrounded by the oaks of the drive.

"My health is quite all right, sir," Henry said frostily. "Thank you for inquiring. Have you thought of what you will do on your return to London, Lord Iddesleigh?"

"Mmm." They'd rounded a curve, and he could no longer see the house. He peered for a moment more, but that chapter of his life was gone. *She* was gone. Best forgotten, really, all of it.

If he could.

"He'll probably want to do the rounds," Christian nattered on blithely. "Catch up on the gossip at Angelo's and the gambling dens and the soiled doves at the more notorious houses."

Simon straightened and closed the window shade. "Actually, I'm going on a hunt. I'll have my nose to the ground, ears flapping, an eager bloodhound racing to find my attackers."

"But wasn't it footpads?" Christian looked puzzled. "I mean, pretty hard to do, track down a couple of lowlifes in London. The city's full of them."

"I have a fairly good idea who they are." Simon rubbed his right index finger with the opposite hand. "In fact, I'm almost sure I've already made their acquaintance. Or at least the acquaintance of their masters."

"Really." Christian stared, perhaps realizing for the first time that he was missing something. "And what will you do when you have them cornered?"

"Why, call them out." Simon bared his teeth. "Call them out and kill them."

Chapter Seven

". . . And I really do think the repairs to the roof over the vestry will last this time. Thomas Jones assured me that he'll do the work himself instead of letting one of his lads bungle it." Eustace paused in his dissertation on the church improvements to carefully guide the horse past a rut in the road.

"How nice," Lucy interjected while she had time.

The sun was out as it had been the previous Tuesday. They drove into Maiden Hill on the road Eustace always took, past the bakery and the same two elderly ladies haggling with the baker. The ladies turned as they had the week before and waved. Nothing had changed. Simon Iddesleigh might never have landed so suddenly in her life only to fly away again.

Lucy felt a mad urge to scream.

"Yes, but I'm not that certain about the nave," Eustace replied.

This was new to the catalogue of church problems. "What's wrong with the nave?"

He frowned, lines etching themselves into his normally

smooth brow. "The roof has begun to leak there as well. Not very much, only enough to stain the ceiling so far, but it will be harder to get to the damage because of the vaulting. I'm not sure even Tom's eldest will enjoy that job. We may have to pay him extra."

Lucy couldn't help it. She threw back her head and laughed, silly peals that were overloud and seemed to echo in the bright winter air. Eustace half smiled in that embarrassed way one does when one isn't quite sure of the joke. The two elderly ladies trotted across the green to see what the commotion was about, and the smith and his boy came out of his shop.

Lucy tried to calm herself. "I'm sorry."

"No, don't apologize." Eustace glanced at her, his coffee-brown eyes shy. "I'm glad to hear your mirth. You don't often laugh."

Which only made her feel worse, of course.

Lucy closed her eyes. She suddenly realized that she should have cut this off ages ago. "Eustace—"

"I wanted—" He started talking at the same time as she, and their words collided. He stopped and smiled. "Please." He indicated she should continue.

But Lucy felt awful now and not eager to start what would no doubt be an uncomfortable discussion. "No, I beg your pardon. What did you mean to say?"

He took a breath, his wide chest expanding under the coarse brown wool of his coat. "I have wanted to speak to you about an important matter for some time now." He turned the carriage behind the church, and suddenly they were secluded.

Lucy had a terrible premonition. "I think—"

But for once Eustace didn't defer to her. He continued

speaking right over her. "I wanted to tell you how much I admire you. How much I enjoy spending this time with you. They're comfortable, don't you think, our little carriage rides?"

Lucy tried again. "Eustace—"

"No, don't interrupt. Let me get this out. You'd think I wouldn't be so nervous, as I know you so well." He inhaled and blew out a gust of air. "Lucy Craddock-Hayes, will you do me the honor of being my bride? There. That's over with."

"I—"

Eustace pulled her to him abruptly, and her voice ended in a squeak. He crushed her gently against his big chest, and it was like being enveloped by a giant, smothering pillow, not unpleasant but not entirely comfortable either. His face loomed above hers before he swooped in to kiss her.

Oh, for goodness' sake! A wave of exasperation crashed over her head. Not, she was sure, what one should be feeling when being kissed by a handsome young man. And to be fair, Eustace's kiss was quite . . . nice. His lips were warm, and he moved them in a pleasing way over her own. He smelled of peppermint—he must have prepared for this kiss by chewing some—and on that thought, Lucy's impatience changed to fond sympathy.

He broke away, looking very pleased with himself. "Shall we tell your father?"

"Eustace—"

"Gadzooks! I should've asked his permission first." His brow crimped in thought.

"Eustace—"

"Well, it can't come as any great surprise, can it? I've

been courting you for a long time now. 'Spect the village considers us already married."

"Eustace!"

He started slightly at the loudness of her voice. "My dear?"

Lucy closed her eyes. She hadn't meant to shout, but he would natter on. She shook her head. Best to concentrate if she was to get through this. "Whilst I am deeply appreciative of the honor you do me, Eustace, I . . ." She made the mistake of looking at him.

He sat there, a lock of brown hair blowing against his cheek, looking perfectly innocent. "Yes?"

She winced. "I can't marry you."

"Of course you can. I really don't think the captain will object. He would've shooed me off long before now if he didn't approve. And you're well past the age of consent."

"Thank you."

He flushed. "I meant—"

"I know what you meant." Lucy sighed. "But I . . . I really can't marry you, Eustace."

"Why not?"

She didn't want to hurt him. "Can't we just leave it at that?"

"No." He drew himself up in an oddly dignified manner. "I'm sorry, but if you're going to reject me, I think I at least deserve to know the reason why."

"No, *I'm* sorry. I didn't mean to lead you on. It's just that"—she frowned down at her hands as she tried to find the words—"over the years, we fell into a kind of habit, one that I no longer questioned. And I should have."

The horse shook its head, jangling the tack.

"I'm a *habit?*"

She winced. "I didn't—"

He placed both his big hands on his knees and clenched them. "All this time I expected that we would marry." His hands flexed. "You've had the expectation of marriage as well; don't tell me you didn't."

"I'm sorry—"

"And now you expect me to give this up on a whim of yours?"

"It isn't a whim." She drew a steadying breath. Crying would be a cowardly way to win his sympathy. Eustace deserved more from her. "I've been thinking and thinking over the last days. I've agonized about what we are to each other. It just isn't enough."

"Why?" Eustace asked the question quietly. "Why should you question what we have, what we are together? It seems nice to me."

"But that's just it." Lucy looked into his eyes. "Nice isn't enough for me. I want—I *need*—more."

He was silent a moment as the wind blew a few left-over leaves against the church door. "Is it because of that Iddesleigh fellow?"

Lucy looked away, took a deep breath, and let it out in a sigh. "I expect it is, yes."

"You know he isn't coming back."

"Yes."

"Then why"—he pounded his thigh suddenly—"*why* can't you marry me?"

"It wouldn't be fair to you. You must know that."

"I think you should let me be the judge of that."

"Maybe so," Lucy conceded. "But then you need to let me be the judge of what is fair to me. And living my life in a compromise, in a *nice* marriage, is no longer tenable for me."

"Why?" Eustace's voice was husky. He sounded close to tears.

Lucy felt moisture prick her own eyes. How could she have brought such a good man so low?

"Do you think you love that fellow?"

"I don't know." She closed her eyes, but the tears overflowed nevertheless. "All I know is that he opened a door into a whole new world I never even knew existed. I've stepped through that door, and I can't return."

"But—"

"I know." She made a slashing motion with her hand. "I know he won't be coming back, that I'll never see or speak to him again. But it doesn't matter, don't you see?"

He shook his head and, once started, couldn't seem to stop. His head swung back and forth in a stubborn, bearlike movement.

"It's like . . ." Lucy raised her hands in a pleading gesture as she tried to think of the analogy. "Like being blind from birth and then one day suddenly being able to see. And not just see, but to witness the sun rising in all her glory across an azure sky. The dusky lavenders and blues lightening to pinks and reds, spreading across the horizon until the entire Earth is lit. Until one has to blink and fall to one's knees in awe at the light."

He stilled and stared at her as if dumbstruck.

"Don't you understand?" Lucy whispered. "Even if one were made blind again in the next instant, one would ever after remember and know what was missed. What could be."

"So you won't marry me," he said quietly.

"No." Lucy let her hands drop, deflated and weary. "I won't marry you."

"Dammit!" Edward de Raaf, the fifth Earl of Swartingham, roared as yet another boy whizzed past. The boy somehow managed to avoid seeing de Raaf's large, waving arm.

Simon stifled a sigh. He sat in his favorite London coffeehouse, his feet—shod in new red-heeled pumps—propped on a nearby chair, and yet he could not drag his mind away from the little town he'd left over a week ago.

"D'you think the service is getting worse?" his companion asked as he was passed over again. The boy must be blind. Or willfully not seeing. De Raaf stood a solid six feet and some inches, had a sallow, pockmarked face, and striking midnight black hair worn in a messy queue. His expression at the moment was enough to curdle cream. He didn't exactly blend into a crowd.

"No." Simon sipped his own coffee thoughtfully. He'd arrived earlier than the other man and was thus already set up. "It's always been this awful."

"Then why do we come here?"

"Well, I come here for the excellent coffee." Simon glanced around the dingy, low-ceilinged coffeehouse. The Agrarian Society, an eclectic, loose-knit club, met here. The only terms of membership were that the man had to have an interest in agriculture. "And, of course, the sophisticated atmosphere."

De Raaf shot him a ludicrously outraged look.

A fight broke out in the corner between a macaroni in a deplorable pink-powdered, three-tailed wig, and a country squire wearing muddy jackboots. The boy scurried past them again—de Raaf didn't even get a chance to raise his hand this time—and Harry Pye stole into the coffeehouse. Pye moved like a cat on the hunt, gracefully and without any sound. Add to that his nondescript appearance—he was of average height and looks and favored a dull brown wardrobe—and it was a wonder anyone noticed him at all. Simon narrowed his eyes. With his physical control, Pye would have made a formidable swordsman. But since he was a commoner, no doubt he had never held a sword; only nobility could wear one. Which didn't stop Pye from carrying a wicked little blade in his left boot.

"My lords." Pye sat in the remaining chair at their table.

De Raaf let out a long-suffering sigh. "How many times have I told you to call me Edward or de Raaf?"

Pye half smiled in acknowledgment at the familiar words, but it was to Simon he spoke. "I am glad to see you well, my lord. We had news of your near murder."

Simon shrugged easily. "A trifle, I assure you."

De Raaf frowned. "That's not what I heard."

The boy slammed a full mug of coffee down beside Pye.

De Raaf's jaw dropped. "How did you do that?"

"What?" Pye's gaze lowered to the empty space on the table before the earl. "Aren't you having a cup today?"

"I—"

"He's decided to give up coffee," Simon cut in smoothly. "Heard it's not good for the libido. Huntington wrote a treatise on it recently, didn't you hear? It especially affects those nearing their middle years."

"Really." Pye blinked.

De Raaf's pale, pockmarked face crimsoned. "What a lot of rot—"

"Can't say I've noticed it affecting me." Simon smiled blandly and sipped his coffee. "But then again, de Raaf is considerably older than I."

"You lying—"

"And he's recently married. Bound to have a slowing-down consequence, that."

"Now see here—"

Pye's lips twitched. If Simon hadn't been watching closely, he'd have missed it. "But I'm newly married as well," Pye interrupted softly. "And I can't say I've noticed any, ah, problem. Must be the age."

Simon felt a strange pang as he realized he was the odd man out. They turned in unison to the earl.

Who sputtered, "Despicable, lying, caddish—"

The boy whirled by again. De Raaf frantically waved his arm. "Ahhh, *damn!*"

The lad disappeared into the kitchen without ever turning his head.

"Good thing you've given up the sacred brew." Simon smirked.

A crash came from the brawl in the corner. Heads swiveled. The country squire had the dandy, sans wig, on his back against a table. Two chairs lay broken nearby.

Pye frowned. "Isn't that Arlington?"

"Yes," Simon replied. "Hard to recognize him without that atrocious wig, isn't it? Can't think why he chose pink. No doubt that's the reason the rural chap is pummeling him. Probably overcome with loathing for the wig."

"They were arguing over swine breeding." De Raaf

shook his head. "He's always been a bit unreasonable about farrowing pens. Runs in the family."

"Do you think we should help him?" Pye asked.

"No." De Raaf looked around for the boy, an evil gleam in his eye. "Arlington could benefit from a beating. Might knock some sense into him."

"Doubt it." Simon raised his mug again, but then lowered it as he saw a slight, scruffy character hesitating in the doorway.

The man scanned the room and spotted him. He started toward them.

"Dammit!" de Raaf exclaimed beside him. "They're ignoring me on purpose."

"Do you want me to get you a coffee?" Pye asked.

"No. I'm going to do it myself or die trying."

The man stopped before Simon. "Took me most of the day, Guv, but I've found him." He proffered a dirty scrap of paper.

"Thanks." Simon gave the man a gold coin.

"Ta." The little man tugged a forelock and disappeared.

Simon opened the paper and read: *The Devil's Playground after eleven.* He crumpled the note and stuffed it in a pocket. And only then realized the other two men were watching him. He raised his brows.

"What's that?" De Raaf rumbled. "Found another one to duel?"

Simon blinked, taken aback. He thought he had kept his dueling secret from de Raaf and Pye. He'd not wanted their interference or their moralizing.

"Surprised we know?" De Raaf leaned back, endangering the wooden chair he sat in. "It wasn't that hard to ferret out how you've been spending the last couple of months, especially after that sword fight with Hartwell."

What was the big man's point? "Not your business."

"It is when you're risking your life with each duel," Pye answered for them both.

Simon stared hard.

Neither man blinked.

Damn them. He looked away. "They killed Ethan."

"John Peller killed your brother." De Raaf tapped a big finger on the table in emphasis. "And he's already dead. You ran him through more than two years ago. Why start again now?"

"Peller was part of a conspiracy." Simon looked away. "A bloody conspiracy from hell. I only found out several months ago, whilst going through some of Ethan's papers."

De Raaf sat back and folded his arms.

"I discovered that fact right before I challenged Hartwell." Simon fingered his index finger. "There were four of them in the conspiracy. Two are left now, and they're all culpable. What would you do if it were your brother?"

"Probably the same as you're doing."

"There you are."

De Raaf grimaced. "The chances you'll be killed increase with every duel you fight."

"I've won both duels so far." Simon looked away. "What makes you think I can't win the next?"

"Even the best swordsman can slip or be distracted for a moment." De Raaf looked irritable. "One moment, that's all it takes. Those are your words."

Simon shrugged.

Pye leaned forward, his voice lowering. "At least let us go with you, be your seconds."

"No. I already have someone else in mind."

"That lad you've been partnering with at Angelo's?" de Raaf cut in.

Simon nodded. "Christian Fletcher."

Pye's gaze sharpened. "How well do you know him? Can you trust him?"

"Christian?" Simon laughed. "Young, I concede, but quite good with a blade. Almost as good as I, in fact. He's beaten me in practice once or twice."

"But would he guard your back in a crisis?" De Raaf shook his head. "Would he even know to look for tricks?"

"It won't come to that."

"Dammit—"

"Besides"—Simon looked from one to the other—"the both of you are in a state of connubial bliss. Think you that I would want to present either of your wives with a dead husband before your first anniversary?"

"Simon—" de Raaf began.

"No. Leave it at that."

"God*damn* you." The big man stood, his chair nearly toppling over. "You had better not be dead the next time I see you." He banged his way out of the coffeehouse.

Simon frowned.

Pye silently emptied his cup. "Since you've reminded me of my lady, I'd best be leaving as well." He rose. "If you have need of me, Lord Iddesleigh, you have only to send word."

Simon nodded. "The kindness of friendship is all I ask."

Pye touched him on the shoulder and then he, too, was gone.

Simon looked at his coffee. It was cold, with a ring of greasy scum floating on the surface, but he didn't order a new cup. At eleven tonight he would track down another of his brother's murderers and challenge him to a duel. Until then, he had nothing in particular to do. No one waited for his return. No one grew anxious as the time wore on. No one would mourn if he did not turn up.

Simon swallowed some of the filthy coffee and grimaced. Nothing was as pathetic as a man who lied to himself. It wasn't that no one would mourn his death—Pye and de Raaf had just now indicated that they would do just that—but that no *woman* would mourn. No, he still lied. *Lucy.* Lucy wouldn't mourn. He mouthed her name and tapped his fingers against the mug. When had he forfeited a normal life, one that included a wife and family? Was it after Ethan had died and he'd suddenly had the title and all the cares it represented thrust on him? Or later, when he'd killed the first one? John Peller. Simon shuddered. His dreams were still haunted by Peller's fingers, falling disconnected to the dewy grass like gruesome flowers newly bloomed.

God.

And he could live with that, could live with the macabre nightmares. After all, the man had killed his only brother. He'd had to die. The dreams had even begun to abate. Until he'd found out there were more men to kill.

Simon raised the mug to his lips before remembering it was empty. Even after dueling Hartwell, it was Peller and his fingers he still dreamed about at night. Strange. It must be some quirk of the mind. Not a normal quirk, to be sure, because his mind was no longer normal. Some men might be able to kill without changing, but he wasn't among their number. And that thought brought him around once again. He'd been right to leave Lucy behind. To decide not to cleave unto a wife, no matter the temptation to let go and live like an ordinary man. He couldn't anymore.

He'd lost that choice when he'd set his course of revenge.

"I DON'T THINK THIS IDDESLEIGH gentleman can be a good acquaintance for you, Christian, viscount or no viscount." Matilda looked pointedly at their only son as she passed him the bread.

Sir Rupert grimaced. His wife's red hair had mellowed over the years of their marriage, lightening with the addition of gray, but her temper had not. Matilda had been the only daughter of a baronet, an old family now impoverished. Before he'd met her, Sir Rupert had thought all aristocratic women were little more than wilting lilies. Not she. He'd found a will of iron underneath Matilda's delicate exterior.

He raised his glass and watched to see how this dinner table confrontation would play out. Matilda was usually a very lenient mother, letting her children choose their own friends and interests. But she had recently gotten a bee in her bonnet about Iddesleigh and Christian.

"Why, Mater, what do you have against him?" Christian grinned charmingly at his mother, his hair the same shade of Titian red that hers had been twenty years before.

"He's a rake, and not a nice one either." Matilda looked over the half-moon spectacles she wore only at home with family. "It's said he killed two men in separate duels."

Christian dropped the bread basket.

Poor lad. Sir Rupert mentally shook his head. He wasn't yet used to prevarication. Fortunately, he was saved by his elder sister.

"I think Lord Iddesleigh a perfectly delicious man," Rebecca said, defiance in her dark blue eyes. "The rumors only add to his appeal."

He sighed. Becca, their second child and the beauty of the family with her classical features, had been at loggerheads with his wife since her fourteenth birthday a decade ago. He'd hoped she would've grown out of her spitefulness by now.

"Yes, dear, I know." Matilda, long used to her daughter's gambits, didn't bother rising to the bait. "Although I wish you wouldn't put it in such a crass way. *Delicious* makes the man sound like a side of bacon."

"Oh, Mama—"

"I can't see what you find to like about him, Becca." Julia, the eldest, frowned down at her roast chicken.

Sir Rupert had long wondered if she'd inherited her mother's nearsightedness. But despite the fact that she considered herself practical, Julia had a vain streak and would have been outraged at the suggestion of spectacles.

She continued, "His humor is not often kind, and he looks at one in such a queer way."

Christian laughed. "Really, Julia."

"I haven't ever seen Viscount Iddesleigh," Sarah, the youngest and most like her father, said. She surveyed her siblings with analytical brown eyes. "I don't suppose he's invited to the same balls as I. What is he like?"

"He's a jolly fine fellow. Very funny and superb with a

sword. He's taught me a few moves. . . ." Christian caught his mother's look and found a sudden interest in his peas.

Julia took over. "Lord Iddesleigh is above average height, but not so tall as our brother. A handsome form and face and he is considered an excellent dancer."

"He dances divinely," Becca tossed in.

"Quite." Julia cut her meat into precise little cubes. "But he rarely dances with unmarried ladies even though he himself is unwed and therefore should be looking for a suitable wife."

"I don't think you can hold his lack of interest in marriage against him," Christian protested.

"His eyes are an unnatural light gray, and he uses them to stare at people in a horrible manner."

"Julia—"

"I can't think why anyone would like him." Julia popped one of the chicken cubes into her mouth and raised her eyebrows at her brother.

"Well, I do like him, despite his unnatural eyes." Christian bulged out his own eyes at his eldest sister.

Becca giggled behind her hand. Julia sniffed and took a bite of creamed potatoes.

"Hmm." Matilda studied her son. She looked unswayed. "We haven't heard your father's opinion of Lord Iddesleigh yet."

All eyes turned to him, the head of this little family. How close he'd come to losing this. To ending in a debtor's prison, his family scattered to the poor sympathy of relatives. Ethan Iddesleigh hadn't had any understanding of that two years ago. He'd recited moral platitudes as if words would feed and clothe a family or keep a decent roof above his children's heads and ensure his daughters married properly. That was why Ethan had been removed.

But that was behind him now. Or should be. "I think Christian is of an age to judge a man's character."

Matilda opened her mouth and then closed it. She was a good wife and knew to defer to his conclusions, even if they did not match her own.

He smiled at his son. "How is Lord Iddesleigh faring?" He helped himself to another piece of chicken from the dish a footman held. "You said he'd been hurt when you left so suddenly for Kent."

"He was beaten," Christian said. "Damn near killed, though he doesn't like to say so, of course."

"My goodness," from Becca.

Christian frowned. "And he knew his attackers, it seems. A strange business."

"Perhaps he lost money at the gaming tables," Sarah said.

"Good Lord." Matilda looked sharply at her youngest. "What do you know of such matters, child?"

Sarah shrugged. "Only what I hear, unfortunately."

Matilda frowned, the soft skin around the corners of her lips crimping. She opened her mouth.

"Yes, well, he's better now," Christian hastily interjected. "He said, in fact, that he had business tonight."

Sir Rupert choked and took a sip of wine to cover. "Really? I thought the recovery would take longer from your initial description."

At least a week, or so he'd hoped. Where were James and Walker tonight? Could he warn them? Damn them anyway—James for fouling up the initial attack on Iddesleigh and Walker for failing to even wing him with his pistol. He glanced at his wife, only to find her looking at him worriedly. Bless Matilda, she didn't miss a thing, but he could do without her shrewdness at the moment.

"No, Iddesleigh's fit enough," Christian said slowly. His eyes were puzzled as he watched his father. "I don't envy whoever it is he's after."

Neither do I. Sir Rupert felt the signet ring in his waist-coat pocket, solid and heavy. *Neither do I.*

Chapter Eight

"You're mad," Patricia pronounced.

Lucy reached for another pink Turkish delight. The candies looked almost inedible, their color was so unnatural, but she was fond of them nevertheless.

"Mad, I tell you." Her friend's voice rose, upsetting the gray tiger cat curled on her lap. Puss jumped down and strutted off in a huff.

They were having tea while Patricia exclaimed over Lucy's failed romance. She might as well, too. Everyone but Papa was watching her sorrowfully these days. Even Hedge had taken to sighing as she went past.

The front sitting room of the little two-story cottage Patricia shared with her widowed mother was sunny this afternoon. Lucy knew for a fact that their finances had been in a dire state since the death of Mr. McCullough, but one would never know it from looking at the sitting room. Clever watercolor sketches lined the wall, painted by Patricia. And if there were brighter patches in the yellow-striped wallpaper, few people would remember that oil paintings had once hung there. Black and yellow cushions were piled on the two settees in a way that was careless and elegant at the same time. One wasn't apt to realize that the furniture beneath the cushions was perhaps a bit worn.

Patricia ignored her cat's defection. "The man has been courting you for three years. *Five,* if you count the time it took him to work up the nerve to actually speak to you."

"I know." Lucy selected another candy.

"Every single Tuesday without fail. Did you know there are some in the village who set their clocks by the vicar's carriage passing by on the way to your house?" Patricia scowled, pinching her lips into an adorable moue.

Lucy shook her head. Her mouth was full of sticky sugar.

"Well, it's true. How will Mrs. Hardy tell the time now?"

Lucy shrugged.

"Three. Long. Years." A gold curl had worked itself loose from Patricia's bun and bounced with each word as if in emphasis. "And Eustace finally, *finally* gets around to asking for your hand in holy matrimony and what do you do?"

Lucy swallowed. "I turn him down."

"You turn him down," Patricia echoed as if Lucy hadn't spoken. "Why? What could you have been thinking?"

"I was thinking that I couldn't stand fifty more years of listening to him talk about the church roof repairs." And that she couldn't stand the thought of living intimately with any man other than Simon.

Patricia recoiled as if Lucy had held up a live spider in front of her nose and suggested she eat it. "Church roof repairs? Haven't you been paying attention the last three years? He always prattles on about church roof repairs, church scandals—"

"The church bell," Lucy cut in.

Her friend frowned. "The churchyard—"

"The tombstones in the churchyard," she pointed out.

"The church sexton and the church pews and the church teas," Patricia trumped her. She leaned forward, china-blue eyes widening. "He's the vicar. He's supposed to bore everyone stiff about the bloody church."

"I'm quite certain you shouldn't use that adjective in conjunction with the church, and I couldn't take it anymore."

"After all this time?" Patricia looked like an outraged titmouse. "Why don't you do what I do and think about hats or shoes while he talks? He's quite happy as long as you interject a 'yes, indeed' every now and again."

Lucy picked up yet another Turkish delight and bisected it with her teeth. "Why don't you marry Eustace, then?"

"Don't be silly." Patricia folded her arms and looked away. "I need to marry for money, and he's as poor as a . . . well, a church mouse."

Lucy paused with the remaining half of the confection hovering before her mouth. She'd never considered Eustace and Patricia before. Surely Patricia didn't actually have a *tendre* for the vicar? "But—"

"We're not discussing me," her friend said firmly. "We're discussing your appalling marriage prospects."

"Why?"

Patricia rolled right over her. "You've already wasted your best years on him. You were, what? Five and twenty last birthday?"

"Four and twenty."

"Same thing." The other woman waved away a full year with a dimpled hand. "You can't start over now."

"I don't—"

Patricia raised her voice. "You'll just have to tell him you've made a terrible mistake. The only other marriageable male in Maiden Hill is Thomas Jones, and I'm almost certain he lets his pigs in the cottage at night."

"You're making that up," Lucy said rather indistinctly because she was chewing. She swallowed. "And who, exactly, are you planning to wed?"

"Mr. Benning."

It was a good thing she'd swallowed the sweet already, because she would've choked on it now. Lucy gave a most unladylike shout of laughter before she looked at her friend and realized she was serious.

"You're the one who's mad," she gasped. "He's easily old enough to be your father. He's buried three wives. Mr. Benning has *grandchildren*."

"Yes. He also has . . ." Patricia ticked off her fingers as she spoke. "A fine manor, two carriages, six horses, two upstairs maids and three downstairs ones, and ninety arable acres, most of it tenanted." She lowered her hands and poured herself more tea in the silence.

Lucy gaped at her.

Patricia sat back on the settee and raised her brows as if they were discussing bonnet styles. "Well?"

"You truly frighten me sometimes."

"Really?" Patricia looked pleased.

"Really." Lucy reached for another sweet.

The other woman slapped her hand away. "You won't fit in your wedding dress if you keep gobbling those."

"Oh, Patricia." Lucy sank into the pretty cushions. "I'm

not going to be married, to Eustace or anyone else. I'm going to become an eccentric spinster and look after all the children you and Mr. Benning will have in his wonderful manor with the three downstairs maids."

"And two up."

"And two up," she agreed. She might as well start wearing a spinster's mobcap at once.

"It's that viscount, isn't it?" Patricia took one of the forbidden Turkish delights and nibbled absently. "I knew he was trouble the moment I saw him eyeing you like Puss does the birds at the window. He's a predator."

"A snake," Lucy said softly, remembering how Simon would smile with just his eyes over his glass at her.

"What?"

"Or a serpent, if you prefer."

"Whatever are you gibbering about?"

"Lord Iddesleigh." Lucy took another candy. She wasn't getting married anyway, so it didn't matter if she couldn't fit into any of her dresses. "He reminded me of a great silver snake. Sort of shiny and rather dangerous. I think it's his eyes. Even Papa saw it, although he took it in a less flattering way. For Lord Iddesleigh, that is." She nodded and ate the sticky confection.

Patricia eyed her. "Interesting. Undoubtedly bizarre, but still interesting."

"I think so, too." Lucy cocked her head. "And you needn't tell me he's not coming back, because I already had that discussion with Eustace."

"You didn't." Patricia closed her eyes.

"I'm afraid so. Eustace brought him up."

"Why didn't you change the subject?"

"Because Eustace deserved to know." Lucy sighed. "He deserves someone who can love him, and I just can't."

She felt slightly queasy. Maybe that last piece of candy hadn't been a good idea. Or maybe the realization that she would spend the remaining years of her life never seeing Simon again had finally caught up with her.

"Well." Patricia set her teacup down and brushed an invisible crumb from her skirt. "Eustace may deserve love, but so do you, my dear. So do you."

SIMON STOOD ON THE STEPS to hell and scanned the crowd of revelers.

The Devil's Playground was London's newest fashionable gaming palace, which was open only for a fortnight. The chandeliers glittered, the paint on the Doric columns was barely dry, and the marble floor still held its polish. In another year, the chandeliers would be blackened with smoke and dust, the columns would show the smears of a thousand greasy shoulders, and the floor would be dull with accumulated grit. But tonight, *tonight,* the girls were gay and beautiful, and the gentlemen surging around the tables had nearly identical expressions of excitement. Every now and again a whoop of triumph or an overloud, near maniacal laugh rose above the general rumble of dozens of voices speaking at once. The air was a thick miasma of sweat, burning candle wax, spoiled perfume, and the odor men secrete when they're on the verge of either winning a fortune or putting a pistol to their head before the night is over.

It had just gone eleven o'clock, and somewhere in this mass of humanity hid his prey. Simon sauntered down the steps into the main room. A passing footman offered a tray of watered-down wine. The libations were free. The more a man drank, the more apt he was to gamble and to stay gambling once started. Simon shook his head, and the footman turned away.

In the far right-hand corner, a golden-haired gentleman leaned over the table, his back to the room. Simon craned to look, but yellow silk obscured his view. A soft, feminine form bumped against his elbow.

"*Pardon moi.*" The demimondaine's French accent was quite good. It almost sounded real.

He glanced down.

She had plump rosy cheeks, dewy skin, and blue eyes that promised things she shouldn't have any knowledge of. She wore a green feather in her hair and smiled artfully. "I shall fetch some champagne in apology, yes?" She couldn't be more than sixteen, and she looked like she belonged on a farm in Yorkshire, milking the cows.

"No, thank you," he muttered.

Her expression revealed her disappointment, but then she'd been trained to show what men wanted. He moved away before she could reply and glanced back at the corner. The golden-haired man was no longer there.

He felt weary.

This was irony: only just past eleven o'clock and he wished he was in his bed, asleep and alone. When had he become an old man with a shoulder that ached if he stayed up too late? Ten years ago he would've barely begun the night. He would've taken the little harlot up on her offer and not even noticed her age. He would've gambled half his allowance away and not flinched. Of course, ten years ago he'd been twenty, finally set up in his own establishment, and a hell of a lot closer in age to the harlot than he was now. Ten years ago he hadn't the sense to be afraid. Ten years ago he hadn't felt fear or loneliness. Ten years ago he'd been immortal.

A gilt head to the left. It turned and he saw a wizened old face wearing a wig. Simon pushed through the crowd slowly, making his way to the back room. That was where the truly reckless gamblers congregated.

De Raaf and Pye seemed to think he had no fear, that he still thought and acted like that stripling lad ten years ago. But it was just the opposite, really. The fear was more intense with each duel, the knowledge that he could—probably would—die more real. And in a way, the fear drove him forward. What kind of a man would he be if he gave in to it and let his brother's murderers live? No, every time he felt fear's icy fingers trailing up his spine, every time he heard her siren call to *just give up, let it be,* he strengthened his resolve.

There.

Golden Hair ducked through black-velvet-lined doors. The man wore purple satin. Simon set his course, sure of the scent now.

"Thought I'd find you here," Christian said from beside him.

He whipped around, his heart nearly stuttering out of his chest. *Ghastly* to be caught so flat-footed. The younger man could have slipped a stiletto between his ribs and he would never have known before he died. Another problem of age—the reflexes slowed. "How?"

"What?" The other man blinked red-tipped eyelashes.

Simon took a breath to control his voice. There was no point in taking out his temper on Christian. "How did you know I'd be here?"

"Oh. Well, I called 'round your place, asked Henry, and voila." Christian spread his arms like a jester performing a trick.

"I see." Simon knew he sounded irritated. It was becoming a habit with Christian to show up unexpectedly, rather like a case of the clap. He took a deep breath. Actually, now that he thought about it, he realized it wouldn't be such a bad thing to have the younger man as company. Made one feel less alone at least. And it was rather soothing to be idolized.

"Did you notice that gel?" Christian asked. "The one with the green feather?"

"She's too young."

"Maybe for you."

Simon glared. "Are you coming with me or not?"

"'Course, 'course, old man." Christian smiled weakly, probably rethinking the advisability of tracking down Simon in the first place.

"Don't call me that." Simon started for the black velvet doors.

"Sorry," Christian muttered behind him. "Where're we going?"

"Hunting."

They'd reached the doors now, and Simon slowed to adjust his eyes to the dim room. There were only three tables here. Each table had four players seated at it. No one looked around at the newcomers. Golden Hair sat at the farthest table with his back to the door.

Simon halted and took a breath. It felt like his lungs couldn't expand enough in his chest to let in the air. Clammy sweat broke out on his back and under his arms.

He suddenly thought of Lucy, her white breasts and her serious amber eyes. What a fool he'd been to leave her.

"I should've at least kissed her," he muttered.

Christian's ears were good. "The green feather girl? Thought she was too young."

"Not her. Never mind." Simon watched Golden Hair. He couldn't tell from this angle—

"Who're you looking for?" Christian at least had the sense to whisper the question.

"Quincy James," Simon murmured, and strolled forward.

"Why?"

"To call him out."

He could feel Christian's stare. "What for? What'd he do to you?"

"Don't you know?" Simon turned his head to meet his companion's clear gaze.

The hazel eyes looked honestly puzzled. Simon sometimes wondered nonetheless. Christian had met him at a crucial point in Simon's life. The younger man had made himself quite friendly in a short period of time, and he didn't seem to have anything better to do than to tail Simon about. But perhaps Simon was being overly fearful, seeing enemies in every shadowy corner.

They reached the far table, and Simon stood behind the golden-haired man. Fear was embracing him now, sucking at his mouth with her frosty lips, rubbing her cold breasts against his chest. If he survived tomorrow's dawn, he was going back for Lucy. What use to play the gallant knight if one died at sunrise without ever tasting the maiden's lips? He now knew he couldn't do this alone anymore. He needed her on some basic level to reaffirm and maintain his humanity even as he summoned up the most bestial part of himself. He needed Lucy to keep him sane.

Simon pasted a smile on his face and tapped the man on the shoulder. Beside him, Christian drew in his breath sharply.

The man looked around. Simon stared for a second, stupidly, before his brain registered what his eyes had already told him. Then he turned away.

The man was a stranger.

LUCY TILTED HER HEAD TO THE SIDE and considered the cartoon she'd begun to draw in her sketchbook. His nose was just a bit off. "Don't move." She didn't need to look up to sense that Hedge, her subject, was trying to sneak away again.

Hedge hated sitting for her. "Awww. I gots things to do, Miss Lucy."

"Such as?" There, that was better. Hedge really had the most extraordinary nose.

They were in the little back sitting room. The light was best here during the afternoon, shining in unobstructed through the tall mullioned windows. Hedge perched on a stool in front of the fireplace. He was attired in his usual rumpled coat and breeches with the addition of an oddly spotted purple neckcloth. Lucy couldn't imagine where he'd gotten it. Papa would have died before wearing such a thing.

"I gotta feed and groom old Kate," the manservant groaned.

"Papa did that this morning."

"Well, then, I should muck out her stall."

Lucy shook her head. "Mrs. Brodie paid one of the

Jones boys to clean Katie's stall only yesterday. She got tired of waiting for you to do it."

"Ain't that cheek!" Hedge looked as indignant as if he hadn't neglected the horse for days. "She knew I was plannin' to do it today."

"Hmm." Lucy shaded in his hair carefully. "That's what you've said the last week. Mrs. Brodie says she could smell the stable from the back door."

"That's only 'cause she's got such a great hooter."

"People in glass houses shouldn't throw stones." She switched pencils.

Hedge wrinkled his brow. "What d'you mean, glass houses? I'm talking about her nose."

Lucy sighed. "Never mind."

"Humph."

There was blessed silence for a moment while Hedge regrouped. She started sketching in his right arm. The house was quiet today with Papa gone and Mrs. Brodie busy in the kitchen baking bread. Of course, it always seemed quiet now that Simon had left. The house was almost lifeless. He'd brought excitement and a type of companionship she hadn't known she was missing until he went away. Now the rooms echoed when she walked into them. She caught herself restlessly wandering from room to room as if she unconsciously searched for something.

Or someone.

"How about that letter to Master David, then?" Hedge interrupted her thoughts. "The captain asked me to post it." He rose.

"Sit back down. Papa posted it on the way to Doctor Fremont's."

"Awww."

Someone banged on the front door.

Hedge started.

Lucy glanced up from the sketch to pin him with her stare before he could make a move. The manservant slumped. Lucy finished the right arm and started on the left. They could hear Mrs. Brodie's quick footsteps. A murmur of voices, then the footsteps neared. *Bother.* She was nearly finished with the sketch, too.

The housekeeper opened the door looking flustered. "Oh, miss, you'll never guess who's come—"

Simon walked around Mrs. Brodie.

Lucy dropped her pencil.

He picked it up and held it out to her, his ice eyes hesitant. "May I talk to you?"

He was hatless, his coat wrinkled, and his boots muddy as if he'd ridden. He'd left off his wig, and his hair was a trifle longer. There were dark circles under his eyes, and the lines bracketing his mouth were deeper. What had he been doing in London this past week to make him look so tired again?

She took the pencil, hoping he wouldn't notice how her hand trembled. "Of course."

"Alone?"

Hedge jumped up. "Right, then, I'll leave." He darted out the door.

Mrs. Brodie looked at Lucy questioningly before following the manservant. She shut the door behind her. Suddenly Lucy was alone with the viscount. She folded her hands in her lap and watched him.

Simon paced to the window and gazed out as if he didn't see the garden at all. "I had . . . business to do this last week in London. Something important. Something that's been preying on my mind for some time now. But I couldn't concentrate, couldn't focus on what needed to be done. I kept thinking of you. So I came here, despite vowing I wouldn't bother you again." He threw a look at her over his shoulder, part frustration, part puzzlement, part something she didn't dare interpret. But it made her heart—already laboring from his entrance—stutter.

She took a breath to steady her voice. "Would you care to sit?"

He hesitated as if considering. "Thank you."

He sat across from her, ran his hand over his head, and abruptly stood up again.

"I should leave, just walk out that door and continue walking until I've put a hundred miles between us, maybe an entire watery ocean. Although I don't know if even that would be enough. I promised myself that I would leave you in peace." He laughed without humor. "And yet, here I am back at your feet, making an ass of myself."

"I'm glad to see you," she whispered. This was like a dream. She'd never thought to see him again, and now he was pacing agitatedly in front of her in her own little sitting room. She didn't dare let herself wonder why he had come.

He swung around and suddenly stilled. "Are you? Truly?"

What was he asking? She didn't know, but she nodded anyway.

"I'm not right for you. You're too pure; you see too much. I'll hurt you eventually, if I don't . . ." He shook his head. "You need to be with someone simple and good, and I am neither. Why haven't you married that vicar?"

He was frowning at her, and his statement sounded like an accusation.

Lucy shook her head helplessly.

"You won't speak, won't tell me," he said huskily. "Are you taunting me? You taunt me in my dreams sometimes, sweet angel, when I'm not dreaming of . . ." He sank to his knees before her. "You don't know me, don't know what I am. Save yourself. Throw me from your house. Now. While you still can, because I've lost my determination, my will, my very honor—what little of it I had left. I cannot remove myself from your presence."

He was warning her, she knew it, but she couldn't tell him to go. "I won't turn you away. You can't ask that of me."

His hands were at either side of her on the settee. They bracketed her but did not touch her. He bowed his head until all she could see was his crown of shorn pale hair. "I'm a viscount; you know that. The Iddesleighs go back a fair ways, but we only managed to pocket a title five generations ago. I'm afraid we have a tendency to pick the wrong side in royal wars. I have three homes. A town house in London, one in Bath, and the estate in Northumberland, the one I told you about when I woke that first day. I said it was a wilderness, and it is, but it's also quite beautiful in a savage way, and of course the land's profitable, but we needn't ever go there, if you don't wish. I have a steward and plenty of servants."

Lucy's eyes were blurred with tears. She muffled a sob. He sounded as if he were . . .

"And there are some mines, copper or tin," he continued, staring at her lap. Was he afraid to look her in the eye? "I can never remember which, and it doesn't really matter because I have a man of business, but they pay quite well. There are three carriages, but one was my grandfather's and is getting rather moldy. I can have a new one made, if you want one of—"

She caught his chin with her shaking hands and tilted his face up so she could see his pale gray eyes, looking so worried, so alone. She placed a thumb over his lips to still the river of words and tried to smile through the tears coursing down her cheeks. "Hush. Yes. Yes, I'll marry you."

She could feel the beat of his pulse against her fingers, warm and alive, and it seemed to echo the wild fluttering of her own heart. She'd never felt joy such as this, and she had the sudden fierce thought, *Make it last, please, Lord. Don't ever let me forget this moment.*

But he searched her eyes, neither triumphant nor happy, only waiting. "Are you sure?" His lips caressed her thumb with the words.

She nodded. "Yes."

He closed his eyes as if terribly relieved. "Thank God."

She leaned down and kissed him softly on the cheek. But when she would've pulled back, he moved his head. His mouth connected with hers.

He kissed her.

Brushing across her lips, teasing her, tempting her, until she finally opened to him. He groaned and licked the inside of her lower lip. She brought her tongue forward at the same time and tangled with his. She didn't know if she was doing it right. She'd never been kissed like this before, but her heart beat loudly in her ears, and she couldn't control the trembling of her limbs. He grasped her head between his hands and held it, angling his face across hers to deepen the embrace. This wasn't like Eustace's gentlemanly kiss. This was darker—hungry and almost frightening. She felt as if she were on the verge of falling. Or of breaking apart into so many pieces she'd never be able to put them back together again. He took her lower lip between his teeth and worried it. What should've been pain, or at least discomfort, was pleasure that went to her very center. She moaned and surged forward.

Crash!

Lucy jerked back. Simon looked over her shoulder, his face taut, a sheen of moisture on his brow.

"Oh my goodness!" Mrs. Brodie exclaimed. A tray of demolished china, oozing cake, and puddling tea lay at her feet. "Whatever will the captain say?"

That's a good question, Lucy thought.

Chapter Nine

"I don't mean to pry, Miss Craddock-Hayes," Rosalind Iddesleigh said nearly three weeks later. "But I've been wondering how you met my brother-in-law?"

Lucy wrinkled her nose. "Please, call me Lucy."

The other woman smiled almost shyly. "How kind. And you, of course, must call me Rosalind."

Lucy smiled back and tried to think whether Simon would mind if she told this delicate woman that she'd found him nude and half dead in a ditch. They were in Rosalind's elegant carriage, and it turned out that Simon did indeed have a niece. Theodora rode in the carriage as well, which was rumbling through the streets of London.

Simon's sister-in-law, the widow of his elder brother, Ethan, looked like she should be gazing from a stone tower, waiting for a brave knight to come rescue her. She had gleaming, straight blond hair, pulled into a simple knot at the crown of her head. Her face was narrow and alabaster white with wide, pale blue eyes. If the evidence wasn't sitting right next to her, Lucy would never have believed she was old enough to have an eight-year-old child.

Lucy had been staying with her future sister-in-law for the last sennight in preparation for her wedding to Simon. Papa had not been pleased by her match, but after grumbling and shouting for a bit, he'd reluctantly given his blessing. During Lucy's time in London, she had visited a bewildering variety of shops with Rosalind. Simon was insistent that Lucy get a completely new trousseau. While she was naturally pleased to have so many fine clothes, at the same time it gave Lucy a niggling worry that she would not make a proper viscountess for Simon. She came from the country, and even dressed in lace and embroidered silks, she was still a simple woman.

"Simon and I met on the lane outside my home in Kent," Lucy hedged now. "He'd had an accident, and I brought him home to recover."

"How romantic," Rosalind murmured.

"Was Uncle Sigh in his cups?" the little girl beside her wanted to know. Her hair was darker than her mother's, more of a gold, and curly. Lucy remembered Simon's description of his brother's curly locks. Theodora obviously took after her dead father in that respect, although her eyes were her mother's wide blue.

"Theodora, please." Rosalind drew her brows together, creasing two perfect lines into her otherwise smooth forehead. "We've discussed the use of proper language before. What will Miss Craddock-Hayes think of you?"

The child slumped in her seat. "She said we could call her Lucy."

"No, dear. She gave me permission to use her Christian name. It wouldn't be proper for a child to do so." Rosalind darted a glance at Lucy. "I'm so sorry."

"Perhaps since I'll soon be Theodora's aunt, she might

call me Aunt Lucy?" She smiled at the girl, not wanting to offend her future sister-in-law but feeling sympathy for the daughter as well.

Rosalind bit the corner of her lip. "Are you sure?"

"Yes."

Theodora gave a small wiggle in her seat. "And you can call me Pocket, because that's what my uncle Sigh calls me. I call him Uncle Sigh because all the ladies sigh over him."

"Theodora!"

"That's what Nanny says," the little girl defended herself.

"It's so hard to keep servants from gossiping," Rosalind said. "And children from repeating it."

Lucy smiled. "And why does your uncle Sigh call you Pocket? Because you can fit in one?"

"Yes." She grinned and suddenly resembled her uncle. She glanced at her mother. "And because I look in his pockets when he comes to visit."

"He spoils her terribly," Rosalind sighed.

"Sometimes he has sweets in his pocket, and he lets me have them," the child confided. "And once he had some lovely tin soldiers, and Mama said that little girls don't play with soldiers, and Uncle Sigh said then it was a good thing I'm a pocket and not a girl." She took a breath and glanced at her mother again. "But he was teasing because he knows I'm really a little girl."

"I see." Lucy smiled. "It's probably things like that that make the ladies sigh over him."

"Yes." Pocket squirmed again. Her mother laid a hand on her thigh and she stilled. "Did you sigh over Uncle Sigh?"

"Theodora!"

"What, Mama?"

"Here we are," Lucy interjected.

The carriage had stopped in the middle of a bustling lane, unable to reach the side of the street because of the crush of carriages, dray carts, hawkers, men on horses, and pedestrians. The first time Lucy had witnessed a scene such as this, her breath had been quite taken away. So many people! All of them shouting, running, *living*. The cart drayers shouting abuses at pedestrians in their path, the hawkers crying their wares, liveried footmen clearing the way for fine carriages, urchins scampering nearly under the hoofs of the horses. She'd not known how to take it all in; her senses were overwhelmed. Now, nearly a week later, she'd become a trifle more used to the city, but even so, she found the constant bustle invigorating to her ears and eyes every time. Perhaps she always would. Could a person ever find London boring?

One of the footmen opened the door and folded down the step before assisting the ladies to alight. Lucy held her skirts well off the ground as they made their way to the shop. A strong young footman walked ahead, both protection and future parcel-bearer. The carriage pulled away behind them. The coachman would have to find a place to stop farther on or circle back.

"This is quite a nice millinery shop," Rosalind said as they entered the establishment. "I think you'll like the trimmings they have here."

Lucy blinked and looked at the floor-to-ceiling shelves of multicolored lace, braid, hats, and trim. She tried not to appear as overwhelmed as she felt. This was a far cry from the single shop in Maiden Hill that had but one shelf of trimmings. After she'd lived for years with a few gray gowns, the variety of color almost made her eyes hurt.

"Can I have this, Mama?" Pocket held up a length of gilt braid and started to wrap it around herself.

"No, dear, although perhaps it would be right for Aunt Lucy?"

Lucy bit her lip. She couldn't really see herself in gilt. "Maybe that lace." She pointed.

Rosalind's eyes narrowed at the pretty Belgian lace. "Yes, I think so. It will go nicely on that rose print sack gown we ordered this morning."

Thirty minutes later, Lucy walked out of the shop, glad that she had Rosalind as a guide. The other woman might look delicate, but she knew her fashions and she bargained like a seasoned housekeeper. They found the carriage waiting in the road, an angry cart driver shouting at the coachman because he couldn't get past. The ladies hurried into the carriage.

"My." Rosalind patted her face with a lace handkerchief. She looked at her daughter, lying on the seat in childish exhaustion. "Perhaps we should go back to the house for some tea and refreshments."

"Yes," Pocket said in heartfelt agreement. She curled up on the seat and was soon asleep, despite the jolting of the carriage and the noise from without. Lucy smiled. The little girl must be used to the city and its ways.

"You aren't what I expected when Simon said he was to be married," Rosalind said softly.

Lucy raised her brows in question.

Rosalind bit her bottom lip. "I don't mean to insult you."

"I'm not."

"It's just that Simon has always kept company with a certain type of lady." Rosalind wrinkled her nose. "Not always respectable but usually very sophisticated."

"And I'm from the country," Lucy said ruefully.

"Yes." Rosalind smiled. "I was surprised, but nicely, at his choice."

"Thank you."

The carriage stopped. There appeared to be some sort of jam in the road. Angry male shouts rose outside.

"Sometimes I think it would be easier to walk," Rosalind murmured.

"Certainly faster." Lucy smiled at her.

They sat, listening to the commotion. Pocket snored softly, unperturbed.

"Actually . . ." The other woman hesitated. "I shouldn't tell you this, but when I first met them—Ethan and Simon—it was Simon I was attracted to at first."

"Really?" Lucy kept her features neutral. What was Rosalind trying to tell her?

"Yes. He had that darkness about him, even before Ethan's death, that I think most women find rather fascinating. And the way he talks, his wit. It can be quite captivating at times. I was enthralled, although Ethan was the more handsome brother."

"What happened?" Had Simon been equally enthralled by this delicate woman? Lucy felt a stab of jealousy.

Rosalind gazed out the window. "He scared me."

Lucy caught her breath. "How?"

"One night, at a ball, I came upon him in a back room. It was a study or a sitting room, rather small and simply decorated except for an ornate mirror on one wall. He was all alone and was standing there, just staring."

"At what?"

"At himself." Rosalind turned to her. "In the mirror. Just . . . watching his reflection. But he wasn't looking at his wig or his clothes like another man might. He was staring into his own eyes."

Lucy frowned. "That's strange."

The other woman nodded. "And I knew then. He wasn't happy. His darkness isn't an act; it's real. There is something that drives Simon, and I'm not sure it will ever let him go. I certainly couldn't help him."

Uneasiness washed over Lucy. "So you married Ethan."

"Yes. And I've never regretted it. He was a wonderful husband, gentle and kind." She looked at her sleeping daughter. "And he gave me Theodora."

"Why did you tell me this?" Lucy asked softly. Despite her calm words, she felt a surge of anger. Rosalind had no right to make her doubt her decision.

"Not to frighten you," Rosalind assured her. "I just felt that it would take a strong woman to marry Simon, and I admire that."

It was Lucy's turn to gaze out the window. The carriage had finally started again. They'd soon be back at the town house where there'd be an array of exotic foods for luncheon. She was famished, but Lucy's mind wandered back to Rosalind's last words: *a strong woman*. She had lived all her life in the same, provincial place where she'd never been challenged. Rosalind had seen what Simon was and prudently turned aside. Was there hubris in her own urge to marry Simon? Was she any stronger than Rosalind?

"SHALL I KNOCK, MA'AM?" the maid inquired.

Lucy stood with the maid on the front steps of Simon's

town house. It rose five stories tall, the white stone gleaming in the afternoon sunshine. The town house was in the most fashionable part of London, and she was conscious that she must look a fool standing here dithering. But she hadn't seen Simon alone for ages now, and she felt a desperate need to be with him. To talk and to find out . . . She laughed nervously under her breath. Well, she guessed she needed to find out if he was the same man he'd been back in Maiden Hill. And so she'd borrowed Rosalind's carriage and come here after their luncheon.

She smoothed a hand down her new gown and nodded at the maid. "Yes, please. Go ahead and knock."

The maid lifted the heavy knocker and let it fall. Lucy watched the door expectantly. It wasn't as if she didn't see Simon—he made sure to dine at least once a day at Rosalind's town house—but they never had a moment alone. If only—

The door was pulled open, and a very tall butler looked down a beak of a nose at them. "Yes?"

Lucy cleared her throat. "Is Lord Iddesleigh in?"

He lifted one shaggy eyebrow in an incredibly haughty way; he must practice nights in front of a mirror. "The viscount is not receiving visitors. If you will leave a card—"

Lucy smiled and walked forward so that the man was forced to step back or let her run into his belly. "I am Miss Lucinda Craddock-Hayes, and I am here to see my fiancé."

The butler blinked. He was obviously in a quandary. Here was his soon-to-be mistress demanding entry, but he probably had orders not to disturb Simon. He chose to bow to the devil in front of him. "Of course, miss."

Lucy gave him a small, approving smile. "Thank you."

They entered a grand hall. Lucy took a moment to look around curiously. She'd never been inside Simon's town house. The floor was black marble, polished to a mirror finish. The walls were also marble, alternating black and white in panels bordered in gilt curlicues and vines, and the ceiling . . . Lucy blew out a breath. The ceiling was all gold and white with painted clouds and cherubs that appeared to hold the crystal chandelier that dangled from the center. Tables and statues were set here and there, all of them in exotic marbles and woods, all decorated lavishly in gilt. A black marble Mercury stood nearby to Lucy's right. The wings on his heels, his helmet, and his eyes were all gold. Actually, *grand* didn't quite describe the hall. *Ostentatious* was the better word.

"The viscount is in his greenhouse, miss," the butler said.

"Then I will see him there," Lucy said. "Is there a place my maid might wait?"

"I will have a footman show her to the kitchens." He snapped his fingers at one of the footmen standing at attention in the hallway. The man bowed and led the maid away. The butler turned back to Lucy. "If you will come this way?"

Lucy nodded. He led her down the hallway toward the back of the house. The passage narrowed and they went down a short set of stairs; then they came to a large door. The butler started to open it, but Lucy stopped him.

"I'll go in alone, if you don't mind."

The butler bowed. "As you wish, miss."

Lucy tilted her head. "I don't know your name."

"Newton, miss."

She smiled. "Thank you, Newton."

He held the door open for her. "If you need anything more, miss, simply call me." And then he left.

Lucy peered into the enormous greenhouse. "Simon?"

If she wasn't looking at it right now with her own eyes, she wouldn't have believed such a structure could exist, hidden in the middle of the city. Rows of benches disappeared into the darkened end of the greenhouse. Every available surface was crowded with green plants or pots of soil. Underneath her feet was a brick walkway that somehow felt warm. Condensation dewed the glass at her shoulders. The glass began at waist height and vaulted overhead. Above her, the London sky had already begun to darken.

Lucy took a few steps into the humid air. She didn't see anyone in here. "Simon?"

She listened but heard nothing. Then again, the greenhouse was awfully big. Perhaps he couldn't hear her. Surely he'd want to keep the hot, moist air in. She pulled the heavy wood door closed behind her and went exploring. The aisle was narrow, and some of the foliage hung over it, forcing her to push through a verdant curtain. She could hear dripping as water condensed and ran off hundreds of leaves. The atmosphere was heavy and still, musty with the smell of moss and earth.

"Simon?"

"Here."

Finally. His voice came from up ahead, but she couldn't see him for the obscuring jungle. She pushed aside a leaf larger than her head and suddenly came out into an open space, lit by dozens of candles.

She stopped.

The space was circular. The glass walls flew up into

a miniature dome, like the ones she'd seen in pictures of Russia. In the center, a marble fountain played softly, and around the outside were more benches with roses. Roses blooming in winter. Lucy laughed. Reds and pinks, creams, and pure whites, the roses' heavy scent filled the air, topping off the sense of wonder and delight. Simon had a fairyland in his house.

"You've found me."

She started and looked in the direction of his voice, and her heart fluttered at the sight. Simon stood at a bench in his shirtsleeves. He wore a long green apron over his waistcoat to protect it, and he'd rolled his sleeves up, exposing his forearms, which were dusted with blond hair.

Lucy smiled at the thought of Simon in working attire. This was an aspect of him that she'd never seen before, and it intrigued her. Since they'd come to London, he'd always been so polished, so very much a man of the world. "I hope you don't mind. Newton showed me in."

"Not at all. Where's Rosalind?"

"I came alone."

He stilled and darted a look at her that she found hard to interpret. "All alone?"

So that was his worry. He'd made it very plain when she first came to London that she was never to leave the house by herself. She'd nearly forgotten the injunction in the intervening week, for nothing had happened as far as she could tell. Obviously, he still worried about his enemies. "Well, except for the coachman and footmen and maid—I borrowed Rosalind's carriage." She smiled easily at him.

"Ah." His shoulders relaxed, and he started to take off his apron. "In that case, may I offer you some tea?"

"You don't have to stop because of me," she said. "That is, if I don't disturb you."

"You always disturb me, sweet angel." He retied his apron and turned back to the workbench.

She saw that he was busy, but they were to be married in less than a week. A thought whispered at the back of her mind, the niggling fear that he'd grown bored of her already, or worse, was having second thoughts. She walked to his side. "What are you doing?"

He seemed to tense, but his voice was normal. "Grafting roses. Not a very exciting chore, I'm afraid, but you're welcome to watch."

"You're sure you don't mind?"

"No, of course not." He stooped over the bench, not looking at her. He had a prickly stick in front of him, presumably part of a rose, and was carefully cutting the end into a point.

"We haven't been alone together in several days, and I thought it would be nice just to . . . talk." She found it hard to speak to him while he was half turned away.

His back was stiff, as if he were mentally pushing her away, but he made no move. "Yes?"

Lucy bit her lip. "I know I shouldn't be calling so late, but Rosalind has me busy all day shopping and finding clothes and such. You wouldn't believe how crowded the streets were this afternoon. It took us an hour to drive home." Now she was babbling. Lucy sat on a nearby stool and took a breath. "Simon, have you changed your mind?"

That got his attention. He looked up, frowning. "What?"

She made a jerky gesture of frustration. "You seem so

preoccupied all the time, and you haven't kissed me since you proposed. I wondered if perhaps you had time to think about it and changed your mind about marrying me."

"No!" He threw the knife down and leaned straight-armed on the bench, head bowed. "No, I'm so sorry. I want to marry you, long to marry you, now more than ever, I assure you. I count the days until we are finally wed. I dream of holding you in my arms as my wedded wife and then must distract my mind or go mad waiting for the day. The problem is mine."

"What problem?" Lucy was relieved but honestly confused. "Tell me and we can work on it together."

He blew out a sigh, shook his head, and turned his face to her. "I don't think so. This problem is all of my own making; dealing with it must be my own cross to bear. Thank God it will disappear in a week when we're bound by the holy vows of matrimony."

"You're deliberately talking in riddles."

"So militant," he crooned. "I can picture you with a fiery sword in one hand, smiting recalcitrant Hebrews and unbelieving Samaritans. They'd cower before your stern frown and frightening eyebrows." He laughed under his breath. "Let's just say I'm having trouble being around you without touching you."

She smiled. "We're engaged. You can touch me."

"No, actually, I can't." He straightened and picked up the paring knife again. "If I touch you, I'm not certain I'll be able to stop." He bent and peered at the rose as he made another deliberate cut in the stem. "In fact, I'm fairly certain I won't stop. I'd be intoxicated by your scent and the feel of your white, white skin."

Lucy felt warmth in her cheeks. She doubted very much

if her skin was so white right now. But he'd hardly touched her at all in Maiden Hill. Surely if he could restrain himself then, he could now. "I—"

"No." He took a breath and shook his head as if clearing it. "I'd have you on your back, your skirts tossed around your shoulders like a common cull before I could think, be in you before I could reflect, and once started, I sure as hell wouldn't stop before we'd both reached heaven itself. Maybe not even then."

Lucy opened her mouth, but no sound came out. *Heaven itself . . .*

He shut his eyes and groaned. "Jesus. I can't believe I said that to you."

"Well." She cleared her throat. His words had made her feel shaky and hot. "Well. That's certainly flattering."

"Is it?" He glanced at her. He had spots of color high on his cheekbones. "I'm glad you're taking your fiancé's lack of control over his animal nature so well."

Oh dear. "Maybe I should go." She made to rise.

"No, stay with me, please. Just . . . just don't come near me."

"All right." She sat back straight and folded her hands in her lap.

His mouth curled down at one corner. "I've missed you."

"And I, you."

They exchanged a smile before he hastily turned away again, but this time she knew the cause and was unperturbed. She watched him set aside the stem and pick up a pot that contained what looked like a small stump. The fountain laughed in the background, and the stars began to fill the sky above the dome.

"You never finished telling me about that fairy tale," she said. "The Serpent Prince. I won't be able to finish the illustrations if you don't tell me the rest."

"Have you been making illustrations?"

"Of course."

"I can't remember where I stopped." He frowned over the ugly stump. "It's been so long now."

"I remember." She settled her bottom more firmly on the stool. "Angelica had stolen the Serpent Prince's skin and threatened to destroy it, but she relented and spared his life in the end."

"Ah, yes." He made a careful V-shaped cut in the top of the stump. "The Serpent Prince said to Angelica, 'Fair maid, since you hold my skin, you hold my very life in your hands. You have but to name it and I will grant you a wish.'"

Lucy frowned. "He doesn't sound very bright. Why does he not simply ask for his skin back without telling her what power she has over him?"

He shot a glance at her from under lowered brows. "Perhaps he was enthralled by her beauty?"

She snorted. "Not unless he was extremely dim."

"Your romantic soul overwhelms me. Now will you let me continue?"

She clamped her mouth shut and nodded mutely.

"Good. It occurred to Angelica that here was a very lucky thing. Perhaps she could meet the prince of the land at last. So she said to the Serpent Prince, 'There is a royal ball being held tonight. Can you take me to the ramparts of the castle so that I may see the prince and his entourage pass by?' Well, the Serpent Prince looked at her out of his gleaming silver eyes and said, 'I can do better than that, I assure you.'"

"But, wait," Lucy interrupted. "Isn't the Serpent Prince the hero of the story?"

"A snake-man?" Simon inserted the pointed end of the stick into the notch he'd made in the stump and began wrapping both with a narrow strip of cloth. "Whatever gave you the idea that he would make a good hero?"

"Well, he is all of silver, isn't he?"

"Yes, but he is also quite nude, and usually the hero of the story has something more to his name."

"But—"

He frowned censoriously at her. "Do you wish me to continue?"

"Yes," she said meekly.

"Very well. The Serpent Prince waved one pale hand, and suddenly Angelica's drab brown rags had turned to a shimmering dress of copper. In her hair were copper and ruby jewels and on her feet, embroidered copper slippers. Angelica twirled in a circle, delighted at her transformation, and she exclaimed, 'Wait until Prince Rutherford sees me!'"

"Rutherford?" Lucy arched an eyebrow.

He stared at her sternly.

"Sorry."

"Prince Rutherford, he of the curling golden hair. But the Serpent Prince did not reply, and only then did Angelica notice that he had sunk to his knees beside the brazier and that the blue-flamed fire within burned lower. For in giving the goat girl her wish, he had depleted his own power."

"Silly man."

He looked up and smiled at her and then seemed to notice the dark sky for the first time. "Good Lord, is it as late as that? Why didn't you tell me? You need to return to Rosalind's town house at once."

She sighed. For a London sophisticate, her fiancé had become lamentably stodgy lately. "All right." Lucy stood and dusted off her skirt. "When will I see you next?"

"I'll come for breakfast." He sounded distracted.

Disappointment shot through her. "No, Rosalind says we must leave early to go to the glover's, and we'll be away for luncheon as well. She's made arrangements to introduce me to some of her friends."

Simon frowned. "Do you ride?"

"Yes," she admitted. "But I haven't a mount."

"I have several horses. I'll come by Rosalind's town house before breakfast, and then we'll ride in the park. We'll be back in time for Rosalind to take you to the glover's."

"I'd like that." She looked at him.

He stared back. "God, and I can't even kiss you. Go on, then."

"Good night." Lucy smiled as she walked back up the aisle.

Behind her she could hear Simon cursing.

"MAY I JOIN YOU?" SIMON COCKED a brow at the cardplayers that night.

Quincy James, seated with his back to him, swung around and stared. A tic started under his right eye. He wore a deep red velvet coat and breeches, and his waistcoat was an eggshell white, embroidered in red to match the coat. Taken with his clubbed guinea-colored hair, he was a pretty sight. Simon felt his lips curve into a satisfied smile.

"'Course." A gentleman in an old-fashioned, full-bottomed wig nodded.

He had the dissipated face of a gambler who'd spent a lifetime at the tables. Simon hadn't been introduced to him, but he'd seen him before. Lord Kyle. The other three men at the table were strangers. Two were in their middling years, nearly identical in white-powdered wigs and with faces flushed from drink. The last was only a youth, his cheeks still spotty. A pigeon in a den of foxes. His mother ought to have kept him safe at home.

But that wasn't Simon's problem.

He pulled out the empty chair next to James and sat. Poor bastard. There wasn't a thing James could do to stop him. Objecting to a gentleman joining an open game simply wasn't done. Simon had him. He allowed himself a moment of congratulation. After spending the better part of a week haunting the Devil's Playground, fending off the advances of infant demimondaines, drinking ghastly champagne, and boring himself stiff moving from gambling table to gambling table, James had finally appeared. He'd begun to worry that the trail had gone cold; Simon had put off hunting while he tended to his marriage arrangements, but now he had James.

He felt an urge to hurry this along, have it over with so that he could get to his bed and maybe be able to greet Lucy for their ride in the morning with a semblance of wakefulness. But that wouldn't do. His cautious prey had finally ventured forth from hiding, and he must move slowly. Deliberately. It was crucial that all of the pieces be in place, that there was no possibility of escape, before he sprung his trap. Mustn't let the quarry slip through an overlooked hole in the net at this juncture.

Lord Kyle flipped cards at each player to see who would deal. The man to Simon's right caught the first jack and gathered the cards to deal. James snatched each card as it was dealt him, nervously tapping the table's edges. Simon waited until all five were dealt—they played five-card loo—before picking them up. He glanced down. His hand wasn't bad, but that didn't really matter. He anted and made the opening lead—an eight of hearts. James dithered and then flung down a ten. The game went around the table, and the pigeon picked up the trick. The youth led again with a three of spades.

A footman entered, holding a tray of drinks. They played in the secluded back room at the Devil's Playground. The room was dim, the walls and door quilted in black velvet to muffle the revels in the main parlor. The men who played here were serious, gambled high, and rarely spoke beyond the demands of the game. This wasn't a social occasion for these gentlemen. This was life or death by cards. Only the other night, Simon had watched a baron lose first all the money he'd had on him, then his one unentailed estate, and then his daughters' dowries. The next morning the man was dead, shot by his own hand.

James grabbed a glass from the waiter's tray, drained it, and reached for another. He caught Simon's gaze. Simon smiled. James's eyes widened. He gulped from the second glass and set it by his elbow, glaring at him defiantly. The play went on. Simon looed and had to ante. James smirked. He played the Pam—the jack of clubs, the high card in five-card loo—and took another trick.

The candles guttered, and the footman returned to trim them.

Quincy James was winning now, the pile of coins to the side of his glass growing. He relaxed in his chair, and his blue eyes blinked sleepily. The youth was down to a couple of coppers and was looking desperate. He wouldn't last another round if he was lucky. If he wasn't, someone would stand him the next hand, and that way lay debtor's prison. Christian Fletcher slipped into the room. Simon didn't look up, but out of the corner of his eye, he saw Christian find a chair at the side of the room, too far away to see the cards. He felt something inside him relax at the sight of the younger man. Now he had an ally at his back.

James won a trick. His lips twisted in a triumphant sneer as he gathered the pot.

Simon shot out his arm and caught the other man's hand.

"What—?" James tried to twist away.

Simon slammed his arm to the table. A jack of clubs fell from the lace at James's wrist. The other players around the table froze.

"The Pam." Lord Kyle's voice sounded rusty from disuse. "What the hell do you think you're doing, James?"

"That's not m-m-mine."

Simon leaned back in his chair and rubbed his right index finger lazily. "It fell from your cuff."

"You!" James jumped up, his chair toppling behind him. He looked like he would strike Simon, but then thought better of it.

Simon raised an eyebrow.

"You s-s-set me up, slipped me the bloody P-p-pam!"

"I've been losing." Simon sighed. "You insult me, James."

"No!"

Simon continued, unperturbed. "I trust swords at dawn—"

"No! Jesus, no!"

"Meet with your approval?"

"God!" James clutched his own hair, the beautiful locks coming out of his ribbon. "This isn't right. I d-d-didn't have the bloody Pam."

Lord Kyle gathered the cards. "Another hand, gentlemen?"

"My God," the boy whispered. He'd gone pale and looked like he might cast up his accounts.

"You can't d-d-do this!" James screamed.

Simon got to his feet. "Tomorrow, then. Better get some sleep, what?"

Lord Kyle nodded, his attention already on the next game. "Good night, Iddesleigh."

"I-I'm done as well. If you'll excuse me, gentlemen?" The pigeon nearly ran from the room.

"Nooo! I'm innocent!" James started sobbing.

Simon winced and walked from the room.

Christian caught up with him in the main parlor. "Did you . . . ?"

"Shut up," Simon hissed. "Not here, idiot."

Thankfully, the younger man kept quiet until they reached the street. Simon signaled to his coachman.

Christian whispered, "Did you . . . ?"

"Yes." God, he was weary. "Do you want a ride?"

Christian blinked. "Thanks."

They got in and the carriage pulled away.

"You'd better find his seconds tonight and arrange the duel." Simon was overcome by a ghastly lethargy. His eyes were full of grit, and his hands were shaking. The morning wasn't that far away. He'd either kill a man or die himself when it came.

"What?" Christian asked.

"Quincy James's seconds. You need to find out who they are, arrange the meeting place and time. All that. The same as the last times." He yawned. "You are going to act as my second, aren't you?"

"I—"

Simon closed his eyes. If he lost Christian, he didn't know what he'd do. "If you aren't, I've got four hours to find another."

"No. I mean, yes," the young man blurted. "I'll be your second. Of course I'll be your second, Simon."

"Good."

There was a silence in the carriage, and Simon fell into a doze.

Christian's voice woke him. "You went there to find James, didn't you?"

He didn't bother opening his eyes. "Yes."

"Is it a woman?" His companion sounded genuinely puzzled. "Has he caused you an insult?"

Simon almost laughed. He'd forgotten that there were men who dueled for such silly things. "Nothing so inconsequential."

"But why?" Christian's voice was urgent. "Why do it that way?"

Jesus! He didn't know whether to laugh or weep. Had he ever in his life been this naive? He gathered his wits to try to explain the blackness that lived in men's souls.

"Because gambling's his weakness. Because he couldn't help himself once I'd joined the game. Because he can't possibly turn me down or worm his way out. Because he's the man he is and I'm the man I am." Simon finally looked at his terribly young friend and gentled his voice. "Is that what you wanted to know?"

Christian's brow was furrowed as if he was working out a difficult mathematical problem. "I didn't realize . . . This is the first time I've been with you when you challenged your opponent. It seems so unfair. Not at all honorable." Christian's eyes suddenly widened as if he'd just realized the insult.

Simon started laughing and found he couldn't stop. Tears gathered in his eyes from the mirth. *Oh God, what a world!*

Finally, he gasped, "Whatever gave you the idea I was honorable?"

Chapter Ten

The predawn mist lay like gray winding sheets, writhing on the ground. It swirled about Simon's legs as he made his way to the agreed-upon dueling place, seeping through leather and linen to chill his very bones. In front of him, Henry held a lantern to light their way, but the mist veiled the light so they seemed to move in a disquieting dream. Christian walked beside him, strangely silent. He'd spent the night contacting and conferring with James's seconds, and gotten little, if any, sleep. Up ahead, another light loomed, and the shapes of four men emerged in the dawn. Each had a nimbus of breath cowling his head.

"Lord Iddesleigh?" one of the men hailed him. It wasn't James, so it must be a second.

"Yes." His own breath billowed forth and then dissipated into the icy morning air.

The man walked toward them. He was of middling years and wore spectacles and a tatty wig. A coat and breeches, several years behind the fashion and obviously well worn, completed his dissolute appearance. Behind him, a shorter man hesitated beside another man who must be the doctor, as evidenced by the bobbed wig of his profession and the black bag he carried.

The first man spoke again. "Mr. James offers his sincere apology for any insult he may have inflicted upon you. Will you accept this apology and avoid a duel?"

Coward. Had James sent his seconds and stayed away? "No, I will not."

"D-d-d-damn you, Iddesleigh."

So he was here. "Good morning, James." Simon smiled thinly.

The reply was another curse, no more original than the first.

Simon nodded to Christian. The younger man and James's seconds went to mark off the dueling space. Quincy James paced back and forth over the frost-killed earth, either to warm his limbs or from nervousness. He wore the same deep red coat he'd had on the night before, wrinkled and stained now. His hair looked greasy, as if he'd been sweating. As Simon watched, the other man dug his fingers through the locks, scratching. Filthy habit. Did he have lice? James must be tired from the late night, but then again, he was an inveterate gambler, used to staying up to all hours. And he was younger. Simon considered him. He'd never seen James duel, but the word at Angelo's academy was that his opponent was an expert swordsman. He wasn't surprised. Despite James's tics and stutters, the man had the grace of an athlete. He was also the same height. Their reaches would be equal.

"May I see your sword?" The spectacled man was back. He held out his hand.

The other second came over. This one was a shorter, younger man in a bottle-green coat who peered around constantly in a nervous manner. Dueling was, of course, against the law. But the law in this case was rarely enforced. Simon unsheathed his weapon and handed it over to Spectacles. Several paces away, Christian retrieved James's sword. He and James's seconds dutifully measured both blades and inspected them before handing them back.

"Open your shirt," Spectacles said.

Simon arched an eyebrow. The fellow was obviously a stickler for proper form. "Do you really think I'm wearing armor under my shirt?"

"Please, my lord."

Simon sighed and shrugged out of his silver-blue coat and waistcoat, pulled his neckcloth off, and unbuttoned the top half of his lace-edged shirt. Henry hurried over to catch the items as they fell.

James loosened his shirt for Christian. "Damn, it's as cold as a Mayfair whore."

Simon pulled apart the edges of his shirt. Goose bumps chased over his bared chest.

The second nodded. "Thank you." His face was wooden, a man without apparent humor.

"You're welcome." Simon smiled mockingly. "Can we get on with it, then? I haven't broken my fast yet."

"And you w-w-won't either." James advanced, sword held ready.

Simon felt his smile disappear. "Brave words for a murderer."

He sensed Christian's swift look. Did the boy know? He'd never told him about Ethan—about the real reason for these duels. Simon raised his blade and faced his opponent. The mist curled about their legs.

"*Allez!*" Christian cried.

Simon lunged, James parried, and the swords sang their deadly song. Simon felt his face stretch into a mirthless grin. He stabbed into an opening, but James deflected the blow at the last minute. And then he was on the defensive, retreating even as he parried slash after slash. The muscles in his calves burned under the strain. James was swift and strong, an opponent to take seriously, but he was also desperate, attacking recklessly. The blood pounded in Simon's veins like liquid fire, making his nerves spark. He never felt so alive and paradoxically so close to death as when he dueled.

"Ah!"

James darted under his guard, aiming a blow at Simon's chest. He deflected the sword at the last minute. His weapon slid, screeching, against his opponent's until they were hilt to hilt, breathing into each other's faces. James pressed against him with all his strength. Simon felt his upper arm bulge. He stood braced, refusing to give ground. He could see the red veins in the other man's eyes and smell his foul breath, reeking of terror.

"Blood," one of the seconds called, and only then did he feel the burn at his arm.

"Do you quit?" Christian asked.

"Hell, no." Simon bunched his shoulders and threw James back, lunging after him. Something dark and animal within him howled, *Now! Kill him now!* He must be careful. If he only wounded his enemy, James would have the right to stop the duel, and then he'd have to go through all this nonsense again.

"There is no need," one of the seconds was shouting. "Gentlemen, throw down your swords. Honor is appeased!"

"Bugger honor!" Simon attacked, slashing and stabbing, his right shoulder sending needles of pain down his arm.

The blades clanged as the men stamped across the green. He could feel warmth trickling down his back and had no idea whether it was sweat or blood. James's eyes widened. He was defending desperately, his face red and gleaming. His waistcoat was stained dark beneath the armpits. Simon feinted high.

And suddenly James turned, lunged, and slashed *behind* his legs. Simon felt the sting at the back of his knees. Horror streaked through him. If James succeeded in cutting the tendons at the back of his legs, he would be crippled, unable to stand and defend himself. But in lunging, James had exposed his chest. The other man drew back to slash at his legs again. Simon pivoted. Put the whole force of his arm behind the blow. And ran James through the chest. Simon felt the jar as his blade hit and grated against bone. His shoulder burned just above his armpit. He saw James's eyes widen in understanding of his own mortality, heard the scream of one of the witnesses, and smelled the acid stink of urine as the dead man lost control of his bladder.

His enemy sank to the ground.

Simon bent for a second, gulping great lungfuls of air. Then he placed his foot on the corpse's chest and pulled his sword out. James's eyes were still open, staring at nothing now.

"Jesus." Christian drew a hand across his white mouth.

Simon wiped the blade of his sword. His hands shook slightly and he frowned, trying to control them. "Could you close his eyes?"

"My God. My God. My God." The short man was nearly

jumping up and down in his agitation. Suddenly, he leaned over and vomited, splattering his shoes.

"Can you close his eyes?" Simon asked again. He didn't know why it bothered him so. James no longer cared that he stared blindly.

The little man was still heaving, but Spectacles passed his hand over James's eyes.

The physician walked over and stared down impassively. "He's dead. You've killed him."

"Yes, I know." Simon shrugged on his coat.

"Christ," Christian whispered.

Simon motioned to Henry and turned to walk back. They no longer needed the lantern. The sun had risen, evaporating the mist and heralding a new day that Quincy James would never see. Simon's hands still shook.

"HE'S OUT? HOW CAN HE BE OUT at this hour?" Lucy stared at Newton.

The sky had just lost the pinkness of dawn. Street sweepers were trundling their carts home across the cobblestones. At the house next door, a maid slammed the door and began vigorously scrubbing her employer's steps. Lucy had arrived at Simon's town house for their early morning ride in the park. She should've waited for him at Rosalind's home, as they'd originally planned. But last night over supper, Rosalind had announced that she would rise unfashionably early to accompany the new cook to the fish market this morning. Cook had served them slightly off fish two nights in a row, and Rosalind thought she needed pointers on selecting a fresh snapper. Lucy had leapt at the chance to ride along and see Simon a little early.

But now she stood on the front stoop like a poor

petitioner before the king. The king, in this case, being
Newton the butler. He was splendidly arrayed in silver
and black livery and an exquisite wig, despite the hour. He
stared back at her down a nose that would have done any
ancient Roman proud.

"I couldn't say, miss." Two spots of red burned in the
butler's otherwise cadaverous cheeks.

Lucy looked at them suspiciously. Her own face began
to heat. Surely Simon wasn't with another woman? No, of
course not. They were to be married in less than a week.
But Lucy felt shaken nonetheless. She hardly knew Simon;
maybe she had misunderstood. Perhaps when he said *dawn*
it had been a fashionable figure of speech, really meaning
ten o'clock. Or maybe she'd confused the day—

A big black carriage rattled up, interrupting her thoughts.
Lucy turned to look. The carriage bore Simon's crest. A
footman jumped down and set the steps. Henry and Mr.
Fletcher descended. Lucy frowned. Why . . . ? Simon
stepped down. Behind her, Newton exclaimed. Simon
was in his shirtsleeves, despite the cold. One sleeve was
streaked with blood, and he held a soaked rag to the upper
arm. Spatters of red arced delicately across his chest. In
strange contrast to the gore, he wore an immaculate white
wig.

Lucy gasped; her lungs wouldn't fill with air. How
badly was he hurt? She stumbled down the steps. "What
has happened?"

Simon stopped and stared at her, white-faced. He looked
as if he didn't recognize her. *"Merde."*

At least he could talk. "Newton, send for a doctor!"

Lucy didn't bother to see if the butler followed her orders. She was afraid if she took her eyes from Simon, he

might collapse. She reached him on the street and held out a hand, hesitant to actually touch him lest she harm him further.

"Where are you hurt? Tell me." Her voice shook.

He took her hand. "I'm fine—"

"You're bleeding!"

"There's no need of a doctor—"

"He killed James," Mr. Fletcher suddenly said.

"What?" Lucy looked at the younger man.

He seemed dazed, as if he'd seen a tragedy. *What had happened?*

"Not out in the street for all the pious listening neighbors to gossip about, please," Simon said. His words dragged as if he were weary to his soul. "We'll hash it out, if we must hash it out, in the sitting room." The fingers clutching her wrist were sticky with blood. "Come inside."

"Your arm—"

"Will be fine as soon as I dose it with brandy—by mouth, preferably." He marched her up the steps.

Behind them, Mr. Fletcher called, "I'm going home. Had enough. Sorry."

Simon paused on the top step and glanced back. "Ah, the golden resilience of youth."

Mr. Fletcher swung around violently. "You killed him! Why did you have to kill him?"

Oh, God. Lucy stared, mute, at Simon's young friend. She felt dread seep into her chest, paralyzing her.

"It was a duel, Christian." Simon smiled, but his voice was still gritty. "Did you think I meant to dance a pretty gavotte?"

"Jesus! I don't understand you. I don't think I even know you." Mr. Fletcher shook his head and walked away.

Lucy wondered if she should echo the sentiment. Simon had just admitted killing a man. She realized—horribly—that the bloodstains on his chest weren't his own. Relief flooded her, and then guilt that she rejoiced at another's death. Simon led her through the door into the great receiving hall. The ceiling, three stories overhead, was painted with classical gods lounging about the clouds, unperturbed by the upheaval below. He dragged her down the hallway and through double doors into a sitting room.

Behind them, Newton groaned. "Not the white settee, my lord."

"To hell with the settee." Simon pulled Lucy down beside him on the immaculate piece of furniture. "Where's that brandy?"

Newton splashed brandy into a crystal glass and brought it over, muttering, "Blood. And it'll never come out."

Simon swallowed half the glass and grimaced, laying his head against the settee back. "I'll have it re-covered, if that'll make you feel better, Newton. Now get out of here."

Henry entered the room, carrying a basin of water and linens.

"But, my lord, your arm—" the butler started.

"Get. Out." Simon closed his eyes. "You, too, Henry. You can bandage, dose, and mother me later."

Henry raised his eyebrows at Lucy. Silently, he laid the basin and bandages beside her and left. Simon still held her wrist. She reached across him with her free hand and carefully pulled back the ripped sleeve. Beneath, a narrow wound seeped blood.

"Leave it alone," he murmured. "It's only a shallow cut.

It looks worse than it is, believe me. I won't bleed to death, at least not right away."

She pursed her lips. "I'm not your butler. Or your valet, for that matter."

"No, you're not." He sighed. "I forgot."

"Well, try to remember in the future that I hold an entirely different role in your—"

"Not that."

"What?"

"I forgot we were to go riding this morning. Stupid of me. Is that why you're here?"

"Yes. I'm sorry. I came early with Rosalind."

"Rosalind? Where is she?" His words were slurred as if he were so fatigued he could hardly speak.

"At the fish market. Hush. It doesn't matter."

He didn't listen. "I will never be able to forgive myself, but do you think you can?"

Silly. Her eyes pricked with tears. How could he deflect her anger with such silly words? "For what? Never mind. I forgive you for whatever it is." She dipped a cloth in the water one-handed. "This would be easier if you let me go."

"No."

She wiped at the blood awkwardly. She really ought to cut the sleeve off altogether. She cleared her throat to steady her voice before she inquired, "Did you really kill a man?"

"Yes. In a duel." His eyes were still closed.

"And he wounded you in return." She squeezed out the cloth. "What did you duel over?" She made sure her tone was even, as if she were asking the time.

Silence.

She looked at the bandages. There was no way she'd be able to tend to him, shackled as she was. "I'm going to need both arms to bandage you."

"No."

Lucy sighed. "Simon, you'll have to let me go eventually. And I really think your arm should be cleaned and wrapped."

"Severe angel." He finally opened his eyes, frost gray and intense. "Promise me. Promise me on your mother's memory that you won't leave me if I give you back your wings."

She blinked and thought about it, but in the end there was really no other answer. "I promise you."

He leaned closer until she could see the shards of ice in his eyes. "Say it."

"I promise on my mother's memory," she whispered, "that I won't leave you."

"Oh, God."

She didn't know whether it was a curse or a prayer, but his mouth came down on hers hard. Biting, licking, sucking. It was as if he meant to consume and draw her into himself so that she might never abandon him. She moaned beneath the onslaught, confused and enthralled.

He angled his head, thrusting his tongue into her mouth. She clutched his shoulders, and then he was pushing her back on the settee, climbing on top of her and shoving her legs apart with his own hard thighs. He settled on her, and even through the multiple layers of her skirt she could feel his hard shaft. She arched against him. Her breath was coming in breathless pants; she couldn't seem to get enough air. He cupped her breast. His hand was so hot she could feel his heat through her bodice, branding her where no man had ever caressed her before.

"Angel." He broke away to whisper against her cheek. "I want to see you, to touch you." He trailed his open mouth over her cheek. "Let me take down your dress. Let me see you. Please."

She shuddered. His fingers molded her shape, stroking and massaging. She felt her nipple bud, and she wanted, *needed,* him to touch it. Naked, with nothing separating their flesh. "Yes, I—"

Someone opened the door.

Simon reared up to glare over the back of the settee at whoever it was. "Get out!"

"My lord." Newton's voice.

Lucy wished she could dissolve this very instant and become a puddle on the settee.

"Get out now!"

"Your sister-in-law is here, my lord. Lady Iddesleigh saw your carriage in front and was concerned as to why you and Miss Craddock-Hayes had not yet gone riding."

Or, she could simply die of mortification.

Simon stilled, breathing heavily. "Damn."

"Yes, my lord," the butler replied stonily. "Shall I put her in the blue sitting room?"

"Damn your eyes, Newton! Put her anywhere but here."

The door closed.

Simon sighed and rested his forehead against her own. "I'm sorry for everything." He brushed his lips against hers. "I'd better leave before Rosalind gets an eyeful. Stay here; I'll send Henry with a shawl." He got up and strode out the door.

Lucy looked down at herself. There was a bloody hand-print on the bodice of her dress.

"OH." POCKET STOOD IN THE DOORWAY to the little sitting room on the third floor of Rosalind's house. She looked at Lucy and placed one foot on top of the other. "You're in here."

"Yes." Lucy raised her head from where she'd propped it on a fist and tried to smile. She'd come to this room after luncheon to think about this morning's events. Rosalind had taken to bed, pleading a headache, and Lucy could not blame her. Rosalind had to have suspected something was wrong when Simon didn't greet her at his own home. He'd hidden in his rooms so she wouldn't see his wound. Add to that Lucy's near silence on the drive back to Rosalind's town house and the poor woman probably thought they were about to break off the wedding. Altogether, it had been a trying morning.

"Is that all right?" Lucy asked Pocket now.

The little girl frowned as if considering. "I guess." Voices from farther down the hallway made her look over her shoulder before scooting into the room. She laid down the wooden box she carried and shut the door very carefully.

Lucy was instantly suspicious. "Aren't you supposed to be in the schoolroom?"

The little girl was dressed in a cool blue gown, her hair in perfect ringlets, giving her an angelic appearance, belied by her calculating eyes. "Nanny's napping." She'd obviously learned her uncle's trick of not actually answering the question.

Lucy sighed and watched Pocket carry the box to the tapestry rug, hitch up her skirts, and sit down cross-legged.

This little back room had an air of abandonment, despite its recent dusting. It was too small to welcome callers, and, besides, it was on the third floor of Rosalind's town house. Above the bedrooms and below the nursery. Yet the one window overlooked the back garden and let the afternoon sun in. The armchairs, one brown and missing an arm, the other a balding rose velvet, were large and comfortable. And the faded rose, brown, and green rug was soothing. Lucy had thought it a perfect place to come and think and be alone.

Clearly, Pocket had, too.

The little girl opened her box. Inside were rows of painted tin soldiers—Simon's forbidden gift. Some were standing, others knelt, their rifles at their shoulders, ready to fire. There were soldiers on horses and soldiers with cannons, soldiers with rucksacks, and soldiers holding bayonets. She'd never seen such an array of tin soldiers. Obviously, this was a superior toy army.

Lucy picked up a little man. He stood at attention, his rifle by his side, a high military hat on his head. "How clever."

Pocket gave her a withering look. "That's a Frenchie. The *enemy*. He's blue."

"Ah." Lucy handed her back the soldier.

"I've four and twenty," the little girl continued as she set up the enemy camp. "I used to have five and twenty, but Pinkie got one and chewed off his head."

"Pinkie?"

"Mama's little dog. You haven't seen him because he lives in Mama's rooms mostly." She wrinkled her nose. "He smells. And he snuffles when he breathes. He's got a pushed-in nose."

"You don't care for Pinkie," Lucy guessed.

Pocket shook her head vehemently. "So now this one"—she held up a headless tin soldier with fearsome teeth marks all over the remaining body—"is a Casualty of Battle, Uncle Sigh says."

"I see."

She laid the mutilated soldier on the carpet, and they both contemplated it. "Cannon fire," Pocket said.

"Pardon?"

"Cannon fire. The ball took his head clean off. Uncle Sigh says he probably didn't even see it coming."

Lucy raised her eyebrows.

"Want to be England?" Pocket asked.

"I'm sorry?"

Pocket looked at her sorrowfully, and Lucy had the sinking feeling that her value might have fallen to the level of Pinkie, the soldier-devouring canine. "Would you like to be England? I'll play France. Unless you *want* to be the Frogs?" She asked the last as if Lucy might just be that dim-witted.

"No, I'll be England."

"Good. You can sit there." Pocket pointed to a space on the rug opposite her, and Lucy realized she was supposed to sit on the floor for this game.

She hunkered down and set up her red tin men under the little girl's critical eye. It was actually rather soothing, and she needed a rest from her thoughts. All day she'd debated whether she should marry Simon. The violent side he'd revealed this morning had been frightening. Not because she thought he might hurt her—she knew, somehow, he would never do that. No, what made her afraid was that her attraction to him remained undimmed, despite what she'd seen.

She'd even rolled about with him on that settee while he was covered with the blood of a man he'd killed. It hadn't mattered. It still didn't matter. If he walked in the room right now, she'd succumb again. And perhaps that was the real problem. Perhaps she feared what he could do to her: make her throw away all the lessons of right and wrong she'd grown up with, make her lose herself. Lucy shivered.

"Not there."

She blinked. "What?"

"Your captain." The little girl pointed to a soldier in a fancy hat. "He should be at the front of his men. Uncle Sigh says a good captain always leads his men into battle."

"Does he?"

"Yes." Pocket nodded decisively and moved Lucy's man forward. "Like that. Are you ready?"

"Um . . ." Ready for what? "Yes?"

"Men, ready your cannon," the little girl growled. She rolled a tin cannon forward and laid her fist beside it. "Fire!" She flicked her thumb, and a marble flew across the carpet and decimated Lucy's soldiers.

Pocket hooted.

Lucy's jaw dropped. "Can you do that?"

"It's war," Pocket said. "Here come the cavalry to flank your army!"

And Lucy realized the English were about to lose the war. "My captain orders his men about!"

Two minutes later the field of battle was a bloodbath. Not a single tin soldier still stood.

"Now what do we do?" Lucy panted.

"We bury them. All brave men deserve proper funerals." Pocket lined up her dead soldiers.

Lucy wondered how much of this game was prescribed by Uncle Sigh.

"We say the Lord's Prayer and sing a hymn." The little girl tenderly patted her soldiers. "That's what we did at my papa's funeral."

Lucy looked up. "Oh?"

Pocket nodded. "We said the Lord's Prayer and threw dirt on the coffin. But Papa wasn't really in there, so we don't have to worry about him drowning in the dirt. Uncle Sigh says he's in heaven and he watches me."

Lucy stilled, imagining Simon comforting this little girl at his brother's graveside, putting aside his own grief to explain in childish terms that her father wouldn't suffocate in the ground. What a tender act. And what was she to do with this new side to Simon? It would be so much easier if he was simply a man who killed, someone who was callous and uncaring. But he wasn't. He was a loving uncle, a man who tended roses all by himself in a glass cathedral. A man who acted like he needed her and made her promise never to leave him.

Never to leave him . . .

"Want to play again?" Pocket was looking at her, waiting patiently.

"Yes." Lucy gathered her soldiers and set them upright.

"Good." Pocket set to work on her own soldiers. "I'm glad you're to be my aunt. Uncle Sigh's the only other one who likes to play soldiers."

"I've always wanted a niece who played soldiers." She looked up at Pocket and smiled. "And I'll be sure to invite you to come and play with me when I'm married."

"Promise?"

Lucy nodded decisively. "Promise."

Chapter Eleven

"Nervous?" de Raaf asked.

"No." Simon paced to the rail, pivoted, and strolled back again.

"Because you look nervous."

"I'm not nervous." Simon angled his head to search down the nave. *Where the hell was she?*

"You do seem nervous." Now Pye was looking at him queerly.

Simon deliberately stilled himself and took a deep breath. It was just past ten o'clock on the morning of his wedding day. He stood in the designated sacred church, arrayed in formal wig, black brocade coat, silver-embroidered waistcoat, and red-heeled shoes. He was surrounded by friends and loving family—well, his sister-in-law and niece anyway. Pocket bounced in the front pew while Rosalind tried to shush her. Christian looked distracted in the row behind. Simon frowned. He hadn't talked to Christian since the duel; there hadn't been time. He'd have to do it later. The vicar was here, a young man whose name he'd already forgotten. Even de Raaf and

Harry Pye had shown. De Raaf looked like a provincial squire in muddy boots, and Pye could have been mistaken for the sexton in plain brown.

The only thing missing was the bride.

Simon suppressed an urge to charge down the aisle and peer out the front doors like an anxious cook awaiting the arrival of the fishmonger with her eels. *Oh, God, where was she?* He hadn't been alone with her since she'd caught him returning from the duel with James, nearly a week ago now, and while she seemed content, while she smiled at him when in the company of others, he couldn't shake off this morbid worry. Had she changed her mind? Had he repulsed her, making love to her while his shoulder dripped gore and he wore the stain of a dead man's blood like a badge of dishonor on his chest? He shook his head. Of course he'd repulsed her, his angel with her strict morals. She must've been horrified. Was it enough to make her break her promise? She'd given her word, on her mother's memory, that she wouldn't leave him.

Was that enough?

Simon walked to a granite pillar that towered to the barrel ceiling fifty feet overhead. A double row of the pink granite columns held aloft the ceiling, decorated with recessed painted squares. Each square was edged in gilt, as if to remind one of the golden afterlife that presumably awaited. Off to the side, he could see into a St. Mary's chapel with a statue of a pubescent Virgin Mary gazing serenely down at her toes. It was a pretty church, lacking only a pretty bride.

"He's pacing again," de Raaf said in a tone he probably thought was quiet.

"He's nervous," Pye replied.

"I am not nervous," Simon said through gritted teeth. He reached to stroke his ring before remembering it was gone. He turned to saunter back and caught Pye and de Raaf exchanging a significant glance. Wonderful. Now he was considered a case for Bedlam by his friends.

A screech came from the front of the church as someone opened the big oak doors.

Simon wheeled. Lucy entered, escorted by her father. She wore a rose-colored gown, pulled back in front to reveal the pale green underskirt. The color made her complexion glow, gave her dusky eyes, brows, and hair a perfect setting, like a rose surrounded by dark leaves. She smiled at him and looked . . . beautiful.

Simply beautiful.

He felt like rushing to her and capturing her arm. Instead, he straightened and moved to stand by de Raaf. He watched her approach, patiently waiting. Soon. Soon, she would be his. He would have no need to fear her loss, her desertion. Lucy laid her hand on the crook of his arm. He refrained from clamping down on it with his other hand. The captain scowled at him and slowly released his daughter's arm. The old man wasn't happy about this. When he asked for her hand, Simon had known that had Lucy been younger or less loved, he would have been out on his ear in an instant. As it was, his angel had prevailed even against her father's clear disapproval. Simon smiled at the older man and gave in to his urge to grasp her hand on his arm. She was his now.

The captain didn't miss the gesture. His ruddy face darkened.

Simon leaned his head close to hers. "You came."

Her face was grave. "Of course."

"I wasn't sure you would after the other morning."

"Weren't you?" She watched him with unfathomable eyes.

"No."

"I promised."

"Yes." He searched her face but couldn't read any more there. "Thank you."

"Are we ready?" The vicar smiled vaguely.

Simon straightened and nodded.

"Dearly beloved," the vicar began.

Simon concentrated on the words that would bind Lucy to him. Perhaps now his fear of losing her would finally die and be laid to rest. No matter what she found out about him, no matter what ghastly mistakes, what grave sins he committed in the future, his angel would have to remain with him.

She was his, now and forever.

"I SHALL SEND UP A MAID TO ASSIST YOU, my lady," Newton intoned from behind Lucy that evening.

She blinked and glanced over her shoulder. "Yes. Ah, thank you."

The butler closed the door softly behind him. Lucy returned to gawking at the room. *Her* room. And she'd thought the bedrooms in Rosalind's town house grand. The walls were covered in rose damask, a warm and soothing color that gave the bedroom the intimate feel of an embrace. Underfoot, the patterned carpet was so thick her heels sank into it. Above, the ceiling was painted with cupids or angels—hard to tell in the dim light of evening—and was edged in gilt. Of course.

And centered between two long windows was a bed.

But to call this piece of furniture a bed was like calling St. Paul's Cathedral a church. This was the gaudiest, the largest, the most sumptuous bed Lucy had ever seen in her life. The mattress was easily three feet off the ground, and on one side were steps, presumably to mount the thing. A massive poster rose from each corner, carved, gilded, and draped with swathes of burgundy velvet. Gold ropes drew back the burgundy drapes to reveal pink gauze underdrapes. The actual bed linens were ecru and made of satin. Lucy hesitantly touched them with one finger.

Someone tapped at the door.

Lucy whirled and stared. Would Simon knock? "Come."

A mobcap peeked around the door. "Mr. Newton sent us, my lady. To help you undress?"

"Thank you." Lucy nodded and watched the little woman trot into the room, trailed by a younger girl.

The older maid immediately began rummaging through the wardrobe. "You'll want the lace chemise, I think, don't you, my lady? On your wedding night?"

"Oh. Yes." Lucy felt a flutter in her stomach.

The maid brought the chemise over and began unhooking the back of Lucy's dress. "They're all talking about the wedding breakfast this morning, my lady, down in the kitchen. How elegant it was. Even that Henry, my lord's valet, was impressed."

"Yes, it was very nice." Lucy tried to relax. Even after a fortnight in London, she still wasn't used to being served quite so intimately. She hadn't had help with her clothes since she was five. Rosalind had assigned one of her maids to look after her, but it seemed that now that Lucy was Simon's wife, she required two.

"Lord Iddesleigh has such a wonderful sense of style." The older maid grunted and bent to undo the last hooks. "And then they say he took you ladies on a tour of the capital after the wedding breakfast. Did you enjoy that?"

"Yes." Lucy stepped out of her gown. She'd been with Simon for most of the day, but they'd never been alone. Perhaps now that they were finally married and the ceremonies over with, they could spend more time together, learn to know one another.

The maid quickly gathered the material and handed it to the younger maid. "Now mind you check that over good. Wouldn't want a stain to set."

"Yes'm," the girl squeaked. She looked no more than fourteen and was obviously in awe of the older woman, although she towered over her.

Lucy took a deep breath as the maid undid her stays. Her underskirts and shift were whisked off and the lace chemise settled over her head. The maid brushed her hair until Lucy could stand it no longer. All this fussing was giving her too much time to think, to worry about the coming night and what would happen.

"Thank you," she said firmly. "That's all I need for the night."

The maids curtsied as they left, and suddenly she was alone. Lucy sank into one of the chairs by the fire. There was a decanter of wine on the table next to her. She stared thoughtfully at it for a moment. The wine might dull her senses, but she was fairly certain it wouldn't calm her nerves. And she knew she didn't want her senses dull tonight, no matter how nervous she was.

A soft tap came from the door—not the one to the hall but the other one, presumably a connecting door.

Lucy cleared her throat. "Come."

Simon opened the door. He still wore his breeches, hose, and shirt, but he'd removed his waistcoat and coat and he was bareheaded. He paused in the doorway. It took her a moment to place his expression. He was uncertain.

"Is that your room in there?" she asked.

He frowned and glanced back. "No, it's a sitting room. Yours, actually. Would you like to see it?"

"Yes, please." Lucy rose, very conscious that she was nude beneath her flowing lace chemise.

He stepped back, and she saw a rose and white room with several settees and armchairs scattered about. There was a door on the farther wall.

"And is your room beyond that?" She nodded to the far door.

"No, that's my sitting room. It's rather dark, I'm afraid. Decorated by some dead ancestor with a gloomy sensibility and a disapproval of any color but brown. Yours is much nicer." He tapped his fingers on the door frame. "Next to my sitting room is my dressing room, equally gloomy, and beyond that, my bedroom, which, fortunately, I've had re-decorated in my own colors."

"Good gracious." Lucy raised her eyebrows. "What a hike you've had to make."

"Yes, I—" He laughed suddenly, covering his eyes with one hand.

She half smiled, not knowing the joke, not knowing in fact how she was supposed to act with him, now that they were finally man and wife and alone in their own rooms. It was all so awkward. "What is it?"

"I'm sorry." He dropped his hand so she could see that

his cheeks had reddened. "This isn't the conversation I'd expected to have on our wedding night."

He's nervous. With that realization, a bit of her own anxiety seemed to fall away. She turned and strolled back into her bedroom. "What would you rather talk about?"

She heard him close the door. "I was going to impress you with my romantic eloquence, of course. I'd thought to wax philosophical about the beauty of your brow."

Lucy blinked. "My brow?"

"Mmm. Have I told you that your brow intimidates me?" She felt his warmth at her back as he moved behind her, but he didn't touch her. "It's so smooth and white and broad, and ends with your straight, knowing eyebrows, like a statue of Athena pronouncing judgment. If the warrior goddess had a brow like yours, it is no wonder the ancients worshiped and feared her."

"Blather," she murmured.

"Blather, indeed. Blather is all I am, after all."

She frowned and turned to contradict him, but he moved with her so that she couldn't quite catch sight of his face.

"I am the duke of nonsense," he whispered in her ear. "The king of farce, the emperor of emptiness."

Did he really see himself so? "But—"

"Blathering is what I do best," he said, still unseen. "I'd like to blather about your golden eyes and ruby lips."

"Simon—"

"The perfect curve of your cheek," he murmured close.

She gasped as his breath stirred the hair at her neck. He was distracting her with lovemaking. And it was working. "What a lot of talk."

"I do talk too much. It's a weakness you'll have to bear

in your husband." His voice was next to her ear. "But I'd have to spend quite a bit of time outlining the shape of your mouth, its softness and the warmth within."

Lucy felt a tightening in her middle. "Is that all?" And she was surprised at the low vibration of her voice.

"Oh, no. Then I'd move to your neck." His hand came around and stroked the air inches from her throat. "How graceful, how elegant, how much I want to lick it."

Her lungs were laboring to fill with air. He caressed her with his voice alone, and she wondered if she would be able to bear it when he used his hands.

He continued, "And your shoulders, so white and tender." His hand hovered over her.

"And then?"

"I'd want to describe your breasts." His tone had dipped and roughened. "But I'd have to see them first."

She drew in a shaky breath. He breathed close to her ear. His presence surrounded her body, but he made no move to touch her. She raised her hand and grasped the ribbon at her throat. Slowly, she pulled it, and the whisper sound of the silk sliding free in the bedroom's quiet was unbearably intimate. His breathing hitched as the edges of her chemise fell apart, baring the upper slopes of her bosom.

"So beautiful, so pale," he murmured.

She swallowed and drew the fabric down her shoulders. Her fingers trembled. She'd never willingly exposed herself to another like this, but the roughened sound of his breathing drove her on.

"I see the soft mounds, the shadowed valley, but not the sweet tips. Let me see them, angel." His voice shook.

Something feminine and primeval leaped within her

at the thought that she could make this man tremble. She wanted to expose herself to him, her husband. She closed her eyes and pulled the chemise down. Her nipples peaked in the chilly air.

He stopped breathing. "Ah, God, I remember them. Do you know what it did to me to turn away from you that night?"

She shook her head, her throat clogged. She remembered as well, his hot gaze on her bare breasts, her own wanton craving.

"It nearly unmanned me." His hands hovered over her breasts, tracing her curves without touching. "I wanted to feel you so badly."

His palms were so close to her skin that she could feel his heat, but he didn't touch her. Not yet. She found herself straining toward his hands, anticipating that first contact. She withdrew her arms from the chemise sleeves but clutched the material at her waist so it wouldn't fall.

"I remember you touched yourself here." His hands cupped the air above her nipples. "May I?"

"I . . ." She shivered. "Yes. Please."

She watched his hands descend and lightly touch her breasts. His warm fingers curved about her. She arched and her breasts thrust themselves into his palms.

"God," he breathed. He stroked in a circle around her breasts.

She looked down at herself and saw his big, long-fingered hands on her skin. They looked unbearably masculine. They looked unbearably possessive. He brought both hands toward the tips of her nipples and gently but firmly squeezed them between his forefingers and thumbs. She inhaled at the shocking sensation.

"Does it feel good?" he asked, his lips in her hair.

"I . . ." She swallowed, unable to answer. It was more than good.

But that seemed answer enough for him. "Let me see the rest. Please." His lips skimmed across her cheek, his palms still cradling her breasts. "Please show me, my wife."

She opened her clenched fists, and her chemise fell to the floor. She was naked. He brushed one hand down to her belly and pulled her back against him so her nude buttocks brushed the fabric of his breeches. They were warm, almost hot, from his body. He pressed against her, and she felt his male organ, long and hard. She couldn't help it. She began to shake.

He chuckled in her ear. "There was more I was going to say to you, but I can't." He pressed into her again and groaned. "I want you too badly, and I've lost the words."

Suddenly he lifted her into his arms, and she could see his eyes, shining silver. A muscle in his jaw flexed. He set her on the bed and put one knee beside her, making the mattress dip. "It will hurt the first time; you know that, don't you?" He reached both arms behind him and pulled his shirt over his head.

She was so distracted by the sight of his bare chest that she hardly heard the question.

"I'll go as slowly as possible." He was lean, the long muscles on his arms and shoulders moving as he climbed into the bed. His nipples stood out in startling contrast to his fair skin, brown and flat and so very naked. A diamond of short, fair hairs grew in the very middle of his chest. "I don't want you to hate me afterward."

She reached to touch his nipple. He groaned and closed his eyes.

"I won't hate you," she whispered.

Then he was on her, kissing her wildly, his hands at either side of her face. She felt like giggling and would have, if his tongue hadn't been in her mouth. It was so wonderful to have him want her like this. She cradled the back of his head in her hands and felt the bristles of his shorn hair against her palms. He lowered his hips to hers and all thought spun away. He was hot. His chest slid across her breasts, damp with sweat. His hard thighs, still encased in his breeches, were nudging her legs apart. She opened her legs, welcoming the weight of his body, welcoming him. He settled against her most vulnerable part, and for a moment she was embarrassed. She was wet and the moisture must be staining his breeches. Would he mind? Then he pressed against her with his maleness and she felt . . .

Wonder.

It was so extraordinary, better even than when she touched herself. Was it always this good, this physical sensation? She thought not. It must be him—her husband—and she gave thanks that she had married such a man. He pressed again, sliding this time, and she sighed.

"I'm sorry." He lifted his mouth from hers, his face tight and without humor.

He fumbled between them, and she realized he must be releasing himself. She skewed her head sideways to look. But he was on her before she could see.

"I'm sorry," he said again, his words sharp and bit off. "I'll make it up to you, I promise. If only"—something nudged against her—"later. *Ahh.*" He closed his eyes as if in pain.

And invaded her. Pushing and widening. *Burning.*

She froze.

"I'm sorry."

She bit the inside of her cheek, trying not to cry. At the same time, she was oddly touched by his apology.

"I'm sorry," he said again.

Something tore quite explicitly, and she inhaled but didn't make a sound.

He opened his eyes, looking stricken and hot and savage. "Oh, God, sweetheart. I promise it will be better next time." He kissed the corner of her mouth softly. "I promise."

She concentrated on steadying her breath and hoped he would finish very soon. She didn't want to hurt his feelings, but this was no longer pleasant for her.

He parted his mouth over hers and licked her bottom lip. "I'm sorry."

His hand moved between them and caressed her lightly where they were joined. She tensed, unconsciously expecting pain, but instead it was pleasant. And then it was more. Heat began to flow from her center. Slowly her thighs relaxed from the rigid arch they'd assumed when he'd entered her.

"I'm sorry," he murmured, his voice deep and lazy.

His thumb brushed against her nubbin of flesh. She closed her eyes and sighed.

He circled. "Sorry."

He moved very slowly within her, sliding. It was almost . . . good.

"Sorry." He thrust his tongue into her mouth, and she sucked it.

She let her legs drop open to give him better access. He groaned into her mouth, incoherent, and suddenly it was beautiful again. She arched her hips to meet that thumb, to demand more pressure and dug her fingers into the hard muscles of his shoulders. He moved faster in reply. He broke their kiss, and she could see his silver eyes, pleading and taking at the same time. She smiled and wrapped her legs about his hips. His eyes widened at her movement and he groaned. His eyelids fluttered closed. Then he was arcing back, the tendons in his arms and neck straining to meet an invisible goal. He shouted and heaved against her. And she watched him, this powerful, articulate man driven to helpless, wordless pleasure by her body. By her.

He fell to her side, his chest still heaving, his eyes closed, and lay there until his breathing calmed. She thought he'd fallen asleep, but he reached out and gathered her to him.

"Sorry." The word was so garbled, she wouldn't have known what he'd said if he hadn't been repeating it all along.

"Shh." She stroked his damp side and smiled secretly. "Go to sleep, my love."

"WHY DID YOU SUMMON ME HERE?" Sir Rupert glanced uneasily around the park. It was very early morning and cold as the devil's heart. No one else was in sight, but that didn't mean Walker hadn't been followed or that some fashionable lordling might not be out riding. He pulled the brim of his hat lower to be on the safe side.

"We can't wait for him to make the next move." Lord Walker's breath steamed as he talked.

He sat his mount like a man who'd been bred to the saddle, as indeed he had. Six generations of Walkers had led the hunt in his home county. The Walker stable was renowned for the hunters that came out of it. He'd probably sat a horse before he could toddle on leading-strings.

Sir Rupert shifted on his gelding. He hadn't learned to ride until he was a young man and it showed. Add to that his crippled leg and he was damned uncomfortable. "What do you propose?"

"Kill him before he kills us."

Sir Rupert winced and looked around again. *Fool.* Anyone listening would have blackmail material at the very least. On the other hand, if Walker could solve this problem for him . . . "We've tried that twice and failed."

"So we try it again. Third time's the charm." Walker blinked at him with bovine eyes. "I'm not waiting like a cockerel to have its neck wrung for the supper pot."

Sir Rupert sighed. It was a delicate balance. As far as he knew, Simon Iddesleigh still wasn't aware of his part in the conspiracy. Iddesleigh most likely thought Walker was the last man involved. And if Iddesleigh could be kept from finding out, if he could bring his revenge to its inevitable bloody conclusion with Walker, well, all and good. Walker wasn't such a very important piece of Sir Rupert's life, after all. He certainly wouldn't be missed. And with Walker gone, there would be no one else alive to connect him to the conspiracy that had led to Ethan Iddesleigh's death. It was a seductive thought. He'd be able to rest, and God knew he was ready for it.

But if Walker talked before Iddesleigh got to him—or, worse, *when* Iddesleigh found him—all would be lost. Because, of course, Iddesleigh was really after Sir Rupert, even if he didn't know it. Hence, Sir Rupert's indulgence of Walker's melodrama and this meeting in the park at dawn. The other man must think they were together in this.

His hand drifted toward his waistcoat pocket where the Iddesleigh signet ring still lay. He should've gotten rid of it by now. He had in fact nearly thrown it into the Thames on two occasions. But each time something stopped him. It was illogical, but he fancied that the ring gave him power over Iddesleigh.

"He married yesterday."

"What?" Sir Rupert focused on the conversation.

"Simon Iddesleigh," Walker said patiently, as if he weren't the slow one. "Married some chit from the country. No money, no name. Maybe the man is insane."

"I think not. Iddesleigh is many things, but insane is not one of them." He squashed an urge to massage his thigh.

"So you say." Walker shrugged and took out his snuffbox. "Any case, she might do."

Sir Rupert stared bemusedly as the other man inhaled a pinch of snuff and sneezed violently.

Walker flapped his handkerchief and then blew loudly. "To kill." He sniffed and wiped his nose before pocketing the handkerchief.

"Are you mad?" He nearly laughed in the other's face. "Remember, it was the death of his brother that set Simon Iddesleigh off in the first place. Killing his new wife isn't likely to stop him, now, is it?"

"Yes, but if we threaten her, tell him if he doesn't cease, we'll kill her." Walker shrugged again. "I think he'll stop. Worth a try at any rate."

"Really." Sir Rupert felt his lip curl. "I think it would be like lighting a powder keg. He'll find you even faster."

"But not you, eh?"

"What do you mean?"

Lord Walker flicked a speck of snuff from the lace at his wrist. "Not you. Made sure to stay out of this, haven't you, Fletcher?"

"My anonymity has served our case well." Sir Rupert met the younger man's gaze steadily.

"Has it?" Walker's heavy-lidded eyes stared back.

Sir Rupert had always found Walker's eyes stupidly beastlike, but that was the problem, wasn't it? It was so easy to discount the intelligence of a big, slow-moving animal. Sweat chilled on his back.

Walker's gaze dropped. "That's what I plan to do at any rate—and I expect you to back me, should I need it."

"Naturally," Sir Rupert said evenly. "We're partners."

"Good." Walker grinned, ruddy cheeks bunching. "Have the bastard over a barrel in no time. Must go now. Left a little dove all cozy in her nest. Wouldn't want her to fly before I got back." He winked lewdly and nudged his horse into a trot.

Sir Rupert watched the mist swallow the other man before turning his own gelding toward home and his family. His leg was giving him the very hell, and he'd pay for this ride by having to put it up for the rest of the day. Walker or Iddesleigh. It didn't much matter at this point.

As long as one of them died.

Chapter Twelve

A soft snoring was the first thing Lucy heard when she woke the day after her wedding. Eyes closed, dreams still drifting in her mind, she wondered who was breathing so sonorously. Then she felt the weight of a hand on her breast and came fully awake. But she didn't open her eyes.

Warm. She couldn't remember ever feeling this deliciously warm in her life, certainly not in winter. Her legs were tangled with masculine, hairy ones, even her toes, which never seemed to totally thaw between October and March, were toasty. It was like having her own private hearth, with the added bonus that this hearth came with smooth skin, snuggled all along her right side. The warm air rising from the covers had a subtle smell. She recognized her own scent mingled with a foreign one she realized must be his. How very primitive. Their body odor had mated.

Lucy sighed and opened her eyes.

The sun was peeking through a crack in the curtains. Was it as late as that? Hard on the heels of that thought was another. Had Simon locked the door? In town, Lucy had become accustomed to a maid drawing the curtains in the morning and stirring the fire. Would the servants have expected Simon to return to his own room last night? She turned her head to frown at the door.

"Shh." Simon squeezed her breast in reprimand at her movement. "Sleep," he mumbled, and his breathing evened out again.

Lucy watched him. Fair stubble glinted on his jaw, there were dark circles under his eyes, and his short hair was smashed to one side. He looked so handsome, she nearly caught her breath. She tilted her head until she could see his hand wrapped around her breast. The nipple poked through between his first and second fingers.

Her face heated. "Simon."

"Shh."

"Simon."

"Back . . . sleep." He brushed a kiss against her bare shoulder without opening his eyes.

She firmed her mouth. This was a serious matter. "Is the door locked?"

"Umm."

"Simon, is the door locked?"

He sighed. "Yes."

Lucy squinted at him. He'd started to snore again.

"I don't believe you." She moved to slide from the bed.

Simon twisted and suddenly he was lying on her. He opened his eyes finally. "I should have expected this when I married a country miss." His voice was gravelly with sleep.

"What?" Lucy blinked up at him. She felt very naked

beneath him. His organ pressed into the softness of her lower belly.

"Early hours." He frowned sternly and shifted so his weight was off her chest. Which only made his hips bear down harder.

Lucy tried to ignore the male anatomy impressing itself onto her stomach. It wasn't easy. "But the maid—"

"Any maid who comes through that door before we quit this room, I'll let go without reference."

"You said it was locked." She tried to frown but was afraid her lips may have curved in the wrong direction. She should've been mortified.

"Did I?" He traced her nipple. "Same thing. No one will interrupt us."

"I don't think—"

He covered her mouth with his, and Lucy forgot her thought. His lips were warm and gentle in contrast to his bristles scraping her chin. Somehow the two different touches were erotic.

"So how will you entertain your new bridegroom," he murmured in her ear, "now that you've woken me, hmm?" He pressed his hips into hers.

Lucy shifted restlessly, then stilled with a gasp—a small one, but he heard it nevertheless.

"I'm sorry." Simon leaped off her. "You must think me a ravenous beast. Does it hurt terribly? Perhaps I should have a maid sent up to tend you. Or—"

Lucy pressed her hand to his lips. She'd never get a word in otherwise. "Shh. I'm all right."

"But surely your—"

"Really." Lucy closed her eyes and contemplated pulling the coverlet over her head. Did all married men speak so frankly to their wives? "I'm just a little sore is all."

He looked at her helplessly.

"It was quite nice." She cleared her throat. How to get him back to her? "When you were lying next to me."

"Come here, then."

She inched closer, but when she would have faced him, he gently turned her so that her back was to his chest.

"Put your head here." He stretched out his arm to make a pillow for her.

She was even warmer than before, cradled and held all around by his body in a comfortable, safe embrace. He brought his legs up behind hers and groaned softly. His erection was against the small of her back, insistent and hot.

"Are you all right?" she whispered.

"No." He chuckled rustily. "But I'll survive."

"Simon—"

He clasped her breast. "I know I hurt you last night." His thumb flicked her nipple. "But it won't be like that again."

"It's all right—"

"I want to show you."

Lucy tensed. What, exactly, did showing her entail?

"I won't hurt you," he whispered in her ear. "It'll feel nice. Relax. Let me show you heaven; you're an angel, after all." His hand smoothed down her torso, tickling across her belly, and reached the hair below.

"Simon, I don't think—"

"Shh." He walked his fingers through her maiden hair. She trembled and didn't know where to look. Thank goodness he wasn't facing her. Finally, she closed her eyes.

"Open for me, sweetheart," he rumbled in her ear. "You're so soft here. I want to pet you."

Surely he wouldn't . . .

He wedged his knee between her thighs, parting them. His hand traced the flanges of her sex. She caught her breath, waiting.

"I'd kiss you here." He stroked up. "Lick and tongue you, memorize your spice, but I think it's too soon for that."

Her brain froze as she tried to imagine. Her hips shied.

"Shh. Be still. It won't hurt. In fact"—he reached the top of her cleft—"I'll make you feel very, very good." He circled that bit of flesh there. "Look at me."

She couldn't. She shouldn't even be allowing him to do this. Surely this wasn't what was normally done between man and wife.

"Angel, look at me," he crooned. "I want to see your beautiful eyes."

Reluctantly she turned her head. Raised her eyelids. He stared at her, silver eyes glittering as he pressed with a finger. Her lips parted.

"God," he groaned. Then he was kissing her, his tongue stroking over hers as his fingers slid more rapidly. She wanted to move her hips, to beg that finger. Instead she arched back, rubbing against him. He mumbled something and bit her bottom lip. She felt her wetness now, seeping, making his fingers slippery.

He pushed his penis hard against her bottom.

She couldn't catch her breath, couldn't think. She shouldn't let this happen. Not in front of him. He thrust his tongue into her mouth and relentlessly circled her below. He was a silver-eyed sorcerer who held her enthralled.

She was losing control. She sucked on the thickness of his tongue and suddenly it happened. She arched and felt pleasure shake her. He moved more slowly then, raised his head to watch her, but she no longer cared. Warmth was diffusing through her, spreading from the center of her body. It did indeed feel good.

"Simon."

"Angel?"

"Thank you." Her tongue felt thick, as if she were drugged, and her words were a mumble. She closed her eyes and drifted for a bit, but then she thought of something. He was still hard against her back. She wiggled her bottom, and he sucked in a breath. Did it hurt him?

Well, of course it must. "Can I . . . ?" She felt her face heat. How to phrase the question? "Can I . . . help you?"

"It's fine. Go to sleep." But his voice was tight, and his male organ was almost burning a hole in her back. Surely that wasn't good for his health.

She turned until she could see his face. She knew her own was flushed with shyness. "I'm your wife. I'd like to help you."

A tinge of red chased across his cheekbones. Funny, he wasn't so sophisticated when it came to his own needs.

The sight strengthened her resolve. "Please."

He looked into her eyes, seemed to search them, and sighed. "I'm going to burn in hell for this."

She arched her eyebrows and touched him gently on the shoulder.

His hand caught hers, and for a moment she thought he would push her away, but he guided her palm under the covers and drew it close to his body. Suddenly she held him. Her eyes widened. He was thicker than she'd imagined. There was no give to his flesh, and strangely his skin was soft. And hot. She wanted very much to look at him but wasn't sure he could take that right now. Instead, very gently, she squeezed.

"Ah, God." His eyelids drooped and there was a dazed look on his face.

It made her feel powerful. "What should I do?"

"Here." His fingers delved into her feminine parts and she jumped. Then he was smearing her moisture over himself. "Just . . ." He wrapped his hand over hers and together they slid up the length of him. And back down again.

And again. This was absolutely fascinating. "May I?"

"Uh. Yes." He blinked and released her hand.

She smiled, secretly pleased that he'd been reduced to monosyllables. She kept up the pace that he'd showed her and watched his dear face. He closed his eyes. A line had burrowed itself between his eyebrows. His upper lip was curled back from his teeth, and his face shone with sweat. Watching him, she felt warmth returning to her sex. But more than that, there was a feeling of control and, underneath, the realization of intimacy that he was letting her do this. That he'd made himself vulnerable to her.

"Faster," he grunted.

She complied, her fingers slipping over his length, gripping his skin, hot and slick beneath her palm. His hips rose to meet her hand now.

"Ahh!" Suddenly his eyes opened, and she saw his irises had darkened to a steel gray. He looked grim and driven and almost as if he were in pain. Then he sneered and his big body began jerking. Cream spurted into her palm. He convulsed again, his teeth gritted, his eyes still staring into hers. She held his gaze, pressing her thighs together.

He slumped back into the bed as if terribly weakened, but she knew already from just last night that this was usual. Lucy withdrew her hand from underneath the covers. On it was a whitish substance. She examined it curiously, spreading her fingers. Simon's seed.

He sighed beside her. "Oh, God. That was unbelievably crass of me."

"No, it wasn't." She bent to kiss the corner of his mouth. "If you can do it to me, surely, then, I can do it to you."

"Wise, my wife." He turned his head to take control of the kiss, his mouth hard and possessive. "I am the luckiest of men."

Moving more slowly than usual, he grasped her wrist and wiped her palm with a corner of the bedding. Then he turned her so her back was once again to his chest.

"Now"—he yawned—"now we sleep."

He wrapped his arms around her and Lucy did just that.

"WOULD YOU LIKE TO DRIVE ABOUT TOWN this afternoon?" Simon frowned at his beefsteak and sawed off a bite. "Or perambulate up and down the paths of Hyde Park? Seems boring, but ladies and gentlemen go there every day, so they must find it enjoyable. Once in a while there's a carriage wreck, which is always exciting."

They were pedestrian suggestions, but he was unsure where else to take Lucy. The sad fact was that he'd never spent much time with a lady. He winced. At least out of bed. Where did married men escort their lovely wives? Not to gambling dens or houses of ill repute, certainly. And the Agrarians' coffeehouse was too grimy for a lady.

Which left the park. Or maybe a museum. He cast a glance at her. Surely she wouldn't want to tour a church?

"That would be nice." She poked a green bean. "Or we could simply stay here."

"Here?" He stared. It was too soon to take her to bed again, although the thought beckoned.

"Yes. You could write or mess about with your roses and I could read or sketch." She pushed the green bean aside and took a bite of the whipped potatoes.

He shifted uneasily in his chair. "Won't you be bored?"

"No, of course not." She smiled. "You needn't think that you must amuse me. After all, I doubt you spent your time driving in parks before you married me."

"Well, no," Simon admitted. "But I'm prepared to make some changes now that I've a wife. I've settled down, you know."

"Changes?" Lucy set down her fork and leaned forward. "Like giving up red heels?"

He opened his mouth, then closed it. Was she bamming him? "Maybe not that."

"Or the ornaments on your coats? Sometimes I feel quite a peahen next to you."

Simon frowned. "I—"

A mischievous smile twitched at the corner of her mouth. "Are all your stockings clocked? I'm sure your hosiery bill must be enormous."

"Are you quite done?"

Simon tried to look stern but had an idea he failed miserably. He was glad to see her merry after last night. When he thought of the pain he must've caused her, he still winced. And then to top that by showing her this morning how to jack him off like a gin whore, it didn't put him in a pretty light. He was corrupting his naive young wife. And the sad thing was that were he to have the opportunity to do it over, he knew he'd place her hand on his cock once again. He'd been so hard, he'd ached. And just the thought of Lucy's cool little hand holding his erection had him aching again. What kind of man became hard at the thought of corrupting the innocent?

"I don't think I want you to change anything at all."

Simon blinked and tried to focus his salacious mind on what his dear wife was saying. He realized that Lucy had become serious.

Her eyebrows were straight and stern. "Except for one thing. I don't want you to duel again."

He inhaled and brought his wineglass to his lips to buy time. *Damn. Damn. Damn.* She wasn't fooled, his angel. She watched him calmly and with no trace of mercy in her eyes.

"Your concern is of course commendable, but—"

Newton slithered into the room, holding a silver plate. *Thank God.* "The post, my lord."

Simon nodded his thanks and took the letters. "Ah, perhaps we are to be invited to a grand ball."

There were only three letters, and he was aware of Lucy still watching him. He glanced at the first. A bill. His lips quirked. "Or perhaps not. You may be right about my red-heeled shoes."

"Simon."

"Yes, my dear?" He laid the bill aside and opened the next. A letter from a fellow rose enthusiast: *a new grafting technique from Spain*, et cetera. It, too, he tossed aside. The third letter had no crest pressed into the red sealing wax, and he didn't recognize the handwriting. He opened it with a butter knife. Then sat blinking stupidly down at the words.

If you have any love for your new bride, stop. Any further duels or threats of duels will be met with her immediate death.

He'd never thought that they might bypass him and go straight to Lucy. He had focused his attention mostly on keeping her safe whilst in his company. But if they were to attack while he wasn't there . . .

"You can't hide behind that note forever," Lucy said.

What if she was hurt—or God forbid *killed*—because of him? Would he be able to live in a world without her and her terrible eyebrows?

"Simon, are you all right? What is it?"

He glanced up belatedly. "Nothing. Sorry. It's nothing at all." He crumpled the note in his fist and stood to toss it in the fire.

"Simon—"

"Do you ice-skate?"

"What?" He'd caught her off guard. She blinked at him in confusion.

"I've been promising Pocket I'd teach her to skate on the frozen Thames." He cleared his throat nervously now. What an idiotic idea. "Would you like to ice-skate?"

She stared at him a moment and then rose suddenly from her chair. She came to him and framed his face with her hands. "Yes. I would be delighted to ice-skate with you and Pocket." She kissed him tenderly.

The first kiss, he thought suddenly and inconsequentially, that she'd offered on her own. He wanted to grab her by the shoulders, wrap her in his arms, and pack her away in some inner room in his house. Somewhere he could keep her safe for always. Instead, he kissed her back, brushing lightly, softly over her lips.

And wondered how he would protect her.

"WHY DON'T YOU TELL ME MORE about the Serpent Prince?" Lucy asked later that evening. She used her thumb to smear the red pastel into a shadow beneath Simon's ear on her sketch.

What a wonderful afternoon they had had with Pocket. Simon had shown himself to be an expert ice-skater. Why that had surprised her, Lucy couldn't tell. He had spun circles around her and Pocket, laughing like a madman. They had skated until the light had begun to dim and Pocket's nose was quite rosy. Now Lucy was pleasantly weary and happy to simply sit and relax with Simon as she sketched him. *This* was what she had hoped their life would be like together. She smiled to herself as she looked at him. Although he could make a better model.

As she watched, Simon shifted in his chair and lost the pose. Again. Lucy caught herself in a sigh. She couldn't very well order her new husband to be still as she would Mr. Hedge, but it was most difficult to sketch him when he kept twitching. They were in her sitting room, the one next to her new bedroom. It was a lovely room, done all in creams and rosy pinks with chairs scattered about. And it faced south, which made for good light in the afternoon, perfect for sketching. Of course, it was evening now, but Simon had lit at least a dozen candles despite her protests about the waste and expense.

"What?" He hadn't even heard her.

What was on his mind? Was it the mysterious letter at

luncheon or her ultimatum about the dueling? That hadn't
been politic, she knew, for a new wife. But she felt too
strongly on the subject to be circumspect.

"I asked you to tell me more of the fairy tale." She
blocked in his shoulder. "About the Serpent Prince. You'd
just gotten to the part about Prince Rutherford. I do think
you should reconsider that name."

"I can't." His fingers stopped tapping against his knee.
"The name comes with the fairy tale. You wouldn't want
me to tinker with tradition, would you?"

"Hmm." She'd wondered for some time now whether
Simon was in fact making the whole story up as he went
along.

"Have you been drawing illustrations for the fairy
tale?"

"Yes."

He lifted his eyebrows. "May I see them?"

"No." She deepened the shadow on his sleeve. "Not
until I'm finished. The story now, please."

"Yes, well." He cleared his throat. "The Serpent Prince
had dressed Angelica all in gleaming copper."

"Wouldn't it weigh an awful lot?"

"Light as a feather, I assure you. The Serpent Prince
waves his hand again and suddenly he and Angelica are
standing at the top of the castle, watching the guests to
the grand ball process by. 'Here,' the Serpent Prince says.
'Wear this and be sure and return by the cock's first crow.'
And he hands her a copper mask. Angelica thanks him,
puts on the mask, and all atremble turns to go into the
ball. 'Remember,' the Serpent Prince called after her. 'The
cock's first crow and no later!'"

"Why? What would happen if she didn't return in

time?" Lucy frowned as she outlined his ears. Ears were always so difficult.

"You'll just have to wait and see."

"I hate it when people say that."

"Do you want to hear this story?" He looked down his long nose at her. He was teasing her, pretending to be haughty, and she abruptly realized she cherished these moments with him. When he teased her like this, she felt as if they had a secret code, one understood only by the two of them. It was silly, she knew, and yet she couldn't help caring for him all the more.

"Yes," she replied meekly.

"Well, the king's ball was a most magnificent affair, as you can imagine. A thousand crystal chandeliers lit the vast hall, and gold and jewels sparkled from the throats of all the beautiful ladies in the land. But Prince Rutherford only had eyes for Angelica. He danced every dance with her and begged her to tell him her name."

"And did she?"

"No. For just as she was about to, the first rays of dawn hit the palace's windows, and she knew the cock would crow soon. She flew from the ballroom, and as she crossed the doorway, she was instantly transported back to the Serpent Prince's cave."

"Hold still." Lucy concentrated on getting the corner of his eye just right.

"I obey your every order, my lady."

"Humph."

He grinned. "Angelica tended her goats all that day, taking a nap now and then, for she was quite weary after dancing the night away. And that evening she went to visit the Serpent Prince. 'What can I do for you now?' he asked her, because he'd been rather expecting her. 'There's another ball tonight,' she replied. 'Can you not make me a new gown?'"

"I think she's become greedy," Lucy muttered.

"Prince Rutherford's golden hair was most alluring," he said innocently. "And the Serpent Prince agreed to conjure a new dress for her. But in order to do so, he must cut off his right hand."

"Cut it off?" Lucy gaped in horror. "But he had no need to do so for the first dress."

Simon looked at her almost sadly. "Ah, but he was only mortal, after all. In order to make another dress for Angelica, he must sacrifice something."

A shiver of unease crept down her spine. "I don't know if I like your fairy tale anymore."

"Don't you?" He got up from his chair and sauntered closer, looking impossibly dangerous.

"No." She watched as he stalked toward her.

"I'm sorry. I wish only to bring you joy." He plucked the pastel from her fingers and set it in the box beside her. "But I can't ignore the ugly realities of life either." He bent his head and brushed his lips down her throat. "No matter how much I'd like to."

"I don't want you to ignore reality," she said softly. She swallowed as she felt his open mouth on the hollow at the base of her throat. "But I don't think we need dwell on the horrors of life. There are plenty of good things, too."

"So there are," he whispered.

He swept her suddenly into his arms before she had time to gather her senses. Lucy clutched at his shoulders as he walked with her into the bedchamber next door and set her on the bed. Then he was over her, kissing her almost desperately.

Lucy closed her eyes at the onslaught of sensation. She couldn't think while he kissed her so deeply, so ravenously, as if he would devour her. "Simon, I—"

"Shh. I know you're sore, I know I shouldn't do this, that I'm a rutting animal to even think of it so soon. But, God, I have to." He raised his head and his eyes were wild. How had she ever thought them cold? "Please?"

How could any woman resist such a plea? Her heart warmed and her mouth curved in a sensuous smile. "Yes."

She had no time to say more. At her consent, he was pulling at her clothes. She heard cloth tear. Her breasts were bare, and he fastened his mouth on one, sucking strongly. She gasped and clutched at his head, feeling the scrape of his teeth. He moved to her other breast but teased the first nipple with his thumb, rubbing and tweaking. She couldn't catch her breath, couldn't assimilate what he was doing to her.

He reared back and stripped off his waistcoat. His shirt drifted to the floor a moment later.

She stared at his bared torso. He was pale and taut. Long ropes of muscle shifted on his arms as he moved. He was breathing rapidly, and the fair hairs on his chest sparkled with sweat. He was such a beautiful man, and he was all hers. A ripple of arousal pulsed through her. He stood and shucked his breeches and hose; then he was unfastening the buttons to his smallclothes.

She held her breath, watching avidly. She'd never seen a man fully naked, and it seemed long overdue. But he climbed atop her, hiding that most interesting part of himself before she could see. And a strange thought ran through her mind: Was he shy? Or was it that he was afraid of shocking her? She raised her eyes to meet his gaze and opened her mouth to disabuse him of that notion—she had, after all, spent her life in the country, where farm animals abounded—but he spoke first.

"You're making me harder, looking at me like that." His voice was rough, almost hoarse. "And it's not as if I need any help to get a cock-stand around you."

Her eyelids drooped at his words. She wanted to taste him, to do things to him that she was only vaguely aware of. *More.* She wanted more.

"I want to put myself in you," he said, guttural. "I want to stay inside you all night, to wake with you around me, to make love to you before you even open your eyes." He knelt above her. His face was not kind, and she gloried in his savagery. "If I could, I'd place you on my lap, darling angel, and hold you throughout dinner, my cock inside you. I'd feed you strawberries and cream and not move. The footmen would come and serve us and never know that my cock was in your sweet cove all the time. Your skirts would cover us, but you'd have to remain very, very still so they wouldn't guess."

She felt a wild pulse of desire at his carnal words. She squeezed her legs together, helplessly listening as he told her wicked, forbidden things.

"And after we'd eaten," he whispered, "I'd order the servants away. I'd take down your bodice and suck your nipples until you came, creaming all over my cock. And I'd still not leave you then."

She shuddered.

He kissed her softly on her neck, his caresses at odds

with his hard words. "I'd place you on the table. Very carefully, oh, so very carefully, so that we never broke contact, and then I'd make love to you until we both screamed." His words brushed her skin. "I can't seem to help myself. I don't know what to do with these feelings. I want to make love to you in the carriage, in my library, my God, outside in the sunshine, lying in green grass. I spent half an hour yesterday calculating how soon it would be warm enough to do so."

His words were so erotic, so dark, it almost frightened her. She'd never thought herself a sensual creature, yet with him her body felt out of control, helpless to feel anything but pleasure. He leaned over her and flipped up her skirts so she was nude below the waist. He looked down at what he'd exposed.

"I want this." He placed his hand over the juncture of her thighs. "All the time. I want to do this"—he parted her legs and lowered his hips until his hardness nestled in her folds—"all the time."

She moaned. What was he doing to her?

"Do you want it, too?" He moved, not entering her but thrusting his erection through her wetness. He was rubbing against her bud.

She arched helplessly, whimpering.

"Do you?" he whispered into the hair at her temple. He thrust his hips again.

Pleasure. "I—"

"Do you?" He bit her earlobe.

"Ohhh." She couldn't think, couldn't form the words that he wanted. She could only feel.

"Do you?" He cradled both her breasts in his hands and pinched the nipples as he thrust over her again.

And she came, grinding her hips against him, seeing stars in the darkness of her eyelids, moaning incoherently.

"God, you're beautiful." He positioned himself and pushed.

She felt a twinge, a slight ache, but she no longer cared. She wanted him inside, as close as possible to her. He wrapped his hand around her knee and hitched up one of her legs and pushed again. She was opening, parting, accepting him. She moaned, listening to his rough breathing. He pushed once more and his entire length came into her.

He groaned. "Do you hurt?"

She shook her head. Why wouldn't he move?

His expression was strained. He bent his head and kissed her softly, brushing over her lips, barely making contact. "I won't hurt you this time."

He pulled her other knee up until she was sprawled open beneath him. Then he ground down on her. She moaned. His pelvis was exactly where it should be, and she was in heaven.

He circled his hips and grunted, "Is it good?"

"Um, yes."

He grinned tightly. And ground down again. Then he kissed her with long, luscious strokes of his tongue, his mouth making love to hers, and always the pressure of his hips, hard and demanding. She was drifting in a sensual haze and didn't know how long he made love to her. Time seemed to have stopped so they could be wrapped together in a cocoon of physical pleasure and emotional rapport. She held him tightly to her. This was her husband. This was her lover.

Then he stiffened and his movements became jerkier, faster.

She gasped and caught his face between her palms, wanting to be connected to him when it happened. He thrust hard against her and she felt his seed, hot inside her, right before her world started swirling. His mouth became slack on hers. She continued kissing him, licking along his bottom lip, tasting his mouth.

He pushed up from her, but she tightened her arms to hold him. "Stay."

He looked at her.

"Stay with me. All night long. Please."

His lips quirked in a small smile before he whispered, "Always."

Chapter Thirteen

"It's not a game for you, is it?" Christian asked several nights later. His voice was low, but Simon glanced uneasily around nonetheless.

Drury Lane Theater was as crowded as a corpse bloated with maggots. He'd procured a gilt-edged box on the second level for himself, Lucy, Rosalind, and Christian. The box was close enough to see the whites of the actors' eyes, high enough that any stray vegetables couldn't reach them, should the play turn sour. The rabble in the stalls below was relatively well behaved. The prostitutes working the floor kept their nipples covered—mostly. The noise was low enough that he could actually hear David Garrick, playing a rather elderly Hamlet, recite his lines. Of course, it helped that the actor had lungs like a fishwife's.

"SBLOOD," Garrick bawled, "do you think *me* easier *played* on than a PIPE?" Spittle glittered in the stage lights.

Simon winced. He much preferred reading Shakespeare to attending it. This was assuming he had to consume the bard at all. He glanced at Lucy. She was enthralled, his angel, her eyes half-closed, her lips parted as she watched the play. Behind her, the crimson velvet curtains lining the box framed her head, making a foil for her pale profile and her dark hair. She was almost unbearably beautiful.

He looked away. "What are you talking about?"

Christian scowled. "You know. The duels. Why are you killing these men?"

Simon arched an eyebrow. "Why do you think?"

The younger man shook his head. "At first I thought it was honor of some kind, that they had insulted a lady close to you." His gaze skittered to Rosalind and away. "I'd heard rumors . . . Well, they were repeated everywhere a couple of years ago, before your brother died."

Simon waited.

"And then I thought perhaps you wanted a reputation. The glory of having dueled and killed."

Simon repressed a snort. *Glory.* God, what a thought.

"But after James"—Christian looked at him, puzzled—"you fought with such ferocity, such viciousness. It had to be personal. What did the man do to you?"

"He killed my brother."

Christian's jaw dropped open. "Ethan?"

"Hush." Simon glanced at Rosalind. Although she was obviously less interested in the play than Lucy, her eyes were still on the stage. He turned back to Christian. "Yes."

"How . . . ?"

"I'm not going to discuss this here." He frowned impatiently. Why should he bother explaining himself at all?

"But you're looking for another one."

Simon rested his chin in his open hand, half covering his mouth. "How do you know?"

Christian shifted impatiently in his velvet and gilt chair.

Simon glanced at the stage. Hamlet was creeping up on

his kneeling uncle. The Danish prince raised his sword, babbled verse, and then sheathed it again, another opportunity for vengeance lost. Simon sighed. He'd always found this particular play tedious. Why didn't the prince just kill his uncle and have done?

"I'm not stupid, you know. I've followed you."

"What?" Simon's attention swung back to the man sitting beside him.

"The last couple of days," Christian said. "To the Devil's Playground and to other sordid places. You go in, don't drink, roam around the room, question the staff—"

Simon interrupted this laundry list of activities. "Why are you following me?"

Christian ignored him. "You're looking for a big man, a titled aristocrat. Someone who gambles, but not as compulsively as James, otherwise you would've found him already."

"Why are you following me?" Simon grit his teeth.

"How could all these men, men of standing and good family, have killed your brother?"

Simon leaned forward until his face was inches from Christian's. Out of the corner of his eye, he saw Lucy glance around. He didn't care. "Why are you following me?"

Christian blinked rapidly. "I'm your friend. I—"

"Are you?" His words seemed to hang in the air, almost echoing.

On stage, Hamlet drove his sword through Polonius. The actress playing Gertrude cried shrilly, "O, what a rash and bloody deed is this!" In the next box someone shrieked with laughter.

"Are you my true friend, Christian Fletcher?" Simon

whispered. "Do you guard my back with a loyal eagle eye?"

Christian looked down and then up again, his mouth grim. "Yes. I am your friend."

"Will you second me when I do find him?"

"Yes. You know I will."

"I'm grateful."

"But how can you keep doing it?" The younger man's eyes were intent. He leaned forward, drawing Lucy's gaze again. "How can you keep killing men?"

"It doesn't matter how I'm able." Simon looked away. *James's open eyes, staring into nothing.* "The only thing that matters is that it's done. That my brother is avenged. Do you understand?"

"I . . . yes."

Simon nodded and leaned back. He smiled for Lucy. "Enjoying the play, my lady?"

"Very much, my lord." She wasn't fooled. Her gaze darted between him and Christian. Then she sighed and looked back to the stage.

Simon scanned the audience. Across from them, a lady in embroidered scarlet turned her lorgnette on him, posing self-consciously. He looked away. Below, a broad-shouldered gentleman pushed his way through the crowd, elbowing a wench. The woman shrieked and shoved back. The man turned and Simon leaned forward to catch sight of his profile. Another man rose to join the argument, and the first man turned aside.

Simon relaxed. Not Walker.

He'd spent the past few days since he'd received the threatening letter searching everywhere for the last man in the group that had killed Ethan. Christian may have followed him to the gaming halls at night, but the younger man hadn't seen Simon during the day at the coffeehouses, at horse auctions, or roaming the tailor shops and other establishments for gentlemen. Walker was nowhere to be seen. And yet, he hadn't gone to ground at his estate in Yorkshire either. Simon had paid ears in that vicinity, and there'd been no reports of Lord Walker. He could, of course, have fled to another county or even overseas, but Simon didn't think so. Walker's family was still in his town house.

On stage, an overlarge Ophelia sang her despair at the desertion of her lover. God, he hated this play. He shifted in his chair. If he could just get it over with. Duel Walker, kill him, put the man in his grave, and let his brother rest at last. Maybe then he could look Lucy in the eye without seeing accusation—imaginary or real. Maybe then he could sleep without fear that he'd wake to the destruction of all his hopes. Because he couldn't sleep now. He knew he woke Lucy at night with his movements, but there seemed no help for it. His dreams, both waking and sleeping, were filled with images of Lucy. Lucy in danger, or injured or— God!—dead. Lucy finding out his secrets and turning from him in disgust. Lucy leaving him. And when he had respite from those nightmares, there were the older ones to haunt him. Ethan imploring. Ethan needing. Ethan dying. He fingered the place where the Iddesleigh signet ring should have lain. He'd lost it. Another failure.

The crowd erupted in shouts. Simon looked up and was just in time to see the final bloodbath that ended the play. Laertes's sword work was particularly egregious. Then the audience applauded—and jeered.

Simon got up to hold Lucy's cloak for her.

"Are you all right?" she asked him under cover of the noise.

"Yes." He smiled for her. "I hope you enjoyed the theater."

"You know I did." She squeezed his hand, a secret wifely touch that made the entire tedious evening worth it. "Thank you for bringing me."

"It was my pleasure." He lifted her palm to his lips. "I shall take you to every one of the bard's plays."

"You're so extravagant."

"For you."

Her eyes grew round and liquid, and she seemed to search his face. Didn't she know the lengths he would go to for her?

"I never know what to make of Hamlet," Christian said behind them.

Lucy glanced away. "I adore Shakespeare. But Hamlet . . ." She shivered. "It's so dark at the end. And I never think he fully realizes the hurt he's done poor Ophelia."

"That business when he jumps into the grave with Laertes." Rosalind shook her head. "I think he felt the most pity for himself."

"Perhaps men never do comprehend the wrongs they've done to the women in their lives," Simon murmured.

Lucy touched her hand to his arm, and then they were moving with the crowd toward the doors. The cold air smacked him in the face as they made the entrance. Gentlemen stood on the wide theater steps, shouting as they ordered footmen to fetch their carriages. Everyone was leaving at once, and naturally there weren't enough runners to go around. Lucy shivered in the winter wind, her skirts whipping against her legs.

Simon frowned. She'd catch a chill if she stayed outside much longer. "Stay here with the ladies," he told Christian. "I'll fetch the carriage myself."

Christian nodded.

Simon shoved through the milling crowd, making slow progress. It wasn't until he'd reached the street that he remembered he shouldn't leave Lucy. His heart jumped painfully at the thought. He glanced back. Christian stood between Rosalind and Lucy at the top of the stairs. The younger man was saying something that made Lucy laugh. They looked fine. Still. Best to be cautious. Simon started back.

Which was when Lucy suddenly disappeared.

LUCY STARED AFTER SIMON as he made his way through the crowd in front of the theater. Something was bothering him, she could tell.

Rosalind shivered on the other side of Mr. Fletcher. "Oh, I do hate these crushes after the theater lets out."

The young man smiled down at her. "Simon will be back soon. He'll be faster than waiting for one of the footmen to get the carriage."

Around them the crowd surged and flowed like the sea. A lady bumped Lucy from behind and muttered an apology. Lucy nodded in reply, still staring after her husband. Simon had disappeared the last couple of nights and had returned late. When she tried to question him, he'd joked, and if she questioned him more, he'd made love to her. Urgently. Relentlessly. As if it was the last time every time.

And tonight during the play he'd been muttering with Mr. Fletcher. She hadn't caught the words, but his face had been grim. Why wouldn't he confide in her? Surely that was part of marriage, for the wife to be a helpmeet to her husband and take some of his cares onto her own shoulders. To provide relief from his worries. She thought when they'd married that she and Simon would become closer. That they would attain that state of harmony that she'd glimpsed in some older couples. Instead they seemed to be growing ever further apart, and she wasn't sure what to do. How to bridge the gap, or was it even bridgeable? Perhaps her marriage ideal was merely the naive dream of a maiden. Perhaps this distance between them was the reality of marriage.

Mr. Fletcher leaned down. "Should have tipped Simon better."

Lucy smiled at his silly jest. She turned to reply and felt a shove from her right. She fell to her knees on the hard marble steps, her palms stinging even through the leather of her kid gloves. Someone grabbed her hair and pulled her head back painfully. Shouts. She couldn't see. Her vision was composed of skirts and the dirty marble beneath her palms. A kick landed on her ribs. She gasped and then her hair was released. Mr. Fletcher was grappling with another man directly over her. She shielded her head as best she could, fearful of being trampled or worse. Rosalind screamed. Another blow to Lucy's bottom and a weight shoved against her back.

Then Simon was there. She could hear his furious shouts even from beneath the pile. The weight left her back, and he pulled her up.

"Are you all right?" His face looked as pale as death.

She tried to nod, but he was lifting her into his arms, carrying her down the steps.

"Did you see where he went?" Mr. Fletcher panted beside them.

"Simon, he meant to kill her!" Rosalind sounded shocked.

Lucy was shivering, her teeth chattering together uncontrollably. Someone had tried to kill her. She'd just been standing on the theater steps and someone had tried to kill her. She clutched at Simon's shoulders, trying to still the violent shaking of her hands.

"I know," Simon said grimly. His hands flexed against her back and legs. "Christian, will you escort Rosalind home? I must take Lucy to a doctor."

"Of course." The young man nodded, his freckles standing out starkly in his face. "Whatever I can do."

"Good." Simon stared intently at the younger man. "And, Christian?"

"Yes?"

"Thank you." Simon spoke low. "You saved her life."

Lucy watched over Simon's shoulder as Mr. Fletcher's eyes widened, and a shy smile lit his face before he turned away with Rosalind. She wondered if Simon knew how much the younger man admired him.

"I don't need a doctor," she tried to protest. Her voice wheezed, which certainly didn't help her case.

Simon ignored her. He strode down the steps, shouldering through the mass of people with impatient arrogance. The crowd thinned when they reached the street.

"Simon."

He quickened his pace.

"Simon, you can put me down now. I can walk."

"Hush."

"But you needn't carry me."

He glanced at her, and she saw to her horror that his eyes were shining. "Yes, I do need."

She subsided then. He kept up the pace across several streets until they reached the carriage. Simon bundled her inside and rapped on the roof. The carriage jolted forward.

He held her across his lap and undid her hat. "Should've had Christian direct the doctor to the town house." He swept off her cloak. "I'll have to summon him when we get back." He turned her just enough to reach her back and began un-buttoning her bodice.

Surely he didn't mean to undress her in a moving carriage? But his face was so serious, so grave, that she asked the question gently. "What are you doing?"

"Finding where you're hurt."

"I told you," she said softly. "I'm all right."

He didn't answer but simply continued working on the buttons. He drew the dress off her shoulders, opened her stays, then stilled, looking at her side. Lucy followed his eyes. A thin line of blood stained her chemise just beside her breast. There was a corresponding tear in the fabric of her dress. Gently, Simon loosened the chemise's tie and pulled it away. A cut lay underneath. Now that she saw it, Lucy suddenly felt the burn. Somehow in all the confusion, she hadn't noticed the pain before. She'd been stabbed, but not deeply.

"He nearly had you." Simon traced underneath the cut. "A few inches farther in and he'd have hit your heart." His voice was calm, but Lucy didn't like the way his nostrils had flared, making white dents beside his nose.

"Simon."

"If his aim hadn't been off . . ."

"Simon—"

"If Christian hadn't been there . . ."

"It's not your fault."

His eyes finally met hers, and she saw that the tears had overwhelmed him. Two trailed unchecked down his cheek. He didn't seem to be aware of them. "Yes, it is. It's my fault. I nearly got you killed tonight."

She frowned. "What do you mean?"

She'd supposed her assailant to be some kind of pickpocket or other thief. Perhaps a madman. But Simon was implying that the attacker had been after her specifically. That he'd wanted to kill her. Simon smoothed his thumb over her lips and tenderly kissed her. Even as she accepted his tongue into her mouth and tasted the salt of his tears, she realized that he hadn't answered her question. And that scared her more than anything else had that night.

HE KNEW HE SHOULDN'T.

Even as he swept Lucy into his arms and carried her into the house, Simon knew he shouldn't. He shouldered aside Newton, who exclaimed in concern, and bore her up the stairs like a Roman plundering a Sabine maiden. He'd pulled Lucy's chemise and gown up without fully hooking the back and had thrown her wrap about her to carry her in. She'd convinced him in the carriage that she really didn't need a physician. The cut over her ribs was the only wound, besides bruising, he could find. Nevertheless, someone had tried to kill her. She was shaken and hurt. Only a cad would demand the rights of a husband now.

Ergo, he was a cad.

Simon kicked open the door to his bedroom, bore her across the silver and black carpet, and deposited her on the bed. She lay on his cobalt-blue cover like an offering. Her hair had loosened and was spread over the silk.

"Simon—"

"Hush."

She gazed up at him with calm topaz eyes as he threw off his coat. "We need to discuss what happened."

He toed off his shoes and nearly ripped the buttons from his waistcoat. "I can't. I'm sorry. I need you too much right now."

"Does what I feel not matter?"

"At the moment?" He tore off his shirt. "Frankly, no."

God, couldn't he stop talking? He seemed to have completely lost the art of prevarication. All his finesse, all his elegant words were gone, and what remained was primitive and essential.

He advanced to the bed, but with a great act of self-control didn't touch her. "If you want me to leave, I will."

Her eyes searched his for a long minute during which he died several times over, and his cock reached monstrous proportions. Then, without speaking, she pulled open the ribbon on her chemise. That was all he needed. He fell on her like a starving man at the sight of a Yorkshire pudding. But despite his urgency, he was careful. Though his hands shook, he pulled her dress from her shoulders slowly. Tenderly.

"Lift," he instructed her, and somehow his voice was hushed.

She raised her hips, and he threw the garment on the floor.

"Do you know how much that cost?" He didn't even care that she sounded amused.

"No, but I can guess." He worked at her slippers and stockings. "I'll buy you a hundred more, a thousand, in every color of rose. Have I told you how much I admire you in rose?"

She shook her head.

"I do. Of course, I admire you even more in nothing. Perhaps I'll let you wear nothing at all. That would solve the expensive dress problem."

"And if I object to such a chilly law?" Her brows arched dangerously.

"I'm your husband." He took the chemise off her at last, revealing her white breasts. For a moment his eyes caught on the shallow cut on her side, and he felt fear again chill his soul. Then his nostrils flared at the sight of her nude. He wasn't altogether successful in keeping the possession out of his voice. "You've promised to obey me in all things. For instance, if I bid you kiss me, you must."

He bent and brushed his lips across her mouth. She responded dutifully, her lips moving under his erotically. He was conscious all the time of her breasts, white and bare and undefended, beneath him. His lust rose, shaking his muscles, but he reined it in. The last thing he needed was for her to see how out of control he really was. How very base he really was.

"I bid you open." His voice was nearly hoarse.

She parted her lips and he at least had that—the warm, moist hollow of her mouth to feast on. His arms suddenly trembled. He drew back and closed his eyes.

"What is it?" she whispered.

He opened his eyes and tried to smile to hide the demons inside. "I need you very badly."

Thankfully, she didn't smile. Instead she looked at him with solemn golden eyes. "Then take me."

He inhaled at her simple, explicit offer. "I don't want to hurt you. You've"—he looked away, unable to meet her gaze—"been hurt too much already tonight."

Silence.

Then she spoke slowly and clearly. "You won't hurt me."

Ah, such trust. It was frightening. If only he could be as confident. He rolled to his back. "Come here."

Those intelligent eyebrows went up again. "Aren't you wearing too much?"

His breeches. "I'll take them off later." Or merely unbutton them.

"May I?"

He gritted his teeth. "Fine."

She rose to her elbow beside him, and her breasts swung with the movement. His cock jumped. Delicately she began unbuttoning him. He felt each small pull of her fingers. He closed his eyes and tried to think of snow. Frost. Sleet. Ice.

A soft sigh.

His eyes popped open. She was leaning over him, her white breasts nearly incandescent in the candlelight. Her gaze was fixed on his ruddy-tipped penis, standing foolishly erect from his breeches. It was the most erotic vision he'd ever seen.

"I wondered if you'd ever let me see him." She didn't move her eyes from his groin.

"I beg your pardon?" He nearly squeaked on the last syllable as she touched her forefinger to his crown.

"I've met him, yes, but never seen him. He's been very shy, this fellow." She ran her finger around the rim.

He nearly came off the bed. She should be shocked, she'd been a naive, country miss. Instead . . .

"And look, here are his companions." She took his balls into her small palm.

God's blood. She was going to kill him.

"Lift."

"What?" He blinked at her dazedly.

"Lift your hips so I may undress you," his budding houri said.

What could he do but obey? She slid off his breeches and made him as naked as she.

"Now it's your turn." Thankfully his voice had returned. He couldn't stand much more of this.

"What would you have me do?" she asked.

"I bid you come here." He held out his arms and tried not to groan when the soft inside of her thigh brushed against his erection.

She climbed over him and carefully sat. His cock bobbed in front of her, touching her belly with each pulse. He wanted nothing more than to bury himself in her, but he had to go slowly.

"I bid you offer your breasts to me," he whispered.

Her eyes widened. Good. At least he wasn't the only one affected. She cupped herself, hesitated, then bent lower. Aphrodite herself couldn't have been more alluring. He watched her face as he sucked a pink nipple into his mouth. She closed her eyes, her mouth helplessly parted. Her mons was pressed against his cock, which was throbbing between them. She trembled and that darkness within him roared with triumph.

He let go of the nipple. "Mount me."

She frowned.

"Please." The word was more an order than a plea, but he was past caring. He needed her pussy around him.

She raised herself. He steadied her with one hand, held his cock with the other, and she slowly sank onto him.

"Hold yourself open for me," he murmured. *Cad.* It made

the way easier, but he also had a wonderful view of her coral wetness.

She gasped and fumbled between their bodies with her fingers. Poor angel. Led into corruption by a selfish devil who cared only for his prick. Ahh. He was half in now, the way tight and warm and soft. He took her hands away, put them on his chest, and used his own fingers to part her folds. To hold her as he worked his way into her tight passage. *Paradise.* He almost smiled. This was as close as he would ever be to heaven. He knew the thought was blasphemy itself, and he didn't care. He was making love to his angel. Tomorrow the world might end, but right now he was balls-deep in wet woman. *His* wet woman.

He thrust and she cried out.

He felt a grin, not a nice one, split his face. He looked down and watched his reddened skin slide into her flesh. Lifted her up and pulled almost out. Saw the glistening moisture of her cunny coating his cock. And slammed back into her. Thrusting into her. Filling her. Claiming her. *My woman. Always. Never to leave. Stay with me.*

Always.

She shook her head wildly. He pressed his fingers against her mound to feel it and to find that special pearl. She moaned, but he didn't relent. He filled her with cock and diddled her clitoris with his thumb, and he knew she couldn't hold out. The walls of her sheath clenched and she came, raining her sweet pleasure on his prick. He buried himself in her until his balls met her bottom. His body convulsed and he felt the pulse of his seed filling her.

Mine.

Chapter Fourteen

Oh, God!

Lucy woke with a start, her breath coming in gasps in the dark of the bedroom. The sheets clung to the cold sweat on her skin like a shroud. She froze and tried to calm her breathing, lying as still as a rabbit on sighting the snake. The dream had been vivid. Bloody. But it was already fading with her consciousness. All she recalled was the fear—and the feeling of hopelessness. She'd been screaming in the dream when she'd woken, and she'd been surprised that the sound was as phantom as the images.

Finally she moved, her muscles aching from being held in tension too long. She reached out to find Simon, to reassure herself that there was life even in the depths of night and nightmare.

He wasn't there.

Maybe he'd gotten up to use the necessary? "Simon?"

No answer. She listened to the silence with the irrational fear that only came after midnight: that all life had died. That she was alone in a dead house.

Lucy shook herself and rose, wincing a bit as the cut

on her side pulled. Her bare toes touched the cold carpet, and she patted her hand in the air, searching for a candle on the bedside table before realizing she'd gone to sleep in Simon's room. The table was on the other side of the bed. She held the bed curtains for a guide and felt with her feet as she rounded the bed. All she remembered of the room from last night was an impression of darkness and the severe colors, an almost black-blue and silver, and that his bed was even bigger than her own. That had amused her.

She held out a hand blindly, felt a book and then the candle. There were still embers glowing in the fireplace, and she crossed to light the candle. The feeble flame hardly revealed the whole of Simon's room, but she already knew he wasn't here. She put on her gown from the theater and pulled a wrap over it to hide the fact that she couldn't do up the back on her own. Then she shoved her bare feet into slippers.

She shouldn't be surprised that he'd disappeared. He'd made a habit of it in the last week, leaving in the evening, only to reappear in the early hours of morning. His nightly wandering seemed to have become more common in the last few days. Sometimes he came to her chamber looking so very weary and smelling of smoke and drink. But he'd never left her bed before, not after making love to her, not after holding her until they both gave in to sleep. And the way he'd made love to her only hours before—so intensely, so desperately—as if he'd never have the opportunity again. She'd actually been afraid at certain points. Not that he'd hurt her, but that she'd lose a part of herself in him.

Lucy shivered.

Their rooms were on the third floor. She checked her

bedroom and sitting room, then descended the stairs. The library was empty. She held her candle high and saw only long, ghostly shadows thrown over the rows of book bindings. A window rattled in the wind from without. She reentered the hallway and debated. The morning room? Highly unlikely, he'd—

"May I help you, my lady?"

Newton's dirgelike tones behind her made Lucy shriek. Her candle went tumbling to the floor, hot wax burning her instep.

"I'm most sorry, my lady." Newton bent and retrieved her candle and lit it with his own.

"Thank you." Lucy accepted the light and held it higher so she could see the butler.

Newton had obviously just come from bed. A nightcap covered his bald pate, and an old coat was thrown over his nightshirt, pulled taut across his small, round belly. She looked down. He wore rather fancy, curl-toed Turkish slippers on his feet. Lucy rubbed one bare foot over the other and wished she'd thought of stockings.

"May I assist you, my lady?" Newton asked again.

"Where is Lord Iddesleigh?"

The butler averted his eyes. "I couldn't say, my lady."

"Can't or won't?"

He blinked. "Both."

Lucy raised her eyebrows, surprised he'd answered with the truth. She studied the butler. If Simon's absence was because of a woman, she was sure Newton would've made excuses for his master. But he hadn't. She felt her shoulders relax from a tension she hadn't even known was there.

Newton cleared his throat. "I'm sure Lord Iddesleigh will return before morning, my lady."

"Yes, he always does, doesn't he?" Lucy muttered.

"Would you like me to warm you some milk?"

"No, thank you." Lucy walked to the stairs. "I'll go back to bed."

"Good night, my lady."

Lucy put her foot on the first tread and held her breath. From behind her, Newton's footsteps receded and a door closed. She waited a moment more, then turned. Quietly she tiptoed back to Simon's study.

This room was smaller than the library but more richly appointed. It was dominated by his massive baroque desk, a recklessly beautiful piece of furniture, picked out in gilt and curlicues. She would've laughed at any other man owning such a piece, but it suited Simon perfectly. There was an arrangement of wingback chairs before the fireplace, and two bookcases flanked the desk, easily accessible to someone sitting at it. Many of the books were on the subject of roses. Simon had shown her this room only the other day, and she'd been fascinated by the detailed hand-colored illustrations in the big tomes. Each rose an ideal of the flower, each part identified and labeled.

So orderly a world.

Lucy settled herself into one of the wing chairs before the fireplace. With the study door open, she had a view into the hallway and all that happened there. Simon would have to pass her by when he came home. She intended to quiz him on his nocturnal ramblings when he did.

APHRODITE'S GROTTO WAS A DEN of howling wolves tonight.

Simon advanced into the main hall of the brothel and looked around. He hadn't set foot in here since before he'd met Lucy, but the place hadn't changed. Half-dressed whores paraded their wares, enticing men, some barely old enough to shave, some toothless with age. Minor royalty rubbed shoulders with upstart merchants and foreign dignitaries. Aphrodite didn't care. As long as the color of the money was gold. In fact, it was rumored that she had just as many female customers as male. Perhaps she charged them both, Simon thought cynically. He looked around for the madam but didn't see her distinctive gold mask. Just as well. Aphrodite frowned on violence in her house, and that was exactly what he was intent on doing.

"What is this place?" Christian whispered beside him.

He'd picked up the younger man two—no, three— houses before. Christian still looked fresh-faced after the theater earlier in the evening, the fight outside it, and the three increasingly seedy gambling places they'd visited before this. Simon very much feared that he himself resembled a newly unearthed corpse.

Damn youth anyway. "Depends." He started up the stairs, dodging the race going on there.

Female jockeys wearing only brief corsets and masks rode bare-chested steeds. Simon winced as a jockey drew blood with her quirt. Although, judging by the bulge in the trousers of her mount, he didn't mind at all.

"On what?" Christian watched wide-eyed as the winning pair galloped up and down the upper hall. The jockey was bare-breasted and bouncing exuberantly.

"On your definition of heaven and hell, I suppose," Simon said.

His eyes felt as if a handful of sand were under each lid, his head ached, and he was tired. So very tired.

He kicked in the first door.

Christian exclaimed something behind him, but he ignored it. The occupants, two girls and a red-headed gentleman, didn't even notice the intrusion. He didn't bother to apologize, just shut the door and moved on to the next. He didn't have much hope of finding Walker. According to his sources, Walker had never patronized Aphrodite's Grotto before. But Simon was getting desperate. He needed to find Walker and get this over with. He needed to make Lucy safe again.

Another door. Shrieks from within—two women this time—and he closed it. Walker was married with a mistress, but he liked the bawdy houses. If Simon visited every single brothel in London, eventually he'd find him, or so he hoped.

"Won't we get thrown out doing this?" Christian asked.

"Yes." *Kick.* His knee was beginning to hurt. "But hopefully not before I find my quarry."

He was at the end of the hall now, at the last door, in fact, and Christian was right. It was only a matter of time before the house thugs arrived. *Kick.*

He nearly turned away, but he looked again.

The man on the bed had his cock buried in a saffron-haired wench on her knees. She was naked, save a demi-mask, and had her eyes closed. Her partner hadn't noticed their interruption. Not that it mattered. He was short and swarthy and black haired. No, it was the *second* man, the one almost in the shadows observing the show, that made the squawk. And a good thing, too, since Simon had almost overlooked him.

"What the hell—"

"Ah. Good evening, Lord Walker." Simon advanced and made a bow. "*Lady* Walker."

The man on the bed started and swung his head around, although his hips still moved instinctively. The woman remained oblivious.

"Iddesleigh, you bastard, what . . . ?" Walker lurched to his feet, his now-limp prick still hanging from his breeches. "That's not my wife!"

"No?" Simon cocked his head, examining the woman. "But she looks like Lady Walker. Particularly that mark there." He pointed with his stick at a birthmark high on her hip.

The man humping her opened his eyes wide. "This 'ere your wife, guvnor?"

"No! Of course not."

"Oh, but I've known your fair lady *intimately* for quite some time, Walker," Simon drawled. "And I'm quite certain this is she."

The big man threw back his head suddenly and laughed, although it sounded a bit weak. "I know your game. You're not going to trick me into—"

"Never had quality before," the stud said from atop the woman. He increased his pace, possibly in appreciation.

"She's not—"

"My acquaintance with Lady Walker goes back many years." Simon leaned on his stick and smiled. "Before the birth of your first child—your heir, I believe?"

"Why, you—"

The black-haired man gave a yell and bucked his hips

into the woman, shuddering as he obviously deposited a load of sperm into her. He sighed and fell off her, revealing a cock that, even half-deflated, was of equine proportions.

"Jesus," Christian said.

"Quite," Simon concurred.

"How the hell did he get that thing in her?" the younger man muttered.

"I'm glad you asked," Simon said as if instructing a pupil. "Lady Walker is quite talented in that regard."

Walker gave a roar and charged across the room. Simon tensed, the blood singing in his veins. Maybe he could finish this tonight.

"See, here," a voice exclaimed from the door at the same time.

The house bullies had arrived. He stepped aside and Walker ran into their waiting arms. The big man struggled ineffectually in their grasp.

"I'm going to kill you, Iddesleigh!" Walker panted.

"Possibly," Simon drawled. God, he was tired to the bone. "At dawn, then?"

The man merely growled.

The woman on the bed chose that moment to roll over. "Would you like a go?" she asked no one in particular.

Simon smiled and led Christian away. They passed a new race on the stairs. The male mounts this time had actual bits in their mouths. One man had blood running down his chin and a cock-stand in his breeches.

He'd have to bathe before he returned to Lucy. He felt like he'd rolled in manure.

Christian waited until they made the front steps before he asked, "Was that really Lady Walker?"

Simon caught himself mid-yawn. "I've no idea."

*   *   *

WHEN LUCY WOKE AGAIN, it was to the sound of Simon entering the study. The room was that gray shade that foretold the dawn of a new day. Simon walked in, carrying a candle. He set it on the corner of his desk and, still standing, pulled out a sheet of paper and began writing.

He never looked up.

At the far side of the room, partially hidden by the arms of the wing chair and in shadows, she must've been nearly invisible to him. She had meant to accost him on his return, to demand answers. But now she merely studied him, her hands curled beneath her chin. He looked tired, her husband, as if he hadn't slept in years. He wore his clothes from the night before: a deep blue coat and breeches with a silver waistcoat, creased and stained now. His wig had lost some of its powder and looked dingy. Shocking, because she'd never seen him—at least in London—other than sartorially correct. Deep lines bracketed his mouth, his eyes were red-rimmed, and his lips had thinned, as if he pressed them together to keep them from trembling. He finished whatever he was writing, dusted it with sand, and straightened the paper on the desk. In doing so, he knocked the pen to the floor. He cursed and bent slowly like an old man to pick it up, placed it carefully on the desk, and sighed.

Then he left the room.

Lucy waited several minutes before rising, listening to his footfalls on the stairs. She padded over to the desk to see what he'd written. It was still too dark to read. She took the note to the window, parted the curtains, and angled the paper to read the still-damp writing. The dawn was just breaking, but she could make out the first lines:

In the event of my death, all my worldly possessions . . .

It was Simon's will. He was leaving his estate to her. Lucy stared at it a moment longer, then replaced the paper on the desk. From the hallway came the sounds of her husband descending the stairs. She moved to stand beside the doorway.

"I'll take my horse," Simon was saying, apparently to Newton. "Tell the coachman I won't have need of him anymore tonight."

"Yes, my lord."

The front door closed.

And suddenly Lucy felt a wave of anger. He hadn't even tried to wake her, else he would've noticed her absence from his bed. She strode into the hall, her skirts swishing about her bare ankles. "Newton, wait."

The butler, his back to her, started and whirled. "M-my lady, I hadn't realized—"

She waved his apology aside and came straight to the point. "Do you know where he's going?"

"I . . . I . . ."

"Never mind," she said impatiently. "I'll simply follow him."

Lucy cautiously opened the front door. Simon's carriage was still sitting out front, the coachman almost asleep on the box. A stable hand was yawning as he returned to the mews.

And Simon was riding away.

Lucy closed the door, ignoring Newton's hissed exclamations behind her, and ran down the steps, shivering in the morning chill. "Mr. Coachman."

The coachman blinked as if he'd never seen his mistress with her hair undone, as indeed he hadn't. "My lady?"

"Please follow Lord Iddesleigh without letting him know."

"But, my lady—"

"Now." Lucy didn't wait for a footman to place the step but scrambled into the carriage. She stuck her head back out again. "And don't lose him."

The carriage lurched forward.

Lucy sat back and pulled a rug over herself. It was bitterly cold. Scandalous of her to be driving about London not fully dressed and her hair down, but she couldn't let modesty keep her from confronting Simon. He hadn't had any decent sleep for days, and he wasn't that long recovered from the beating. How dare he continue to risk his life and not think she should know about it? Cut her off, in fact, from that part of himself. Did he think she was a doll to be taken out and played with and then packed away again when he had other matters to see to? Well, it was long past time that she discuss with him exactly what she considered came under the duties of a wife. Her husband's health, for one thing. Not keeping secrets from her, for another. Lucy harrumphed and folded her arms across her chest.

The December sun had finally dawned, but the light was poor and didn't seem to affect the cold at all. They turned in to the park, the cobblestones changing to gravel beneath the carriage's wheels. A mist hung eerily about the ground, shrouding the trunks of trees. From the small carriage window, Lucy couldn't see any movement and had to trust that the coachman was still following Simon.

They rolled to a halt.

A footman opened the door and peered in at her. "John Coachman says if he gets any closer, his lordship will see."

"Thank you."

With the man's help, Lucy alighted and turned to where he pointed. About a hundred yards away, Simon and another man faced each other like figures in a pantomime. At this distance, she could only tell it was Simon from the way he moved. Her heart seemed to stop dead. Dear Lord, they were ready to begin. She wasn't in time to persuade Simon to stop this terrible rite.

"Wait for me here," she ordered the menservants, and walked toward the scene.

There were six men in all—four others stood apart from the duelists, but none looked in her direction or even seemed to notice her at all. They were too involved in this masculine game of death. Simon had removed his coat and waistcoat, as had his opponent, a man Lucy had never seen before. Their white shirtsleeves were almost ghostly in the gray morning mist. They must be cold, but neither man shivered. Instead Simon stood still, while the other man swooshed his sword about, perhaps in practice.

Lucy stopped maybe twenty yards away in the shelter of some bushes. Her bare feet were already frozen.

Simon's adversary was a very big man, taller than him, with greater breadth of shoulder. His face was ruddy against his white wig. In contrast, Simon's face was pale as death, the weariness she'd noticed at the house more pronounced in daylight, even at this distance. Both men stood still now. They bent their legs, raised their swords, and paused like a tableau.

Lucy opened her mouth.

Someone shouted. She flinched. Simon and the big man lunged together. Violence sang in the speed of their thrusts, in the awful sneers on their faces. The clatter of their swords rang in the still air. The big man advanced, his sword stabbing, but Simon sprang away, parrying the thrusts. How could he move that fast when he was so tired? Could he keep it up? Lucy wanted to run forward, to shout at the combatants, *Stop it! Stop it! Stop it!* But she knew that her mere appearance might be enough to startle Simon into dropping his guard and getting killed.

The big man grunted and attacked low. Simon stumbled back and repelled the other man's blade with his own.

"Blood!" someone cried.

And only then did Lucy notice the stain on her husband's middle. *Oh, God.* She didn't realize she'd bitten her lip until she tasted copper. He still moved. Surely if he'd been run through he'd fall? But he backed instead, his arm continuing to work as the other man herded him. She felt bile rise in her throat. *Dear Lord, please don't let him die.*

"Throw down your swords!" another man cried.

Lucy looked and realized one of the men was young Mr. Fletcher. The other three men shouted and gesticulated at the combatants, trying to end the duel, but Mr. Fletcher merely stood, an odd smile on his face. How many of these pointless battles had he attended? How many men had he witnessed her husband kill?

Lucy suddenly hated his fresh, open face.

The bloody stain at Simon's middle spread. He looked like he wore a scarlet sash about his waist now. How much blood was he losing? The big man grinned and swung his sword with even greater speed and force. Simon was lagging. He turned away the other man's blade again and again. Then he stumbled and almost lost his footing. Another stain appeared on his shirt, this one above the wrist of the hand that held his sword.

"Goddamn." She heard his voice faintly. It sounded so weak, so very weary to her ears.

Lucy closed her eyes and felt tears leak beneath them. She rocked her body to contain the sobs. *Must not make a noise. Must not distract Simon.* Another shout. She heard Simon's husky voice swearing. She almost didn't open her eyes. But she did. He was on his knees, like a sacrifice to a vengeful god.

Oh, my sweet Lord.

The other man wore a look of grotesque triumph on his face. He lunged, his sword flashing, to stab Simon. To kill her husband. *No, please, no.* Lucy ran forward as if in a dream, not making a sound. She knew she'd never get to them in time.

Simon raised his sword at the very last second and impaled the other man through the right eye.

Lucy bent and vomited, hot bile splattering her bare toes. The big man screamed. Awful, high shrieks that sounded like nothing she'd ever heard before in her life. She heaved again. The other men shouted words she couldn't comprehend. She looked up. Someone had removed the sword from where the big man's right eye had been. Black stuff dripped down his cheek. He lay on the ground moaning, his wig fallen from his shaved head. A man with a physician's black bag was bent over the wounded man, but he merely shook his head.

Simon's opponent was dying.

She choked and heaved once more, the taste of acid on her tongue. Only a yellow thread emerged from her sore throat.

"Iddesleigh," the dying man gasped.

Simon had risen, although he seemed to be trembling.

Blood was splashed on his breeches. Mr. Fletcher was working at his shirt, trying to bandage him, his face averted from the man on the ground.

"What is it, Walker?" Simon asked.

"Another."

Her husband suddenly straightened and pushed Mr. Fletcher away. Simon's face sharpened, the lines carving ditches into his cheeks. In one stride he stood over the fallen man. "What?"

"Another." The big man's body shook.

Simon dropped to his knees beside him. "Who?"

The man's mouth moved before sound emerged. "Fletcher."

Mr. Fletcher swung around, confusion on his face.

Simon didn't take his gaze from the dying man. "Fletcher is too young. You can't trick me that easily."

Walker smiled, his lips coated with the gore from his destroyed eye. "Fletcher's—" A convulsion of coughing cut off his words.

Simon frowned. "Bring some water."

One of the other men proffered a metal bottle. "Whiskey."

Simon nodded and took it. He held the flask to his enemy's lips and the man gulped. Walker sighed. His eyes closed.

Simon shook him. "Who?"

The fallen man was still. Was he already dead? Lucy began to whisper a prayer for his soul.

Simon swore and slapped his face. *"Who?"*

Lucy gasped.

Walker half opened his eyes. "Faa-therrr," he slurred.

Simon stood and looked at Christian. The man on the ground sighed again, the breath rattling from his throat.

Simon didn't even glance down. "Your father? He's Sir Rupert Fletcher, isn't he?"

"No." Christian shook his head. "You're not taking the word of a man you killed?"

"Should I?"

"He lied!"

Simon simply looked at the younger man. "Did your father help kill my brother?"

"No!" Christian threw up his hands. "No! You're unreasonable. I'm leaving." He strode away.

Simon stared after him.

The other men had moved off.

Lucy wiped her mouth with the back of her hand and stepped forward. "Simon."

Her husband turned and met her eyes across the body of the man he'd just killed.

Chapter Fifteen

Jesus God.

Lucy.

"What are you doing here?" Simon couldn't help it; the words came out a hiss.

Lucy *here,* her hair undone, her face ghastly white. She clutched her cloak to herself, shoulders hunched, huddling, the fingers under her chin bluish with cold.

She looked as if she'd seen a horror.

He glanced down. Walker's body lay at his feet like a bloody prize. There was a gaping hole where his eye had been, and his mouth sagged open, life no longer holding it shut. The doctor and seconds had backed away as if they were afraid to deal with the corpse while its killer still stood over it. *Jesus God.*

She *had* seen a horror.

She'd seen him fight for his life, seen him kill a man by running him through the eye, seen the blood spurt. He was covered in gore, his own and the other man's. *Jesus God.* No wonder she looked at him like he was a monster. He was. He could hide it no longer. He had nowhere to turn. He'd never wanted her to see this. Never wanted her to know he—

"What are you doing here?" he shouted, to make her back down, to drown out the chant in his mind.

She stood firm, his angel, even in the face of a screaming, bloodied madman. "What have you done?"

He blinked. Raised his hand, still clutching the sword. There were wet, reddish stains on the blade. "What have I . . ." He laughed.

She flinched.

His throat was raw, aching with tears, but he laughed. "I've avenged my brother."

She looked down at Walker's ruined face. Shuddered. "How many men have you killed for your brother?"

"Four." He closed his eyes, but he still saw their faces against his eyelids. "I thought four was all. I thought I was done, but I'm told there is a fifth."

She shook her head. "No."

"Yes." He didn't know why he continued. "There will be another."

She pressed her lips together, whether to hold back a sob or to contain her revulsion, he did not know. "You can't do this, Simon."

He pretended stupidity, though he wanted to sob. "Can't? I've already done it, Lucy. I'm still doing it." He spread his arms wide. "Who is there to stop me?"

"You can stop yourself." Her voice was low.

His arms dropped. "But I won't."

"You will destroy yourself."

"I am already destroyed." And he knew, deep, deep in his blackened soul that he spoke the truth.

"Vengeance is for the Lord."

So calm. So sure.

He sheathed his sword, still bloody. "You don't know what you're talking about."

"Simon."

"If vengeance is for the Lord, then why does England have courts of law? Why do we hang murderers every day?"

"You aren't a court of law."

"No." He laughed. "A court of law wouldn't touch them."

She closed her eyes as if weary. "Simon, you can't just take it upon yourself to kill men."

"They murdered Ethan."

"It's wrong."

"My *brother*, Ethan."

"You're sinning."

"Would you have me sit back and let them savor their kill?" he whispered.

"Who are you?" Her eyes snapped open, and her voice held a hysterical edge. "Do I even know who you are?"

He stepped over Walker's battered corpse and grabbed her by the shoulders, leaned down so that his no-doubt foul breath washed over her face. "I am your husband, my lady."

She turned her face away from him.

He shook her. "The one you promised to obey always."

"Simon—"

"The one you said you'd cleave to, forsaking all others."

"I—"

"The one you make love to at night."

"I don't know if I can live with you anymore." The

words were a whisper, but they rang in his head like a death knell.

Overwhelming fear froze his gut. He jerked her body tight against his own and ground his mouth down on hers. He tasted blood—either hers or his, it didn't matter and he didn't care. He would not—*could* not—let her go. Simon raised his head and stared her in the eye. "Then it's too bad you no longer have a choice."

Her hand trembled as she wiped a smear of blood from her mouth. He wanted to do it for her, wanted to say he was sorry. But she'd probably bite his fingers right now, and the words wouldn't come anyway. So he simply watched her. She pulled her soiled cloak together and turned and walked away. He watched as she made her way across the green. She climbed into the carriage and drove off.

Only then did he pick up his coat and mount his horse. The London streets had filled with people going about their business. Costermongers with carts, urchins on foot, lords and ladies in carriages and riding horses, shopkeepers and whores. A mass of breathing beings starting a new day.

But Simon rode apart.

Death had taken him into the company of the damned, and his bond with the rest of humanity was broken.

THE STUDY DOOR SLAMMED AGAINST THE WALL.

Sir Rupert looked up to see his son standing in the doorway, pale, disheveled, and his face gleaming with sweat. He started to rise from his desk.

"Did you do it?" In contrast to his appearance, Christian's voice was low, almost calm.

"Do what?"

"Did you kill Ethan Iddesleigh?"

Sir Rupert sat back down. If he could, he would've lied; he made no bones about it. He'd found that deception was often the best way. More often than not, people wanted to be lied to; they didn't like the truth. How else to explain why they fell for lies so quickly? But his son's face showed that he already knew the truth. His question was rhetorical.

"Shut the door," Sir Rupert said.

Christian blinked, then did as ordered. "My God. Did you, Father?"

"Sit down."

His son slumped into a carved and gilded chair. His ginger hair was matted with sweat, and his face shone greasily. But it was his tired expression that bothered Sir Rupert. When had his son's face become lined?

Sir Rupert spread his hands. "Ethan Iddesleigh was a problem. He had to be removed."

"Dear God," Christian groaned. "Why? Tell me why you would kill a man."

"I didn't kill him," he said irritably. "Do you think your father so foolish? I simply arranged for his death. I was involved in a business venture with Ethan Iddesleigh. It consisted of myself, Lord Walker—"

"Peller, James, and Hartwell," Christian interrupted. "Yes, I know."

Sir Rupert frowned. "Then why do you ask, if you know already?"

"I only know what Simon has told me, and that has been precious little."

"Simon Iddesleigh was no doubt prejudiced in his account, however small it was," Sir Rupert said. "The facts are these: We had invested in tea and stood to lose everything. We all agreed to a course of recovery. All, that is, but Ethan. He—"

"This is about money?"

Sir Rupert looked at his son. Christian wore an embroidered silk coat that would provide food and shelter for a laborer's family for the better part of a season. He sat in a gilt-painted chair a king wouldn't be ashamed to own, in a house on one of the best streets of London.

Had he any idea at all? "Of course it's about money, dammit. What did you think it was about?"

"I—"

Sir Rupert slammed the flat of his hand down on his desk. "When I was your age, I worked from before the sun rose until past dark of night. There were days that I fell asleep over my supper, my head on a plank table. Do you think I would ever go back to that?"

"But to kill a man over gold, Father."

"Don't you sneer at gold!" Sir Rupert's voice rose on the last word. He brought it under control again. "Gold is the reason you have no need to labor as your grandfather did. As I did."

Christian ran a hand through his hair. He seemed dazed. "Ethan Iddesleigh was married with a little daughter."

"Think you I would choose his daughter over mine?"

"I—"

"We would've lost the house."

Christian looked up.

"Yes." Sir Rupert nodded. "It was as bad as that. We would've had to retire to the country. Your sisters would've lost their seasons. You would've had to give up that new carriage I'd bought you. Your mother would've had to sell her jewels."

"Were our finances so dire?"

"You have no idea. You get your quarterly allowance and never think where it comes from, do you?"

"Surely there are investments—"

"Yes, investments!" Sir Rupert pounded on the desk again. "What do you think I'm talking about? This was an investment—an investment upon which our entire future depended. And Ethan Iddesleigh, who never had to work a day in his life, who had his entire fortune handed to him on a silver platter when he was but a babe, wanted to stand on principle."

"What principle?" Christian asked.

Sir Rupert breathed heavily. His leg was hurting like the very devil and he needed a drink. "Does it matter? We were on the brink of destruction. Our *family*, Christian."

His son merely stared at him.

"I told the others that if we got rid of Iddesleigh, we could go ahead. It was a short step from there to getting Iddesleigh to call out Peller. They dueled and Peller won." He leaned forward and pinned his son with his gaze. "We won. Our family was saved. Your mother never even knew how close we'd come to losing it all."

"I don't know." Christian shook his head. "I don't know if I can accept that you saved us this way and left Ethan Iddesleigh's daughter fatherless."

"Accept?" A muscle in his leg spasmed. "Don't be a fool. Do you want your mother in rags? Me in the poor-house? Your sisters taking in washing? Principles are all well and fine, lad, but they don't put food in your mouth, do they?"

"No." But his son looked doubtful.

"You are as much a part of this as I am." Sir Rupert fumbled in his waistcoat pocket before rolling the ring across the table at his son.

Christian picked it up. "What's this?"

"Simon Iddesleigh's ring. James had it taken from him when his thugs almost killed him."

His son raised incredulous eyes at him.

Sir Rupert nodded. "Keep it. It will remind you of whose side you stand on and what a man must do for his family."

He'd raised Christian to be a gentleman. He'd wanted his son to feel at home in the aristocracy, to never fear that he'd make a faux pas and give away his plebeian origins— as he himself had feared as a young man. But in giving him this confidence, this assurance that he need not worry about finances, had he weakened his son?

Christian stared at the ring. "He killed Walker this morning."

Sir Rupert shrugged. "It was only a matter of time."

"And now he'll come after you."

"What?"

"He knows about you. Walker told him that you were the fifth man."

Sir Rupert swore.

"What are you going to do?" His son pocketed the ring.

"Nothing."

"Nothing? What do you mean? He's tracked down the others and forced them to call him out. He'll do the same to you."

"I doubt it." Sir Rupert limped around the desk, leaning heavily on his cane. "No, I sincerely doubt it."

WHEN SIMON ENTERED THE BEDROOM that night, the house was quiet and dark. Lucy had begun to wonder if he was coming home at all. She'd spent the afternoon waiting, futilely trying to read a book she didn't even remember the title of. When he hadn't arrived home at their usual dinner hour, she'd supped alone. And then, determined to speak to him when he did return, she'd gone to bed in his rooms. Now she sat up in his big mahogany bed and wrapped her arms around her knees.

"Where have you been?" The question was out before she could stop it. She winced. Maybe she didn't want to hear where he'd been.

"Do you care?" He set a candelabra on a table and shrugged off his coat. The blue silk was gray in places, and she saw at least one tear.

She tamped down her anger. It wouldn't help right now. "Yes, I care." And it was true. No matter what, she loved him and cared about him and what he did.

He didn't reply but sat down on a chair by the fire and removed his boots. He stood again and took off his wig, placing it on a stand. Rubbing both hands vigorously over his head, he made the short hair stand on end.

"I was about." He stripped off his waistcoat, throwing it on a chair. "Went 'round the Agrarians'. Looked at a bookstore."

"You didn't go hunting for Mr. Fletcher's father?" That had been her fear all this time. That he was off making the arrangements for another duel.

He glanced at her, then stripped off his shirt. "No. I like to take a day of rest between my slaughters."

"It's not funny," she whispered.

"No, it's not." In only his breeches, he poured out a basin of water and washed.

She watched him from the bed. Her heart ached. How could this man, moving so wearily yet gracefully, have killed another human this morning? How could she be married to him? How could she still care for him?

"Can you explain it to me?" she asked softly.

He hesitated, one arm raised. Then he washed under his arm and along that side as he spoke. "They were a group of investors: Peller, Hartwell, James, Walker, and Ethan, my brother." He dipped the cloth he used in the basin, wrung it out, and rubbed his neck. "And apparently Christian's father as well. Sir Rupert Fletcher." His eyes met hers as if he expected an objection.

She made none.

He continued. "They bought a shipment of Indian tea together. Not just one, but several shiploads. Hell, a bloody fleet, as if they were merchant princes. The price of tea was rising, and they stood to make a fortune each. Easily. Quickly." He moved the cloth across his chest in circles, wiping away blood and sweat and dirt.

She watched him and listened and made no sound, fearful of interrupting this story. But inside she was quaking. She felt pulled to the man washing himself so mundanely, despite the blood, and at the same time, was repelled by the stranger who had killed a man just this morning.

Simon splashed water on his face. "The only risk was the ships sinking at sea or wrecking in a storm, but that's a risk any investor takes. They probably thought about it a minute and discounted it. After all, there was so much money to be made." He looked at the basin of scummy water, emptied it into a slops jar, and refilled it.

"But Ethan, always correct Ethan, talked them into taking out insurance against the ships and the arrival of the tea. It was expensive, but he said it was the smart thing to do. The responsible thing to do." He ducked his head into the basin and sluiced the water over his hair.

She waited until he'd palmed the water from his hair and straightened. "What happened?"

"Nothing." He shrugged and picked up a cloth and toweled his clean hair. "The weather was fine, the ships fit, and, I suppose, the crew competent. The first ship arrived in port without problem."

"And?"

He spent some time carefully folding the towel before laying it beside the basin. "The price of tea had fallen in the meantime. Not just fallen, but plummeted. It was one of those quirks of the market that they couldn't have foreseen. There was a sudden glut of tea. Their tea wasn't worth the cost of unloading the crates from the ship." He walked into the next room, his dressing room.

"So the investors lost their money?" she called.

"They would've." He returned with a razor. "But then they remembered the insurance. The insurance that Ethan had made them take out. So ridiculous at the time and their only hope now. If they sank the ships, they could recoup their loss."

She frowned. "But Ethan . . ."

He nodded and pointed the razor at her. "But Ethan was the most honorable man I ever knew. The most honest. The most sure of himself and his morals. He refused. Damn the loss of money, damn their anger, damn the possibility of ruin, he would not take part in a fraud." He soaped his face.

Lucy thought about Ethan's honesty—how naive he must have been and how hard for a man like Simon to live up to. Simon's voice was flat. Perhaps to someone else he would sound unemotional, but she was the woman who cared for him, and she heard the pain under the words. And the anger.

Simon set the edge of the razor against his throat and made the first stroke. "They determined that they must get rid of Ethan. Without him, they could wreck the ships and recover; with him, all was lost. But it's not so easy to kill a viscount, is it? So they spread bloody, bloody rumors that were impossible to disprove, impossible to fight." He wiped the lather from his razor onto a cloth.

"Rumors about him?" Lucy whispered.

"No." He stared down at the razor in his hand as if he'd forgotten what it was. "About Rosalind."

"What?"

"About Rosalind's virtue. About Pocket's birth."

"But Pocket looks just like you . . ." She trailed away, the implication hitting her. *Oh, dear Lord.*

"Exactly. Just like me." His lips twisted. "They called Rosalind a whore, said I'd debauched her, that Pocket was a bastard and Ethan a cuckold."

She must've gasped.

He turned to her, his eyes pained, his voice finally strained. "Why do you think we haven't attended any London balls or parties or damned musicales, for God's sake? Rosalind's reputation was ruined. Absolutely ruined. She hasn't been invited anywhere in three years. An impeccably virtuous lady and she was cut dead on the street by married women who'd had too many liaisons to count."

Lucy didn't know what to say. What an awful thing to do to a family, to do to brothers. *Poor, poor Rosalind.*

Simon took a deep breath. "They left him no choice. He called out Peller, the one they'd chosen to talk the loudest. Ethan had never fought a duel, barely knew how to hold the sword. Peller killed him in less than a minute. Like leading a lamb to slaughter."

She drew in her breath. "Where were you?"

"Italy." He raised the razor again. "Seeing the ruins and drinking." *Stroke.* "And wenching, I'll admit as well." *Wipe.* "I didn't know until a letter was sent. Ethan, steady, boring Ethan—Ethan the good son—my brother, Ethan had been killed in a duel. I thought it was a joke; I came home anyway." *Stroke.* "I'd wearied of Italy by that time. Fine wine or no, there are only so many ruins one can see. I rode to the Iddesleigh family estate and . . ."

He took some time wiping the blade this time. His gaze was averted from hers, but she could see his Adam's apple move as he swallowed.

"It was winter and they'd preserved his body for my return. Couldn't hold the funeral without me, it seems. Not that there were many mourners waiting, only Rosalind, nearly prostrate with shock and grief, and Pocket and the priest. No one else was there. They'd been shunned. Ruined." He looked up at her, and she noticed that he'd cut himself under the left earlobe. "They did more than just kill him, Lucy, they destroyed his name. Destroyed Rosalind's reputation. Destroyed Pocket's hopes of ever marrying well, although she's too young to know that yet."

He frowned and finished shaving without saying anything else.

Lucy watched him. What was she to do? She could understand his reasons for wanting vengeance only too well. If someone had done such a wrong to David, her brother, or to Papa, she, too, would seethe with indignation. But that still didn't make killing right. And what of the cost to Simon, in both body and soul? He couldn't have fought all those duels without losing a part of himself. Could she simply sit by while he annihilated himself in vengeance for a dead brother?

He washed his face and dried it off and then walked to where she sat. "May I join you?"

Did he think she'd refuse him? "Yes." She scooted backward to make room.

He shucked his breeches and blew out the candle. She felt the bed dip as he climbed in. She waited, but he didn't move toward her. Finally she rolled against him. He hesitated, then put his arm around her.

"You never finished the fairy tale you were telling me," she whispered against his chest.

She felt his sigh. "Do you really want to hear it?"

"Yes, I do."

"Very well, then." His voice floated to her in the dark. "As you recall, Angelica wished for another dress even more beautiful than the first. So the Serpent Prince showed her a sharp silver dagger and bade her cut off his right hand."

Lucy shivered; she'd forgotten that part.

"The goat girl did as he told her, and a silver dress trimmed with hundreds of opals appeared. It looked like moonlight." He stroked her hair. "And she went off and had a jolly good time at the ball with pretty Prince Rutherford and returned late—"

"But what about the Serpent Prince?" she interrupted. "Wasn't he in great pain?"

His hand paused. "Of course." He resumed stroking. "But it was what Angelica wanted."

"What a selfish girl."

"No. Just poor and alone. She couldn't help demanding beautiful clothes any more than the snake could help having scales. It's simply the way God made them."

"Hmm." Lucy wasn't convinced.

"Anyway." He patted her shoulder. "Angelica returned and told the Serpent Prince all about the ball and pretty Rutherford and how everyone admired her gown, and he listened silently and smiled at her."

"And I suppose the next evening she wanted a new dress for silly Rutherford."

"Yes."

He stopped and she listened to his breathing in the darkness for a few minutes.

"Well?" she prompted.

"But of course it must be even more beautiful than the last."

"Of course."

He squeezed her shoulder. "The Serpent Prince said nothing was easier. He could get her the most beautiful dress she'd ever seen, the most beautiful dress in the world."

Lucy hesitated. This didn't sound good for some reason. "She must cut off his other hand?"

"No." He sighed wistfully in the dark. "His head."

Lucy jerked back. "That's awful!"

She felt his shrug. "The most beautiful dress, the ultimate sacrifice. The Serpent Prince knelt before the goat girl and presented his neck. Angelica was appalled, of course, and she did hesitate, but she was in love with Prince Rutherford. How else could a goat girl win a prince? In the end, she did as the Serpent Prince instructed and cut off his head."

Lucy bit her lip. She felt like weeping over this foolish fairy tale. "But he comes alive again, doesn't he?"

"Hush." His breath brushed across her face. He must've turned his head toward her. "Do you want to hear the story or not?"

"Do." She snuggled against him again and was still.

"This time the dress was truly magnificent. It was made all of silver with diamonds and sapphires strewn over it so that Angelica looked as if she were wearing light itself. Prince Rutherford was overcome with ardor or perhaps greed when he caught sight of her and immediately fell to his knees and proposed."

Lucy waited, but he was silent. She poked him in the shoulder. "Then what happened?"

"That's it. They married and lived happily ever after."

"That can't be the end. What about the Serpent Prince?"

She felt him turn toward her. "He died, remember? I suppose Angelica shed a few tears for him, but he was a snake, after all."

"No." She knew she was foolish to object—it was only a fairy tale—but she felt unreasonably mad at him. "He's the hero of the story. He transformed himself into a man."

"Yes, but he's still part snake."

"No! He's a prince." She knew somehow that what they

were arguing about had nothing to do with the fairy tale. "That's what the story's called, *The Serpent Prince*. He should marry Angelica; he loved her, after all."

"Lucy." He gathered her into his arms, and she let him even though she was angry with him. "I'm sorry, angel, but that's the fairy tale."

"He doesn't deserve to die," she said. Tears pricked at her eyes.

"Does anyone? Whether he deserves it or not is neither here nor there; it's simply his fate. You can no more change that than you can change the course of the stars."

The tears had escaped and were rolling into her hair and, she very much feared, his chest. "But the fate of a man. That can be changed."

"Can it?" he asked so low she almost didn't hear.

She couldn't answer, so she closed her eyes and tried to contain the sobs. And she prayed, *Please, God, let a man be able to change his fate.*

Chapter Sixteen

The dream woke her again in the early hours of the next morning.

Lucy opened her eyes in the gray light and stared at the embers in the fireplace without moving. This time she recalled fragments. She'd dreamed that Christian had dueled Lord Walker while Simon took tea and looked on. Lord Walker had already lost his eye, and he was quite angry, although it didn't affect his swordsmanship. Which had made it all the more gruesome. Then Lucy had been there at the table with Simon. She poured the tea and sipped and then looked into her cup. The tea had been made of rose petals. It was red, like blood. And she'd been horrified. Maybe it really was blood. She'd put her cup down and refused to drink any more, although Simon urged her to. But she knew she couldn't trust him because when she looked down, where his legs should have been there was a tail. A snake's tail . . .

Lucy shivered.

She'd woken covered in sweat, and now her flesh was chilled. Her hand crept across the silk coverlet, and she touched a warm arm. Warm male skin. Despite the fact that they had their own bedrooms, each large enough to house an entire family, Simon had slept with her every night since their wedding, whether in her own room or, as tonight, in his. Lucy had the feeling that this wasn't quite done in the *ton,* for a man to sleep with his wife, but she was glad. She liked having his warmth next to her. She liked hearing his deep breathing at night. And she liked the smell of him on her pillows. It was nice.

"Hmmph?" He rolled toward her and flung a heavy arm over her waist. His breathing deepened again.

Lucy didn't move. She shouldn't wake him just for a nasty dream. She snuggled her nose into his shoulder, inhaling his scent.

"What is it?" His voice was gravelly, low, but more awake than she'd thought.

"Nothing." She ran her hand over his chest, feeling the hairs tickle her palm. "Just a dream."

"Nightmare?"

"Mmm."

He didn't ask what about. Merely sighed and gathered her into his arms. Her legs slid along his, and she felt his erection bump her hip.

"Pocket used to have nightmares." His breath blew against the top of her head. "When I stayed with them after Ethan's death."

He smoothed his hand down her back and patted her bottom, then settled there, warm and possessive.

"She had a nanny, but the woman must've slept soundly, because Pocket would slip past her and find her mother's room." He chuckled, his voice rusty. "And a couple of times she came to me. Scared the wits out of me the first time. Cold little hand touching my shoulder in the middle of the night, a high voice whispering my name. Nearly took a vow to swear off drink before bed."

Lucy smiled against his shoulder. "What did you do?"

"Well." He rolled to his back, still holding her, and stretched one arm over his head. "First of all, I had to figure out a way to put on my breeches. Then I sat with her in a chair by the fire. Wrapped a blanket about both of us."

"Did she fall back asleep?"

"No, she did not, the imp." He scratched his chest. "Much like you, she wanted to talk."

"I'm sorry. I can stop."

"No," he whispered. "I like talking to you like this." He linked his fingers with hers on his chest.

"What did you talk about?"

He seemed to think for a bit. Finally, he sighed. "She told me Ethan used to talk to her when she had a bad dream. He'd tell her about, oh, dolls and puppies and her favorite sweets. Things like that. Things to take her mind off the nightmare."

Lucy smiled. "So you talked to her about puppies?"

"Actually, no." She saw his quick grin in the brightening room. "More like how to drive a phaeton. What to look for in horseflesh. The proper way to brew coffee and where, exactly, it comes from."

"Where does coffee come from?" She pulled the coverlet over her shoulder.

"I told her Africa, where Pygmy workers train crocodiles to climb the trees and whack the coffee beans down with their tails."

Lucy laughed. "Simon . . ."

"What else was I to say? It was three o'clock in the morning."

"Is that how you'll comfort me?"

"If you wish." His fingers flexed against hers. "We could discuss tea, Chinese versus Indian, and where it grows and whether it's true that it must be picked only by perfect female children below the age of six wearing crimson silk gloves and working by the light of a blue moon."

"And if I'm not interested in tea and its production?" Lucy drew her foot across one of his calves.

He cleared his throat again. "Then perhaps you'd be entertained by discussing various breeds of horses. Those best for carriages and those best for—"

"No." She disengaged her hand from his and stroked down over his belly.

"No?"

"Definitely, no." She touched his manhood, running her fingers up its length and smoothing over the head. She loved touching him.

For a moment he breathed heavily. Then he spoke. "Do you—"

She gently squeezed.

"*Ah*, have some other idea in mind?"

"Yes, I think I do." Holding firmly to his erection, she turned her face and bit his shoulder. He tasted of salt and musk.

Apparently that was his breaking point. He suddenly rolled toward her. "Turn over." His voice was husky.

She complied, rubbing her bottom against his groin.

"Minx," he muttered. He arranged her over his lower arm so she lay in his embrace.

"I think you should tell me about rose culture," she murmured solemnly.

"Do you, indeed?" He draped his upper arm over her and ran his hand across her breasts.

"Yes." She'd never tell him, but she found his voice unbearably sensuous sometimes. Feeling him all along her back and hearing him, but not seeing his face, made her shiver with a sudden erotic chill.

"Well, soil is most important." He pinched a nipple.

She watched his elegant fingers against her flesh and bit her lip. "Dirt?"

He squeezed harder, making her gasp with the sharp prick of desire. "We rose enthusiasts prefer the word *soil*. It sounds so much more serious."

"How is soil different from dirt?" She bumped back against him. His hardness slid over her bottom and lodged in the groove. She felt surrounded by his hot body. It made her feel small. Feminine.

"Ahh." He cleared his throat. "It just is. Now listen. Manure."

She bit back an inappropriate giggle. "That's not romantic."

He gently pulled her nipple, and she arched in reaction. "The choice of topic was yours." His fingers wandered to her other breast and tweaked the tip there.

She swallowed. "Even so—"

"Hush." He inserted his leg between her own and rubbed up.

His thigh caressed her just there, and she closed her eyes. "Mmm."

"Manure is the key to good soil. Some suggest ground cattle bones, but they are heretics fit only for raising turnips."

His hand skimmed over her belly and down. "The manure must be applied in the fall and allowed to overwinter. Too late application causes burning of the plant."

"R-really?" All her attention was on that hand.

He traced one finger delicately through the crease between thigh and mons, almost tickling her. He brushed her maiden hair and came to the other crease, hesitating. She squirmed impatiently. She could feel herself warming, growing wet with just the anticipation of what he would do next.

"I see you understand the significance of good manure. Now, think of your excitement"—his hand darted down and parted her lips—"when I discuss compost."

"Oh." He'd inserted a finger right into her.

"Yes." She felt him nod behind her but she hardly cared. "You have the makings of a great rose horticulturist."

She tried to tighten her thighs around his hand, but his leg prevented her. "Simon . . ."

He withdrew the finger and speared her again. She clenched helplessly around him.

"Compost, according to Sir Lazarus Lillipin, should consist of one part animal manure, three parts straw, and two parts vegetable remains."

Another finger found her pearl of flesh and she moaned. It seemed almost decadent that a mere man could bring her such pleasure.

"These," he still nattered on behind her, "to be placed in layers within a pile until said pile reaches the height of a short man. Lillipin makes no mention of how wide the pile should be, a grave omission in my own, rather learned opinion."

"Simon."

"My angel?" He flicked his finger, but not quite hard enough.

She tried to arch into his hand, but he still kept her imprisoned between his legs. She cleared her throat, but her voice still emerged huskily. "I don't want to talk about roses anymore."

He tsked behind her, although his own breathing had roughened. "It can be a dull subject, I admit, but you have been a very good pupil. I think you deserve a reward."

"A reward?" She would've smiled if she could've. Was that how he saw it? Vain man. She had a sudden flash of tender affection that made her want to turn and kiss him.

But he raised her top leg over both of his. "A reward only given to the best lasses. The ones who listen to their horticultural masters and know their roses well."

He was at her entrance. He parted her lips with his fingers and shoved a little in. She gasped and would've wriggled if he had let her. She'd forgotten how large— He pushed again. From this angle, she could feel every inch, widening, invading her.

"Only the best?" She hardly recognized her own voice; it was so low she seemed to purr.

"Uh, yes." Her husband panted behind her.

"And am I the best?"

"God, yes."

"Then, Simon?" she asked. A primitive sort of power filled her.

"Hmm?"

"I deserve more. I want more. I want all of you." And she did. She wanted both man and mind, his body and his soul, and she was shocked at her own greed.

"Oh, God," he groaned, and shoved his entire length into her.

She moaned and tried to close her legs. She felt so full of him. He kept her legs splayed open with his own, his clever fingers found that spot on her again, and he started thrusting. *So good.* She wanted him like this forever, his flesh merged with hers, his attention totally on her. No conflict could trouble them here when they were together. She arched her head back, under his own, and found his mouth. He kissed her deeply as he continued to thrust in and out of her, his flesh rubbing against and invading hers. A wail rose in her throat but he swallowed it. He pinched her gently on that vulnerable peak. And she fell apart, his manhood dragging in and out of her all the while as she gasped and panted.

Suddenly he withdrew. He flipped her to her belly, raised her hips a little, and thrust in again. *Dear Lord.* She was almost flat on her belly, and she could feel every inch of him. This position felt primitive, and with her recent release, it almost overwhelmed her senses.

"Lucy," he groaned above her. He slowly drew himself out until only his tip lodged in her opening, wide and hard. And thrust heavily again. "My darling Lucy." He panted against her ear, and then his teeth scraped her earlobe. "I love you," he whispered. "Don't ever leave me."

Her heart quaked. He was all around her. His weight against her back, his scent invading her senses as his flesh invaded her flesh. This was domination, pure and simple, and she found it unbearably erotic. A wave of pleasure rose again within her. *Oh, let this moment continue. Let us be together forever.* She was weeping, her physical ecstasy mixed and confused with a terrible feeling of impending loss she could not control.

"Lucy, I . . ." He thrust more roughly. Faster. He levered off her and pounded into her vulnerable body, and she felt his sweat spray her back. "Lucy!"

He grunted and shook, and she felt the warmth spread in her and couldn't tell it apart—her climax from his seed planted within her.

THE FIRST THING SIMON NOTICED about Sir Rupert's study was the prints on the walls. Botanical prints.

Behind him, Fletcher's butler said, "Sir Rupert will see you shortly, my lord."

He nodded, already advancing on an engraving that depicted a gnarled branch with delicate flowers above and, incongruently, the fruit below. On the bottom of the picture, in archaic script, was the legend, *Prunus cerasus*. Sour cherry. He looked at the next, framed in gilt: *Brassica oleracea*. Wild cabbage. The leaves were so ornately curled they might have been exotic bird plumes.

"I'd heard you had an interest in horticulture," Sir Rupert said from the door.

Simon didn't move. "I didn't know you had one as well." He turned to face his enemy.

Sir Rupert was leaning on a crutch.

Simon hadn't expected that. Here only five minutes and he'd been surprised twice already. This wasn't going as planned. But then he hadn't really known how to plan this, the final confrontation. He thought he'd already finished everything when he'd faced Walker. He hadn't dreamed there was another to pursue until the dying man confessed as much. He didn't dare discuss it with Lucy. After this morning's sweet lovemaking, he didn't want to upset their fragile truce. Yet he still had to see that she was safe, which meant eliminating the last man. Please, God, soon. If he could do that without Lucy finding out, perhaps they still stood a chance.

"Would you like to see my conservatory?" Sir Rupert cocked his head, eyeing him like an amused parrot.

He was older than the other conspirators, had to be in order to have fathered Christian. But still, Simon hadn't braced himself for the lines on the man's face, the slight stoop to his shoulders, and the bit of flesh that wobbled under his chin. All proclaimed him a man over fifty years. Otherwise he would make a formidable opponent. Although shorter than he, Sir Rupert's arms and shoulders were heavy with muscle. Were it not for his age and the cane . . .

Simon considered the offer. "Why not?"

The older man preceded him from the room. Simon watched Sir Rupert's painful progress down the marble hall, his crutch echoing each time it hit the floor. Alas, the limp was not faked. They turned down a smaller hall, one that ended in an ordinary oak door.

"I think you'll like this," Sir Rupert said. He produced a key and inserted it into the lock. "Please." His arm swept in front of him, indicating Simon should go first.

Simon raised his eyebrows and stepped over the threshold. Humid air bearing the familiar smells of loam and rot enveloped him. Above those scents floated a lighter aroma. It was an octagonal room made of glass from the floor upward. Around the edges and in clusters in the middle were every kind of fruiting citrus tree, each in its own enormous pot.

"Oranges, of course," Sir Rupert said. He limped to his side. "But also limes and lemons and various subgroups of orangelets. Each has its own particular taste and smell. Do you know, I believe if you blindfolded me and gave me a fruit, I could tell which it was merely by scoring the skin?"

"Remarkable." Simon touched a shiny leaf.

"I'm afraid I spend too much time and money on my little hobby." The older man caressed a fruit, still green. "It can be consuming. But so, for that matter, can revenge." Sir Rupert smiled, a kind, fatherly man surrounded by his artificial garden.

Simon felt a welling of hatred and carefully suppressed the emotion. "You seize the bull by its horns, sir."

Sir Rupert sighed. "There seems little point in pretending I don't know why you've come. We're both too intelligent for that."

"Then you admit you conspired to kill my brother." Simon deliberately broke off the leaf he'd been caressing.

"Tcha." The older man made an irritated sound. "You reduce it to the simplicity of a babe knocking over play blocks, when it was nothing of the sort."

"No?"

"No, of course not. We stood to lose a fortune—all the investors, not just I."

"Money." Simon's lips twisted.

"Yes, money!" The older man thumped his stick. "You sound like my son, sneering over money like it dirties your hands. Why do you think we all, your brother included, went into the venture in the first place? We needed the money."

"You killed my brother because of your own greed," Simon hissed, unable to contain all of his rage.

"We killed your brother for our families." Sir Rupert blinked, breathing heavily, perhaps surprised by his own candor. "For my family. I'm not a monster, Lord Iddesleigh. Don't make that mistake. I care for my family. I would do anything for my family, including, yes, removing an aristocrat who would've let my family go to the poorhouse so he could stand on his noble principles."

"You make it seem like the investment was sure to make money all along, yet it was a gamble from the start. It was hardly Ethan's fault the price of tea fell."

"No," Sir Rupert agreed. "Not his fault. But it would've been his fault had he kept us from reaping the insurance money."

"You killed him to commit a fraud."

"I killed him to preserve my family."

"I don't care." Simon lifted his lip in a sneer. "I don't care what excuses you've made, what reasons you have in your own mind, what sorrows you seek to win my pity with. You killed Ethan. You've admitted the murder yourself."

"You don't care?" The older man's voice was soft in the still, oppressive air. "You, who have spent a year avenging your own family?"

Simon's eyes narrowed. A bead of sweat ran down his back.

"I think you do understand," Sir Rupert said. "Do care, in fact, for my reasons."

"It doesn't matter." Simon fingered another leaf. "You tried to have my wife killed. For that alone I will see you dead."

Sir Rupert smiled. "There you are wrong. The attempt on your wife's life was not my fault. That was the work of Lord Walker, and you've already killed him, haven't you?"

Simon stared at the other man, tempting him with this hope of redemption. How easy it would be to just let it go. He'd killed four men already. This one said he wasn't a threat to Lucy. He could walk away, go home to Lucy, and never have to duel again. So easy. "I cannot let my brother's death go unavenged."

"Unavenged? You've avenged your brother to the tune of four souls. Isn't that enough?"

"Not while you still live." Simon tore the leaf.

Sir Rupert flinched. "And what will you do? Make war on a crippled man?" He held up his crutch like a shield.

"If need be. I'll have a life for a life, Fletcher, cripple or no." Simon turned and walked to the door.

"You won't do it, Iddesleigh," the old man called behind him. "You're too honorable."

Simon smiled. "Don't count on it. You're the one who pointed out how very similar we are." He closed the door and walked out of the house, the scent of hothouse citrus following him.

"YOU NEED TO HOLD STILL, THEODORA DEAR, if you want Aunt Lucy to draw your portrait," Rosalind chided that afternoon.

Pocket, in the act of swinging her leg, froze and darted an anxious glance at Lucy.

Lucy smiled. "Almost done."

The three of them sat in the large drawing room at the front of Simon's town house—her town house as well, now that they were wed. She must start thinking of it that way. But truthfully, Lucy still considered the house and servants Simon's. Perhaps if she stayed—

She sighed. What nonsense. Of course she would stay. She was married to Simon; the time for doubts had long since passed. No matter what he did, she was his wife. And if he didn't duel anymore, there was no reason why they couldn't grow ever closer. Just this morning, Simon had made urgent love to her, had even told her he loved her. What more could a woman ask from her husband? She should've felt safe and warm. Why, then, did she still have this feeling of impending loss? Why hadn't she said she loved him as well? Three simple words that he must've been expecting, yet she'd been unable to form them.

Lucy shook her head and concentrated on the sketch. Simon had insisted this room be remade for her, despite her protests. Though she had to admit now that it really was lovely. With Rosalind's help, she'd chosen the colors of a ripe peach: delicate yellows, sunny pinks, and rich reds. The result was lively and soothing at the same time. And in addition, the room had the best light in the house. That alone would've made it Lucy's favorite. She looked at her subject matter. Pocket was dressed in turquoise silk that provided a beautiful contrast for her flaxen locks, but she sat stiffly hunched as if frozen in mid-wiggle.

Lucy hastily made a few more strokes with her pencil. "Done."

"Huzzah!" Pocket exploded off the chair she'd been posed on. "Let me see."

Lucy turned her sketchbook.

The little girl tilted her head first one way and then

another, then scrunched her nose. "Is that what my chin looks like?"

Lucy examined her sketch. "Yes."

"Theodora."

Brought up short by her mother's warning tone, Pocket bobbed a curtsy. "Thank you, Aunt Lucy."

"You're most welcome," Lucy replied. "Would you like to see if Cook is finished with her mincemeat pies yet? They're for Christmas dinner, but she might have one for you to sample."

"Yes, please." Pocket paused only long enough to seek her mother's approving nod before darting out of the room.

Lucy began to put away her pencils.

"It's very kind of you to indulge her so," Rosalind said.

"Not at all. I enjoy it." Lucy glanced up. "You and Pocket will be coming to dine with us on Christmas morning, won't you? I'm sorry my invitation is so late. I forgot Christmas is only a few days away until Cook started baking pies."

Rosalind smiled. "That's quite all right. You are newly married, after all. We will be delighted to join you."

"Good." Lucy watched her hands placing the pencils in a jar. "I'm wondering if I can ask you something personal. Very personal."

There was a pause.

Then Rosalind sighed. "Ethan's death?"

Lucy looked up. "Yes. How did you know?"

"It consumes Simon." Rosalind shrugged. "Sooner or later I expected you to ask about it."

"Do you know he's been fighting duels over Ethan's

death?" Her hands were trembling. "He's killed two men that I'm aware of."

Rosalind gazed out the window. "I'd heard rumors. The gentlemen never like to tell us of their affairs, do they? Even when it involves us. I'm not surprised."

"Didn't you ever think to stop him?" Lucy grimaced at her own lack of tact. "Forgive me."

"No, it's a natural question. You're aware that he's dueling partly for my honor?"

Lucy nodded.

"I tried after Ethan's death when I first heard the gossip about duels to talk to him about it. Simon laughed and changed the subject. But the thing is"—Rosalind leaned forward—"it really isn't about me. It's not even about Ethan, God rest his soul."

Lucy stared. "What do you mean?"

"Oh, how can I explain?" Rosalind got up to pace. "When Ethan was killed, it cut off any way for the brothers to come to terms with each other. For Simon to understand and forgive Ethan."

"Forgive him? For what?"

"I'm expressing myself badly." Rosalind stopped and frowned.

Outside, a cart rumbled by and someone shouted. Lucy waited. She knew somehow that Rosalind held the key to Simon's single-minded quest for revenge.

"You must comprehend," her sister-in-law said slowly. "Ethan was always the good brother. The one everyone liked, the perfect English gentleman. Simon almost by default took the only other role. That of the wastrel, the ne'er-do-well."

"I've never thought him a wastrel," Lucy said softly.

"He isn't, really." Rosalind looked at her. "I think some of it was merely youth, some of it reaction to his brother and how their parents saw the both of them."

"How did their parents see them?"

"When the brothers were very young, their parents seemed to decide that one was good and the other bad. The viscountess was especially rigid in her thinking."

How awful to be branded the bad brother at so young an age. "But"—Lucy shook her head—"I still don't understand how that affects Simon now."

Rosalind closed her eyes. "When Ethan let himself be murdered, Simon was forced to assume both roles. Both the good and the bad brother."

Lucy raised her eyebrows. Was what Rosalind said possible?

"Just listen." Rosalind held out her hands. "I think Simon felt guilty that Ethan had died defending Simon's name in a way. Remember the rumors were that Simon was my lover."

"Yes," Lucy said slowly.

"Simon had to avenge him. Yet, at the same time, he must feel terrible anger at Ethan for dying in such a way, for leaving me and Theodora to his care, for being the good brother and martyring himself." She stared down at her open palms. "I know I do."

Lucy looked away. This was a revelation. Everything she'd heard about Ethan pointed to how good he'd been. It had never occurred to her that Rosalind might feel anger toward her late husband. And if she did . . .

"It took me many months to let Ethan go," Rosalind said quietly, almost to herself. "To forgive him for dueling a man he knew was the better swordsman. It's only been recently that . . ."

Lucy looked up. "What?"

Her sister-in-law blushed. "I . . . I have been driving with a gentleman."

"Forgive me, but Simon said your reputation was—"

"Ruined." Rosalind's complexion was quite rosy now. "Yes, in the *ton* it was. My gentleman is a solicitor at the law house that helped settle Ethan's estate. I hope you don't think the less of me?"

"No. No, of course not." Lucy caught Rosalind's hand. "I'm happy for you."

The fair woman smiled. "Thank you."

"I only wish," Lucy whispered, "that Simon could find such peace."

"He's found you. At one time I wasn't sure he would ever let himself marry."

"Yes, but I can't talk to him. He doesn't listen, won't admit what he's doing is murder. I . . ." Lucy looked blindly away, her eyes full of tears. "I don't know what to do."

She felt Rosalind's hand on her shoulder. "Maybe there isn't anything you can do. Perhaps this is something only he can defeat."

"And if he doesn't?" Lucy began, but Pocket charged back into the room at that moment, and she had to turn away to hide her eyes from the little girl.

The question hung there, unanswered.

If Simon couldn't defeat his demons, if he didn't stop killing other men, he would destroy himself. Maybe Rosalind was right; maybe there truly wasn't anything she could do to stop his deadly path. But she had to at least try.

Surely there was someone else who felt as she did, someone who didn't want this duel with Sir Rupert. She'd go to Christian if she could, but from his reaction at the Lord Walker duel, he would not have sympathy for her cause. Few would have the same feelings as a wife. Lucy straightened. A *wife*. Sir Rupert was married. If she could win his wife to her side, perhaps between the two of them they could stop—

"Aunt Lucy," Pocket cried, "won't you come taste Cook's pies? They're ever so good."

Lucy blinked and focused on the little girl tugging at her hand. "I'm afraid I can't right now, dear. I must go see a lady."

Chapter Seventeen

Simon snipped off a dead leaf from a *Rosa mundi*. Around him the smells of the conservatory floated in the humid air—rotted leaves, earth, and the faint scent of mildew. But the perfume of the rose in front of him overpowered them all. She had four blooms on her, all different, the streaks of white swirling into the crimson on her petals. *Rosa mundi* was an old rose but a favorite nonetheless.

The leaf he'd snipped fell to the white-painted table, and he picked it up and threw it in a bucket. Sometimes a dead leaf carried parasites and, if forgotten by the horticulturist, would infect the healthy plants as well. He made it a habit to clean up as he went. Even the smallest of leftovers might later prove the doom of an entire table of plants.

He moved to the next rose, a *Centifolia muscosa*—common moss rose—its leaves glossy green with health, its perfume almost cloyingly sweet. The petals in her flowers spilled over themselves, lush and billowy, shamelessly revealing the green sepals at their center. If roses were women, the moss rose would be a tart.

Sir Rupert was a leftover. Or perhaps the last of a series of labors. Whichever way one looked at it, he had to be dealt with. Clipped and cleaned up. Simon owed it to Ethan to finish the job. And to Lucy, to make sure she was safe from his past and his enemies. But Sir Rupert was also a cripple; there was no getting away from that fact. Simon hesitated, studying the next rose, a York and Lancaster, which bore both pink and white flowers on the same plant. He balked at dueling a man with such uneven odds. It would be a killing, pure and simple. The older man wouldn't have a chance, and Lucy didn't want him dueling. She would probably leave him, his stern angel, if she found out he was even contemplating issuing another challenge. He didn't want to lose her. Couldn't imagine never waking again with her. His fingers shook at even the thought.

Four dead, wasn't that enough? *Is it enough, Ethan?*

He turned over a healthy-looking leaf on the York and Lancaster and found a swarm of aphids, busily sucking the life from the plant.

The door to the conservatory crashed open.

"Sir, you're not allowed—" Newton's voice, outraged and fearful, admonished the intruder.

Simon turned to confront whoever disturbed his peace.

Christian charged down the aisle, his face pale and set.

Newton dithered. "Mr. Fletcher, please—"

"That's all right—" Simon started.

Christian punched him in the jaw.

He staggered back, falling against the table, his vision blurred. *What?*

Pots crashed to the floor, the shards skittering in the walkway. He straightened and brought his fists up to defend himself as his eyes cleared, but the other man was simply standing there, his chest heaving.

"What the *bloody* hell," Simon began.

"Duel me," Christian spat.

"What?" Simon blinked. Belatedly his jaw began to throb with pain. He noticed that the moss rose was in pieces on the floor, two of the main stems broken. Christian's boot crushed a bloom underfoot, the perfume rising from the dead rose like a eulogy.

Newton hurried out of the room.

"Duel me." Christian raised his right fist in threat. "Do I have to hit you again?" His expression was without humor, his eyes wide and dry.

"I wish you wouldn't." Simon felt along his jaw. He couldn't talk if it was broken, could he? "Why would I want to duel you?"

"You don't. You want to duel my father. But he's old and his leg is bad. He can hardly walk. Even you might feel a twinge of guilt at running through a cripple."

"Your father killed my brother." Simon let his hand fall.

"So you have to duel him." Christian nodded. "I know. I've seen you kill two men now, remember? I've watched you enact your sense of family—of honor, though you refuse to use that word—over the last few weeks. Do you really expect any less from me? Duel me as my father's surrogate."

Simon sighed. "I don't—"

Christian hit him in the face again.

Simon fell on his arse. "Shit! Stop that." He must look a complete idiot, sitting in mud in his own greenhouse. Pain bloomed across his cheekbone. Now the entire left side of his face felt on fire.

"I'll keep doing it," the younger man said from above him, "until you agree. I've seen you badger two men into dueling. I've learned well."

"For God's—"

"Your mother was a dockside whore, your father a bastard!" Christian shouted, red-faced.

"Christ." Was the boy mad? "My fight is with your father, not you."

"I'll seduce your wife—"

Lucy! a primitive part of his brain screamed. He shook it away. The boy was playing his own game. "I don't want to duel you."

"And if she won't submit, I'll kidnap and rape her. I'll—"

No. Simon surged to his feet, backing Christian against a bench. "Stay away from her."

The younger man flinched but kept talking. "I'll parade her naked through the streets of London."

Dimly, Simon saw Newton coming down the aisle, Lucy's ghost-white face behind him. "Shut up."

"I'll brand her a slut. I'll—"

Simon backhanded him, throwing him against another table. "Shut your mouth!"

The table quaked under Christian's weight. More pots exploded on the floor. Simon flexed his hand. His knuckles stung.

The younger man shook his head. "I'll sell her for tuppence a pop to any man who'll have her."

"Shut your bloody mouth, goddamn it!"

"Simon." Lucy's voice, quavering.

"Shut it for me," Christian whispered, his teeth red with blood. "Duel me."

Simon took a slow breath, fighting down his demons. "No."

"You love her, don't you? Would do anything for her." Christian leaned close enough that blood-flecked spittle struck him in the face. "Well, I love my father. There is no other way for us."

God. "Christian—"

"Duel me or I'll make sure you'll have to." The boy looked him straight in the eye.

Simon stared at him. Then his gaze traveled over the other man's head to Lucy's face. Straight, severe brows, mahogany hair pulled back in a simple knot, lips compressed in a line. Her beautiful topaz eyes were wide, pleading. Absently he noted that she still wore her cloak from an outing. Newton must've just caught her as she returned home.

Impossible to chance her safety.

"Very well. The morning after tomorrow. That will give you and me enough time to find seconds." His eyes flicked back to Fletcher. "Now get out."

Christian turned and left.

Too late. Lucy stood in the greenhouse and watched her world crumble around her, despite all the efforts she'd gone to this afternoon. She'd arrived home from her mission too late.

Her husband's face had turned to graven stone. His eyes had lost any color they once might've had. They were as cold now as the midnight frost that kills sparrows in their sleep. Mr. Fletcher brushed past her, but Lucy couldn't tear her gaze from Simon's expression. She hadn't heard their conversation, but she'd seen him hit the younger man and seen the blood on Simon's cheek.

"What happened? What have you done to Mr. Fletcher?" She didn't mean the words to sound so accusatory.

Behind her she heard the door close. They were alone in the conservatory. Newton had left as well.

"I don't have time to talk." Simon rubbed his hands together as if washing away imaginary dirt. They trembled. "I need to find seconds."

"I don't care. You must talk to me." She felt almost dizzy from the perfume of the roses smashed on the floor. "I went to meet Lady Fletcher. She and I—"

He looked up, his expression unchanged, and cut her off. "I'm to duel Christian Fletcher in two days."

"No." Not again. She couldn't take another fight, another man dead, another portion of Simon's soul burned away. Oh, God, no more.

"I'm sorry." He made to walk past her.

She grabbed his arm and felt it flex beneath her hand. She had to stop him. "Simon, don't do this. Lady Fletcher has agreed to talk to her husband. She thinks he will see reason, that there might be another way—"

He cut her off, his head bowed, his eyes not meeting hers. "It's Christian I'm dueling, Lucy, no longer his father."

"But the hope remains the same," she insisted. She'd made the effort, come up with a plan, gained Lady Fletcher's trust. It'd all seemed so close, so possible half an hour before. Why didn't he understand? "You can't do this."

"But I shall." His eyes were still averted.

"No." They—their marriage—wouldn't survive this.

Couldn't he see? "I'll talk again with Lady Fletcher. We'll find another way to settle—"

"There is no other way." He raised his head finally and she saw anger and despair in his eyes. "This is not your business. Talking to Lady Fletcher will solve nothing."

"We must at least try."

"Enough, Lucy!"

"You can't just kill people!" She flung his arm away, her mouth twisting bitterly. "It's not right. Don't you know that? It's immoral. Simon, it's evil. Don't let evil destroy your heart, your soul. I beg you, don't do this!"

His jaw clenched. "You don't understand—"

"Of course I don't understand!" Her chest was constricted. She couldn't catch her breath. The heavy, humid air seemed too thick to inhale. She leaned forward and said fiercely, "I went to church as a little girl. I know that's considered provincial to a sophisticated man like yourself, but I did. And the church says—the *Bible* says—that it is a sin to take the life of another." She had to stop to gasp, tasting the scent of roses on her tongue. "And I believe that. It's a mortal sin, to murder a fellow human being, even if you try to hide it by dueling. It's murder, Simon. In the end, it's murder, and it will consume you."

"Then I'm a sinner and a murderer," he said quietly. He walked past her.

"He's your friend," she called desperately.

"Yes." He stopped at that, his back toward her. "Christian is my friend, but he's also Fletcher's son. The son of Ethan's murderer. He challenged me, Lucy, not the other way around."

"Listen to yourself." She fought against tears. "You're planning to kill a friend. A man you've eaten with, talked with, laughed with. He admires you, Simon. Did you know that?"

"Yes, I know he admires me." He finally swung around, and she saw a sheen of sweat on his upper lip. "He's spent the last month following me around; he apes my clothes and my mannerisms. How could I miss that he admires me?"

"Then—"

He shook his head. "It does not matter."

"Simon—"

"What would you have me do?" he asked through gritted teeth. "Refuse to duel?"

"Yes!" She held out her palms, pleading. "Yes. Walk away. You've already killed four men. Nobody will think the less of you."

"I will."

"Why?" Desperation made her voice quaver. "You've avenged Ethan already. Please. Let's go to Maiden Hill or to your country estate or anywhere else. It doesn't matter, just as long as we leave."

"I can't."

Angry, hopeless tears blurred her vision. "For God's sake, Simon—"

"He threatened you." He stared into her eyes, and she saw tears and awful determination in his gaze. "Christian threatened you."

She swiped at the wetness on her cheeks. "I don't care."

"I do." He stepped close and grabbed her upper arms. "If you think I'm the sort of man to walk away from a threat to my wife—"

"He only said it to make you fight."

"*Even* so."

"I will follow you." She choked and her voice quavered. "I'll follow you to the dueling place, and I'll run between you if I have to. I'll find a way to stop you when you duel. I can't let you do this, Simon, I—"

"Hush. No," he said gently. "We won't duel at the last place. You'll have no knowledge of the meeting spot. You can't stop me, Lucy."

She sobbed. He pulled her against his chest, and she felt his heartbeat, so strong under her cheek. "*Please, Simon.*"

"I need to finish this." His lips were on her forehead, murmuring against her skin.

"Please, Simon," she repeated like a prayer. She closed her eyes, felt the tears burn her face. "Please." She clutched his coat, smelled wool and his scent—the scent of her husband. She wanted to say something to persuade him, but she didn't have the words. "I'll lose you. We'll lose each other."

"I can't change who I am, Lucy," she heard him whisper. "Even for you."

He let her go and walked away.

"I NEED YOU," SIMON SAID TO EDWARD DE RAAF an hour later in the Agrarians' coffeehouse. He was surprised at how rusty his voice sounded, as if he'd been imbibing vinegar. Or sorrow. *Don't think of Lucy.* He had to concentrate on what needed to be done.

De Raaf must've been surprised, too. Or maybe it was the words. He hesitated, then waved at the empty chair next to him. "Sit down. Have some coffee."

Simon felt bile rise in his throat. "I don't want any coffee."

The other man ignored him. He gestured to a boy who, strangely, looked up and nodded. De Raaf turned back to him and frowned. "I said sit down."

Simon sat.

The coffeehouse was nearly empty. Too late for the morning crowd, too early for the afternoon drinkers. The only other patron was an elderly man by the door in a dusty, full-bottom wig. He was mumbling to himself as he nursed a cup. The boy slammed down two mugs, snatched de Raaf's first, and whirled away before they could even thank him.

Simon stared at the steam drifting from the cup. He felt oddly cold, although the room was warm. "I don't want any coffee."

"Drink it," de Raaf growled. "Do you good. You look as if someone's kicked you in the bollocks, then told you your favorite rose died while you were still on the ground writhing."

Simon winced at the image. "Christian Fletcher has challenged me to a duel."

"Humph. You're probably shaking in your red-heeled shoes." De Raaf's eyes narrowed. "What have you done to the boy?"

"Nothing. His father was in the conspiracy to kill Ethan."

De Raaf raised his black eyebrows. "And he helped?"

"No."

De Raaf looked at him.

Simon's lips twisted as he fingered his mug. "He fights for his father."

"You would kill an innocent man?" de Raaf asked mildly.

Christian was innocent of his father's crime. Simon took a sip of coffee and swore as it burned his tongue. "He's threatened Lucy."

"Ah."

"Will you second me?"

"Hmm." The other man set his own mug down and leaned back in his chair, making it squeak with his weight. "I knew this day would come."

Simon raised his eyebrows. "When you could get a lad to bring you coffee?"

De Raaf pretended not to hear. "When you would come crawling to me for help—"

Simon snorted. "I'm hardly crawling."

"Desperate. Your wig unpowdered and full of nits—"

"My wig is not—"

De Raaf raised his voice to talk over him. "Unable to find any other to help you."

"Oh, for Christ's sake."

"Pleading, begging, *Oh, Edward, help me, do.*"

"Jesus," Simon muttered.

"This is indeed a wonderful day." The other man lifted his cup again.

Simon's mouth curved in a reluctant smile. He took a careful sip of his coffee. Hot acid.

De Raaf grinned at him, waiting.

Simon sighed. "Are you going to second me?"

"'Course. Be happy to."

"I can see that. The duel isn't until the morning after tomorrow. You have a full day, but you should get started.

You'll need to go 'round Fletcher's house. Find out who his seconds are and—"

"I know."

"Get a reputable physician, one who doesn't let blood at the drop of a hat—"

"I am aware of how to second a duel," de Raaf interrupted with dignity.

"Good." Simon drained the coffee cup. The black liquid burned all the way down. "Try to remember your sword, will you?"

De Raaf looked insulted.

He stood.

"Simon."

He turned back around and raised his brows.

De Raaf looked at him, all trace of humor gone from his face. "If you need me for anything else?"

Simon looked at the big, scarred man for a moment and felt his throat swell. He swallowed before replying. "Thanks."

He strode from the coffeehouse before he started blubbering. The old man in the full-bottomed wig was snoring, facedown on the table, when he passed him. The bright afternoon sun hit Simon as he walked out. Despite the sunlight, the air was so cold his cheeks burned. He swung up on his gelding and guided him into the busy street. *I must tell Lucy—*

Simon cut the thought short. He didn't want to think about Lucy, didn't want to remember the fear and hurt and rage on her face when he'd left her in the greenhouse, but it was near impossible. Thinking of Lucy was ingrained in his bones now. He turned down a street lined with various small shops. She hated that he was dueling. Perhaps if he had something to give her tonight. He'd never given her a wedding present . . .

Half an hour later, he exited a shop with a rectangular paper-wrapped parcel in his hand and a larger, bulkier one under his arm. The larger parcel was for his niece. He'd noticed a toy shop on the street and remembered he ought to have something for Pocket on Christmas. His mouth twitched as he thought of what his sister-in-law would think of his present for her daughter. He remounted the horse, carefully juggling the parcels. No doubt Lucy would still be angry, but at least she would know that he was sincerely sorry that he'd caused her distress. For the first time that day, he allowed himself to think about the next days. If he survived the duel, it would finally be over. He'd be able to sleep in peace.

He could love Lucy in peace.

Maybe he would agree to her idea of travel. They could go to Maiden Hill for their first Christmas together and visit with the captain. He had no need to see the old coot again so soon, but Lucy might be missing her father by now. After the New Year they could tour Kent, then journey north to his lands in Northumberland, assuming the weather wasn't too bad. He hadn't been to the manor there in ages. It probably needed refurbishing, and Lucy could help him with that.

He looked up. His town house was ahead. For a moment he was disoriented. Had he ridden this far and not even noticed? Then he saw the carriage. His carriage. Footmen carried trunks down the front steps. Others were heaving them onto the back of the carriage, swearing from the weight. The coachman already sat on the box. Lucy appeared at the front door, mantled and hooded like a religious penitent.

He dismounted the horse ungracefully, hurriedly, panic welling in his chest. The rectangular package fell to the cobblestones and he left it.

She was descending the stairs.

"Lucy." He caught her by the shoulders. "Lucy."

Her face was cold and white beneath the hood. "Let me go, Simon."

"What are you doing?" he hissed, knowing he looked a fool. Knowing the servants, Newton, passing strangers, and the neighbors watched. He didn't give a damn.

"I'm going to Papa."

A ridiculous spurt of hope. "Wait and I'll—"

"I'm leaving." Her cold lips barely moved as she mouthed the words.

Horror fisted around his vitals. "No."

For the first time she met his eyes. Hers were red-rimmed but dry. "I have to leave, Simon."

"No." He was a little boy denied a sweet. He felt like falling down and screaming.

"Let me go."

"I can't let you go." He half laughed here in the too-bright, cold London sun before his own house. "I'll die if I do."

She closed her eyes. "No, you won't. I can't stay and watch you tear yourself apart."

"Lucy."

"Let me go, Simon. Please." She opened her eyes, and he saw infinite pain in her gaze.

Had he done this to his angel? Oh, God. He unclasped his hands.

She brushed past him and walked down the steps, the wind playing with the hem of her mantle. He watched her climb into the carriage. The footman shut the door. Then the coachman slapped the reins, the horses stepped out, and the carriage pulled away. Lucy didn't look back. Simon watched until the carriage was lost in the bustle of the street. And still he stared.

"My lord?" Newton spoke beside him, probably not for the first time.

"What?"

"It's cold, my lord."

So it was.

"Perhaps you'd like to go in," his butler said.

Simon flexed his hand, surprised that his fingertips were numb. He looked around. Someone had taken away his horse, but the rectangular package still lay on the cobblestones.

"Best come inside, my lord."

"Yes." Simon started down the steps.

"This way, my lord," Newton called as if Simon were a senile old man in danger of toddling into traffic.

Simon ignored him and picked up the package. The paper was torn at the corner. Perhaps he could have it re-wrapped, this time in pretty paper. Lucy would like pretty paper. Except Lucy wouldn't ever see it. She'd left him.

"My lord," Newton still called.

"Yes, all right." Simon went inside, the package in his hand.

What else was there to do?

Chapter Eighteen

"Who's there?" Papa called from the doorway, his night-cap pulled down almost to his ears. He wore an old coat over his nightshirt and buckle shoes on his feet, wiry ankles poking out. "It's past nine o'clock. Decent folk are all in their beds by now, y'know."

He held a lantern high to throw light into the gravel drive before the Craddock-Hayes house. Behind him, Mrs. Brodie in mobcap and shawl peered over his shoulder.

Lucy opened the carriage door. "It's me, Papa."

He squinted, trying to see her in the gloom. "Lucy? What's Iddesleigh thinking to travel this late at night? Eh? Must've gone mad. There's highwaymen about, or doesn't he know that?"

Lucy descended the carriage steps with the help of a footman. "He isn't with me."

"Mad," her father repeated. "The man's mad to let you travel alone, footmen or no. And at night. Bounder!"

She felt a contrary urge to defend Simon. "He didn't have a say in it. I've left him."

Mrs. Brodie's eyes widened. "I'll make tea, shall I?" She turned and hurried into the house.

Papa merely harrumphed. "Come home in a tiff, have you? Smart gel. Keeps a man on his toes when he doesn't know what a gel will do next. No doubt good for him. You can stay a couple of days and go home after Christmas."

Lucy sighed. She was tired to her bones, tired to her soul. "I'm not going back to him. I've left Simon for good."

"What? What?" Her father looked alarmed for the first time. "Now see—"

"Jaysus, don't anybody sleep around here?" Hedge came around the corner, his nightshirt escaping from his breeches, gray hair poking out from a greasy tricorne. He caught sight of Lucy and stopped dead. "Is she back already? Thought we just got her packed off the place."

"I'm pleased to see you, too, Mr. Hedge," Lucy said. "Perhaps we can continue this conversation inside, Papa?"

"That's right," Hedge muttered. "I've been here nearly thirty years—the best years of my life, too—and does anyone care? No, they do not. I'm still not to be trusted."

"See to the horses, Hedge," Papa ordered as they went inside.

Lucy heard Hedge groan. "Four big beasties. My back's not good . . ." Then the door closed behind them.

Papa led the way into his study, a room that she wasn't used to entering. Papa's study was his own domain; even Mrs. Brodie wasn't allowed to clean it. Not, at least, without a lot of fussing first. Papa's great oak desk was placed at an angle to the fire, too close really, as was attested by the blackened wood on the leg nearest the hearth. The surface of the desk was obscured by piles of colorful maps. They were held in place by a brass sexton, a broken compass, and a short length of rope. To the side of the desk was an enormous globe of the world on its own stand.

"Now, then," her father started.

Mrs. Brodie bustled in with a tray of tea and buns.

Papa cleared his throat. "Best see if there's some of your good steak and kidney pie left from dinner, Mrs. Brodie, if you will."

"I'm not hungry," Lucy began.

"Looking pale, poppet. Steak and kidney pie do you good, eh?" He nodded at the housekeeper.

"Yes, sir." Mrs. Brodie hurried out.

"Now, then," Papa began again. "What's happened that you've come running home to your father?"

Lucy felt her cheeks heat. Put like that, her actions sounded childish. "Simon and I have had a difference of opinion." She looked down as she carefully pulled her gloves off, one finger at a time. Her hands were shaking. "He is doing something that I cannot agree with."

Papa slammed his hand down on his desk, making her and the papers lying there jump. "Cad! Hasn't been married more than a few weeks and already messing with ladies of low repute. Ha! When I get my hands on that bounder, that scoundrel, that . . . that *rake,* I'll see him horsewhipped—"

"No, oh, no." Lucy felt a bubble of hysterical laughter well up inside her. "That's not it at all."

The door opened and Mrs. Brodie came in again. She looked sharply at the two of them. She must've heard their voices in the hall, but she didn't say anything. She set her tray on a table at Lucy's elbow and nodded. "Have a bite of that, Miss Lucy. It'll make you feel better. I'll have the fire laid in your old bedroom, shall I?" Without waiting for an answer, the housekeeper bustled out.

Lucy looked at the tray. There was a slice of cold meat pie, a bowl of stewed fruit, a bit of cheese, and some of Mrs. Brodie's fresh bread. Her stomach rumbled. She'd declined supper at an inn on the way home, and she hadn't known she was hungry until now. She picked up a fork.

"Then what is it?"

"Hmm?" Mouth full of tender pie, Lucy didn't want to think about Simon, his danger, or their failed marriage. If she could just go to bed . . .

But Papa was stubborn when he wanted to be. "Why'd you leave the man if he wasn't carrying on with soiled doves?"

"Duels." Lucy swallowed. "Simon has killed four men already. In duels. He calls them out and then kills them, and I can't take it anymore, Papa. He's destroying himself slowly, even if he survives the encounters. He won't listen to me, won't stop, so I left him." She looked down at her pie, oozing brown gravy, and suddenly felt nauseous.

"What for?"

"What?"

Papa scowled. "Why's he killing these fellows? Don't like your husband, never have and, make no bones about it, probably never will. But he doesn't strike me as a loony. Popinjay, yes; loony, no."

Lucy almost smiled. "He's killing the men responsible for his brother, Ethan's, death, and I know what you're going to say, Papa, but however noble the reason, it's still murder and a sin in the Bible. My conscience can't abide it, and I don't think Simon's can either in the end."

"Ha," her father grumbled. "Glad to know I'm so easily read by my daughter."

Lucy bit her lip. This wasn't how she'd imagined coming home. Her head was beginning to pound, and apparently her father wanted an argument. "I didn't mean—"

"I know. I know." He waved away her apology. "You didn't mean to insult your old pater. But the fact is you did. Think all men feel the same, do you, gel?"

"No, I—"

"'Cause we don't." Papa leaned forward and stabbed a finger at her nose to emphasize the point. "Don't think killing for revenge is the thing at all. Seen too many men die for too little reason to condone it."

Lucy bit her lip. Papa was right; she'd been too hasty in her judgment. "I'm sorry—"

"Doesn't mean I don't understand the man, though," he said over her words. He sat back in his chair and stared at the ceiling.

Lucy flipped over the pie crust. The inside was rapidly congealing, white puddles of fat hardening on the surface of the gravy. She wrinkled her nose and set the plate aside. Her head had begun to pound in earnest now.

"Understand and even sympathize," Papa suddenly said, making her jump. He popped up from his chair and began pacing. "Yes, sympathize with the man, damn him. Which is more than you do, my dear."

Lucy stiffened. "I think I understand Simon's reasons for dueling these men. And I can sympathize with the loss of a loved one."

"But can you sympathize with the man? Eh?"

"I don't quite see the difference."

"Ha." Papa stared at her a moment, his brows beetling.

She had the sinking feeling that she'd somehow let her father down. Sudden tears threatened. She was tired, so tired from traveling and the argument with Simon and all of the things that had happened before. Somewhere in the back of her mind she'd thought surely Papa of all people would take her part in this catastrophe.

Papa stalked to the window and looked out, although he couldn't have seen anything but his reflection. "Your mother was the finest woman I ever knew."

Lucy frowned. What?

"Was two and twenty when I met her—a very young lieutenant. She was a bonny lass, all dark curls and light brown eyes." He turned and looked at her over his shoulder. "Same color as yours, poppet."

"So I've been told," she whispered. She still missed Mama—the soft voice, the laughter, and the steady light she'd been to her family. Lucy looked down, her eyes filling. It must be the fatigue.

"Mmph," Papa grunted. "Could've had her pick of any of the gentlemen hereabouts. In fact, it was very close at one point with a dragoon captain." He snorted. "Scarlet uniform. Always turned the ladies' heads—*and* the bastard was taller."

"But Mama chose you."

"Aye, she chose me." Papa shook his head slowly. "Could've knocked me over with a feather, I was that surprised. But we were wed and we settled down here."

"And you lived happily ever after." Lucy sighed. She'd heard the tale of her parents' courtship and marriage many times before when she was a girl. It'd been a favorite bedtime story. Why couldn't her own marriage—

"No, there you're wrong."

"What?" Lucy frowned. She couldn't have understood Papa correctly. "What do you mean?"

"Life's not like a fairy tale, my girl." Papa turned fully around to face her. "In our fifth year of marriage, I came home from sea to find your mother had taken a lover."

"A lover?" Lucy sat up straight in her amazement. Her mother had been kind and gentle and wonderful. Surely . . . "You must be wrong, Papa."

"No." He pursed his lips, frowning at his shoes. "She near threw the fact in my face."

"But, but . . ." She tried to digest this information and failed completely. It was simply unbelievable. "Mama was good."

"Yes. She was the finest woman I ever knew. Already said that." Papa gazed down at the globe as if he were seeing something entirely different. "But I was away at sea for months at a time, and she had two small babies to take care of, all alone in this little village." He shrugged. "She told me she was lonely. And mad at me."

"What did you do?" Lucy whispered.

"Got angry. Stormed about, cursing a blue streak and yelling. You know me." Papa spun the globe. "But in the end I forgave her." He looked up. "Never regretted it either."

"But . . ." Lucy frowned, groping for the words. "How could you forgive such an offense?"

"Ha. Because I loved her, that's why." Papa tapped the globe, skewering Africa with his finger. "And because I realized that even the finest of women is only human and can make a mistake."

"How . . . ?"

"She was a woman, not an ideal." Papa sighed now. He

looked old, standing there in his nightshirt and cap, but at
the same time stern and commanding. "People make mistakes. Ideals don't. Think that's the first lesson that must
be learned in any marriage."

"Simon has murdered." Lucy drew a deep, shuddering
breath. No matter what Papa thought, their cases were very
different. "And he plans on doing it again. He's going to
duel a dear friend, a man who looks up to him, and Simon
will probably kill him. I know he's not an ideal, Papa, but
how do you expect me to forgive that?" How could he expect her to live with a man so bent on destruction?

"I don't." Papa spun the globe a final time and stumped
to the door. "Well past your bedtime, gel. And mine. Get
some rest."

Lucy stared after him, uncertain, tired, and confused.

"But remember this." He turned at the door to spear her
with a look. "I might not expect you to forgive, but God
does. Says so right in your Bible. Think on that."

IT HAD ALWAYS BEEN INEVITABLE, really, that Lucy should
leave him, Simon mused. The only surprise was how long
it had taken her to go. He ought to be thankful he'd had the
few weeks of their marriage together, the days of happy
companionship and the nights of sweet lovemaking. He
carefully poured himself a tumbler of brandy. Carefully,
because it was his second or perhaps third, and because his
hands had begun to shake like a palsied old man.

But that was a lie.

His hands had been shaking ever since Lucy had left
yesterday afternoon. He trembled as if he had the ague, as
if all the demons inside him had decided to make themselves physically felt. Demons of rage, demons of pain,

demons of self-pity, and demons of love. They shook and rattled his frame, demanding acknowledgment. He'd lost the ability to contain them anymore, and they had free rein of his soul now.

He grimaced to himself and swallowed a gulp of the amber liquor. It burned his throat all the way down. He probably wouldn't be able to hold his sword on the day of the duel. Wouldn't that be a surprise for Fletcher? To find him standing there, shaking and trembling, his sword fallen to his feet, useless. Christian would merely have to gut him and go home for breakfast. Hardly worth his time, when you thought about it. And Simon had nothing—nothing at all—to do between now and the duel on the morrow's dawn.

He picked up his glass and wandered from his study. The hall was dark and cold, even if it was only afternoon. Couldn't anyone keep enough fires lit to warm him? He had so many servants; he was a viscount, after all, and he'd be ashamed to have less than fifty souls toiling over his every whim, night and day. He thought to bellow for Newton, but the butler had been hiding the entire day. Coward. He turned down the hall, his footsteps echoing in his big, lonely house. What had made him think for even a second that he and an angel could ever be united? That he'd be able to hide from her the rage in his heart or the stain on his soul?

Madness, pure madness.

Simon reached the doors to his conservatory and paused. Even from without he could smell them. Roses. So serene, so perfect. As a young boy, he'd been mesmerized by the swirl of velvet petals that led to a secret center, hidden and shy, at the flower's heart. The thing about roses was that even when not in bloom, they required constant care. The leaves must be inspected for blight, mildew, and parasites. The soil must be carefully tended, weeded, and improved. The plant itself should be cut back in autumn, sometimes quite savagely, in order that it might bloom again in the spring. A demanding, selfish flower, the rose, but one that rewarded with spectacular beauty when well cared for.

He had a sudden memory of himself, young and unmade, sneaking into the rose garden to hide from his tutor. The gardener, Burns, tending to the roses, not noticing the boy stealing behind. Only, of course, the gardener must have noticed. Simon smirked. The old man had merely pretended not to know the boy was in the garden, ducking his studies. In that way both could coexist in the place they loved best without any to blame should they be discovered.

He laid his hand on the door feeling the cedar wood, imported specially when he'd had this adult refuge made. Even as a grown man he went to the rose garden to hide.

Simon pushed open the door, and the humid air caressed his face. He could feel the sweat start along his hairline as he took a gulp of brandy. Newton had made sure the greenhouse was tidied again within an hour of Christian's departure. One would never know that there had been a fight here. He moved farther in and waited for the smell of loam and the sweet perfume of the roses to bring back his serenity. To return his soul to his body and make him whole again—less a demon and more a man. They did not.

Simon stared at the long row of benches, at the neatly ordered pots, at the plants, some mere thorny sticks, some flamboyantly in bloom. The colors assaulted his eyes, every shade of white and pink and red and all the imaginable hues in between: flesh pink, cold white, black crimson, and a rose the exact shade of Lucy's lips. It was a dazzling display that had taken him most of his adult life to collect, a masterpiece of horticulture.

He looked up to where the glass ceiling came to a perfect angle overhead, protecting the delicate plants within and keeping the chill London wind without. He looked down to the carefully laid bricks beneath his feet, arranged in a herringbone pattern, orderly and neat. The greenhouse was exactly as he'd envisioned it ten years before, when he'd had it built. It was in every way the culmination of all his dreams of refuge, of peace. It was perfect.

Except that Lucy was not here.

There would never again be peace for him. Simon tossed back the rest of the brandy, raised his tumbler high, and threw it to the bricks. Glass shattered across the path.

THE DARK CLOUDS HANGING LOW in the sky threatened rain or maybe even snow. Lucy shivered and chafed her hands together. She should've worn mittens. Hoarfrost had delicately entombed the garden this morning, delineating each dead leaf, each frozen stem with white fur. She touched a withered apple and watched the frost melt in a perfect circle under the warmth from her fingertip. The apple beneath was still dead.

It was really too chill to be outside, but she was restless today, and the house felt confining. She'd tried sitting inside, working on a sketch of a country kitchen still life: big earthen bowl, brown eggs, and Mrs. Brodie's freshly baked bread. The eggs had turned misshapen under her fingers, and her charcoal had broken against the paper, making a messy blotch.

Strange. She'd left Simon because she couldn't stand his choices. She'd felt herself in turmoil, living with him while he killed or sought death himself. Lucy knit her brows. Perhaps she hadn't acknowledged it before, that part of her flight was fear—the constant, agonizing worry that he might die in one of his duels. Yet here, in the quiet of her childhood home, the turmoil within herself was much worse. The silence, the very lack of drama, was almost oppressive. At least in London she could flail against Simon, argue his revenge. She could make love to him.

Here, she was alone. Simply alone.

She missed Simon. She'd expected that there would be some yearning, the ache of loss when she'd left him. After all, she cared for him very much. What she hadn't expected was that the ache would be a gigantic hole in the fabric of her life, a hole in her very being. She wasn't at all sure she could live without him. And while that sounded melodramatic, it was also sadly true. She very much feared that she would return to her husband not because of the morally sound argument put forth by her father—that one should forgive the sinner—but because of a mundane truth.

She could not live apart from him.

No matter what he'd done, no matter what he would do in the future, no matter what he was, she still missed him. Still wanted to be with him. How appalling.

"Goodness, it's freezing out here. Whatever are you doing, haunting the garden like the ghost of a wronged woman?"

Lucy swung around at the irritable voice.

Patricia hopped from one foot to the other behind her.

She'd pulled her hood around her face and held a fur muff to her nose, obscuring all but her china-blue eyes. "Come inside right now before you turn to ice."

Lucy smiled at her friend. "Very well."

Patricia heaved a sigh of relief and scurried in the back door without waiting for her. Lucy followed behind.

When she came inside, Patricia already had her cloak and muff off. "Remove that." The other woman gestured at Lucy's hood. "And let's go in the sitting room. I've already asked Mrs. Brodie for tea."

Soon they were seated in the little back room, a steaming pot of tea before them.

"Ahh." Patricia held her cup before her face, nearly bathing in the warm liquid. "Thank goodness Mrs. Brodie knows how to heat the water properly." She took a sip of tea and set down her cup in a businesslike manner. "Now tell me about London and your new life."

"It's very busy," Lucy said slowly. "London, that is. There is so much to see and do. We went to the theater not long ago and I adored it."

"Lucky." Patricia sighed. "I'd love to see all the people in their finest clothes."

"Mmm." Lucy smiled. "My sister-in-law, Rosalind, is quite kind. She's taken me shopping and shown me her favorite places. I have a niece as well. She plays with tin soldiers."

"Very unique. And your new husband?" Patricia asked in a too-innocent tone. "How is he?"

"Simon is well."

"Because I did notice that you came visiting without him."

"He's busy—"

"On Christmas Eve." Patricia arched an eyebrow. "Your *first* Christmas Eve together. And while I am aware that you are a deplorably unsentimental woman, I'm nevertheless somewhat suspicious."

Lucy took care while pouring herself a second cup of tea. "I don't believe it's any of your business, Patricia."

Her friend looked shocked. "Well, of course it isn't my business. If I confined my curiosity to matters strictly my business, I should never learn anything. Besides," Patricia said more prosaically, "I care about you."

"Ah." Lucy looked away to hide the tears that pricked at her eyes. "We did have a difference of opinion."

"A difference of opinion," Patricia repeated neutrally.

There was a pause.

Then Patricia thumped the cushion beside her. "Did that bastard take a mistress already?"

"No!" Lucy frowned at her, appalled. "Why does everyone immediately think that?"

"Do they?" Patricia looked interested. "Probably because he has that air about him."

"What air?"

"You know"—Patricia circled her hand vaguely—"as if he knows far more than he should about women."

Lucy blushed. "He does."

"Makes him near irresistible." Patricia sipped her tea. "So it's all the more alarming that you were able to part from him. Especially, as I say, at Christmas."

A sudden thought struck Lucy. She set her cup down. "I haven't finished his present."

"What?"

Lucy stared at her friend. "I meant to illustrate a book for him, but it isn't finished."

Patricia looked satisfied. "You must be expecting to see him tomorrow, then . . ."

Her friend continued, but Lucy wasn't listening. Patricia was right. Sometime in the last few minutes, she had made her decision: She would return to Simon, and they would somehow fix this problem between them.

"And that reminds me," Patricia said. She pulled a small box from her pocket and held it out.

"But I haven't anything for you." Lucy pulled off the lid. Inside was a lady's handkerchief embroidered with her new initials. The letters were lopsided, it was true, but quite lovely anyway. "How thoughtful. Thank you, Patricia."

"I hope you like it. I'm afraid I punctured my fingers as often as the cloth." Her friend held out her right hand in evidence. "And you do, you know."

"Do what?"

"Have a present for me." Patricia withdrew her hand and inspected her fingernails.

Lucy looked at her, puzzled.

"I recently received an offer of matrimony, and since you had previously declined the gentleman in question and actually gone so far as to marry someone else—"

"Patricia!" Lucy jumped up to hug her friend, nearly knocking over the tea tray in the process. "You mean you're engaged?"

"Indeed."

"And to Eustace Penweeble?"

"Well—"

"What happened to old Mr. Benning and his ninety arable acres?"

"Yes, that is sad, isn't it?" Patricia pinned a gold curl back into place. "And that grand manor. It really is a shame.

But I'm afraid that Mr. Penweeble quite overwhelmed all my good sense. I think it must be his height. Or perhaps his shoulders." She took a pensive sip of tea.

Lucy nearly giggled, only managing to control the impulse at the last moment. "But how did you get him to propose so fast? It took him three years with me."

Patricia looked demure. "It might've been my fichu."

"Your fichu?" Lucy glanced at the innocent bit of lace about Patricia's neck.

"Yes. Mr. Penweeble had taken me for a drive and somehow"—Patricia's eyes widened—"it came undone. Well, I couldn't get it tucked back in properly. So I asked him."

"Asked him what?"

"Why, to tuck it back in my bodice for me, naturally."

"Patricia," Lucy breathed.

"For some reason he felt compelled to propose to me after that." Patricia smiled like a cat with a saucer of cream. "We're to have an engagement party on Boxing Day. You'll stay for that, won't you?"

Lucy carefully set her teacup down. "I wish I could, dear. But I must get back to Simon. You're right. I should spend Christmas with him."

Now that she had made the decision, she felt an urge to be off at once. It was important somehow to return to Simon as soon as possible. Lucy stilled the impulse and folded her hands in her lap. Patricia was talking about her forthcoming marriage and she should listen. The drive to London took hours.

Surely a few minutes more would make no difference either way.

Chapter Nineteen

"What is going on?" his wife demanded before Sir Rupert had even crossed his own threshold.

He frowned, startled, as he handed the sleepy footman his hat and cloak. "What do you mean?" It couldn't be much past five in the morning.

With Walker and James gone, his investments had become precarious. He'd spent the night, as he had the last several, working to ensure they wouldn't topple. But what was Matilda doing up at this hour?

His wife's eyes darted to the footman, trying hard not to appear as if he were listening. "May I speak to you in your study?"

"Of course." He led the way to his sanctuary and immediately sank into the chair behind the desk. His leg ached terribly.

His wife closed the door softly behind her. "Where have you been? You've hardly spoken the last several days. You've secluded yourself in here. We don't even see you at meals. That is what I am referring to." She advanced toward him, back militarily erect, the green batiste of her gown shushing across the carpet. He noticed that the skin around her jawline had softened, sagging a bit, creating a plump pouch under her chin.

"I'm busy, my dear. Merely that." He absently rubbed at his thigh.

She wasn't fooled. "Don't palm me off. I'm not one of your business cronies. I'm your wife. Lady Iddesleigh called on me two days ago." She frowned as his curse interrupted her words, but continued. "She told me a fantastic story about you and the viscount. She said that he was intent on calling you out. Cut line and tell me the problem."

Sir Rupert leaned back in his chair, the leather creaking beneath his rump. It was a good thing Matilda was a female; she would have been a frightening man. He hesitated, considering. He'd spent the time since Iddesleigh had threatened him in contemplation. Pondering how he could eliminate a viscount without being implicated. The problem was that the best way had already been used with Ethan Iddesleigh. That plan had been so simple, so elegant. Distribute rumors, force a man into calling a much better swordsman out . . . death had been inevitable, and it hadn't been traced back to him personally. Other ways—hiring killers, for instance—were much more apt to be brought home to him. But if Iddesleigh persisted, the risk might have to be taken.

Matilda lowered herself into one of the armchairs before his desk. "Think on it all you want, but you must at least bestir yourself enough to go look for Christian."

"Christian?" He looked up. "Why?"

"You haven't seen him in the last two days, have you?" She sighed. "He's been almost as dour as you, moping about the house, snapping at his sisters. And the other day he came home with his lip bloodied—"

"What?" Sir Rupert stood, fumbling for his cane.

"Yes." His wife's eyes widened in exasperation. "Hadn't you noticed? He said he'd stumbled and fallen, but it was quite obvious he'd been in some type of fisticuffs. Not at all what I expect from our son."

"Why wasn't I told?"

"If you would bother to talk to me . . ." Matilda's gaze sharpened. "What is it? What are you keeping from me?"

"Iddesleigh." Sir Rupert took two steps to the door and stopped. "Where is Christian now?"

"I don't know. He never came home last night. That is why I've waited up for you." Matilda had stood, clasping her hands before her. "Rupert, what—?"

He swung on her. "Iddesleigh did indeed mean to call me out."

"Call out—"

"Christian knew. God, Matilda." He thrust his hands into his hair. "He might've challenged Iddesleigh to prevent him dueling me."

His wife stared at him. The blood slowly left her face, leaving it pasty and crumpled, showing every one of her years. "You must find him." Her lips hardly moved. "You must find him and stop him. Lord Iddesleigh will kill him."

He stared for a moment, frozen by the horrible truth.

"Dear husband." Matilda held out her hands like a supplicant. "I know you have done things. That there are dark actions in your past. I've never questioned you before, never wanted to know just what you did. But, Rupert, don't let our boy die for your sins."

Her words were a spur, galvanizing him into action. He limped to the door, his cane knocking loudly against the marble in the hall. Behind him, his wife had begun to sob, but he heard her nonetheless. "Don't let Christian die for you."

A CAT—OR MAYBE A RAT—RAN ACROSS the path of his horse as Simon rode up the street. Not yet dawn, the blackest part of the night, this was the dominion of Hecate, goddess of crossroads and barking dogs. It was that strange place in between night and day when the living felt not quite safe. The only sound in the deserted street was the muffled clop of his gelding's hoofs. The corner drabs had already taken to their sad beds, the street mongers were not yet up. He could've been riding through a necropolis. A frozen necropolis, snowflakes weeping silently from the sky.

He'd ridden more than half the night away, meandering from the white town houses of Grosvenor Square to the stews of Whitechapel. Strangely, he'd not been accosted, prime pickings though he most obviously was—an aristocrat stinking of drink and not aware of his surroundings. A pity that. He could've used the distraction of a nasty robbery, and it might've solved all his troubles. But instead, here he was alive just before dawn with a duel to fight.

De Raaf's town house was up ahead. Somewhere. Or at least he thought so. He was so exhausted, weary unto death. Sleep no longer comforted him, no longer brought him a measure of peace. He hadn't slept since Lucy had left him two days before. Perhaps he'd never sleep again. Or sleep forever, after this dawn. Simon smirked at his own small wit. The horse turned in to a mews, and he

straightened a bit in the saddle, looking for the back of de
Raaf's town house. As he neared, a shape separated itself
from the black shadows by a gate.

"Iddesleigh," de Raaf murmured, his low voice startling
the gelding.

Simon gentled the horse. "De Raaf. Where's your
mount?"

"'Round here." The big man opened the gate and
ducked inside.

Simon waited, noticing for the first time the bite of the
winter's wind. He glanced up. The moon was down, but it
would've been covered with clouds had it still hung in the
sky. The coming day would be bleak. Just as well.

De Raaf returned, leading his ugly bay. A soft bag was
strapped to the back of the beast behind the saddle. "You're
not wearing a wig. You look naked without one."

"No?" Simon ran his hand over his short hair before
he remembered. The wig had fallen off in a lane during
the night, and he'd not bothered to retrieve it. No doubt
it now decorated the head of some urchin. He shrugged.
"No matter."

De Raaf eyed him in the dark before mounting his
horse. "I can't think your new bride will approve of you
trying to get your gut perforated on Christmas morn of all
days. Does she know what you intend to do?"

Simon raised his eyebrows. "How does your own lady
feel about you attending a duel on Christmas?"

The big man winced. "No doubt Anna would hate it. I
hope to be home before she wakes and finds me gone."

"Ah." Simon turned his horse's head.

De Raaf nudged his horse into a walk beside him. They
rode abreast back to the lane.

"You didn't answer my question." The big man broke the silence, his breath steaming in the light from a window they passed.

"Lucy's feelings are moot." Something inside Simon tore at the thought of his angel. He flexed his jaw before admitting, "She's left me."

"What did you do?"

Simon scowled. "How do you know it was my fault?"

De Raaf simply lifted one eyebrow.

"She disapproves of dueling," Simon said. "No, that's not right. She disapproves of killing. Of murder."

The other man snorted. "Can't see why."

It was Simon's turn to give a speaking look.

"Then why are you dueling, man?" de Raaf barked impatiently. "Christ, it isn't worth losing your wife over."

"He threatened her." The memory still made his hands clench. Friend or no, Christian had threatened to rape Lucy. He could not be allowed to get away with that offense.

De Raaf grunted. "Then let me handle Fletcher. You won't even have to get involved."

Simon glanced at him sideways. "Thank you, but Lucy is my wife."

The big man sighed. "You're sure?"

"Yes." Simon squeezed the gelding into a trot, forestalling any further conversation.

They wound their way through more dingy streets. The wind whistled its remorse around corners. A cart passed, rumbling on the cobblestones. Simon finally saw movement on the sidewalk. Silent shapes, still infrequent, that slunk or scurried or loped. The denizens of the day had begun their rounds, careful in the dark that still concealed the dangers of night. Simon looked at the sky again. It had barely lightened to a nasty gray-brown. The snow lay in a thin, white layer on the street, covering filth and foul odors, giving it the illusion of purity. Soon the horses would stir it into muddy slush and the illusion would be gone.

"Damn, it's cold," de Raaf huffed from behind.

Simon didn't bother replying. They entered the path into the green. Here, the landscape was quiet. No human had disturbed the pristine snow yet.

"Are his seconds here?" De Raaf broke the quiet.

"They must be."

"You don't have to do this. Whatever—"

"Stop." Simon glanced at the other man. "Be still, Edward. It's past the time for that."

De Raaf grunted, frowning.

Simon hesitated. "If I'm killed, you'll look after Lucy, won't you?"

"Christ—" De Raaf bit off whatever he was going to say and glared. "'Course."

"Thank you. She's with her father in Kent. You'll find her direction and a letter on my desk. I'd appreciate it if you could deliver the letter to her."

"What the hell is she doing in Kent?"

"Repairing her life, I hope." Simon's mouth quirked sadly. Lucy. Would she mourn for him? Would she wear the dingy weeds of a widow and weep sweet salt tears? Or would she forget him soon and find consolation in the arms of the country vicar? He found to his surprise that he could still feel jealousy.

Lucy, my Lucy.

Two lanterns flickered against dim figures ahead. They were actors in an inevitable drama. The boy, who until a few days ago he'd regarded as a friend, the men who would watch him kill or be killed, the doctor who would pronounce a man dead.

Simon checked his sword, then nudged his horse into a trot. "We're here."

"MY LADY." NEWTON'S FACE RELAXED almost into a smile before he recovered and bowed, the tassel of his nightcap flopping over his eyes. "You've returned."

"Naturally." Lucy pulled back her hood and stepped over the threshold into her town house. Good Lord, did all the servants know her—*their*—business? Silly question. Of course they did. And, judging from Newton's hastily covered surprise, they hadn't expected her to come back to Simon. Lucy leveled her shoulders. Well. Best put that notion out of their heads. "Is he here?"

"No, my lady. His lordship left not half an hour ago."

Lucy nodded, trying not to show her disappointment. She had come so close to seeing him before he did this thing. She would've liked to wish him luck at least. "I'll wait for him in the study."

She laid the blue leather-bound book she carried on the hall table next to a rather battered brown paper package and gave it a small pat.

"My lady." Newton bowed. "May I wish you merry Christmas?"

"Oh, thank you." She'd set out late from Kent, despite Papa's protests, and made the last leg of the journey through the dark of night, thankful for the hired footmen clutching the back of the carriage. In all the whirl, she'd almost forgotten what day it was. "A merry Christmas to you as well, Mr. Newton."

Newton bowed again and glided away in his Turkish

slippers. Lucy picked up a candelabra from the hall table and entered Simon's study. As she crossed to a chair before the fireplace, the candle flames lit two small prints in the corner that she hadn't noticed before. Curious, she wandered over to inspect them.

The first was a botanist's rendition of a rose, full-blown and pink, its petals spread shamelessly wide. Underneath the rose was its dissection, showing the various parts, all properly labeled, as if to bring decorum to the sprawl of the flower above.

The second print was medieval, probably one of a series that would have illustrated the Bible. It depicted the story of Cain and Abel. Lucy held the candelabra up to study the horrible little etching. Cain's eyes were wide, his muscles bulging bestially as he struggled with his brother. Abel's face was calm, unalarmed as his brother killed him.

She shivered and turned away. It was horrible to have to wait for him like this. She'd never known before what he was doing. But now . . . She'd vowed to herself that she would not argue with him, even if she hated what he was about to do, even if he killed a friend, even if she was in terror for his very life. When he returned, she would welcome him as a loving wife should. She would get him a glass of wine, she would rub his shoulders, and she would make it clear that she was staying with him forever. Whether he dueled or not.

Lucy shook herself. Best not to think of the duel at all. She set her candelabra on the desk and went to one of the elegant rosewood bookcases to look at the titles. Perhaps she could distract herself with reading. She scanned the spines: horticulture, agriculture, roses, and more roses, with a single treatise, probably valuable, on fencing. She selected a large volume on roses and placed it on the edge of the desk. She was about to open it, perhaps learn enough to be able to discuss the flower with her husband, when she glanced at the blotting paper before the desk chair. There was a letter on it. Lucy angled her head.

Her name was scrawled across the top.

She stared for a moment, her neck still crooked; then Lucy straightened and walked around the desk. She hesitated a second longer before snatching up the letter, ripping it open and reading:

My Dearest Angel,

Had I known what despair I would bring you, I swear I would've done my damnedest not to be left half dead almost at your doorstep that afternoon, so long ago now. But then I wouldn't have met you—and already I am forsworn. For even knowing the pain I've brought you, I do not regret loving you, my angel. I am a selfish, uncaring cad, but there it is. I cannot unmake myself. Meeting you was the most wondrous thing that has ever happened to me. You are the closest I will ever come to heaven, either here on Earth or in the afterlife, and I will not regret it, not even at the cost of your tears.

So I go to my grave an unrepentant sinner, I'm afraid. There is no use in mourning one such as I, dearest. I hope you can resume your life in Maiden Hill, perhaps marry that handsome vicar. De Raaf has my business papers and will look after you as long as you need him.

—Your Husband, Simon

Lucy's hands were shaking so badly the paper cast wild shadows against the wall, and it took her a moment to see the postscript at the bottom:

P.S. Actually, there is one thing I regret. I would've very much liked to have made love to you one more time. Or three. —S

She laughed, horribly, through the tears blurring her vision. How like Simon to make salacious jokes even while writing a farewell love letter. For that was what the note was: a good-bye in case he died. Had he written letters like this before all of his duels? There was no way of telling; he would've destroyed them on his return.

Oh, God, she wished she'd never entered the room.

Lucy dropped the letter back on the desk and hurried out the door, snatching up the candelabra on her way out. Somehow reading Simon's words as if he were already dead made the waiting far worse. It was just another duel, she tried to reassure herself. How many had he fought now? Three? Five? She'd lost count and he must have, too. He'd won each before. He'd returned to her bloodied but alive. *Alive.* Any argument, any problem they had, could be resolved if he just returned to her alive. Lucy looked up and found that her feet had taken her to Simon's conservatory. She placed her palm against the wooden door, so solid and comforting, and pushed. Perhaps if she strolled the greenhouse with its rows of pots—

The door swung open and she froze. Broken glass glittered everywhere.

Simon's conservatory had been destroyed.

*   *   *

"IF YOU DON'T MIND, MY LORD?" one of Christian's seconds asked. The man was narrow-chested with large, bony hands springing strangely from the delicate wrists of a girl. He blinked nervously in the lantern light and almost shied when Simon turned to him.

Oh, grand. The end of his life would be presided over by a boy hardly old enough to shave. "Yes, yes," Simon muttered impatiently. He tore open the neck of his shirt, popping a button off. It landed in the fluff of snow at his feet and sank, creating a short tunnel. He didn't bother retrieving it.

The second peered at his chest, presumably to confirm that he wasn't wearing chain mail under his shirt.

"Let's get on with it." Simon swung his arms, trying to keep warm. There was no point in donning his waistcoat and coat again. He'd be sweating soon enough, even in shirtsleeves.

Twenty feet away, he could see de Raaf. The big man grunted and gave Christian back his sword. The younger man nodded and walked toward Simon. Simon studied him. Christian's face was white and set, his ginger hair like a dark flame. The boy was tall and handsome. No lines marred his cheeks. Only months ago at Angelo's academy, Christian had walked toward him as he did now. Simon's regular sparring partner had reneged, and Angelo had sent him Christian to practice against instead. On that occasion, the young man's face had betrayed nervousness, curiosity, and a little awe. Now his face was expressionless. He'd learned well in just a few months.

"Ready?" Christian's voice was without inflection.

The thin-wristed second approached to give Simon

back his sword. "Ought we to wait until it's brighter? The sun isn't even up."

"No." Simon took his sword and pointed with the tip. "Put the lanterns to either side of us."

He watched as de Raaf and the other seconds followed his directions.

Simon flexed his knees and raised his left hand behind his head. He caught de Raaf's eye. "Remember Lucy."

De Raaf nodded grimly.

Simon turned to face his opponent. "Ready."

"Allez!"

Christian sprang like a fox—healthy, young, and feral. Simon brought his sword up just in time, swearing under his breath. He parried the blow and retreated, his rear foot sliding in the crust of snow. He stabbed under the other man's guard, almost catching him in the side, but Christian was too fast. Steel rang as his sword was deflected. Simon's breath rasped loudly in his own ears. The air bit his lungs with cold on each inhale. He grunted and parried another attack. Strong and swift, Christian moved like an athlete of old. Simon grinned.

"You find this amusing?" the younger man panted.

"No." Simon coughed as the cold air seemed to drive too deeply into his lungs and fell back again under a flurry of slashes. "I merely admire your form." His wrist ached and the muscle on his upper arm was beginning to burn, but it was important to make a good show.

Christian looked at him suspiciously.

"Really. You've improved enormously." Simon smiled and darted at an opening.

Christian leaned back. The tip of Simon's sword grazed

his left cheek, leaving a scarlet line behind. Simon's smile widened. He hadn't thought he would make contact.

"Blood!" Christian's second called.

De Raaf didn't even bother. Both duelists ignored the shout.

"Bastard," the younger man said.

Simon shrugged. "Something to remember me by."

Christian struck at his flank.

Simon pivoted, his feet slipping again in the icy snow. "Would you have hurt Lucy?"

Christian sidestepped, his arm still moving easily despite the blood painting half his face. "Would you have killed my father?"

"Maybe."

The younger man ignored his answer and feinted, drawing Simon's blade down. Fire slashed across his brow.

"Damn!" Simon jerked his head back. The blood was already running into his right eye, blinding it. He blinked, his eye stinging. He heard de Raaf swearing in a low, steady monotone.

"Something to remember *me* by." Christian repeated his words without smiling.

"I won't have long."

Christian stared, then lunged forward violently. Simon blocked the blow. For a second they were locked together, Christian bearing down, Simon holding him off with the strength of his shoulder. Then, slowly—*incredibly*—Simon's arm gave. The sword point slid, screeching, toward him. De Raaf shouted hoarsely. The sword point stabbed into Simon, high on his right chest. He gasped and felt the steel scrape against his collarbone, felt the jar as the point hit his shoulder blade and stopped. He brought

his own sword up between their sweating, surging bodies
and saw Christian's eyes widen as he understood the peril.
The younger man jumped back, the hilt of his sword slipping out of his grasping hand. Simon cursed as the buried
sword tip pulled like a damned viper, but remained stead-
fastly planted in his flesh.

It wasn't time yet.

Simon ignored the agony in his shoulder and slashed
at Christian, keeping the man away from the bobbing hilt.
Sweet heaven, he must look like a puppet with a stick jutting from his shoulder. What an ignoble way to die. His opponent stared at him, out of reach but unarmed. The sword
in his chest sagged, dragging on his muscle. Simon tried to
reach the hilt. He could just grasp it but hadn't the leverage
to pull it from his own body. Blood soaked his shirt, growing colder with each passing minute. Christian's second
was standing shocked in the bloody, churned snow. Christian himself seemed nonplussed. Simon understood the
other man's dilemma. To win the duel, Christian must pull
his sword from Simon's shoulder. But in order to reach his
sword, he must first face Simon's sword unarmed. And yet
what could Simon do with the damn thing sticking out in
front of him? He couldn't pull it out, and he couldn't really
fight with it weaving and bobbing before him.

Impasse.

De Raaf had grown silent, but now he spoke. "It's
over."

"No," Simon hissed. He kept his eyes on the younger
man. "Take it."

Christian eyed him warily—as well he should.

Meanwhile, de Raaf still pleaded. "He was your friend.
You can end this, Fletcher."

Christian shook his head. Blood from the cut on his cheek already stained his collar. Simon wiped the gore from his eye and smiled. He would die today; he knew it. What point in living without Lucy? But he would have an honorable death. He would make the boy work for his kill. Despite the blood soaking his shirt, despite the fire eating at his shoulder, despite the weariness weighing down his soul, he would have a real fight. A real death.

"Take it," he repeated softly.

Chapter Twenty

The light from Lucy's candles shone on the conservatory floor. Glass shards sparkled there like a carpet of diamonds. Lucy stared dazedly at them a moment before she noticed the chill. She looked up. The wind was whistling through what had once been a glass roof, making her candle flames flicker and threaten to go out. She held the candelabra higher. Every pane in the greenhouse was jagged and broken. The sky, graying with the threat of day, hung too low.

Who . . . ?

She moved into the greenhouse almost without volition. The glass crunched beneath her boots, scraping against the brick walk. Terra-cotta pots were in drifts on the tables, broken and crushed, as if a great, angry wave had tossed them there. Lucy stumbled down the aisle, the bits of glass sliding beneath her shoes. Upturned roses in various states of bloom were scattered everywhere. One ball of roots hung from a windowpane overhead. Pink and red blooms bled petals on the floor, their familiar perfume curiously absent. Lucy touched a flower and felt it melt and shrivel beneath the warmth of her hand. It was frozen. The bitter winter air had been let in to savage the sheltered blooms. Dead. All the roses were dead.

Dear God.

Lucy reached what had been the dome in the middle of the conservatory and stopped. Only a skeleton, bits of glass skin still clinging here and there, remained. The marble fountain was chipped and cracked as if a giant hammer had been taken to it. A frozen plume of ice stood in the fountain, stilled in mid-splash. More ice spilled from a crack in the fountain and widened into a frozen lake around it. Beneath the ice, shards of glass glittered, horribly beautiful.

Lucy swayed in shock. A gust of wind moaned through the conservatory and blew out all but one of her candles. Simon must have done this. He'd destroyed his fairyland conservatory. *Why?* She sank to her knees, huddled on the cold floor, her one remaining flame cradled in her numb palms. She'd seen how tenderly Simon had cared for his plants. Remembered the look of pride when she'd first discovered the dome and fountain. For him to have smashed all this . . .

He must have lost hope. All hope.

She'd left him, even though she'd promised not to on her mother's memory. He loved her and she'd left him. A sob tore at her throat. Without hope, how could he survive the duel? Would he even try to win? If she knew where he would duel, she might stop him. But she had no idea where this duel would take place. He'd warned her that he would hide the dueling rendezvous from her and he had. She couldn't stop him, she realized achingly. He was going to duel; he might be there already, preparing to fight in the cold and dark, and she couldn't stop him. She couldn't save him.

There was nothing for her to do.

Lucy looked around the ruined conservatory, but there was no answer here. Dear God, he would die. She would lose him without ever having the chance to tell him how much he meant to her. How much she loved him. *Simon.* Alone in the dark, destroyed greenhouse she wept, her body shaking with sobs and the cold, and she finally acknowledged what she had kept hidden deep in her heart. She loved her husband.

She loved Simon.

Her last candle flickered and went out. She drew a breath and wrapped her arms about herself, bent as if broken. She lifted her face to the gray sky as silent, ghostly snowflakes dropped and melted on her lips and eyelids.

Above her, the dawn broke on London.

DAWN WAS BREAKING ON LONDON. The expressions on the faces of the men around Simon were no longer in shadow. Daylight filtered across the dueling green. He could see the desperation in Christian's eyes as he darted forward, his teeth clenched and bared, his red hair matted with sweat at the temples. Christian grabbed the sword in Simon's shoulder and wrenched at it. Simon gasped as the blade sawed at his flesh. Scarlet drops fell to the snow at his feet. He leveled his own sword and swung blindly. Violently. Christian ducked to the side, almost losing the hilt of his sword. Simon slashed again, felt the blade connect. A spray of blood decorated the snow, then was trampled underfoot, mixing with Simon's scarlet drops until all was a muddy mess.

"Goddamn," Christian moaned.

His breath blew in Simon's face, foul with fear. His face was white and scarlet, the wash of blood on his left cheek only a shade darker than the freckles underneath. *So young.* Simon felt an absurd urge to apologize. He shivered; his blood-soaked shirt was freezing. It had begun to snow again. He looked at the sky over Christian's head and thought, ridiculously, *I shouldn't have to die on a gray day.*

Christian sobbed hoarsely.

"Stop!"

The shout came from behind him. Simon ignored it, bringing his sword up one last time.

But then de Raaf was there, his own sword drawn. "Stop, Simon." The big man interposed his blade between them.

"What are you doing?" Simon panted. He was dizzy and only just kept from reeling.

"For the love of God, stop!"

"Listen to the man," de Raaf growled.

Christian froze. *"Father."*

Sir Rupert limped slowly through the snow, his face nearly as white as his son's. "Don't kill, him, Iddesleigh. I concede. Don't kill my boy."

"Concede what?" Was this a trick? Simon glanced at Christian's horrified face. Not on the son's part, at least.

Sir Rupert was silent, using his breath to laboriously walk closer.

"Jesus. Let's get this skewer out of you." De Raaf placed a fist on Simon's shoulder and tugged Christian's sword out with one swift motion.

Simon couldn't keep a moan from escaping his lips. His

vision darkened for a second. He blinked fiercely. Now wasn't the time to faint. He was vaguely aware that blood was pouring from the wound on his shoulder.

"Christ," de Raaf muttered. "You look like a butchered pig." He opened the bag he'd brought with him and took out a handful of linens, wadding and shoving them into the wound.

God's balls! The pain was near unbearable. "Didn't you get a doctor?" Simon asked through gritted teeth.

De Raaf shrugged. "Couldn't find one I trusted." He pressed harder.

"Ouch." Simon inhaled a hissing breath. "*Goddamnit.* So I have you to physic me?"

"Yes. Aren't you going to thank me?"

"Thank you," Simon grunted. He looked at Sir Rupert, refusing to flinch as de Raaf tended his shoulder. "What do you concede?"

"Father," Christian began.

Sir Rupert made a slashing motion with his hand, cutting him off. "I concede I am responsible for your brother's death."

"*Murder,*" Simon growled. He gripped his sword tighter, although de Raaf stood between him and the others, blocking the movement of his blade. The big man chose that moment to put his other hand at his back and press his palms together, squeezing the shoulder. Simon bit back an oath.

De Raaf looked pleased. "You're welcome."

Sir Rupert nodded. "Your brother's murder. I am to blame. Punish me, not my son."

"No!" Christian shouted. He lurched forward, limping like his father.

Simon saw the other man's right leg was blood-soaked below the thigh. His sword had found its mark. "Killing your son would punish you most satisfactorily," Simon drawled.

Edward, facing him, lifted his eyebrow so only he could see.

"Killing Christian also takes an innocent life," Sir Rupert said. He leaned forward, both hands on the head of his cane, his eyes fixed on Simon's face. "You've never killed an innocent before."

"Unlike you."

"Unlike me."

For a moment no one spoke. The snow fell silently. Simon stared at his brother's murderer. The man admitted it—all but crowed the fact that he'd arranged Ethan's death. He felt hatred rise in him like bile at the back of his throat, nearly overwhelming reason. But however much he might loathe Sir Rupert, he was right. Simon had never killed an innocent man.

"What do you have in mind?" Simon asked finally.

Sir Rupert took a breath. He thought he'd won a concession, damn him. And he had. "I will pay you the price of your brother's life. I can sell my London home."

"What?" Christian burst out. Snowflakes had melted on his eyelashes like tears.

But Simon was already shaking his head. "Not enough."

His father ignored Christian, intent on persuading Simon. "Our country estates—"

"What about Mother and my sisters?" Christian's thin-wristed friend approached and tried to tend his wound, but Christian waved him away impatiently.

Sir Rupert shrugged. "What about them?"

"They haven't done any wrong," his son said. "Mother adores London. And what of Julia, Sarah, and Becca? Will you beggar them? Make it impossible that they ever marry well?"

"Yes!" Sir Rupert shouted. "They are women. What other avenue would you have me consider?"

"You would sacrifice their futures—their very happiness—to prevent me dueling Simon?" Christian stared incredulously.

"You are my heir." Sir Rupert held out a shaking hand to his son. "You are the most important. I cannot chance your death."

"I don't understand you." Christian pivoted away from his father, then gasped and wavered. His second hurried to him and offered his support.

"It doesn't matter," Simon interrupted. "You cannot pay for my brother's death. His life has no price."

"Damn you!" Sir Rupert drew a sword from his cane. "Will you duel a crippled man, then?"

"No!" Christian pulled away from his second.

Simon raised his hand, stopping the younger man's surge forward. "No, I will not duel you. I find that I have lost my taste for blood."

Long lost it, if the truth were known. He had never liked what he'd had to do, but now he knew: He could not kill Christian. He thought of Lucy's fine, topaz eyes, so serious, so right, and almost smiled. He could not kill Christian because it would disappoint Lucy. So small a reason, but a crucial one nevertheless.

Sir Rupert lowered his sword, a smirk forming on his lips. He thought he'd won.

"Instead," Simon continued, "you will leave England."

"What?" The smile died from the older man's face.

Simon raised an eyebrow. "You prefer a duel?"

Sir Rupert opened his mouth, but it was his son who replied. "No, he doesn't."

Simon looked at his former friend. Christian's face was as white as the snow falling around them, but he stood straight and tall. Simon nodded. "You will accept banishment from England for your family?"

"Yes."

"What?" Sir Rupert blustered.

Christian turned savagely on his father. "He has offered you—*us*—an honorable way out, without bloodshed or loss of fortune."

"But where would we go?"

"America." The young man turned to Simon. "That meets with your approval?"

"Yes."

"Christian!"

Christian kept his eyes on Simon, ignoring his father. "I will see it done. You have my word."

"Very well," Simon said.

For a moment, the two men stared at each other. Simon watched an emotion—regret?—chase across the other's eyes. He noticed for the first time that Christian's eyes were almost the same shade as Lucy's. *Lucy.* She was still gone from his life. That made two souls he had lost in as many days.

Then Christian straightened. "Here." He held out his open palm. On it lay the Iddesleigh signet ring.

Simon took it from him and screwed the ring on his right index finger. "Thank you."

Christian nodded. He hesitated for a moment, looking at Simon as if he wanted to say more, before he limped away.

Sir Rupert frowned, white lines etching themselves between his brows. "You'll accept my banishment in return for Christian's life?"

"Yes." Simon nodded curtly, his lips thinning as he wavered on his feet. A few seconds more, that was all he needed. "You have thirty days."

"Thirty days! But—"

"Take it or leave it. If you or any member of your family is still in England after thirty days, I will challenge your son again." Simon didn't wait for a reply; the other's defeat was already etched in his face. He turned away and walked toward his horse.

"We need to get you to a physician," de Raaf rumbled sotto voce.

"So he can bleed me?" Simon almost laughed. "No. A bandaging will suffice. My valet can do it."

The other man grunted. "Can you ride?"

"'Course." He said it carelessly, but Simon was relieved when he actually pulled himself atop his horse. De Raaf shot him an exasperated glance, but Simon ignored it, turning toward home. Or what had once been home. Without Lucy there, the town house became merely a building. A place to store his neckcloths and shoes, nothing more.

"Do you want me to accompany you?" de Raaf asked.

Simon grimaced. He held his horse to a gentle walk, but the movement still jarred his shoulder. "It would be nice to have someone here, should I fall ignominiously from my mount."

"And land on your arse." De Raaf snorted. "Naturally,

I'll ride you to your town house. But I meant when you go after your lady."

Simon turned painfully in the saddle to stare at him.

De Raaf raised an eyebrow. "You are going to bring her back, aren't you? She's your wife, after all."

Simon cleared his throat while he pondered. Lucy was very, very mad at him. She might not forgive him.

"Oh, for God's sake," de Raaf burst out. "Don't tell me you're just going to let her go?"

"Didn't say that," Simon protested.

"Mope about in that great house of yours—"

"I don't mope."

"Play with your flowers while you let your wife get away from you."

"I don't—"

"She is too good for you, granted," de Raaf mused. "But still. Principle of the thing. Ought to at least try to bring her back."

"All right, all right!" Simon nearly shouted, causing a passing fishmonger to look at him sharply and cross to the other side of the street.

"Good," de Raaf said. "And do pull yourself together. Don't know when I've seen you looking worse. Probably need a bath."

Simon would have protested that as well, except he did indeed need a bath. He was still thinking of a suitable reply when they arrived at his town house. De Raaf dismounted his gelding and helped Simon swing down from his horse. Simon bit back a groan. His right hand felt leaden.

"My lord!" Newton ran down the front steps, wig askew, pot belly jiggling.

"I'm fine," Simon muttered. "Just a scratch. Hardly bled at—"

For the first time in his employment, Newton interrupted his master. "The viscountess has returned."

HER FINGERS WERE SPREAD OVER HER CLOSED EYES. *Dear Lord.* A shudder racked her frame. *Protect him.* Her knees were numb from the cold. *I need him.* The wind whipped against her wet cheeks.

I love him.

A scrape came from the end of the aisle. *Please, God.* Footsteps, slow and steady, crunched on the broken glass. Were they coming to tell her? *No. Please, no.* She curled within herself, huddled on the ice, her hands still shielding her eyes, blocking out the dawning day, blocking out the end of her world.

"Lucy." It was a whisper, so low she should not have been able to hear it.

But she did. She dropped her hands, raised her face, hoping, but not daring to believe. Not yet. He was bareheaded, ghastly white, his shirt covered in gore. Blood was crusted down the right side of his face from a cut on his brow, and he cradled one arm. But he was alive.

Alive.

"Simon." She clumsily wiped her eyes with the heels of her hands, trying to get rid of the tears so she could see, but they kept coming. "Simon."

He stumbled forward and dropped to his knees before her.

"I'm sorry—" she started, and then realized she was speaking over his words. "What?"

"Stay." He'd grasped her shoulders with both hands,

squeezing as if he couldn't believe her solid. "Stay with me. I love you. God, I love you, Lucy. I can't—"

Her heart seemed to expand with his words. "I'm sorry. I—"

"I can't live without you," he was saying, his lips skimming her face. "I tried. There isn't any light without you."

"I won't leave again."

"I become a creature with a blackened soul—"

"I love you, Simon—"

"Without hope of redemption—"

"I love you."

"You are my salvation."

"I love you."

He finally seemed to hear her through his own confession. He stopped still and stared at her. Then he cradled her face in his hands and kissed her, his lips moving tenderly over hers, wanting, comforting. She tasted tears and blood and didn't care. He was alive. Her sob was caught in his mouth as he opened it over hers. She sobbed again and ran her hands across the back of his head, feeling his short hair tickle her palms. She'd nearly lost him.

Lucy tried to pull back, remembering. "Your shoulder, your forehead—"

"It's nothing," he murmured over her lips. "Christian pricked me, that's all. It's already bandaged."

"But—"

He suddenly lifted his head, his ice eyes staring into hers, melting. "I didn't kill him, Lucy. We dueled, it's true, but we stopped before anyone was killed. Fletcher and his family will go to America and never return to England."

She stared at him. He hadn't killed, after all. "Are there more duels?"

"No. It's over." He blinked and seemed to hear what he'd said. "It's over."

Lucy laid a hand on his cold, cold cheek. "Darling."

"It's over." His voice broke. He bowed his head until his forehead rested on her shoulder. "It's over and Ethan is dead. Oh, God, my brother is dead."

"I know." Gently she stroked his hair, feeling the sobs that he would not let her see shake his frame.

"He was such a pompous ass, and I loved him so much."

"Of course you did. He was your brother."

Simon choked on a laugh and raised his face from her shoulder. "My angel." His gray eyes swam with tears.

Lucy shivered. "It's cold here. Let's go inside and get you into bed."

"Such a practical woman." He struggled to rise.

Lucy stood stiffly and put her arm about him to help him up. "And I insist on a physician this time. Even if I have to drag him away from his Christmas breakfast."

"Christmas." Simon stopped short, nearly knocking her down. "Is it Christmas?"

"Yes." Lucy smiled up at him. He looked so confused. "Didn't you know? It's all right. I don't expect a present."

"But I have one for you, and one for Pocket as well," Simon said. "A toy naval ship complete with sailors and officers and rows of little cannons. It's really quite clever."

"I'm sure it is. Pocket will adore it, and Rosalind will not approve, and I expect that's your intention." Lucy's eyes widened. "Oh, my goodness, Simon!"

He frowned. "What?"

"I invited Pocket and Rosalind to Christmas breakfast.

I forgot." Lucy stared up at him horrified. "What should we do?"

"We'll inform Newton and Cook and leave it to them." He kissed her forehead. "Rosalind is family, after all. She'll understand."

"Maybe so," Lucy said. "But we can't let them see you like this. We'll at least have to get you cleaned."

"I bow to your every wish, my angel. But humor me and open your present now, please." He shut the conservatory door behind them and slowly made his way to the hall table where she'd earlier set the blue book. "Ah, it's still here." He turned with the battered rectangular package and held it out, looking suddenly uncertain.

Lucy's brow wrinkled. "Shouldn't you at least lie down?"

He offered the package mutely.

Her mouth curved in a smile that she could not suppress. Impossible to be stern with him while he stood in front of her like an earnest child. "What is it?" She took the package. It was rather heavy, so she laid it on the hall table again to unwrap it.

He shrugged. "Open it."

She began working at the string.

"I should've given you a wedding present before now," he said beside her. She could feel his hot breath on her neck.

Lucy's mouth twitched. Where was her sophisticated London aristocrat now? Funny that Simon would be so nervous about giving her a Christmas present. She unwound the string.

"You're a viscountess, now, for God's sake," Simon was muttering. "I should've bought you jewels. Emeralds or rubies. Sapphires. Definitely sapphires and maybe diamonds."

The paper fell away. A flat, cherrywood box lay before her. She looked at him questioningly. He raised his brows back at her. She opened the box and froze. Inside were rows of pencils, plain and colored, as well as charcoal, pastels, a tiny ink bottle, and pens. A smaller box held watercolors, brushes, and a little bottle for water.

"If you don't like it or if something is missing, I can have the art supplier make another," Simon said very rapidly. "Maybe a bigger one. And I've ordered several bound sketchbooks to be made, but they aren't ready yet. Of course, I'll be giving you jewels as well. Lots of jewels. A treasure trove of jewels, but this is just something small—"

Lucy blinked back tears. "It's the most wonderful thing I've ever seen." She wrapped her arms about his shoulders and hugged him close, glorying in the familiar smell of him.

She felt Simon's arms lift to embrace her, but she remembered then. "I've got something for you as well." She handed him the blue book.

He opened it to the title page and smiled widely. "The Serpent Prince. However did you finish it so fast?" He began leafing through the pages, studying her watercolor pictures. "I suppose I ought to give this to Pocket. It was for her that I commissioned it, after all, but—" He choked as he reached the last page.

Lucy glanced at it, admiring the handsome silver-haired prince she'd painted next to the pretty goat girl. It really was a fine piece of work, even if she did say so herself.

"You've changed the ending!" Simon sounded outraged.

Well, she didn't care. "Yes, it's much better now that Angelica marries the Serpent Prince instead. I never did like that Rutherford."

"But, angel," he protested. "She'd chopped off his head. I don't see how he could recover from that."

"Silly." She pulled his face down to hers. "Don't you know true love heals all?"

He paused just before their lips met, his eyes a silvery gray misted with tears. "It does, you know, your love for me."

"*Our* love."

"I feel whole when I'm with you. I didn't think that was possible after Ethan and Christian and . . . everything. But you swept into my life and redeemed me, ransomed my very soul from the devil."

"You're being blasphemous again," she whispered as she stood on tiptoe to reach his mouth.

"No, but really—"

"Hush. Kiss me."

And he did.

A masked avenger dressed in a harlequin's motley protects the innocents of St. Giles at night.

When a rescue mission leaves him wounded, the kind soul who comes to his rescue is the one woman he'd never have expected . . .

Please turn this page
for a preview.

Chapter One

LONDON, ENGLAND
MAY 1738

The body in the road was the absolute cap to the day. Isabel Beckinhall, Baroness Beckinhall sighed to herself. Her carriage had come to a standstill in the worst part of London—the dirty streets of St. Giles. And *why* was she in St. Giles as dark descended? Because she'd volunteered to represent the Ladies' Syndicate for the Benefit of the Home for Unfortunate Infants and Foundling Children at the final inspection of the new Home for Unfortunate Infants and Foundling Children, more fool she.

Never volunteer. Not even when pleasantly filled with warm scones and hot tea. Warm scones were obviously the work of the Devil or perhaps Lady Hero Reading, one of the two founding patronesses of the home. Lady Hero had refilled her teacup and looked at Isabel with wide gray eyes, asking prettily if Isabel would mind meeting with Mr. Winter Makepeace, the home's dour manager, to look over the new building. And Isabel had blithely agreed like some scone-filled mindless cow.

And the damned man hadn't even shown!

"Moo," Isabel muttered to herself just as the carriage door opened to admit her lady's maid, Pinkney.

"Ma'am?" Pinkney asked, her blue eyes wide and startled. Of course Pinkney's eyes were nearly always wide and startled. She was one of the most sought-after lady's maids in London, a paragon of the latest fashion, but Isabel had privately begun to wonder if her new maid wasn't a bit dim.

"Nothing," Isabel replied, waving aside her bovine utterance. "Did you find out why it's taking so long to move the dead man?"

"Oh, yes, my lady," Pinkney said. "It's because he's not dead." Her pretty dark blond brows drew together. "Well, not yet anyway. Harold the footman is having a time pulling him aside, and you wouldn't credit it, ma'am, but he's a comic actor."

It was Isabel's turn to blink. *"Harold?"*

"Oh, no, my lady!" Pinkney giggled until she caught Isabel's steady gaze. "Er…" The maid cleared her throat. "The not-yet-dead-man is. He's dressed as a harlequin, mask and all—"

Isabel was no longer listening. She'd opened the door and climbed from the carriage. Outside the gray day was growing grimmer still with the advent of nightfall. Fires flared to the west and she could hear the rumbling of the rioters from that direction. They were getting closer. Isabel shivered and hurried to where Harold and the other footman were bent over a figure on the ground. Pinkney was such a ninny she'd probably mistaken the costume or the man or the mask or—

But no.

Isabel drew in a sharp breath. She'd never seen the notorious Ghost of St. Giles in person, but she had no doubt that this must be he. The prone man wore black and red motley. His floppy, brimmed hat had fallen from his head and she could see that his brown hair was tied back simply. A short sword was sheathed at his side and a long sword lay by one of his broad hands. A black half mask with a ridiculously long nose covered the upper half of his face, leaving his square chin and wide mouth revealed. His lips were parted over straight white teeth, the upper lip a little bigger than the bottom, and sensuously curved in unconsciousness.

Isabel snapped her attention up to her coachman. "Is he alive?"

"He's still breathin' at least, my lady." Harold shook his head. "Don't know for how long, though."

A shout came from nearby and the sound of smashing glass.

"Put him in the carriage," Isabel said. She bent to pick up his hat.

Tom, the second footman, frowned. "But, my lady—"

"*Now.* And don't forget his sword."

Already she could see a mass of people rounding the corner down the street. The footmen glanced at each other then as one lifted the Ghost. Harold grunted under the weight, but he made no complaint.

A crowd gathered at the end of the street, and then someone gave a shout.

The rioters had spotted the carriage.

Isabel picked up her skirts and trotted after her footmen. Harold gave a great heave and dumped the Ghost and his sword into the carriage. Isabel scrambled rather inelegantly inside. Pinkney was staring wide-eyed at the Ghost, who was in a heap in the corner of the carriage, but for the moment Isabel ignored him. She tossed the hat on top of the Ghost, lifted her seat, and withdrew two pistols from the hidden compartment underneath.

Pinkney squeaked in alarm.

Isabel turned and handed the pistols to the footmen at the carriage door. "Don't let anyone climb the carriage."

Harold's jaw tightened. "Yes, my lady."

He took the pistols, gave one to Tom, and mounted the carriage.

Isabel closed the carriage door and knocked on the roof. "Fast as you can, John!"

The carriage started forward with a lurch just as something hit the side.

"My lady!" Pinkney cried.

"Hush," Isabel said.

There was a lap robe on the maid's seat and Isabel pulled it over the Ghost. She sat back on her own seat, clutching the window as the carriage rocked around a corner. Something knocked against the carriage. A grimacing face appeared suddenly at the window, tongue smearing against the glass lewdly.

Pinkney screamed.

Isabel stared at the man, her heart racing, but her gaze steady as she met his eyes. They were bloodshot and filled with maddened rage. The carriage jolted and the man fell away.

One of the pistols fired.

"My lady," Pinkney whispered, her face white, "the dead man—"

"Not-quite-dead man," Isabel muttered, eyeing the

robe. Hopefully anyone glancing inside would see a robe thrown carelessly in the corner, *not* the hidden Ghost of St. Giles. She braced herself as the carriage swung wildly around a corner.

"Not-quite-dead man," Pinkney obediently repeated. "Who is he?"

"The Ghost of St. Giles."

Pinkney's robin's egg blue eyes widened. "Who?"

Isabel stared at her lady's maid in exasperation. Really, the chit was something of an idiot. "The Ghost of St. Giles? The most notorious footpad in London? Goes about in a harlequin's costume, either ravishing and murdering or rescuing and defending, depending on whose stories you believe?"

If Pinkney's eyes got any bigger they might fall out of her head altogether.

"No?" Isabel waved a hand toward the window and the shouting and screaming outside and said sweetly, "The man that mob wants dead?"

Pinkney stared horrified at the robe. "But...why, my lady?"

The second pistol fired with a deafening *BOOM*! Pinkney jumped and looked wildly at the window.

Dear God, they were out of ammunition. Isabel prayed the footmen were safe—and that they could hold off the rioters without their guns. She was an aristocrat, but that meant little to a mob such as this. Just last year a viscount had been dragged from his carriage and robbed in St. Giles.

Isabel took a deep breath and felt under the robe until she found the hilt of the Ghost's sword. She drew it out and put the heavy thing across her lap. If nothing else she could hit someone over the head with it if need be. "They want him dead because this morning he cut Charming Mickey O'Connor down from the gallows."

Pinkney actually brightened at this. "Oh, Charming Mickey, the pirate! *Him* I've heard of. They say he's handsome as sin and dresses better than the king himself."

Of course her lady's maid had heard of a well-dressed pirate.

"Quite," Isabel flinched as something hit the window, cracking the glass. "They probably chased him all the way from Tyburn gallows, poor man."

"Oh." For a moment Pinkney bit her lip. Then she looked timidly at Isabel. "But, my lady, if the mob wants him and he's in our carriage...ah..."

Isabel drew on all her strength to smile firmly. Her hand tightened on the hilt of the sword across her lap."That's why we're not going to let them know we have the Ghost, are we?"

Pinkney blinked several times as if working through this logic, and then she smiled. The child really was quite pretty. "Oh, yes, my lady."

The lady's maid sat back as if quite confident that they were all out of danger now that everything had been explained.

Isabel twitched aside the curtains to peer through the cracked glass. She wasn't nearly as sanguine. Many of the streets in St. Giles were narrow and twisting—the reason that her carriage had been traveling so slowly earlier. A mob could move much faster afoot than they. But the mob was beginning to fall away. John Coachman had found a straight stretch of road and was urging the horses into a trot.

Isabel let fall the curtain with a heartfelt sigh of relief. *Thank God.*

Half an hour later the carriage was pulling up before her neat town house.

"Bring him inside," she ordered Harold when he pulled open the doors.

He nodded wearily. "Yes, my lady."

"And Harold?" Isabel descended the carriage still clutching the sword.

"My lady?"

"Well done. To both you and Tom." Isabel nodded to Tom.

A shy grin split Harold's broad face. "Thank you, my lady."

Isabel permitted herself a small smile before she swept into her town house. Edmund, her dear late husband, had bought Fairmont House for her shortly before he'd died, and had gifted it to her on her twenty-eighth birthday. He'd known that the title and estates would go to a distant cousin and had wanted her properly settled with her own property free of the entail. Isabel had immediately redecorated on moving in four years ago. Now the entry hall was all white marble, with soaring gilded Corinthian columns along the edges emphasizing the height of the room.

"Thank you, Butterman," Isabel said as she tucked the sword under her arm and pulled off her gloves and hat, handing them to the butler. "I need a bedroom readied immediately."

Butterman, like all her servants, was impeccably trained. He didn't even blink an eye at the abrupt order—or the sword she carelessly held. "Yes, my lady. Will the blue room do?"

"Quite."

Butterman snapped his fingers and a maid went hurrying up the stairs.

Isabel turned and watched as Harry and Tom came in with the Ghost between them.

Butterman raised his eyebrow a fraction of an inch at the sight of the unconscious man, but merely said, "The blue room, Harold, if you please."

"Yes, sir," Harold panted.

"If you don't mind, my lady," Butterman murmured, "I believe Mrs. Butterman may be of assistance."

"Yes, thank you. Please send Mrs. Butterman up as quickly as possible." Isabel followed the footmen up the stairs.

The maids were still turning back the sheets on the bed in the blue room, when the footmen arrived with their burden, but at least the fire on the grate was lit.

Harold hesitated, probably because the Ghost was quite dirty and bloody, but Isabel gestured to the bed. The Ghost groaned as the footmen laid him on the spotless counterpane.

Isabel propped his sword in a corner of the room and hurried to his side. His eyes were closed. His hat had been left in the carriage, but he still wore his mask, though it was askew on his face. Carefully she lifted the thing over his head and was surprised to find underneath a thin black silk scarf covering the upper part of his face from the bridge of his strong nose to his forehead. Two eyeholes had been cut into the material to make a second, thinner mask. She examined the harlequin's mask in her hand. It was leather and stained black. High arching eyebrows and the curving grotesque nose gave the mask a satyrlike leer.

She set it on a table by the bed and looked back at the Ghost. He lay limp and heavy on the bed. Blood stained his motley leggings above his black jackboots. She bit her lip. Some of the blood looked quite fresh.

"Butterman said 'twas a man injured," Mrs. Butterman said as she bustled in the room. She went to the bed and stared at the Ghost a moment, hands on hips, before nodding decisively. "Well, nothing for it. We'll need to undress him, my lady, and find out where the blood's coming from."

"Oh, of course," Isabel said. She reached for the buttons of the Ghost's fall as Mrs. Butterman began on the doublet.

Behind her, Isabel heard a gasp. "Oh, my lady!"

"What is it, Pinkney?" Isabel frowned as she worked at a stubborn button. Blood had dried on the material, making it stiff.

"'Tisn't proper for you to be doing such work." Pinkney sounded as scandalized as if Isabel had proposed walking naked in Westminster Cathedral. "He's a *man*."

"I assure you I have seen a nude man before," Isabel said mildly as she peeled back the man's leggings. Underneath, his smallclothes were soaked in blood. Good God. Could a man lose so much and survive? She began working at the ties to his smallclothes.

"He has bruising on his shoulder and ribs and a few scrapes, but nothing to cause this much blood," Mrs. Butterman reported as she spread the doublet wide and raised the ghost's shirt to his armpits.

Isabel glanced up and for a moment froze. His chest was delineated with lean muscles, his nipples brown against his pale skin, black, curling hair spreading between. His belly was hard and ridged, his navel entirely obscured by that same black curling hair. Isabel blinked. She had seen a man—men, actually—naked, true, but Edmund had been in his sixth decade when he died and had certainly never looked like this. And the few, discreet lovers that' she'd taken since Edmund's death had been aristocrats— men of leisure. They'd hardly had more muscles than she. Her eye caught on the line of hair trailing down from his navel. It disappeared into his smallclothes.

Where her hands were.

Isabel swallowed and untied the garment, a little surprised by the tremble of her fingers, and drew them down his legs. His genitals were revealed, his cock thick and long, even at rest, his bollocks heavy.

"Well," Mrs. Butterman said, "he certainly looks healthy enough *there*."

"Oh, my, yes," Pinkney breathed.

Isabel looked around irritably. She'd not realized the maid had come close enough to see the Ghost. Isabel drew a corner of the counterpane over the Ghost's loins, feeling protective of the unconscious man.

"Help me take off his boots so we can bare his legs completely," Isabel told Mrs. Butterman. "If we can't find the wound there, we'll have to turn him over."

But as they stripped his breeches further down his legs a long gash was revealed on the man's muscled right thigh. Fresh blood oozed and trickled over his leg as the sodden material was pulled away.

"There 'tis," Mrs. Butterman said. "We could send for the doctor, my lady, but I've a fair hand with the needle and thread."

Isabel nodded. She glanced again at the wound, relieved

it was not nearly as bad as she'd feared. "Fetch what you'll need, please, Mrs. Butterman, and take Pinkney with you to help. I have the feeling he won't be much pleased by a doctor."

Mrs. Butterman hurried out with Pinkney.

Isabel waited, alone in the room save for the Ghost of St. Giles. He was unconscious, but still he was a commanding presence, his big body sprawled upon the dainty bed. Isabel looked at him. He was a man in the prime of his life, strong and athletic, nearly bare to her gaze.

All except his face.

Her hand moved almost without thought. She stretched toward the black silk mask still covering the upper part of his face. Was he handsome? Ugly? Merely ordinary looking?

Her hand began to descend toward the mask.

His flashed up and caught her wrist.

His eyes opened, assessing and quite clearly brown. "Don't."

Even the most refined lady
craves an untamed man
to release her passion . . .

Please turn this page
for an excerpt from

*To Taste
Temptation*

Available now.

Chapter One

Now Iron Heart got his name from a very strange thing. Although his limbs and face, and indeed all the rest of his body, were exactly like every other man created by God, his heart was not. It was made from iron, and it beat on the surface of his chest, strong, brave, and steadfast....
—from *Iron Heart*

LONDON, ENGLAND
SEPTEMBER 1764

"They say he ran away." Mrs. Conrad leaned close to impart this bit of gossip.

Lady Emeline Gordon took a sip of tea and glanced over the rim of the cup at the gentleman in question. He was as out of place as a jaguar in a room full of tabby cats: raw, vital, and not quite civilized. Definitely not a man she would associate with cowardice. Emeline wondered what his name was as she thanked the Lord for his appearance.

Mrs. Conrad's afternoon salon had been paralyzingly dull until *he* had sauntered in.

"He ran away from the massacre of the 28th Regiment in the colonies," Mrs. Conrad continued breathlessly, "back in fifty-eight. Shameful, isn't it?"

Emeline turned and arched an eyebrow at her hostess. She held Mrs. Conrad's gaze and saw the exact moment when the silly woman remembered. Mrs. Conrad's already pink complexion deepened to a shade of beet that really didn't become her at all.

"That is ... I ... I—" her hostess stammered.

This was what one got when one accepted an invitation from a lady who aspired to but didn't quite sail in the highest circles of society. It was Emeline's own fault, really. She sighed and took pity. "He's in the army, then?"

Mrs. Conrad grasped the bait gratefully. "Oh, no. Not anymore. At least I don't *believe* so."

"Ah," Emeline said, and tried to think of another subject.

The room was large and expensively decorated, with a painting on the ceiling overhead depicting Hades pursuing Persephone. The goddess looked particularly vacuous, smiling down sweetly on the assembly below. She hadn't a chance against the god of the underworld, even if he did have bright pink cheeks in this portrayal.

Emeline's current protégé, Jane Greenglove, sat on a settee nearby, conversing with young Lord Simmons, a very nice choice. Emeline nodded approvingly. Lord Simmons had an income of over eight thousand pounds a year and a lovely house near Oxford. That alliance would be very suitable, and since Jane's older sister, Eliza, had already accepted the hand of Mr. Hampton, things were falling into place quite neatly. They always did, of course, when Emeline consented to guide a young lady into society, but it was pleasing to have one's expectations fulfilled nevertheless.

Or it should be. Emeline twisted a lace ribbon at her waist before she caught herself and smoothed it out again. Actually, she was feeling a bit out of sorts, which was ridiculous. Her world was perfect. Absolutely perfect.

Emeline glanced casually at the stranger only to find his dark gaze fixed on her. His eyes crinkled ever so slightly at the corners as if he was amused by something—and that something might be her. Hastily she looked away again. Awful man. He was obviously aware that every lady in the room had noticed him.

Beside her, Mrs. Conrad had started prattling, evidently in an attempt to cover her gaffe. "He owns an importing business in the Colonies. I believe he's in London on business; that's what Mr. Conrad says, anyway. And he's as rich as Croesus, although you'd never guess it from his attire."

It was impossible not to glance at him again after this information. From midthigh up, his clothing was plain indeed—black coat and brown-and-black-patterned waistcoat. All in all, a conservative wardrobe until one came to his legs. The man was wearing some type of native leggings. They were made from an odd tan leather, quite dull, and they were gartered just below the knees with red, white, and black striped sashes. The leggings split in the front over the shoes with brightly embroidered flaps that fell to either side of his feet. And his shoes were the strangest of all, for they had no heels. He seemed to be wearing a type of slipper made of the same soft, dull leather, with beading or embroidery work running from ankle to toe. Yet even heelless, the stranger was quite tall. He had brown hair, and as far as she could tell from half-way across the room, his eyes were dark. Certainly not blue or green. They were heavy-lidded and intelligent. She suppressed a shiver. Intelligent men were so hard to manage.

His arms were crossed, one shoulder propped against the wall, and his gaze was interested. As if they were the exotic ones, not he. His nose was long, with a bump in the middle; his complexion dark, as if he'd lately come from some exotic shore. The bones of his face were raw and prominent: cheeks, nose, and chin jutting in an aggressively masculine way that was nevertheless perversely attractive. His mouth, in contrast, was wide and almost soft, with a sensuous inverted dent in the lower lip. It was the mouth of a man who liked to savor. To linger and taste. A dangerous mouth.

Emeline looked away again. "Who is he?"

Mrs. Conrad stared. "Don't you know?"

"No."

Her hostess was delighted. "Why, my dear, that's Mr. Samuel Hartley! Everyone has been talking about him, though he has only been in London a sennight or so. He's not quite acceptable, because of the . . ." Mrs. Conrad met Emeline's eyes and hastily cut short what she'd been about to say. "*Anyway*. Even with all his wealth, not everyone is happy to meet him."

Emeline stilled as the back of her neck prickled.

Mrs. Conrad continued, oblivious. "I really shouldn't have invited him, but I couldn't help myself. That form, my dear. Simply delicious! Why, if I hadn't asked him, I would never have—" Her flurry of words ended on a startled squeak, for a man had cleared his throat directly behind them.

Emeline hadn't been watching, so she hadn't seen him move, but she knew instinctively who stood so close to them. Slowly she turned her head.

Mocking coffee-brown eyes met her own. "Mrs. Conrad, I'd be grateful if you'd introduce us." His voice had a flat American accent.

Their hostess sucked in her breath at this blunt order, but curiosity won out over indignation. "Lady Emeline, may I introduce Mr. Samuel Hartley. Mr. Hartley, Lady Emeline Gordon."

Emeline sank into a curtsy, only to be presented with a large, tanned hand on rising. She stared for a moment, nonplussed. Surely the man wasn't that unsophisticated? Mrs. Conrad's breathy giggle decided the matter. Gingerly, Emeline touched just her fingertips to his.

To no avail. He embraced her hand with both of his, enveloping her fingers in hard warmth. His nostrils flared just the tiniest bit as she was forced to step forward into the handshake. Was he *scenting* her?

"How do you do?" he asked.

"Well," Emeline retorted. She tried to free her hand but could not, even though Mr. Hartley didn't seem to be gripping her tightly. "Might I have my appendage returned to me now?"

That mouth twitched again. Did he laugh at everyone or just her? "Of course, my lady."

Emeline opened her mouth to make an excuse—any excuse—to leave the dreadful man, but he was too quick for her.

"May I escort you into the garden?"

It really wasn't a question, since he'd already held out his arm, obviously expecting her consent. And what was worse, she gave it. Silently, Emeline laid her fingertips on his coat sleeve. He nodded to Mrs. Conrad and drew Emeline outside in only a matter of minutes, working very neatly for such a gauche man. Emeline squinted up at his profile suspiciously.

He turned his head and caught her look. His own eyes wrinkled at the corners, laughing down at her, although his mouth remained perfectly straight. "We're neighbors, you know."

"What do you mean?"

"I've rented the house next to yours."

Emeline found herself blinking up at him, caught off guard once again—a disagreeable sensation as rare as it was unwanted. She knew the occupants of the town house to the right of hers, but the left had been let out recently. For an entire day the week before, men had been tramping in and out of the open doors, sweating, shouting, and cursing. And they'd carried...

Her eyebrows snapped together. "The pea-green settee."

His mouth curved at one corner. "What?"

"You're the owner of that atrocious pea-green settee, aren't you?"

He bowed. "I confess it."

"With no trace of shame, either, I see." Emeline pursed her lips in disapproval. "Are there really gilt owls carved on the legs?"

"I hadn't noticed."

"*I* had."

"Then I'll not argue the point."

"Humph." She faced forward again.

"I have a favor to ask of you, ma'am." His voice rumbled somewhere above her head.

He'd led her down one of the packed gravel paths of the Conrads' town house garden. It was unimaginatively planted with roses and small, clipped hedges. Sadly, most of the roses had already bloomed, so the whole looked rather plain and forlorn.

"I'd like to hire you."

"*Hire* me?" Emeline inhaled sharply and stopped, forcing him to halt as well and face her. Did this odd man think she was a courtesan of some sort? The insult was outrageous, and in her confusion she found her gaze wandering over his frame, crossing wide shoulders, a pleasingly flat waist, and then dropping to an inappropriate portion of Mr. Hartley's anatomy, which, now that she noticed it, was rather nicely outlined by the black wool breeches he wore under his leggings. She inhaled again, nearly choking, and hastily raised her eyes. But the man either hadn't observed her indiscretion or was much more polite than his attire and manner would lead one to believe.

He continued. "I need a mentor for my sister, Rebecca. Someone to show her the parties and balls."

Emeline cocked her head as she realized that he wanted a chaperone. Well, why hadn't the silly man said so in the first place and saved her all this embarrassment? "I'm afraid that won't be possible."

"Why not?" The words were soft, but there was an edge of command behind them.

Emeline stiffened. "I take only young ladies from the highest ranks of society. I don't believe your sister can meet my standards. I'm sorry."

He watched her for a moment and then looked away.

Although his gaze was on a bench at the end of the path, Emeline doubted very much that he saw it. "Perhaps, then, I can plead another reason for you to take us on."

She stilled. "What is that?"

His eyes looked back at her, and now there was no trace of amusement in them. "I knew Reynaud."

The beating of Emeline's heart was very loud in her ears. Because, of course, Reynaud was her brother. Her brother who had been killed in the massacre of the 28th.

VISIT US ONLINE AT

WWW.HACHETTEBOOKGROUP.COM

FEATURES:

**OPENBOOK BROWSE AND
SEARCH EXCERPTS**

•

AUDIOBOOK EXCERPTS AND PODCASTS

•

AUTHOR ARTICLES AND INTERVIEWS

•

**BESTSELLER AND PUBLISHING
GROUP NEWS**

•

SIGN UP FOR E-NEWSLETTERS

•

**AUTHOR APPEARANCES AND TOUR
INFORMATION**

•

SOCIAL MEDIA FEEDS AND WIDGETS

•

DOWNLOAD FREE APPS

BOOKMARK HACHETTE BOOK GROUP
@ WWW.HACHETTEBOOKGROUP.COM

THE CLUB OF ANGELS

Luis Fernando Verissimo

The club
of
Angels

Translated from the Portuguese by
MARGARET JULL COSTA

A NEW DIRECTIONS BOOK

Published by arrangement with Dr. Ray-Güde Mertin, Literarische Agentur, Germany, and
the Harvill Press, London.

Internal illustrations by Nelly Dimitranova, courtesy of the author and Eastwing

Manufactured in the United States of America
New Directions Books are printed on acid-free paper.
First published by New Directions in a cloth edition in 2002.
Published simultaneously in Canada by Penguin Books Canada Limited.

Library of Congress Cataloging-in-Publication Data

Verissimo, Luis Fernando, 1936-
        [Clube dos anjos. English]
        The club of angels / Luis Fernando Verissimo ; translated from the Portuguese
        by Margaret Jull Costa.
                p. cm.
        ISBN 0-8112-1500-8
                I. Costa, Margaret Jull.   II. Title

        PQ9698.32.E73 C5813 2002
        869.3'42—dc21   2001054673

New Directions Books are published for James Laughlin
by New Directions Publishing Corporation
80 Eighth Avenue, New York 10011

All desire is a desire for death.

A possible Japanese maxim

THE CLUB OF ANGELS

1 *The Meeting*

LUCÍDIO IS NOT ONE OF THE DEVIL'S 117 NAMES, nor did I conjure him up from the depths so that he could punish us. When I first mentioned him to the group, someone said: "You're making this up!", but it's not true, I'm innocent – well, as innocent as an author can be. Mystery stories always consist of tedious searches for the guilty party, when it's obvious that there is only one guilty party. Don't bother glancing at the last page of the book, dear reader, for the name is on the cover: it's the author. In this instance, you might suspect that I am rather more than the mere intellectual author of the crimes described within, that my fingers not only tapped out their lugubrious dance over the keys, but also added the poison to the food and interfered rather more in the plot than they should have done. Such suspicions are based on logic, or, rather, on the peculiar logic of mystery stories: if only one person is left alive at the end, there is your criminal; if two people are left alive, but one is invented, the other one must be the criminal. Lucídio and I are the only survivors of this story, and if I didn't invent him, and as it's highly unlikely that he invented me, he is obviously the guilty one, given that he was the cook and everyone died, in one way or another, from what they ate. If I invented him, then the guilt falls entirely on me. I cannot even allege that if Lucídio is an invention, then the whole story is an invention, and that there are, therefore, no crimes and no criminals. Fiction is not an extenuating circumstance. Imagination is no excuse. We all have murderous thoughts, but only that monster, the author, sets his crimes down on paper and publishes them. I may not have killed my nine confrères and brothers-in-obsession, but I am guilty of the fiction of having killed them. In order to prove that I am innocent of these terrible crimes, I must convince you that I did not invent Lucídio. I also need to convince you that the story is true in order to prove that I am innocent of having created a fiction. An invented crime is far worse than any real crime. A real crime could, after all, be accidental or the product of a moment of passion, but whoever heard of an unpremeditated fictitious crime?

I can give the time, day, month and place of our first meeting. If you want witnesses, go and ask the people at the wine merchant's. They know me; I spend a small fortune on wine in their shop every month. Ask them about Dr Daniel, the fat fellow who likes St-Estèphe wines. I'm not, in fact, a doctor, but I am rich, which is why they deferentially call me "Doctor". When he approached me in their Bordeaux section, in February, exactly nine months ago, they must have noticed the contrast between Lucídio and me. He's short and thin, with a head much too big for his body, but he's always very elegantly dressed in suit and tie. I'm tall and stout, I wear a baggy shirt outside my trousers and have even been known to wear espadrilles to the Ducasse de Paris. The people in the shop must have noticed the disparity between us and commented on it. And they will tell you that the place was empty and that we started talking by the Bordeaux and walked around the entire shop together, and that, by the time we had reached the Chilean wines, we were like old friends. They might recall that I bought a Cahors, which I would never normally buy, on his recommendation. And that we left the shop together. We were seen. Lucídio exists. I swear it. Ask at the wine merchant's.

The people at the shop don't know that, afterwards, we went and had a coffee in the shopping mall and sat down to continue our conversation, since we had so many interests in common. Not that we actually got beyond food and drink during that first encounter. Lucídio moves very discreetly and makes very few gestures. He sits with his back straight and keeps his head almost perfectly still. I don't so much sit down on a chair or at a table as moor there. A difficult process, given the scarcity of tug boats. On that day, before settling safely on the chair and calling for the waiter, I managed to knock over a sugar bowl, almost overturn the table and drop the wine. Poor Lívia, my girlfriend, says that I'm not aware of how much space I take up, and that this comes from my having been a spoiled, fat child. Something to do with being an only child for whom no one ever set any boundaries. Poor Lívia is a psychologist and a nutritionist and has been trying to save me for years now. I'm not so much a lover as a cause. I've had three wives, all three of whom were after my money. Lívia isn't after my money. She wants to be the woman who rescues me, which strikes me as a much more self-interested and frightening ambition. Perhaps that is why I resist marrying her, whereas I put up no resistance at all to marrying the others, even though I knew perfectly well that they didn't love me for my belly. We live separately, but she takes care of my apartment and my clothes and tries, in vain, to take care of my diet too. I am convinced that, if she could, she would limit my food intake to the milk from her breasts and to fibre, lots of fibre. I also talk too loudly and too much, another consequence of a childhood without boundaries. Lívia has persuaded me that the whole tragedy of my life can be put down to the lack of someone who would tell me: "Daniel, stop it!"

I remember that I did nearly all the talking during that first meeting with Lucídio. I told him about our club. I told him the names of all the members, and Lucídio responded to each name with an "Ah" or an "Hm", to show that he was impressed. After all, I did cite nine of the best-known families in the state. And, finally, I told him my name, which also impressed him. Or rather, he made some other polite noise, always maintaining the same, tight little smile. Oddly enough, Lucídio never shows his teeth.

Wait, now that I think of it, he said "I know!" When I gave him my full name, Daniel, plus my family name, he said "I know!" Which only proves, you must be thinking, that the meeting was not pure chance. But he might have recognized me from a photograph. Years before, when Ramos was in charge of our lives, we were often mentioned in the press – in the society pages or in specialist food and drink magazines. He might have recognized us from photographs, all ten of us, from photographs and by reputation. We still met once a month for supper. For ten months of the year, from March to December. We ate at a different member's home each month, and that member was responsible for providing supper. We would be starting a new season in March, and I was in charge of the first supper of the year. But there was a possibility that the season would not even begin. Lucídio asked why.

"The group is falling apart. We've lost our pizzazz."

"How long have these meetings been going on?"

"Twenty-one years. Twenty-two this year."

"Always with the same members?"

"Yes. No. One died and was replaced. But there are always ten members."

"Are you all more or less the same age?"

From the tone of his questions, Lucídio might have been making notes on the table. At the time, however, I didn't notice that interrogational tone. I told him everything. I told him the history of the Beef Stew Club. Lucídio only interrupted his otherwise constant, tight-lipped smile to say "Ah" or "Hm".

We were all about the same age. We were all pretty rich, although our fortunes had fluctuated over the past twenty years. They were all inherited fortunes, subject to the inconstancies of our characters and of the market. Mine had survived three disastrous marriages and a life devoted to strange stories, which I collect, and to graceless idleness, but only because my father pays me not to drag any of the family businesses into my destructive orbit. Apart from Ramos, we were all about the same age and from the same social class. And apart from Samuel and Ramos, we had all grown up together. Pedro, Paulo, Saulo, Marcos, Tiago, João, Abel, and me. From almost daily get-togethers in Alberi's bar during adolescence, and Alberi's beef stew with egg *farofa* and fried banana which, for years, defined our culinary tastes, we had progressed to weekly suppers at different restaurants, then to monthly meetings in our respective homes. And with time and Ramos' lectures, we had refined our tastes. However, Samuel still insisted that nothing in life could compare with a fried banana.

"Does the host always do the cooking?"

"Not necessarily. He can if he wants, or he can serve up food made by someone else. But he is responsible for the quality of the meal. And of the wines."

"So what happened? I don't understand."

"What do you mean, what happened?"

"The pizzazz. You said you'd lost your pizzazz."

"Oh, right. I think it happened when Ramos died . . . because Ramos was the one who died. He was our organizer. He drew up the statutes, had the headed notepaper and the cards printed. He even designed the club's coat of arms. He took it all very seriously. After he died . . ."

"Of AIDS."

"That's right. Everything changed. The final supper of the season last year was terrible. It was as if we were all sick to death of each other's faces. It took place at the Chocolate Kid's apartment, at Tiago's. The meal was excellent, but the supper ended badly. A fight even broke out amongst the women. And that was the last supper of the year, which is always a special occasion. Around Christmas time. I think that in the last two years since Ramos died . . ."

"You've been losing motivation."

"Yes, motivation, oomph, pizzazz."

"Everything but your hunger."

"Everything but our hunger."

The late-night shoppers were beginning to arrive. We ordered two more coffees. As usual, I filled mine with sugar, spilling some in the saucer. I realized that I was recounting not only the slow disintegration of our group, but also the biography of our hunger, what had happened to it and to us over a period of twenty-one years.

In the beginning, it wasn't just the pleasure of eating, drinking and being together that united us. There was a degree of ostentation as well. Once we had exchanged Alberi's beef stew for finer things, our suppers turned into rituals of power, even though we didn't know it at the time. We could afford to eat and drink well, and so we ate and drank only the best and made a point of being seen and heard exercising that privilege. But it wasn't only that either. We weren't just stupid s.o.b.'s. We were different and, at those noisy celebrations of our shared tastes, we revelled in our friendship and our singularity. We had a greater appreciation of life and its pleasures, and what truly united us was the certainty that our hunger represented all the appetites which the world would, one day, arouse in us. We were so voracious, at the start, that anything less than the world would have been tantamount to coitus interruptus. We wanted the world, but we ended up as mere city-bound failures, rolling around in our own shit. But I'm getting ahead of myself. Daniel, stop it! We're still in the café in the shopping mall, and I'm sitting opposite Lucídio, pouring my life out onto the table, along with the sugar.

On the night that Ramos decided to formalize the foundation of the Beef Stew Club – named in honour of our past lives as ignorant gourmands – Marcos, Saulo and myself had just set up our public relations agency, once, that is, I had persuaded my father that my days of idleness were over and that I deserved some financial backing, or at least several years' worth of allowances in advance, in order for me to start my own business. We were full of plans. In no time at all, we would be the stars of the PR world. Marcos with his artistic talents, me with my writing skills and Saulo with his gift for getting on with people, for selling things and for creative flimflam. Paulo had been elected city councillor. He had liberal views which sat uneasily with his bank balance and with having us as friends – he used to call us all damn reactionaries – but he was very bright. We were sure that, within the constraints of the time, he would enjoy a brilliant political career, greatly helped by the fact that he had a brother high up in the national security police. Tiago was beginning to make a name for himself as an architect. Pedro had finally taken over the running of the family firm, after spending a year in Europe with Mara (with whom we were all in love), on a honeymoon that lasted many moons, despite his family's repeated calls for him to come home. João, our clever João, who taught us to invest in the stock market and was our supplier of cigars and jokes, began to earn "obscene" amounts of money, to use Samuel's word. Abel, our kind, sensitive Jesuit, who specialized in grilled meat and fish, had recently left his father's legal practice to open his own. Like Pedro, he too had just got married. At the time, his sense of euphoria was a mixture of the guilt he felt at having broken free from his father's domination, his enthusiasm for the new practice, and the sexual shock of marriage to Norinha. Unbeknown to him, she had already slept with two other members of the group, and had even come on to Samuel once. Abel was the one who would occasionally interrupt our self-celebrations by exclaiming: "Magic moment, everyone, magic moment!", thereby, of course, ruining the magic of the moment. Samuel thought that this need for constant epiphanies was a remnant of Abel's religious past.

Samuel. The best and the worst of us. The one who ate the most, but never got fat. The one who loved us most and most insulted us, and whose favourite word was "bastard" which he used to describe everyone, from the waiter ("Oh, Monsieur Bastard!") to the Pope ("His Bastardness"). He was the most lucid and the most obsessive of us all; he was the last to die, this month, right before my eyes, and the one who suffered the most painful death. And finally, there was Ramos, who convinced us that our hunger was not just physical hunger, that we were enlightened beings, that our voracity was the voracity of a generation, or, at the very least, that we weren't just utter bastards. Ramos – "our Holy Bastard" as Samuel called him – always gave the speeches at our meetings. Everything had started with him. He was the one who had brought a certain solemnity to our ordinary suppers and had formed the club out of "the ten people who are sitting around this table, and only these ten", until death or women did us part. Then he dipped chunks of bread in the wine so that we would all chew together and swallow together, as if making a holy vow of loyalty. It was a ceremony whose eucharistic references Abel found most moving.

In the beginning, Ramos was the only true gourmet of the group. He catechized us and imposed order and style on our hunger. He convinced us that the Beef Stew Club's first act should be finally to renounce Alberi's beef stew as a parameter of gastronomic quality. There was some resistance to this. For years afterwards, whenever he wanted to annoy Ramos, Samuel would defend the virtues of the fried banana. But Samuel would eat anything. And, we suspected, anyone. Ramos taught us that we were practising a unique art, and that gastronomy was a cultural pleasure like no other, for no other brought with it the same philosophical challenge by which appreciation demanded the destruction of the thing appreciated and where veneration and consumption were one; no other art could equal eating as an example of the sensory perception of an art, any art, with the one exception, he thought, of actually stroking Michelangelo's David's butt. He had lived for some years in Paris, and the trips to Europe were his idea, with visits to famous restaurants and vineyards, which he himself organized with, according to Samuel, "typical poovy meticulousness". And he was the one who warned us that the moment we allowed women to join the club, everything would go wrong. It had to be those ten people and only those ten, otherwise the charm would be lost and so would we. He really was something of a prophet.

I don't know why I told all this to someone I barely knew. Perhaps because I had never before had such an attentive listener. Lucídio sat utterly still, his hands folded on the table, like a neat parcel which he only unwrapped in order to take another sip of coffee. The tight-lipped smile never left his face. It was getting late. I needed to go home and phone Lívia, who worries about my lone visits to the shopping mall. I lived close enough to walk there and back, and she used to say that, given my lumbering bulk, the only reason

I didn't get mugged in the street was because muggers feared that such an easy target could only be some kind of set-up. I invited Lucídio up to my apartment. I wanted to show him my wines. And I wanted to continue telling him our story. I don't know why. At our Christmas supper, Samuel had quoted a phrase in Latin, from *The Satyricon*. Everything ends in shipwreck. Or something like that. Lucídio had found me in mid-shipwreck, when I was almost under, with only my mouth still above water, full of the desperate garrulousness of the dying. I needed to tell someone about the tragedy of my life and of my friends' lives and I had finally found an attentive listener. Someone who would not recommend that I eat more fibre.

Only much later did it occur to me: How did Lucídio know that Ramos had died of AIDS? Was it simply a hunch? Had he known Ramos and the cause of his death and inadvertently let this information slip? Or was he giving me the first clue as to why he had arrived in our lives in order to poison us?

2 The Fish Scale

SOMETIMES I THINK THAT I DID WITH MY apartment what I would like to do with my brain. I got rid of all the clutter. The apartment consists of two vast empty rooms that look as if they were ready for a ball that never actually begins. On the bare parquet floor, against the white walls, are two long white sofas forming a right angle, and at the enormous windows hang beige curtains, my one and only concession to colour. Or, rather, to Lívia. When the group suppers are, or were, held in my apartment, I would place the big table in the middle of the larger of the two rooms. The table remains dismantled for the rest of the year, the chairs piled up out on the balcony, and I eat at the kitchen table. Lucídio, still with that half-smile on his lips, examined everything and said nothing. The only possible response to those two great empty rooms.

On the other hand, in my study, with its walls panelled

in wood from top to bottom, I have done my best to imitate the home of a pair of squirrels remembered from an illustration in a children's book and which, all my life, has been my ideal of warm domesticity. It is just as if I too lived inside a tree trunk, surviving on nuts stored up for the winter, and I know that the reason all my marriages went wrong was because none of my three wives understood that their role in my life was that of Mrs Squirrel. Even the lampstands are made of knotty wood, just like those of Mr and Mrs Squirrel. Everything I love is in this room, in a jumble that has resisted Lívia's frequent civilizing incursions. Newspapers and magazines scattered about the floor. My brandy glasses. My bottles of cognac and armagnac. My cigars. In short, my winter store of nuts. Oh, and my computer on which I write the nonsense that so alarms Lívia – like my endless tale of the Lesbian Siamese twins – and on which I am typing these words while I await Mr Spector's second visit. But I'm getting ahead of myself again. My tree trunk is also home to my television, my video recorder, my tapes, my sound system, my CDs, everything I need to withstand the siege of snow and wolves. And a few books. Just a few, on gastronomy and wines, and some unread volumes about advertising that date from the time when, with Marcos and Saulo, I opened the agency and closed it after a mere eight months. Ramos was the only one in the group who read a lot. Tiago would read and re-read the detective novels that filled his house and of which he was a compulsive buyer. Once Paulo had given up Marxism and abandoned politics to work at Pedro's company, he stopped reading altogether. I don't know where Samuel got his culture from, or where he acquired the erudition he deployed in his insults, like the time he compared Abel's suffering after his divorce from Norinha with that of Philoctetes, whose gaping, suppurating wound so disgusted his companions on the Odyssey that they abandoned him on a desert island. "Keep your stench to yourself, Philoctetes," Samuel would say to the snivelling Abel, while we did our best to console him. Yet it was to Samuel, during long nights in bars or walking the streets, that Abel poured out his hurt and anger until he had managed to purge Norinha from his life. "There's nothing quite like the confessional, even for a lapsed Catholic," Samuel said. I never saw Samuel with a book. Just as Ramos never gave us the slightest glimpse of his life as a homosexual, so Samuel concealed his intellectual life from the rest of the gang.

In my study, the only decorations are Marcos' paintings, given to me by Saulo. Marcos' horrible paintings are everywhere. Instead of shelves there are two temperature-controlled wine stores, which I had painted with imitation veins and knots, as would befit a squirrel's wine store. I placed the bottle of Cahors I bought from the wine merchant's in one of these and chose an Ormes de Pez '82 to drink right away, despite Lucídio's protests. Just as I was opening the wine, the phone rang. Lívia. I had forgotten to ring her to report on my day.

"What have you been up to?"

"Nothing."

"This is the third time I've phoned. Where were you?"

"I got chatting to someone at the shopping mall. I've got a friend with me at the moment."

"Not Samuel!"

Lívia had a horror of Samuel. He was the only one who regularly visited the other club members between suppers and tried to keep the group together and our friendship alive, even though his somewhat gloomy figure only served to remind us of what time had done to us all, and even though his sole concern during those visits was to speak ill of everyone else. Samuel still had the appetite of a young man, but with the passing of time he had grown ever thinner. His neglected teeth and the dark circles under his eyes gave him a decadent air which he positively flaunted, as if forcing us to face up to our own reality. Samuel's body was bowed by our failures, his face etched with all our broken promises. Twenty years before, none of us had had the success with women enjoyed by the misogynistic Samuel, with his deep-set eyes and gruff voice. Not even Paulo, who, according to Samuel, referred to his own prick as the Vote Catcher and used it to recruit female voters of every age and type, anywhere and at any time, the bastard. Once, we had had to bring our collective influence to bear in order to get Samuel out of jail because a woman he had beaten up turned out to have friends in high places and had complained to the police. Pedro had argued that we should just leave him there, to teach him a lesson. Perhaps he knew that Samuel had done what everyone else in the group, with the exception of Ramos, had wanted to do: to screw Pedro's wife, Mara, she of the white skin and the long, straight hair. We vetoed the idea of any kind of exemplary punishment for Samuel. The Beef Stew Club looked after its own. It wasn't just a question of getting Samuel off the hook. It was a matter of testing our influence in the city. Samuel had already told me that he was impotent and that even beating up a woman no longer excited him. He even brandished his impotence as a condemnation of all the experiences we had missed out on in the past twenty years. "I did it for you, you bastards. My flaccid cock is the Christ of this group, dead on the cross. It became impotent for your sakes!" Lívia was convinced that Samuel was a malignant worm who wanted to grab me by the ankle and drag me into his subterranean labyrinth, close to hell and far from her. "He even looks like a worm," she used to say.

"No, Lívia, it's not Samuel."

"So who is it, Zi?"

Zi is short for Zinho which is short for Danielzinho. I have found my Mrs Squirrel.

18

"No one you've met."

I almost told her that the person with me was, in fact, an anti-Samuel. A new friend who was polite, kind and elegant, who was also, I presumed, possessed of a good set of teeth, and was no threat to anyone.

Little did I know.

That was the night, towards the end of February last year, when Lucídio showed me the fish scale. A small laminated fish scale, about two centimetres long, with an ideogram painted in white on the plastic, in contrast to the red of the fish scale itself. He removed it carefully from his wallet. I don't know if he always carried the fish scale about in his wallet or if he had rehearsed that moment. Lucídio held the fish scale before my eyes and said:

"I am the only man in the Western World who has one of these."

"What is it?"

"It's a scale from a fugu fish. I belong to a secret society that meets once a year in Kushimoto in Japan to eat fresh fugu. I and a Chinese man are the only non-Japanese members of the society. Or, rather, we were. He died at the last meeting."

"How?"

"He was poisoned. The fugu is a poisonous fish. If it's not prepared by an expert, trained to cut up the fish in a certain way, it can kill within minutes. The Chinese man took eight minutes to die. It was a horrible death."

I smiled. At least, I think I did. Just to see if this was all a joke. But Lucídio's half-smile had vanished. It was no joke. He went on:

"It takes three years to train a fugu chef. Every year, the society sets a kind of final examination to find out who will receive the title of fugu master. It's always a class of ten students. Each student uses a volunteer to taste the fresh fugu he has prepared for the examination. If the fish has been badly prepared, the volunteer dies in a matter of minutes."

"And what happens to the student?"

"He repeats the year."

"And the society is made up of these volunteers . . . "

"Exactly. A society of ten members. Since the failure rate on the course is thirty per cent, and an average of three volunteers dies at each examination, the membership is constantly being renewed. But there's a waiting list of people wanting to join the society. I had to wait seven years."

"Does the volunteer gain anything from taking part in the test?"

He smiled. This time it was almost a proper smile.

"I wouldn't have expected such a question from you . . . "

"So why . . . "

"There is nothing in the world that can compare with the taste of raw fugu, Daniel. And the pleasure of eating fugu is tripled by the risk you run of dying. The prospect of dying at any moment, in seconds, produces a chemical reaction that heightens the flavour of the fugu. In Japan, anyone can eat fugu prepared by specialist chefs and with minimal risk. But only in Kushimoto, once a year, can you eat fugu with a real possibility of not surviving the first mouthful. There is no comparable gastronomic experience. That is why it is a secret society. It is the most exclusive gourmet club in the world. Officially, the examination doesn't even exist."

"How did you find out about it?"

"I happened to say to a Japanese friend that I had tried everything there was to try and that I thought it highly unlikely that I would ever have a new gastronomic experience. And he said: 'Do you want to bet?' Oddly enough, we too met by chance in a wine merchant's."

"And he was a member of the society."

"Yes. By a stroke of irony, I took his place. He died happy. He had two fish scales."

"Two?"

"Anyone who survives ten meetings, that is, ten years, is given a fish scale like this. He had survived twenty years of fugu tempered with fear."

"What's that written on the plastic?"

"It's a Japanese ideogram which can be translated in various ways. It could be: 'All desire is a desire for death' or 'Hunger is a deaf coachman' or 'The sage and the wise man eat with the same teeth'."

"All that in one ideogram?"

"You know what these orientals are like."

"How many of these examinations have you taken part in?"

"Seventeen."

Lucídio leaned forward as if to whisper a secret.

"And it gives me a bigger hard-on every time."

We drank two bottles of Ormes de Pez and several glasses of cognac, but Lucídio did not for an instant relax his rigid pose or lose his solicitous half-smile, he did not even loosen his tie. When I said I was hungry, he offered to make an omelette and he made an omelette the like of which I had not tasted in a long time. Browned to perfection on the outside, moist inside, sliding on to the plate with the consistency of the nectar of the gods. He had learned how to cook omelettes in Paris, where he had lived for some time. We talked for more than an hour about omelettes and their secrets. I asked what his speciality was, apart from omelettes, and he said that he specialized in classic French cuisine and that, amongst other things, he made a very respectable *gigot d'agneau*. I can't remember now whether I mentioned to him then that, coincidentally, this was my favourite dish. Now I know it was no coincidence. I told him I was worried about the Beef Stew Club's first supper of the season the following month, for which I was responsible. It was an important supper. This was the year that the Club would either emerge from its

22

post-Ramos depression or go under. Following the disastrous Christmas supper at Tiago's house, it might even be difficult to get all ten of us round the same table again, let alone the women. In twenty-one years, the ten members had had exactly twenty wives or partners between us, including my three and Gisela, the adolescent girl whom Abel had adopted after his divorce from Norinha, and the two women Pedro had been with since Mara, including the one who burst into hysterical tears when she was introduced to Samuel, whom she had obviously met before. At that moment, as far as I knew, six of the members had partners. Lívia refused to have anything to do with the suppers and had often asked me to leave the group and use that rupture as a starting point for going on a proper diet and attempting to rebuild my life. If I wanted to, I could go back to work or publish my strange stories.

Lucídio offered to help me with the supper. I accepted, largely because I wanted to introduce him to the others. He said that he would prefer to remain anonymous. He would not be a member of the Club. He would stay in the kitchen. I suggested that he make the *gigot d'agneau*, but he said something which, at the time, I found intriguing.

"No, I'll leave that to the end."

And he went round the kitchen making an inventory of my pots and pans.

*

23

Five minutes after Lucídio had left my apartment, refusing my offer to call him a taxi ("I live nearby") and shaking my hand, at the same time time performing a brief, formal bow, feet together, despite the degree of intimacy which I felt we had already achieved, Lívia phoned. She always phoned late at night to find out what I had eaten and if the wolves had been kept at bay.

"Who was it you had with you, Zi?"

"I'll tell you later."

"Was it a woman?"

"No, it wasn't. I'll tell you about it later."

Who was it exactly who had been there?

Before leaving, and after noting down my telephone number, Lucídio had asked if he could give me a piece of advice. About the supper.

"Yes, of course, go ahead."

"Don't invite the women."

3 The First Supper

THE FOLLOWING DAY, THERE WAS A PHONE CALL from Lucídio. He started explaining who he was, "I made you an omel..." and I broke in. "Yes, yes, how are you?" He said that he was already gathering the ingredients for the supper, even though it was still two weeks off. He had already decided what he would make. *Boeuf bourguignon.*

"Oh, Abel will enjoy that. It's his favourite."

"Yes, I know."

Did he say: "Yes, I know"? I don't know. He asked if I had in my kitchen a particular utensil he would need, and I said I did. Then he asked what arrangements we made about serving the food, would there be anyone there to help? I said that my stepmother would send over some of her own staff. He said he would rather work alone. He would cook and I would serve. I said: "Fine." I said that

I wanted to pay for the ingredients he was buying. He said: "We'll settle up later." And then:

"Have you spoken to the others yet?"

"Not yet."

"Begin with Abel."

That was all I needed. Another Lívia ordering me around and trying to organize my life. But I confess that I rather liked him meddling. He was an interesting man, despite his formality and that awful fixed smile. I could hardly wait to introduce him to the others and see their reaction to his story about the fugu and the secret society. What other stories would he have up his sleeve? I love weird stories. The more incredible they are, the more likely I am to believe them. And it would be good not to have to face that first supper of the new season alone, and to have a novelty to present to my fellow members. Perhaps this was exactly what we were lacking. Perhaps Lucídio would sort out all our lives. Yes, a man who would risk his life for the taste of a deadly fish was precisely what we needed to restore our sense of unity and to haul us out of that spiral of bitterness and mutual recrimination into which Ramos' death had plunged us. After all, we were gastronomes, not a cursed generation or a religious order riven by doubt. Even if he had invented that story about the fugu, it was an inspiration. And if you could judge someone by an omelette alone, the supper would be excellent.

*

26

I began with Abel, who, as I had expected, showed little enthusiasm for the Club's continued existence.

"I don't know, Daniel, perhaps we should give it a rest for this year."

"Abel . . ."

"That last supper was excruciating."

"The main course will be *boeuf bourguignon*, Abel."

"Oh, really?"

He didn't need much more persuading.

"Will you make that dessert of yours? The banana one?"

"Yes, Abel."

"The usual time, then, nine o'clock?"

"The usual time."

Then I phoned João, who also proved reluctant. He might come or he might not. He was actually thinking of leaving the Club. The Christmas supper had demonstrated to him that it was time to stop. "Otherwise, I'm going to end up punching Paulo." In twenty-one years, the only time João had missed a Club supper was when he had had to go into hiding in order to escape some people whose money he had lost and who wanted to kill him, and who thus, according to Samuel, revealed an appalling ignorance of the capitalist ethos. Samuel suggested to the creditors that rather than killing João, they should simply break several of his bones, apart from those he needed in order to recover their money. And he even drew up a list of the bones João would not require in order to earn enough money to pay them all off. But he was also the one who helped João the most, going so far as to conceal him in his own apartment from the furious creditors. From there he would bring us periodic news of the asylum seeker. "He's in excellent spirits. I can't even persuade him to commit suicide." And he concluded with one of his obscure quotations: "One of man's greatest self-delusions is the existence of remorse."

"Why not give it another go, João," I said. "After all, we have been together twenty-one years."

"I don't know . . . "

From his place of asylum in Samuel's apartment, João eventually reached an agreement with his creditors. But he didn't reform. He had been a liar ever since he was a boy and he relied on his inborn talent to elicit money from people and then come up with an explanation as to why the money had disappeared. That had been only the first of the many difficult times that had destroyed his marriage and his good name, but not his good humour and his capacity for telling jokes. At our Christmas supper, Paulo had yelled out: "Oh, no!" when João had launched into yet another joke, and Paulo had accused him of being the perfect stereotype of the Brazilian elite, someone who strolls through the ruins, even the ruins of his own life, brandishing his own inconsequentiality as a safe-conduct pass, as a prior absolution, and he said that to tell one more of his jokes at that precise moment would be

28

simply monstrous. João clearly wasn't contrite, but he might have the decency to stop telling jokes. To which João responded that at least he wasn't a communist who had ended up licking the boots of Pedro, our industrialist, and defending Pedro's company against strikers as vehemently as he had once attacked capitalism during his time as a deputy. When Abel had attempted to calm them down, he too got a mouthful from Paulo, who said he wasn't prepared to put up with his saintly tones for another minute, especially given that Abel was not only known to be one of the wiliest and most scoundrelly lawyers in the whole of Rio state, but was also a paedophile . . . The argument had ended with Gisela chasing after Paulo in order to rub his nose in her ID card proving that she was eighteen years old. In the end, Samuel quoted a Latin phrase: "*Si recte calculam ponas, ubique naufragium est*", which, seeing everyone's aggressively expectant faces, impatient with his damned erudition, he had translated as: "However accurate your calculations, everything ends in shipwreck. Petronius, *The Satyricon*." After a long silence, Paulo said: "Oh, go fuck yourself, Samuel." And Samuel had raised his glass and said: "And a Happy Christmas to you too, Paulo." The supper had ended with Paulo's new wife and the young Gisela almost coming to blows.

"Nine o'clock, then, João."

"We'll see."

*

29

By the end of that dreadful Christmas supper, only myself, Paulo, his wife and Tiago, our host, were left, all of us very drunk, conducting a post-mortem of the night's events. Paulo had taken my face in his hands and said:

"What have I done with my life, Daniel? What have I done with my life?"

I could barely keep my eyes open. Paulo's wife was asleep on the sofa. Tiago, the Chocolate Kid – the only member of the group who was nearly as fat as me – was dancing, clasping a bottle of cognac to his chest.

"I'm just a pile of shit," shouted Paulo, still clutching my face in his hands.

"No, *I'm* a pile of shit!" Tiago shouted. "Do you know what I am?"

"No, *I'm* a pile of shit!" insisted Paulo.

"Do you know what I am? A complete failure."

"Look, *I'm* a pile of shit!"

"I'm a failed pile of shit. I'm a bigger pile of shit than you are."

Paulo had let go of my face in order to grab Tiago's head.

"Look, I'm a bigger pile of shit than any of you!"

"Why?"

"Because I was better than all of you. I was the best! It didn't take much for you lot to become piles of shit, but I had a long way to fall. That's why I'm the biggest pile of shit of the whole lot of you."

Tiago then clasped my face in his hands and asked my opinion, having first thrown the cognac bottle to the floor.

"Daniel, who do you think is the biggest pile of shit?"

But I was in no condition to make an objective judgement. We were all piles of shit. Years before, there had been a rumour that Paulo had given the security police the names and addresses of colleagues of his in hiding. We had never attempted to find out the truth. The Beef Stew Club looks after its own.

To my surprise, everyone came to the first supper of the new season. Lucídio had asked me for everyone's address and had sent each member a copy of the menu, which he had tastefully produced on a computer and decorated with an old-fashioned vignette, beneath which was a sentence declaring that the supper would be for men only. We hadn't done anything so fancy since Ramos' death. For two weeks, Lucídio came in and out of my apartment, always very proper and very elegant, preparing everything for the big night, showing a devotion to detail that bordered on the obsessive, except that it was a discreet, methodical obsession. Luckily, none of his visits coincided with one of Lívia's visits of inspection. In fact, when I think about it, Lívia has never once seen Lucídio. On the day of the supper, he arrived at seven in the morning and spent all day in the kitchen, which, in obedience with his instructions, I would enter only once, in order to prepare my banana dessert. That was when I saw that he was wearing a huge, almost ankle-length apron and a proper chef's hat. And a tie, of course.

The first to arrive was André, who had taken Ramos' place in the Club. He owned a pharmaceutical company and was possibly the richest of us all, given João's latest financial setbacks and the near-bankruptcy of Pedro's firm. Despite the two years he had been a member of the Club, he was still not properly integrated into the group and had a certain terror of Paulo's verbosity, of Samuel's aggression and of the group's growing tendency towards chaos. He had been proposed as a member by Saulo, who was the public relations officer for his company, and he had had us over for supper at his mansion twice, serving *paella*, his speciality, on both occasions. He was a shy, refined man, much older than the rest of us. The skin on his wife's face was taut from too much plastic surgery, and, at the Christmas supper, she had reacted indignantly to a remark Samuel made to her husband, until André explained that "bastard" was a term of affection. Samuel was using "bastard" in the good sense of the word. Poor André had joined the group hoping to find the pleasant company of civilized people, "*le crème de le crème*" as his wife had said when she first met us, getting the definite article wrong, and he had found himself instead at an endless private party full of resentful guests, watched anxiously

32

by Saulo, who worried about the repercussions our eccentricities might have on their business relationship. I don't know why André didn't just leave the group. Not even the food made up for his evident discomfort in our midst, for the suppers got progressively worse as our misunderstandings grew. But then, as Saulo put it, one could hardly expect good critical sense from someone whose culinary benchmark was *paella*.

"I liked the printed menu," André said.

Samuel arrived shortly afterwards, brandishing the same menu.

"Whose kitsch idea was this? It's precisely the sort of thing Ramos would have done."

By coincidence, João and Paulo arrived at the same time. They obviously hadn't spoken to each other in the lift. João stayed in the living room, and Paulo went into my study. He didn't want to talk to anyone. Tiago was also in a gloomy mood and slumped down on one of the sofas. Saulo and Marcos turned up together as usual and Saulo warned me that he might have to leave early. Abel's first question was to ask if Paulo had arrived, because he wanted to steer well clear of him. He said he was only there for my sake, because it was my supper, but he was seriously thinking of leaving the group. The last to arrive was Pedro, preceded by the smell of his shaving lotion. He lived with his mother, and we suspected that his mother, Dona Nina, still gave him his daily bath. When Pedro came in, some of the group

33

were in the study, watching television in silence, and the others were sprawled on the white sofas in the living room, sad and still, as if resigned to the fact that no one would ask them to dance. If I had to choose a picture to sum up the melancholy end of the Beef Stew Club, that would be it. Only André and I were talking, he out of nervousness and me out of politeness or compulsion. Once Pedro was there, I called everyone into the living room and went to get the champagne. In the kitchen, Lucídio indicated the large tray of canapés he had prepared and ordered me to come back for it once I had served the champagne. In the living room, we gave our usual, but this time somewhat constrained toasts. First, "To hunger", then "To Ramos". Samuel proposed a third, "To our friendship", which was seconded only by André, until he realized that the remark was intended to be ironic. I went to fetch the tray of canapés and offered them to each guest. Paulo asked who was preparing the meal, since there were some very promising smells issuing from the kitchen. I started to say that it was a surprise, but I stopped because, at that moment, I caught sight of João's face. João had just gulped down one of Lucídio's canapés.

To say that his face lit up would be a literary cliché, but João's face did exactly that. He blushed with pleasure. Today, when I think of that first supper and of its consequences, that is the moment I remember most clearly. I was moved by João's emotion, and it still moves me now. For the first time in many years, I had rediscovered an emotion, that of taking pleasure in the pleasure of a friend, and I thought: we can still outwit time, this group can still be saved, I can still be saved. Not everything, after all, ends in shipwreck. I don't know if João was any more of a son-of-a-bitch than the rest of us. That depends on subjective criteria that change with each generation. At that moment, I thought of the João of twenty-one years before, when he had not yet learned that the effect of jokes was lost if he started laughing before the end, with the rest of us round the table hitting him to try and halt his fit of laughter and the whole restaurant bursting into applause when he finally managed to get out the punchline: "No, my cassock isn't made of bronze!" I looked at Abel. Poor Abel. At that moment, he was in such ecstasy that, like João, he couldn't speak. It was Pedro who said: "This canapé's delicious!" followed by approving "ums" and "ahs" from everyone else. I tried one. It was made from grated onion and cheese, but there must have been more to it than that. Whatever it was, I then understood the reason for João's glowing face and Abel's beatific expression. When Abel finally managed to speak, it was to say: "Magic moment, everyone, magic moment!"

The whole supper was marvellous. The canapés were followed by artichoke hearts *à la vinaigrette*. And when I brought in the *boeuf bourguignon* from the kitchen, provoking a "My God" from Abel when he saw it, I was received by an enthusiastic clamour from around the table. They wanted to know who the mysterious chef was. I told them about Lucídio, or the little I knew. Our meeting at the wine merchant's. His perfect omelette, which had led me to accept his offer to cook for the group. And his story of the fugu and the secret society. Someone said: "The guy doesn't exist, you're making this up!" Paulo said that he had read something about such a society, but only in a novel. "It's not true," said Pedro, his mouth full of meat. "He's kidding you." Tiago said that Lucídio might well be a con artist, he could even be an invention of mine, but he was a great cook. Marcos said: "The man's a genius!" and insisted that I bring him out from the kitchen to prove that he existed and to receive the group's applause. "Calm down," I said, having absolutely no intention of leaving my place without first finishing the best *boeuf bourguignon* I had ever tasted in my life. Abel was chewing with his eyes closed. He said again: "My God!" and when he had finished eating, he declared solemnly, provoking loud laughter: "Now I can die." The loudest laughter came from Paulo. The group was reconciled. Lucídio had dragged us back from the brink.

In the kitchen, Lucídio told me that there was just enough *boeuf bourguignon* left for one person and for one person only. I passed the information on. Did anyone want seconds? Some didn't even reply, they just groaned, to indicate that enough was enough. But Abel said:

"I can't resist. I want more."

And I brought the final helping of *boeuf bourguignon* from the kitchen and set it down in front of him, to applause from the other guests. Abel emptied the plate in seconds.

I hadn't stinted on my Bordeaux for that special supper. When I brought in the dessert, with the announcement that our chef would soon make his appearance, there was an almost palpable halo of pleasure hovering over the group round the table. My banana dessert did not disappoint and was extravagantly praised. "What a meal!" exclaimed Marcos, and João got up from his chair to plant a kiss on the top of my head. "What a shame Ramos isn't here," said Abel, with tears in his eyes, and everyone agreed. I served the coffee as well as the cigars and cognac. This had traditionally been Ramos' moment, the moment when he would always get to his feet in order to make a speech, with a glass of cognac in one hand and a cigar in the other, which he waved about theatrically. After his death, no one had replaced him as orator in that moment of plenitude, which had never again been the same. Once, ten years before, Ramos had got to his feet and stood for a long time, gazing round at us affectionately before speaking. He looked at us one by one, as if bestowing a blessing on us. Then he said: "Hold on to this moment. One day, we will remember it and we will say: 'It was our best moment.' We will compare it with other moments in our lives and we will say that no moment was ever again quite like this one. We will sate our appetites again, of course, because that is the blessed nature of appetite. It isn't every day that we want to see a syrupy Van Gogh or hear a piquant fugue by Bach, or make love to a succulent woman, but every day we want to eat; hunger is the recurring desire, the only recurring desire, for sight, sound, sex and power all come to an end, but hunger goes on, and while one might weary of Ravel for ever, one could only ever weary of ravioli for, at most, a day." He may have said "Pachelbel" and "béchamel" rather than "Ravel" and "ravioli", I'm quoting from memory. Ramos: "But even if we do sate our appetites as we have now, we will never be sated in the same way as we are now, replete with our own virtues and our pleasure in friendship, food, life – and cognac." Then he had raised his glass and made everyone else do the same. "Gentlemen, rejoice! We are at our peak." Everyone drank. Then he said: "Gentlemen, weep. Our decline has just begun." And we all drank again, feeling jollier than ever. On that night, it was five o'clock in the morning by the time we left the table.

Abel got to his feet. For the first time since Ramos' death, someone was about to make a speech while we drank our cognac.

"I just have one thing to say about your supper, Daniel."
We all waited expectantly. Abel emphasized each syllable:
"It was fucking marvellous!"

Everyone applauded. André was moved. We had recovered our fascination in his eyes. Now this was more like the Beef Stew Club he had heard so much about. Cognac glasses were raised to Abel. In a way, he had echoed Ramos' "Discourse on Plenitude". We might not have reconquered our peak, ten years after Ramos' blessing, but we had come close, close to our best moment, close to our lost lives, close to Ramos. That was what, in a nutshell, Abel had said. Poor Abel. The first to die, just as in the Bible.

Months later, after the sixth death, after the July wake, I had reminded Samuel of the phrase Lucídio had come out with when he finally made his triumphal appearance in the dining room that night, to cheers from the group. João had got up from his chair, knelt down in front of Lucídio and asked to kiss his hand. And Lucídio had said:

"'Let me wipe it first; it smells of mortality.'"
"It was a quotation," said Samuel. "From *King Lear*."
Damn Samuel.

4 *The Discourse on Sexual Desire*

MY STEPMOTHER ALWAYS PROVIDES ME WITH servants whenever I need them. I know that she and Lívia meet periodically to discuss my life. She has a kind of horror of being around me – I think it's my sandals that do it – and prefers to play her part from a distance, detailing staff from her cleaning and maintenance platoon to help me out as necessary. We had agreed that she would send round some people to wash the dishes, clean the kitchen and tidy up the apartment on the morning after the supper. I was dredged up from the depths of sleep by the buzzing of the intercom and brought slowly to the surface like a recalcitrant fish. I was still groggy after opening the door to two startled young women who did their best not to stare at my gaping underpants, when the phone rang. It was Lívia wanting to know how the supper had gone.

"Wonderful. Absolutely marvellous. The best *boeuf bourguignon* I've ever tasted."

I told her how well everything had turned out. The atmosphere. The reconciliations. The hit Lucídio had made with the group. The talking into the small hours. The general air of animation. All this greatly disappointed Lívia, who glumly hung up the phone. Her prayers had not been answered. The Beef Stew Club had acquired a new lease of life and would continue.

I was just getting ready to plunge back into sleep when the phone rang again. It was Tiago. He had just heard the news from Gisela. Abel was dead.

We were all at the wake, apart from André. Gisela was standing weeping in the middle of a bunch of strange women. Presumably her family. We didn't know where Abel had found Gisela. We didn't know anything about her. She had never made much of an impression on us and treated us with a certain disdain, shocking us on one occasion by bringing along to one of our suppers a covered plate containing a steak *a la milanesa* and mashed potatoes, saying that she was fed up with pretentious food. I glanced round for Abel's parents, but I couldn't see them. Abel had argued with his father when he had left the old man's practice, and his mother had never forgiven him for leaving the church. Norinha was there, clinging to the son she had had with Abel. Her son is only slightly younger than Gisela.

Abel's six brothers were seated in various parts of the chapel. Not one of them came over to us. Samuel seemed even more sombre than usual. As always, he had taken care of everything. When Ramos was dying, even we, accustomed to Samuel's contradictions and to his cruelty, had been shocked by his insensitivity. "I'm not visiting a queer," he had said, to explain why he hadn't gone to see Ramos in the hospital, on the last day of his life. Yet he was the one who had arranged Ramos' funeral, and grief had made the dark shadows under his eyes and the lines on his face even more pronounced. When I started testing out theories about the death of the whole group, it even occurred to me that Samuel had been left to last so as to take care of the funerals and to register the loss of each one on his face, as on an ancient papyrus.

"Was it his heart?" I asked.

"I think so," said Samuel. "He must have had a problem already, but never told us. Lolita over there says he started feeling ill around dawn and then was horribly sick. He didn't want her to call a doctor. I bet you he died on top of her, the bastard."

"It couldn't have been the food," said Saulo. "We all ate the same, and I didn't feel a thing. Did any of you?"

No one had felt anything. It was true that no one had eaten as much as Abel, and no one had slept with Gisela afterwards. It must have been his heart. Nevertheless, I went looking for a phone and called André. No, he hadn't

42

felt anything either. He didn't know Abel had died, no one had told him, how unfortunate, he would try to be there for the funeral later that afternoon. I said it wasn't necessary, the group was well represented. He said he would come anyway. Then he asked:

"Will next month's supper still go ahead?"

The previous night, we had agreed that André should be the following month's host. He had suggested that Lucídio should again make the supper. Or was that Lucídio's suggestion? Whoever it was who came up with it, the idea was received with enthusiasm by the group, especially by poor Abel.

"Oh yes," I replied.

In twenty-one years, we had never cancelled a supper because of a death. Not even for the death of my mother. Not even for Ramos. At the first supper held after Ramos' death, his place was set at the table, and I recited the "Discourse on Sexual Desire" – or what I remembered of it – which he had delivered at the truffle supper. And ever since then we had drunk the champagne toasts we always drank before each supper, toasting hunger, as always, and Ramos too. Yes, the second supper cooked by Lucídio would go ahead, and a toast to poor Abel would be added to the ritual of the newly resuscitated group.

I rejoined the other members at the wake. I told them that André was fine and then, just for the sake of saying something, asked if anything had happened. I'm no good at keeping quiet. João said that, apart from Abel leaping out of the coffin, dancing a few tango steps around the chapel before lying down again, no, nothing had happened at all. From behind her family guard, Gisela was pointing at us. I heard her say:

"It was at that fat guy's house."

Only Samuel and I stayed until the end of the wake. The others left and returned when it was time for the funeral. About mid-afternoon, Lívia arrived to see if I was all right and if I needed anything. She left again having looked neither at the dead man nor at Samuel. Then, suddenly, my heart gave a flutter. Mara appeared. She kissed me on both cheeks and ignored Samuel. The last time I had seen her was when Ramos had died. She grew lovelier with each funeral. I followed her out of the chapel and she asked me about the man standing next to me, and only then did I realize that she hadn't even recognized Samuel.

"Oh, no one you know," I said.

"Did you see that?" said Samuel afterwards. "She pretended not to have noticed me."

When it was time for the funeral, Abel's father and mother appeared and stood to attention next to the coffin. A priest was about to speak. Gisela was standing with her heels together and her arms out, like a ballerina, supported

44

by the presumed women of her family. Norinha stood behind her son, her hands resting on his shoulders. I guessed that the priest was an old friend of the family. He said that Abel's priestly vocation had been lost to the Church, but that at that very moment, his doubtless contrite spirit was returning to it. Abel's mother nodded in confirmation. Poor Abel.

When she walked past us, her arms about her son, Norinha did not even look at us. Gisela glared at us angrily. The Beef Stew Club has left a long trail of resentful women behind it. We have ruined a number of marriages, but this was the first time we had killed someone's husband at the supper table.

For two weeks, I heard nothing from Lucídio. I had given his number to André, so that they could arrange the next supper. It would be a *paella*, that much had been agreed on the night of the first supper, but it would be a *paella* such as had never been seen in Spain or in the Western World. According to Lucídio, his recipe came from an island in the Indian Ocean that had been colonized by the Spanish, and where *paella* had evolved quite differently and had ended up utterly unlike the original, the difference being based largely on the type of garlic used and a kind of spice, a lemon-flavoured grass found only on the island. Luckily, Lucídio had some of that spice, as well as plenty of the giant garlic he needed and which now only grows in East Africa. When, after two weeks, he phoned me, I asked jokingly if any of the ingredients were poisonous, like the fugu. Lucídio did not reply to my question, but said instead:

"I was so sorry to hear about Abel."

"I was only joking."

"It was his heart, wasn't it? That's what André told me."

"Apparently. But you know what it's like, a young wife and . . ."

"I wanted to ask you a favour."

Lucídio has no sense of humour. His smile is permanent, but his lips never part. What favour? He would prefer it if that second supper could take place in my apartment. Things were obviously going to be difficult at André's house. His wife would interfere. She had already made it clear to her husband that she would not hand over her kitchen to Lucídio and she had demanded that she be allowed to supervise his activities, with a right to veto. Lucídio would be unable to work in such conditions, especially since his *paella* – as well as being outside his usual speciality, classic French cuisine – involved unconventional procedures for which my kitchen would be much better equipped. I said that if that was all right with André, it was all right with me. It was agreed that it would still be André's supper, that he would pay for everything and bring the wines, but that it would take place in my empty rooms.

Everyone came. André arrived in the late afternoon, bringing his wines with him. Lucídio allowed him into the kitchen, but only for five minutes, in order to inspect the ingredients. Then we sat in the study while Lucídio was cooking, and André asked me all kinds of questions about Abel. Had I known him long? Since childhood, I said. Almost everyone in the group had known each other since childhood. Marcos and Saulo had been my neighbours, they had lived in the same street as me. They were inseparable. We used to call them the Siamese Twins. Tiago, Pedro, Abel, João and Paulo had also lived in the same part of town. During adolescence, the group had become somewhat dispersed. Abel was deeply involved with the Church. We knew he would have no truck with wild behaviour and we suspected that he was still a virgin. Despite our insistence, he hadn't even wanted to meet Milene, whom all of us had screwed. Paulo became a student leader and distanced himself from the rest of the group, who despised politics. Pedro wasn't around much either. He led a cloistered existence. He didn't go to school, but had private teachers, and was being groomed to take over the management of the family firm. Apart from that, his mother, Dona Nina, was paranoid about contagion. She could not bear the idea of her little Pedro coming into contact with the impurities of the world, amongst which she included us. Especially me. Not for nothing had I borne since childhood the nickname, the Talking Sleazebag. When I saw Mara with Pedro for the first time, I guessed that she had been chosen by Dona Nina to be the wife of her son. No one was whiter or, apparently, cleaner. Samuel had insinuated himself into the group, though no one knew where he had come from. He didn't live in the same part of town, and we never found out anything about his family. He entered our lives as Four Eggs Samuel, for he had been caught in flagrante by Saulo in Alberi's bar, the group's informal headquarters, eating four fried eggs at a time. From then on, our admiration for the scrawny lad with the voracious appetite had never ceased to grow. Samuel never studied, but he knew everything. He never worked, but he was never short of cash. He played dice for money with a group of older boys, in the backroom of Alberi's bar, losing more often than he won. He drank as much as he ate and he was into drugs. Once he had slept with Milene, she wanted nothing more to do with the rest of us and followed him everywhere, despite the beatings our idol gave her. And it was Samuel who introduced us to Ramos, years later, when the group, persuaded by Samuel that it was important, indeed predestined, exchanged the beef stews of Alberi's bar for weekly suppers in good restaurants. That was when Abel, Pedro and Paulo rejoined us, for they had not been part of the smaller group who formed the supper group – Tiago, the Chocolate Kid, the Siamese Twins, myself, João and Samuel. It was as if Samuel, having initiated us, had then handed us over to Ramos, in order for him to complete our sensual education and for us to become a legend. At the time, we still thought we would become a legend, that the city was too small for our appetites. We were bastards, yes, but great bastards, princely bastards. We knew hardly anything about Ramos either. He was older than us, had a private income and, as he put it one day, knew a great deal about Shakespeare and about sauces. His relationship with Samuel was a mystery that we made no attempt to plumb.

Our rite of passage from adolescence to maturity took place round a table in a restaurant, when Ramos explained to us why an overdone steak ceased to be a delicacy and became instead a useful object, like the sole of a shoe. This caused a revolution in the life of Abel, our pious griller of meat. According to Samuel, it was then that Abel began to lose his faith. The revelation that the raw was superior to the overcooked functioned as a kind of catechesis in reverse for Abel. There was an intrinsic incompatibility between rare meat and metaphysics, and Abel opted for the bleeding flesh.

I don't know how interested André was in my affectionate recapitulation of the facts or if he was merely trying to show how sorry he was about Abel's death. Once he had discovered that we were not, after all, *"le crème de le crème"*, he had shown no interest in our stories and displayed an almost physical disgust for, in descending order of horror,

Paulo's leftist histrionics, Samuel's slow decomposition and my belly. Now I'm sorry that I didn't let him talk more that night, while we were waiting for the others and while, in the kitchen, Lucídio was preparing the last *paella* of André's life.

A memorable *paella*. Preceded by champagne toasts to Ramos and to Abel and by scallops served with a delicate salmon mousse. We were all in a euphoric mood, despite Abel's death. That first supper cooked by Lucídio had convinced us that the Beef Stew Club could be saved by our appetites, even if we no longer loved each other as we once had and even if we had thrown away our lives. No one mentioned Abel during supper. Abel had once again become one of his family's saints, and it was up to us to preserve what remained alive amongst us, what had been salvaged from the shipwreck: our animal affinity, our group hunger, dating back to the days when we used to grunt like pigs as we munched our way through Alberi's beef stew. All we had in common now was our hunger. I hardly stopped talking, even when my mouth was full. André kept saying how sorry he was that his wife wasn't there; she did, after all, have Spanish blood and was bound to have had something to say about this very unusual *paella*. Then João said that banning women from the suppers had been a great decision. A wise decision. It was the women who had been responsible for our decline. It was the women who had got us turfed out of Paradise; without them, our rituals would regain their adolescent purity, we were once again the contented pigs we had been when we used to eat at Alberi's bar. When Lucídio brought in the second dish of *paella* with large bulbs of garlic arranged around the edge, he was greeted with howls of recognition. He was the person responsible for our resurrection. André tried to protest, without much conviction. His Bitinha should be there, she who loved *paella*, she who had studied *paella*. His protests were buried beneath our ferocious grunting. I remembered the "Discourse on Sexual Desire" that Ramos had made over the cognac, after the memorable truffle supper. We owe both truffles and civilization to female sexual desire, Ramos had said, raising his glass and proposing a toast to the female of the species and their glands. The truffles smelled like the pheromones of male pigs, and the sows in heat and in pursuit of love would search out the truffles and frantically dig them up. "Instead of a husband, they found a kind of vegetable nodule – as many young women do today," Ramos had said. The marvellous truffles we had eaten were the result of the amorous frustration of anonymous sows. According to Ramos, all gastronomic pleasure was a co-opted form of sexual desire. We interrupt the organic process of a plant or animal in order to eat it and we exhaust our own voluptuousness, our own perverted sexual desire, in the pleasure of eating. We were gathered there thanks to the destruction of the forests in the Pliocene period when our ancestors, obliged to live on the open grasslands, formed into groups for protection and began to exchange the natural sexuality of animals for human sexuality with all its concomitant terrors. Human history had begun when, instead of coming into season like other animals, the female hominid became sexually available on a permanent basis, a change that had brought with it the menstrual cycle, lunar time and the long flight from the open vulva that was civilization. All male societies like ours – and here, with the hand holding the cigar, Ramos made a circling gesture that included the table, the leftovers and his nine sated fellow members – were small reconstituted forests, artificial refuges in the midst of the grasslands, Paradise regained by man, before the historic decline and fall of the oestrus. When I recounted Ramos' theory to Lívia, she said that, basically, Ramos thought more highly of sows than he did of women. Her indignation only increased when I told her how much we had paid for the truffles.

Lucídio announced that there was still some *paella* left. Enough for one. Who would like it? André hesitated, then raised his hand.

"Could I take it home for Bitinha?"

"NO!" we all roared in unison. A roar from the forest.

André resigned himself to eating the rest of the *paella*

alone. He left the garlic bulbs to the end, crushing the last two with the back of his fork and squeezing out their creamy flesh, which he ate along with the skins. Sitting beside him and pretending to inspect each forkful with close, scientific interest, Samuel said:

"'The gods are just, and of our pleasant vices ...'"

Lucídio, standing at the table, completed the quotation, as if they had rehearsed it:

"'Make instruments to plague us.'"

I know now, though I didn't know it then, that this is another quotation from *King Lear*. But Samuel and Lucídio did not even look at each other when they spoke these words. It was as if they had rehearsed it.

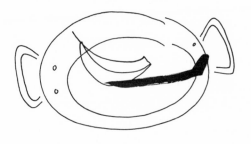

5 *The Lesbian Siamese Twins*

THERE WAS A SMELL OF GARLIC AT THE WAKE. I don't know whether it came from the dead man or not. The eight of us stood in the middle of the chapel, forming a separate ragged rectangle, like a Roman phalanx ready for attack from every side. Perhaps the smell was coming from us. We didn't know anyone there, apart from the widow, who looked ghastly sitting there beside the coffin, her face bare of make-up, the absence of which revealed the scars left behind by various plastic-surgery operations. She did not look up to receive our condolences. Each of us had to pick up her right hand from her lap, squeeze it, and then carefully replace it. André had died in the night. Of a heart attack.

Tiago was at my side. He whispered in my ear, but everyone else in our group heard.

"First Abel, then André . . . If we're dying in alphabetical order then . . ."

The next would be Daniel. Everyone looked at me.

"Mere coincidence."

"Possibly, but if I were you, I'd skip the next supper."

"Or take an antidote for poison with you," suggested Samuel.

The following month's supper would be given by Samuel. We had agreed that Lucídio would again be the chef and that the supper would again be held in my apartment, where Lucídio now felt at home in my kitchen.

"What do you mean? No one's been poisoned in my apartment."

"Well, I don't know about that."

"Abel died screwing Gisela. André died of a heart attack."

"Both of them died after a Club supper," said Saulo.

"At which the main course was their favourite dish," added João in my other ear.

"That's just a coincidence. If there was something in the food, why wasn't anyone else affected?"

"I don't know."

The funeral was well attended. There were three graveside speeches. André had, after all, been a leading light of the pharmaceutical industry. The governor sent a representative; Saulo sidled up to him during one of the speeches and introduced himself. He offered his card. With André gone, he might lose his position as public relations officer for the company and he needed to secure his future.

I noticed that the governor's representative accepted the card, but quickly moved away, making no attempt to disguise his embarrassment at this approach. We were the object of everyone's reproving or merely curious glances. We were an incomprehensible part of André's life. Years before, when the Beef Stew Club's meetings used to make the society pages, many of the people there would have dreamed of one day belonging to our group. Now, however, we were a curiosity, a nuisance. I realized then how odd we had all become. Not just me in my baggy shirt and my sandals, or the gloomy, cadaverous Samuel. Or Tiago, who could never manage to squeeze his chocoholic's body into conventional clothes. Pedro, though a business-man like most of the other men there, looked equally out of place; his immaculately groomed and perfumed appearance seemed almost aggressive, an exaggerated parody of elegance. Saulo had always been a follower of fashion, but somewhere along the line he had lost all sense of proportion, and everything about him jarred with the surrounding sobriety. We looked like a group of invaders from another species who had not yet realized that their disguise wasn't working, and that their tails were showing. I imagine that this was more or less what André's wife used to say to him, once she had discovered that we were not the sophisticates she had taken us for. They're not our kind of people, André. Leave that club of madmen. Yes, in the last twenty-one years, we had all become very peculiar.

Saulo and Marcos were cousins. They had been brought up together, but they couldn't have been more different. Marcos was the sensitive, introverted artist. Saulo was the exact opposite, he had had the soul of a PR man ever since he was a child. When we set up our agency, DSM, the idea was that Marcos would take care of the artwork, I would write the texts and Saulo would get the contacts, but none of us had the one indispensable talent that would ensure that the business was a success – none of us was an administrator. Despite their differences, though, Saulo and Marcos were inseparable. Our nickname for them was the Siamese Twins, later abbreviated to Twin 1 and Twin 2. They used to be my best friends. The increasing bitterness of the last years had corroded our former friendship, and even though Saulo has shown me over and over that he was not to be trusted, I miss them nonetheless. Of all the people who have died, they are the ones I miss the most. Damn, I've just spilled a glass of Cahors over the keyboard. I'm writing this in the middle of the night. Whatever comes into my head. That is why I was left until last, so that I could write it all down. Now I know why I escaped. I am the sacred recorder of this strange story.

Drawing my inspiration from Saulo and Marcos, I began inventing stories about Siamese twins, brothers with completely different ambitions, one wanting to succeed in life as a high jumper or as a dancer, while the other wanted to pursue his monastic vocation; the stories then evolved into the adventures of two lesbian Siamese-twin sisters, stories on which Marcos, Saulo and I worked during the long, idle afternoons at the agency. We had counted on the support of relatives and family friends to help get the agency off the ground. What we didn't know is that everyone considered us a bunch of irresponsible good-for-nothings, with absolutely no experience of the advertising world, and the only support they were willing to give us were a few encouraging words spoken out of consideration for our parents. While we waited for clients to appear, Marcos spent his time painting a mural on his office wall, Saulo in his room, with the door closed, interviewing candidates for the post of receptionist, while I sat in my office writing strange stories or talking on the phone. I talked more than I wrote. I can never keep quiet for long. Then, at the end of the afternoon, the other members of the group would arrive. We had spent a large part of our initial capital on a stock of whisky to offer our clients, but the stock ran out after only a month of after-hours meetings with Club members in Saulo's room, where a candidate or two for the receptionist's job would often agree to stay on in order to meet what Saulo called the agency's shareholders, "the men with the money". Samuel always had the most success with the girls. Anyone who judged the agency by the number of times the lights stayed on late into the night would have assumed that we were working furiously and that our success was guaranteed. But in its eight brief months of life, the agency only carried out one commission, a campaign for a company owned by Pedro's father; the three of us thought it was brilliant, but the old man paid for it and never used it. Still, it allowed us to pay off our back rent and my enormous phone bill. We closed the agency, feeling misunderstood and misjudged, on the day that Saulo's minibar went phut. Without ice, we concluded, we simply couldn't go on.

For Lívia, the stories of the lesbian Siamese twins are a symbol of my squandered life and talent. Saulo and Marcos and, unintentionally, other members of the group contributed incidents and details to the saga of the Siamese twins, but most of the stories are mine. The unfortunate sisters Zenaide and Zulmira, unable to consummate the intense sexual attraction they felt for each other, tried to make up for their frustration by having affairs with other women, difficult, dramatic affairs that were always ultimately destroyed by jealousy. Since they could never be alone with their lovers, one always had to submit to the criticisms and complaints of the other, putting up with the other's muffled laughter whenever she made some slightly extravagant declaration of love or with having her lovemaking interrupted by impatient questions like: "Have you two finished yet?" But the lesbian Siamese twins did not only have sexual adventures. Sometimes one of the group would ring me up with an idea – "Zenaide and Zulmira versus 007" or "Zenaide and Zulmira chosen for the national football team" – which I would then develop. Once I had an argument with Paulo, who accused Zenaide, Zulmira and myself of political and social apathy when the country was living through one of the blackest periods in its history, under a dictatorial regime, with a censored press, with people being imprisoned and tortured, and all those other things which, in our group, only Paulo cared about. As a riposte, I came up with "Zenaide and Zulmira, disillusioned with the political process, go off to join the guerrilla movement", which was a great success with the group of six at the agency, and whose tragic ending was supplied by Paulo himself: in her excitement at government plans to build the Transamazonian highway, Zenaide gives up the armed struggle and surrenders to government forces, neglecting to mention that Zulmira does not agree with her and beneath her skirt is concealing a bomb which explodes as the two of them are being welcomed by the authorities in Brasília. The explosion kills the President and all the military ministers, thus changing the direction of Brazilian history and, more importantly, separating the twin sisters, who can, at last, love each other as they always wanted to, in the midst of the ruins of the Planalto Palace.

*

I continued to make up stories about the lesbian Siamese twins; even today, I'm holed up in my tree trunk writing about them, but the stories are growing increasingly sombre in tone. In my stories, the twins are still Siamese twins, but with time and the twins' increasing age, their condition has become an allegory which I myself can barely comprehend. An allegory of a terrible duality, of our horror of that unavoidable other which is our body and of that excess of flesh which is not us, but with which we share our biography and which takes us with it at the end when it dies, of that ... I can hear Lívia saying: "Oh, Daniel, stop it!" She had found the lesbian Siamese twins quite sick enough when they were merely comical, irresponsible figures. She doesn't want me to tell her what they got up to before we met. Lívia says they are a manifestation of the group's pathological misogyny, which is the black hole from which she wants to save me. I have become a very strange person indeed.

The one member of the group who never understood the lesbian Siamese twins was João. He just couldn't see anything funny about them. He liked proper jokes, not what he called "oh-ha-ha" humour, that made people smile and say "oh-ha-ha" just to show they had understood, instead of giving a good belly laugh. João, our brilliant con man, who had survived for years in the murky, semi-legal world of financial advice and had never once lost his good humour, despite being condemned to death by more than one ruined client. I was thinking about his laughter and his invariable optimism in any situation when I asked Lucídio what the menu would be for Samuel's supper. Would it perhaps be *gigot d'agneau*, my favourite dish? This was another way of asking if the person chosen to die was me, assuming the order of death was alphabetical. No, replied Lucídio. Sautéed mushrooms Provençal – if, that is, we hadn't had enough of garlic after poor André's *paella* – followed by duck *à l'orange*.

Duck *à l'orange* was João's favourite dish.

I phoned Saulo.

"It's duck *à l'orange*."

"What is?"

"That's what Lucídio's going to cook for the next supper."

"So?"

"It's João's favourite."

A silence. Then:

"Phone him."

I phoned João.

"About the supper Lucídio is cooking for Samuel."

"Yes?"

"It's duck *à l'orange*."

A silence. Then:

"Thank you."

João was the first to arrive for Samuel's supper. He saw the look of surprise on my face and said:

"Duck *à l'orange* cooked by Lucídio – you don't think I'd miss that, do you?"

Marcos and Saulo arrived soon afterwards and they too were surprised to see João. Saulo looked at me. I threw up my hands, denying all responsibility.

"I warned him."

"Do you want to die, João?" asked Saulo.

"You're forgetting," said João, "that there are two hypotheses. One: the deaths are in alphabetical order, in which case it's Daniel's turn. Two, the person to die . . . "

João had to stop because Lucídio had just come into the room to check something on the table, which was already set. When Lucídio returned to the kitchen, João went on:

"Two: the person to die is the one whose favourite dish is the main course. There's a third hypothesis too, of course: that we're all completely mad, and the deaths have nothing whatever to do with the suppers."

"Well, we'll find out tonight," said Marcos.

Samuel always served champagne at his suppers. Before and during. We started drinking champagne with Lucídio's marvellous canapés. We toasted Ramos and Abel and, after some hesitation, André too. Then João raised his glass in my direction and said:

"May the worst man die."

Marcos said: "Shh!" Lucídio might hear us from the kitchen.

Our chef had a problem with my oven. He had calculated he would need three ducks for the group of eight, but he could only get two ducks in the oven at a time. He would cook the third duck while we were demolishing the first two. The duck was perfect. João moaned at every mouthful. He had never tasted an orange sauce like it. And I must confess that the possibility of dying definitely increased my pleasure in the food. What Lucídio had said about the fugu was true, the risk of dying really did have an effect on the taste buds; flavours took on an extraordinary clarity, and one ate in a state of exaltation, of near euphoria. I remembered Ramos' theory, which he expounded at the last supper before his own death, that there is something in our errant cells that envies the condemned man because he knows when he will die. João must have been feeling something similar. He too was blessed with a destiny, he too was enjoying the strange delight of eating a meal on death row. When I went to fetch the third duck, I noticed that Lucídio had placed a few slices with some sauce on a separate plate and put it to one side. João and I had taken it upon ourselves to finish off the third duck; this was an act of deference on the part of the other guests to the person who, regardless of what criterion was being used, was, hypothetically, about to die.

Saulo sighed and said:

"I'm the one who should die . . . "

He had been fired from André's company. He had been unable to find another job. He had no money and, as well as what he owed his ex-wife, he had to support Marcos too. He looked enviously at João and myself.

We continued to eat like two condemned men.

Lucídio came in with what was left of the duck. He approached the table somewhat solemnly, wrapped in that comical, ankle-length apron. We were silent, eight expectant mutes seated before three carcasses. We knew that we had entered the rarefied zone of grave decisions. From then on it would be the Beef Stew Club against Fate, seconds out, and our adolescence was a long way off. Lucídio said:

"There's a little bit left over. Would anyone like it?"

And João and I looked at each other. I said:

"No, I'm full actually. It was delicious but . . . "

João held out his hand for the plate.

"I'll have it."

King Lear quotation of the night. I looked it up afterwards. Having explained that the secret of his duck *à l'orange* was the Calvados he added and that the sauce was the product of an *"entente cordiale"* – said without a scintilla of humour – between the apple and the orange, Lucídio remarked that he hoped we had enjoyed it.

"'I would much rather be attacked for want of wisdom

than praised for harmful mildness.'"

I'm not quite sure how Samuel reacted to those words. I have a vague recollection of a smile, a shaking of the head, like someone who cannot quite believe what he is hearing.

In the latest of my stories about the lesbian Siamese twins, Zulmira, by now an old woman who has experienced the love of all kinds of women, has an affair with a vampiress. She is bitten on the neck and she too turns into a vampiress. She becomes obsessed with the idea of biting Zenaide on the neck, and Zenaide is forced to remain constantly vigilant against her sister's canine teeth, and the unfulfilled love between them turns into hatred. The metaphor, if I understand myself rightly, depicts the horror of a destiny lying in wait for us, as opposed to a fate which, while terrible, is also clear and certain. Lívia puts her hands over her ears whenever I try to tell her these stories. She is trying to persuade me to turn my hand to children's literature instead.

6 *The Fish Scale II*

JOÃO WAS THE FIRST OF THE GROUP TO DRIVE A car. He stole his father's car, crammed seven of us inside and took us for a ride that ended with the car landing in someone's back garden, having first cleared a wall higher than the car itself – quite how we never knew. We fled to Alberi's bar, and, shortly afterwards, the owner of the house, one Homero, turned up accompanied by a police officer. We were all out of breath, and João was bleeding from a cut to the head caused by a garden gnome which – again inexplicably – had flown in through the car windscreen. And it was then that Alberi said the words that we would repeat for years afterwards, whenever we recalled the episode: "They're all angels here." We were not just innocent of having invaded Homero's garden, but, given Alberi's tone of voice, we would always be innocent whatever we did. It wasn't an absolution, it was a curse.

It wasn't a transient condition, a lie, it was a category. And no one looked more like an angel than Marcos, Twin 2, with his delicate features and his liquid, basset-hound eyes. He had fallen flat on his face when he got out of the car and was still shaking and covered in mud, but he was the one who confirmed Alberi's words to Homero and the policeman. We had been in the bar for the last two hours, we didn't know anything about a car, we were innocent. Marcos' eyes saved us that night. We all got off apart from João, when the car was identified as belonging to his father. João's punishment kept him off the roads for more than a month. And now Marcos was the one who was shedding most tears at João's wake. The May wake.

"It's a punishment," said Marcos.

He had grown mystical. Only his weight prevented him from levitating; he too had become peculiar over time. Once, he had tried to drag Saulo off to Tibet and had only given up when Saulo, having used every possible argument to dissuade him, had spread wide his arms so that Marcos could have a good look at him; he had even spun round so that Marcos could take in every detail of his immaculate clothes and underclothes and his ostentatious red tie, and said: "Can you honestly imagine me in the Himalayas?" Marcos had given up the Tibet idea. The two were never apart. Marcos was an orphan and had been brought up by his aunt, Saulo's mother. When Marcos married Olguinha, thus disappointing all the other girls who had fallen in love with his romantic profile and his puppy-dog eyes – or, as Samuel put it, the eyes of a "repentant libertine" – João's remark: "I wonder who will sleep in the middle" was not far from the truth. Saulo went with them on their honeymoon, although he swore he had slept in a separate room. Saulo protected Marcos. He insisted that his cousin was a great painter, even when the rest of the group had accepted that Marcos was, in fact, a mediocrity. He would secretly buy Marcos' paintings, so that Marcos would think that his exhibitions were a success. We all had several paintings by Marcos in our homes, given to us by Saulo. When Olguinha left Marcos for a Uruguayan, Saulo swore revenge, but not just against Olguinha and the Uruguayan. He also dreamed up ways of harming Uruguay by organizing boycotts and anti-Uruguay demonstrations. Marcos was the baby of the group. Not even Samuel could insult him with any conviction, limiting himself to such remarks as: "The libertine could yet become a saint, or vice versa." Marcos was the only one of my friends whom Lívia liked. Once, she had even managed to persuade him to follow one of her dietary programmes. Exercise, planned meals and lots and lots of fibre. It didn't last long. What she did not realize was that Marcos' angelic exterior concealed a diabolical appetite. With the passage of time, our romantic artist had grown fat and ugly and more and more ethereal. He only returned to reality for brief visits, and to eat. He created mystical paintings – banal allegories – but, fortunately, he could no longer find anyone prepared to exhibit them. We got them as presents from Saulo.

"It's a punishment," said Marcos at João's funeral, once he had stopped crying.

"What do you mean?" I asked.

"We're being punished."

"But why?"

Those liquid eyes, the eyes of a now ageing puppy-dog.

"Why? Why? How can you still ask why?"

We were whispering in a corner. The only other sounds in the chapel were the sobs coming from João's family. I looked around me, searching for some satisfied face, but none of the investors that João had conned out of their money was there.

"Look, no one's been poisoned in my apartment," I said.

But Marcos went on:

"We're being punished for our sins, for our corrupt souls."

Saulo gripped Marcos' arm:

"Calm down, Marcos."

At the last supper before his death, Ramos had spoken to us of the secret envy we all feel for the condemned man. He had already known then that he was going to die. So had we. The supper had taken place at my apartment, and

Samuel was in charge of the food and drink. We served Ramos' favourite dishes, medallion of lobster with mayonnaise and lamb with mint sauce. According to him, mint sauce was England's sole contribution to Western civilization, apart from Shakespeare and parliamentarianism, though he never quite managed to convince us of this. Ramos was the only member of the group who liked mint sauce. Ramos said that our lives were like badly told murder stories, lacking any of the symmetry or the epiphanies of art. We knew who the murderer was right from the start. He was born with us. We were born bound to our own assassin. Yes, just like – and he blessed me from afar with the hand holding the cigar – Daniel's Siamese twins. We grow up with our murderer; the identity of our murderer was no mystery. We had the same appetites and weaknesses and committed the same sins. But we never knew when he would kill us, we never knew what game he was playing. Knowing the hour and manner of our death was like being presented with a plot, with a denouement, with all the advantages that detective fiction has over life. Knowing our fate was like stealing a glance at the last page of the book. We read our lives differently, as the accomplices of both the author and the murderer. We had symmetry, meaning and logic. Or, rather, irony, which was a literary form of logic. The only intelligent way of reading a detective story was by beginning at the end, said Ramos, smiling sadly at the protests of Tiago, the Chocolate

Kid, amongst whose many obsessions was an addiction to both chocolate and detective fiction. What we envy in the condemned man is the privilege he enjoys of knowing how and when his life will end. We envy him for being a better reader than we are. There are no casual readers on death row, concluded Ramos. All writers, all critics and all gastronomes ought to live in a permanently terminal state. On that night, for the first time since the Beef Stew Club was founded, Ramos did not call for a toast with the cognac. We all knew that this was the last time we would have supper together. We did not know, however, that the end would come so soon. The following day, Ramos was in the hospital, where he died just before midnight.

Samuel got to his feet and made the toast, raising his glass to Ramos.

"To our own Holy Bastard."

The May wake was the most troubled of all. João's family could find no explanation for his death. He had returned home after the supper, half-drunk, and had refused to go to bed. He had refused to sit down. He said that he wanted to be on his feet when "he" arrived. Who was "he"? João was very agitated. Only as day was breaking did he finally agree to lie down on the sofa. He did not wake up again. A heart attack. He who had never had a day's illness in his life, who had never lost his good humour, who had survived crises, threats of legal action and death and the prospect of imminent ruin, all with the blood pressure of a boy. Of a boy, his mother repeated, indignantly. How was it possible?

Lívia came into the chapel, greeted João's mother and wife and walked over to me as if she were about to hit me.

"What is going on, Zi?"

"Calm down. This isn't the place."

"What is going on? What's happening?"

"Look, no one has been poisoned in my apartment."

How was it possible? Three suppers, three deaths, what was going on? I asked Lívia to lower her voice, but João's wife, realizing that she had acquired an ally, came over and planted herself next to Lívia, right under my nose. She demanded an explanation for what had happened. The Beef Stew Club closed ranks behind me. The Beef Stew Club looks after its own. Samuel said that no one needed to explain anything. It was Fate. Saulo also began to defend us, but he had to stop when he saw that Marcos was no longer at his side. Marcos was standing next to the coffin and had started making a speech to the dead man:

"Sinner . . ."

Saulo managed to drag him away before he got any further, but João's mother had already thrown back her head in shock, gasping for air. We thought it best to withdraw *en masse*, the seven survivors, before we were thrown out. As we left, we heard someone mention a post-mortem. Things couldn't go on like this.

Lívia, with the aid of my stepmother's troops, cleaned my whole kitchen from top to bottom. She changed all the pots and pans and disinfected the balcony. And she demanded to know more about "this Lucídio" who was cooking our suppers. Where had he sprung from? The murderous germs might be on his hands.

I tried to change the subject, but Lívia insisted. She wanted to be there when he next cooked supper for the group. Always assuming we were mad enough to continue with the suppers after three deaths.

A fortnight after João's funeral, Lucídio phoned me.

"I'm so sorry about João."

"Hm."

"Was it his heart?"

"Apparently. There was talk of carrying out a post-mortem, but I don't think they did."

"A post-mortem?"

"To find out what killed him. I mean, he might have been poisoned."

"Poison in the food, you mean?"

"That's right."

He said nothing, and suddenly I was seized by panic. I didn't want him to take this the wrong way, hang up the phone and disappear from our lives for ever. Not before he had made my *gigot d'agneau*. I said:

"Are you still there?"

"Yes."

"Shall we discuss the June supper?"

We had agreed that the June supper would be paid for by Paulo, but held in my apartment, as the other suppers had been.

"Of course," he said.

I gave a sigh of relief.

"What are you thinking of cooking?"

"I'll do quiche as the main course."

"Right."

Quiche. Marcos was mad about quiche.

I gave Lívia the wrong date for the supper so that she wouldn't run into Lucídio in the kitchen while he was preparing the meal. Lucídio complained that the pans had been changed. Luckily, Lívia had replaced my quiche dishes with new ones, though he preferred the old ones. On the night of the supper, once everyone had arrived, I gathered them all together in my study and locked the door. If Lucídio came out of the kitchen, where he had spent the whole afternoon preparing the supper, he would not catch us unawares. We talked in low voices so that he wouldn't be able to hear us through the door. We needed to talk.

"Abel, André, João . . . If it's by alphabetical order, then he's missed you out, Daniel. Why would he do that?"

"It isn't by alphabetical order," said Marcos.

"What order is he following, then?"

"It's by order of sin. Abel was the first of the ten because he left the Church. Isn't 'Thou shalt honour the Lord thy God' the first commandment?"

We all exchanged glances. No one knew the order of the ten commandments.

"What was André's sin, then, apart from being a bore, of course?" asked Samuel.

"And João? The commandments don't really cover being a liar, a usurer, a conman and a teller of terrible jokes. Or do they?"

"It's by alphabetical order," said Pedro.

"Or no order at all. He chooses one person to die and makes that person's favourite dish."

We were all looking at Marcos. Given that he fulfilled both criteria, it was his turn.

"If it is by alphabetical order, why did he miss out Daniel?" insisted Marcos.

"Because Daniel owns the apartment and the kitchen and he's the one who introduced him to us. By any criterion, Daniel will be the last to die."

"The one who dies," said Pedro, "is always the one who asks for more."

"Dies how?" I asked.

"What do you mean 'how'? By being poisoned."

"Look, no one's been poisoned in my apartment."

"Oh, Daniel, wake up. He's poisoning us one by one. It must be the poison from that fish."

"What fish?"

"That Japanese fish he told us about."

"You don't actually believe that story, do you?" asked Samuel.

"Why shouldn't we? He told us that he studied cooking in Paris, and the dishes he produces prove that that's true. He said he has access to a deadly poison and the three mysterious deaths after the suppers cooked by him prove that that is true too. And then there's the fish scale."

"The fish scale doesn't prove anything," said Samuel.

"Why not?"

And Samuel took out his wallet and produced a fish scale identical to the one Lucídio had shown us.

"Because I've got one too."

According to Samuel, these laminated fish scales could be bought in any shop selling Japanese artefacts, and the ideogram didn't mean "All desire is the desire for death" or "Hunger is a deaf coachman" or any other such nonsense, it was simply the ideogram for "sea". And the scale came from a fish that might or might not be poisonous, but it was more likely to be from some ornamental fish. Pedro said that this didn't prove anything either, because the fact was that Lucídio was poisoning us, and Marcos was obviously the chosen victim for tonight's supper, and we needed to decide what to do. What do you think, Marcos?

But Marcos had his head up and there was a faint smile on his lips. He hadn't heard a word we had been saying.

"Just smell that," Marcos said.

"What?" asked Saulo.

"The smell of quiche."

Gorgeous canapés. Giant asparagus, bought who knows where, in Hollandaise sauce. And the quiches lorraines . . . Delicate, delicious, divine. Two per person, filling the whole plate. All the plates returned to the kitchen empty. The only discordant note of the evening was struck by Paulo's wines. Paulo worked for Pedro, who was bankrupt. According to Samuel, the rule in such a situation is for the employees' wines to get worse as the owner's wines get better, because the owner, in order to console himself, starts spending more on luxuries than on his failed business and his employees. The wine was Brazilian wine, which provoked Samuel into insulting both Paulo and Pedro. Samuel was just threatening to dissolve the sleeve of Paulo's sweater by soaking it in the wine, when Lucídio appeared from the kitchen with a quiche on a plate and said:

"There's one left. Who would like it?"

There followed a long, deep silence. Marcos and Saulo were looking at each other. Finally, Saulo said:

"You don't want it, do you, Marcos?"

In order to change the subject, Tiago asked what was for dessert, but Lucídio did not reply. Samuel said:

"Leave it, Marcos."

"Yeah," said Pedro, "let's move on to dessert."

Marcos still said nothing. He looked at the quiche, then back at Saulo, then at the quiche. He sighed and said:

"I want it."

Saulo hesitated, then said:

"Then I'll have a piece too."

Lucídio went back into the kitchen and brought out another plate. He divided the quiche into two equal portions and placed the plates on the table in front of Marcos and Saulo. All this happened in absolute silence. Marcos and Saulo ate in silence and we sat in silence until they had both eaten. Lucídio was standing by the table. When they had finished, Samuel, whose lined face seemed to have grown more lined as the night progressed, remarked:

"'The worst is not, so long as we can say "This is the worst.'"

King Lear. Act IV, Scene 1.

And Lucídio smiled his tight-lipped smile.

7 Wanton Boys

ONCE, WE SPENT THE ENTIRE AFTERNOON AT THE agency, Marcos, Saulo and myself, discussing the perfect woman. I was courting my first wife at the time, the one who, when we subsequently parted, touchingly insisted on keeping a little statuette that we had bought together, as "a souvenir of our good times"; when she got to the front door, she turned and hurled the statuette at my head. We had all had girlfriends, steady and not so steady, apart from Samuel, who despised "nice" girls and was a regular visitor to the city's bordellos. But none of those girl-friends had possessed even one of the attributes which we agreed made up the perfect woman. That afternoon, we described her hair and her skin and even specified what her teeth should be like, agreeing that having slightly prominent incisors which pushed out the upper lip – just a touch – would only increase her perfection. We chose tone of voice, breasts, legs, even the thickness of her ankles. However, only when we had described the whole woman and were arguing about whether we would share her or fight to the death over her, did we realize that we had described Mara, Pedro's wife. We quickly devised a name for our ideal which was nothing like that of our friend's wife: Verônica Roberta. We would dream of Verônica Roberta whenever we dreamed of Mara, whom we could never have.

In twenty years, Mara had lost none of her tranquil beauty. She had a few grey hairs, which she made no attempt to cover up. Her body had grown thicker and heavier, but her figure was still our passionate ideal. She looked at Saulo's face in the coffin, then stood for a long time looking at Marcos' face, who, in death, seemed to have regained his youth and his angelic looks. Marcos had always been her favourite. "Marcos is the only one of all of you who is worth anything," she had said to me once, after her affair with Samuel and her divorce from Pedro. She came over to me. Samuel was beside me. The wake for Twin 1 and Twin 2 was going very smoothly, in marked contrast to the turbulence of João's wake, and despite the shock caused by the cousins' simultaneous death and the growing perplexity concerning the tragedies besetting the Beef Stew Club, which had lost fifty per cent of its membership in only four months, Mara greeted me. I hesitated, then said:

"You remember Samuel, don't you?"

She drew back.

"Samuel!"

He was smiling, taking care not to open his mouth and reveal his rotten teeth. The dark circles under his eyes looked as if they had been badly shaded in with charcoal.

"How are you, Mara?"

She was lost for words. They looked at each other, Mara open-mouthed, Samuel's forced smile making his hollow cheeks seem even hollower. Then he shrugged, as if exempting himself of all blame for the passage of time and apologising for being the third corpse at the wake. And Mara burst into tears.

We never knew whether Pedro ever suspected that Mara had deceived him with Samuel. For us it was traumatic. It was simply beyond our imaginings that the perfect woman could possibly have an affair with Four Eggs Samuel, however irresistible he might be. It didn't bother us to think of Mara and Pedro in bed together. Ever since we were boys, we had happily granted Pedro the right to all the privileges of his birth without feeling in any way diminished. When he began having all his lessons at home, we regretted the loss of a classmate, but we didn't reject him or envy him. When his mother forbade him to mix with us, we understood her concern: we really were unhygienic and dangerous. When Pedro was given his first car for his eighteenth birthday, we agreed to the conditions he laid down if we were to travel in it: only two at a time so as not to strain the suspension and with clean shoes on, and we all felt genuinely delighted with the new car. And when Pedro introduced us to his girlfriend, Mara, with her long, straight hair, very white skin and slightly imperfect incisors – but only imperfect to the point of perfection – we concluded that this was merely another entirely deserved prize that Fortune had bestowed on our Dauphin. Pedro and Mara's honeymoon in Europe lasted almost a year, and we accompanied them in our imaginations from bed to bed. When they returned, Pedro took up his place in his father's company, later replacing his father as director when his father died. In the next twenty years, he destroyed the company, as we had expected he would, and he lost Mara, for which we never forgave him. When the Beef Stew Club made its first trip to Europe, Pedro and Mara were not yet divorced, but he took another woman with him instead, thus denying us Mara's company. We had to content ourselves with dreams of Verônica Roberta, who never disappointed us. Verônica Roberta, for example, would never have had an affair with Four Eggs Samuel.

It was on that first trip to Paris with the Beef Stew Club that Ramos spoke to me, for the first and only time, of his homosexuality. We were strolling along the banks of the Seine late one afternoon, and he told me about his Parisian experiences. He had visited Paris regularly ever since he was a young man, and, at one point, had lived for four years in an apartment in Montparnasse. He went back to Paris every year, sometimes more than once. He had a friend in Paris. A very close friend. Then he corrected himself, as if he had come to a decision.

"No, he's not a friend, he's my lover."

"Ah," I said, just to say something.

"We met right here. He's Brazilian."

"Ah."

"I haven't been to see him this time. It's all a bit complicated . . . "

I glanced surreptitiously at Ramos' face, trying to find some reason for that sudden need for confidences. It was pure chance that we happened to be walking along together. We had no special affinity, apart from the affinities of the group as a whole. He was our organizer and teacher and we all admired him, but we knew very little about him. Samuel had introduced him to the group, but not even Samuel seemed to know much about his private life. Samuel always referred to him as "queer", because of his eccentricities and affected mannerisms. But years later, when Ramos was in hospital dying of Aids, Samuel seemed the most bitter about that confirmation of Ramos' homosexuality, which put an end to our assumption that they were lovers.

"Ah."

"I have another friend in Brazil."

"Ah."

"Am I boring you?"

"No, no."

"Love affairs are always boring, especially complicated ones."

"No, no."

"The infinite variety of human behaviour is not as fascinating as people say. Rather, it is the cause of all our sorrows."

"Ah."

I did not feel comfortable in the role as Ramos' confidant. Why me? Since I was a compulsive talker, I was hardly the most confidential of confidants.

"If they were both sensible people, it would be different, but they're not. They're foolish and cruel."

"Do they know each other?"

"Oh yes, and they hate each other."

Then he added:

"They're my 'wanton boys'..."

I thought he said "my wonton boys" and imagined it must have something to do with Chinese food, but Ramos explained that "wanton" was an English word meaning "naughty", "mischievous", "bad". "Wanton boys" was a quotation from Shakespeare.

That night, we dined round a large table in one of the oldest restaurants in Paris, and Ramos' speech over the cognac was conducted in French, to the dismay of the majority of the members. And Samuel almost caused an incident by insisting on calling the waiters "Monsieur Bastard". After that day in Paris, Ramos never again talked to me about his private life, and I never asked him about it.

At the funeral of the Siamese Twins, a man came over to me and introduced himself. I thought he said he was an Inspector and, before he had asked me anything, I said:

"Look, no one has been poisoned in my apartment, Inspector."

But I had misheard. He corrected me.

"No, not Inspector, Spector. My card."

His name was Eugênio Spector, and the only other thing on his card, apart from his phone number, was the word "Events". He would like to talk to me, when it was convenient. He had a proposition to make which I might find interesting. He asked me to phone him. "As soon," he said, making an episcopal gesture that took in everything around us, "as you have recovered from your grief." Mr Spector was here a few days ago and . . . But I'm getting ahead of myself again. Daniel, stop it!

After the funeral, we went back to my apartment, where we gathered in the study. The full complement of the surviving Beef Stew Club membership: all five of us. At the funeral, Lívia kept saying: "This is madness, Zi, madness.

You must stop holding these suppers." The matter to be discussed was, should we stop holding the suppers or not? The next host would be Pedro. In alphabetical order – since Saulo had chosen to die out of order – Paulo should be the next to die.

"So, do we cancel the supper?" I asked.

"No," said Paulo without a moment's hesitation.

"I think we should take a vote," said Samuel.

"I'm the main interested party," said Paulo. "The supper will go ahead."

Pedro suggested that he, rather than Lucídio, should choose the menu. Paulo disagreed. Lucídio would decide what to make. I suggested that we supervise the making of the meal, especially the last fateful portion. Paulo vetoed that too. Lucídio must have full freedom in which to do his work.

"Be honest," said Paulo, "the deaths aside, have you ever eaten so well in your entire life as at Lucídio's suppers?"

"No, but . . ."

"And there's another thing. If we start interfering in his work, he'll disappear. He'll go away. He'll leave us."

"We're the ones who are disappearing," said Tiago. "One by one. One a month. The Beef Stew Club will come to an end not for lack of a cook, but for lack of members. We're all dying!"

And then Paulo leaned back on the sofa – beneath one of Marcos' paintings which, according to the artist, depicted the struggle of the One Being to free itself from the duality of body and spirit – and said:

"Well, I don't know about you, but I don't really care."

Lívia phoned me to find out how I was. I said I was fine and was going to try and get some sleep. She asked if there was anyone with me. "No," I lied. Samuel had stayed behind after the others had gone. He was deeply depressed by the deaths of Marcos and Saulo and by his meeting with Mara.

"Stop this madness, Zi!"

"Of course."

"Stop these suppers. Denounce that cook!"

"Of course, of course."

When I hung up, Samuel was studying one of Marcos' paintings – one of many donated to me by Saulo – that adorned the walls of my study.

"Do you think Marcos killed himself as an act of self-criticism?"

"Is that what we're doing, killing ourselves?"

"I'm not, are you?"

I remembered the euphoria I had felt as I ate the duck à l'orange when there was a possibility that I might be the one chosen to die. The feeling that Ramos had described, of entering a privileged territory where everything was clear and inevitable and one's senses were heightened to the nth degree. The territory of the condemned man, or of the taster of fugu as described by Lucídio.

"Samuel, tell me something."

"What?"

"How come you've got a fish scale identical to Lucídio's?"

"Ask Lucídio how come he's got a fish scale identical to mine. And he lied about that, by the way."

"Where did you get yours?"

"It was a present."

"Why do you think Lucídio lied about the fish scale?"

"He wanted to arouse your curiosity. That whole story about the fugu fish is an invention. He just wanted to get you interested. He knew about your taste for the bizarre."

"How did he know?"

"Someone must have told him."

"Do you think he did it all just so that I would invite him to cook for us, just so that he could poison us?"

"Well, it worked."

"But why is he poisoning us?"

"You're asking the wrong question."

"What's the right question?"

"Why are we allowing ourselves to be poisoned?"

Paulo was the last to arrive for the supper at which he would be poisoned. Lucídio had confirmed that the dish of the evening would be *blanquette de veau*. Paulo's favourite. The condemned man arrived with a large piece of red cloth draped over his shoulders, like a cape. He had been looking for something from his past life as a political activist to bring to his sacrifice and had found nothing, apart from a few mouldy books. He had improvised a red flag and he wore it over his shoulders throughout the evening, during which he was the only one to speak. He gave an account of his political commitment from his days as a student, passing through his time as a councillor, the period spent in hiding, the demonstrations, the secret missions on behalf of the Party, prison, and his election as deputy. And he spoke too of his betrayal. Yes, it was true. He had betrayed his colleagues, had turned them in. While we were living our mediocre lives entirely lacking in grandeur, never even experiencing the exaltation of some great act of infamy, some terrible guilt, he had been on the barricades and had grovelled in the filth. What we had in common was our hunger and our failure, but he had touched the extremes, he was better than us, better than all of us, including those who had died. And while he was talking, he busily devoured canapés, then an onion tart, then several helpings of veal accompanied by a dry white Bordeaux that Pedro had disinterred from his cellar for his collaborator's last supper. And when Lucídio brought in the terrine containing what was left of the blanquette of veal, he did not need to ask who wanted more. Paulo snatched the hot terrine from his hands, noisily lapped up the white sauce from the terrine itself, then put it down on the table and ate the meat with his hands, grunting, just as if he were eating Alberi's beef stew. While the others were having dessert, Paulo sat hunched in his chair, silent at last, head lolling, eyes fixed on the table cloth. He did not look up, not even when Lucídio, to everyone's surprise, proposed making the final toast, Ramos' toast, over the cognac.

"You can't," protested Samuel. "You're not a member of the Club."

But Pedro, Tiago and myself persuaded him to let Lucídio speak. After all, the Club barely existed any more.

Lucídio raised his glass of cognac. It was the first time he had accepted a cognac. It was the first time he had not remained standing by the table, merely responding to questions about the food he had served. He had frustrated the hopes I had had that he would turn out to be a good storyteller, and that he would have other stories like the one about the fugu club to recount. He behaved like a chef grateful to be treated as an equal by his masters and to be invited to sit at the table, but who nevertheless knew his place and maintained due respect. Now he was going to speak. He raised his glass of cognac and, looking at Samuel, he said:

"'All friends shall taste the wages of their virtue, and all foes the cup of their deservings.'"

Samuel raised his glass to Lucídio and said:

"'What you have charged me with, that have I done, and more, much more; the time will bring it out: 'tis past, and so am I. But what art thou that hast this fortune on me?'"

And Lucídio:

"'I am a man more sinned against than sinning.'"

"I don't understand a word," said Paulo, suddenly reviving. That was the last thing he said.

"'Nothing will come of nothing,'" said Samuel.

And he and Lucídio drank down their cognac in one, at the same time.

We agreed that the next supper would be organized by Tiago, but with the same format – in my apartment, with Lucídio in the kitchen. Tiago began to say: "And who will be pois . . . ", but he stopped himself in time. Lucídio exchanged his apron for an elegant jacket, bade a formal goodbye to everyone except Samuel, and left. Tiago left immediately afterwards. Pedro gave Paulo a lift home. Before leaving, Paulo gave me a long embrace, but Samuel refused to embrace him and said: "Get out of here, you bastard." Samuel lay down on one of the sofas in the living room. He asked if he could sleep there that night. I said he could. His chin was buried in his chest and he was staring fixedly at one of my bare walls. I said:

"Lucídio knew that Ramos died of AIDS. How?"

"Someone told him."

"You and Lucídio have met before."

He did not reply.

"Why didn't you say something the first time you saw him here?"

He took a while before replying. Then he closed his eyes, sighed and said:

"I wanted to see how far he would go."

"Why?"

But Samuel was already waving me away, indicating that he would say nothing more that night.

8 *The Chocolate Kid – Detective*

AFTER THE DEATH OF HIS FATHER, PEDRO HAD asked his mother to go and live with him and his third wife. Dona Nina had quickly taken over the running of the house and had ended up getting rid of her daughter-in-law, though not without first accusing her of various crimes against hygiene, home and husband. We were convinced that Dona Nina still gave Pedro his daily bath and told him what to wear, but, on the day of Paulo's funeral, Dona Nina had clearly failed in her duty. Pedro turned up at the July wake tieless and unshaven. I felt we were being deliberately excluded, and that the only reason we had not been thrown out was because they did not consider us worthy of the fuss that would involve. Pedro, Tiago and myself stood in a corner, far from the coffin, and the other people kept shooting us censorious, uncomprehending glances. Pedro's ill-kempt appearance did not help, not to mention the woollen socks I wore with my sandals and the fact that I too had not shaved since receiving the news of Paulo's death that morning. Samuel did not come to the wake. By the time I woke up to open the door to my stepmother's cleaning troops, he had already left. Lívia arrived at my apartment along with the cleaners, saying: "I just don't believe it, Zi, I just don't believe it. You actually held another supper. I just don't believe it. Who's going to die next?" Hadn't I sworn that there would be no more suppers? No, I hadn't, I . . . Then the phone rang with the news of Paulo's death. He had lain down wrapped in the red flag and he had done another curious thing: around his neck were slung the trainers he used to wear to play five-a-side football, even though he hadn't played it since he was a boy, and that is how he had died. When he found out about the trainers, Pedro said: "I wonder what I should do?"

"What do you mean?"

"I'm going to do something similar. I'm going to discuss it with Mara."

"What are you talking about, Pedro?"

"Mara will know what I should do, how I should die."

His eyes were bloodshot, his face puffy and his hair dishevelled. For the first time since I had met him when we were twelve years old, I was seeing Pedro out of control of his own image, Pedro discovering what the world would be like without Dona Nina.

"I'll be next, you know," said Pedro.

And he sounded almost proud.

Mara was not at the July wake, but Mr Spector was. He waved to me from afar and said, by dint of gestures and grimaces, that our business could wait, that now was not the moment, that he would look me up later, later. Gisela was there, and she came over to tell us that after all these suspicious deaths, she had begun investigating Abel's death. She would order the body to be exhumed. And we had better prepare ourselves because she was going to kick up a terrific fuss. I remembered what Ramos once said, over the cognac, about women challenging men. All women come from one of two different lines, the Judaeo-Christian and the Greek. Those from the Judaeo-Christian line were descended from Eve, whom God had made from Adam's rib in order to serve man, tempt him and accompany him in his fall and ruin. Those from the Greek line were descended from Athena, whom Zeus had plucked from his own brain, and those women never missed a chance to remind men that they were sprung from the head of a god and had nothing to do with men's insides or with their damnation. Gisela belonged to the latter group.

Lívia was not at the wake either, but she was waiting for me in my apartment after the funeral. And she had recruited an unexpected figure to try and force me to confront my own madness and bring me to my senses, a figure I rarely saw: my father. He did most of the talking during this meeting intended to save me from myself, against a background of Lívia's litany of "I don't believe it, I don't believe it", varying only in the stress placed on the "don't" and the "believe". My father was doing his best to understand. Did I know what people were saying about us? That we had gone mad and were engaged in some kind of gastronomic Russian roulette, that the undertakers were beating a path to our door every time we got together. This had to stop. We were just lucky that there had been no police investigation up until now, or a trial, or a scandal in the press. This had to stop!

And then I said something that surprised even me. I said:

"To stop now would be unfair on those who have already died."

"What?"

"I don't believe it," said Lívia. "I don't believe it. I don't believe it."

My father lost patience with me. This normally happens after we have been talking to each other for about ten minutes. On that day it took a little longer. He told me to get a grip on myself. Was I still writing? Did I want to publish a book? Lívia said I had talent. He would pay to have the book published. Perhaps I fancied a trip abroad? Anything to make me stop this madness. I made a supreme effort and said nothing. Finally, he lost patience. If I wanted to continue with this insane behaviour, then fine, but I wasn't going to do it with his money. If I wanted to kill myself, then I should go ahead and kill myself, but he wouldn't finance it. And I couldn't count on any further help from my stepmother to clean up the mess after one of our macabre orgies.

My father left. Lívia stayed.

"I don't believe it. I *don't* believe it. I don't be*lieve* it."

"You don't understand."

"No, I don't, Zi."

"It's a group thing. All this is a, it's a . . . "

What was it? I could not explain something that I myself did not understand. Lívia said:

"Oh, don't talk to me about the group. A pack of useless failures who have never done anything but stuff their faces and ruin other people's lives. Tell me one of them that has ever done anything worthwhile. Poor Marcos tried, but you lot stopped him. Pedro managed to bankrupt the family business, João was a well-heeled conman, Paulo was simply unbearable . . . And Samuel is sick, mad. He ought to be locked up. I'm sure this is all his idea. I'm sure of it. I wonder if this Lucídio even exists. I bet you he's just someone Samuel invented."

"No, Lívia. You don't know what we were like before . . . before this."

"Oh, don't start talking to me about Ramos, please. From what you've told me, he was the sickest of you all."

Lívia had not known us before. She couldn't understand. She had not taken part in the rituals. After Ramos' death, the women had started coming to the suppers, and all they ever heard about was Ramos, about his speeches over the cognac, about the unforgettable tour of Burgundy he had taken us on, about the time when . . . In the end, Pedro's last wife had protested: "You sound like the apostles talking about Christ! Will you stop going on about that Ramos man!"

On that same day, after Lívia had left, having extracted from me a promise that I would stop holding the suppers, would undergo some psychological treatment and eat fibre, lots of fibre, all under her guidance, Tiago arrived at the apartment. Or was that on another day? No, it was the same day. I'm not being very rigorous about writing this; for a few hours now, I've been drinking glass after glass of wine; I can't remember everything, but this, I swear, is how it all happened, more or less anyway. Tiago came to the apartment and told me that, after Pedro's supper, he had followed Lucídio home. Discreetly, of course. We wouldn't want to do anything that might frighten off our brilliant chef or suggest that the deaths might have something to do with him or show any interest in his life beyond what his formality allowed. But did I know where Lucídio lived?

"Where?"

"In Ramos' apartment."

"What do you mean?"

"The same building, the same apartment. I saw his name outside."

Tiago, the inveterate reader of detective novels, had decided to investigate the deaths of our fellow Club members. It didn't surprise me that an obsessive like Tiago should already know so much – did I know, for example, that João had had cancer, and that not even his family knew? Tiago was the most obsessive of us all. He wasn't just addicted to chocolate itself. He knew everything there was to know about chocolate, its history, its composition, the possible chemical explanations for his dependency on it. He belonged to an international society of chocoholics who exchanged information about their common passion. On one of our trips to Europe, he had left the group to meet up with a correspondent of his living in Brussels, and he had returned in a state of wonderment. He had been invited to spend the night at the man's house, and not only was there a kind of chest beside the bed full of chocolate, but the chest itself was made of chocolate, just in case supplies ran short and the person woke up in the middle of the night craving chocolate. The occasion on which Milene, who had provided all the other group members with their first sexual experience, had offered herself to Tiago in exchange for a bar of chocolate had long been part of group folklore, for Tiago had chosen to keep both his virginity and the chocolate. Years later, he had sacrificed a big contract in order to attend a chocolate festival in Switzerland, and his reputation as an architect had never recovered. But then he was obsessive about everything. In his house, he had one room entirely devoted to his detective novels, which filled the bookshelves lining the walls and were piled up on the floor and on tables. Once, Ramos said: "Man is the only animal who always wants more than he needs. Man is man because he wants more." The Chocolate Kid wanted everything and wanted to know everything. Even his curiosity was voracious. He told me that he had looked into the story of the poisonous fish. There was a city called Kushimoto in Japan, and a fish called fugu that could kill if not properly prepared, but there was no secret brotherhood of fugu tasters, unless, of course, it was very, very secret. He had not found the laminated fish scale in any shop selling Japanese artefacts, but he had described it and been told that it might be a scale from a hermaphrodite fish, and that the scale was often carried by homosexuals, a bit like the cocoa bean Tiago had on his key ring to identify him as a chocoholic to other chocoholics. Always assuming, warned Tiago, that the Japanese man in the shop wasn't just making this up.

The Chocolate Kid and I went to the building. It was near enough to my apartment to go there on foot.

It was growing dark. It was cold. Only the curiosity Tiago had aroused in me could have prised me from my squirrel's dray, which, lately, I had only left in order to buy wines in the shopping mall and to go to the monthly wake. There was Lucídio's name as the occupant of number 617, Ramos' old apartment. The porter eyed us mistrustfully, largely because of my sandals and socks, but he yielded to Tiago's amiably insistent questions and began to talk. The young man in 617 had moved into the building recently, about a year ago. It seems he had inherited the apartment from Ramos. Before that, he had apparently lived in Paris. I described Samuel – which was easy enough, I just had to describe a death's head – and I asked the porter if he had seen him coming in and out of the building. He said: "You mean Senhor Samuel? Of course. He often used to come here when Senhor Ramos was alive, but not now." Senhor Lucídio was a very reserved man, always very polite, but very reserved. He didn't go out much and he never had guests. No, he didn't seem to have any family. He was probably at home right now. Would we like him to tell Senhor Lucídio we were there? No, thank you. We asked him not, on any account, to tell Lucídio we had been there and we beat a hasty retreat. The last thing we wanted was for Lucídio to think we were prying into his life.

Days later, I got a phone call from Mara. Be still, my heart. She was worried about Pedro. He had got in touch with her for the first time in many years. He wanted to plan his wake and he thought she would be able to help.

"Plan his wake?"

"He says it's a privilege. Knowing the day and manner of your death and being able to plan your end gives meaning to your life, he says. He wants to prepare everything, and he wants me to help him arrange the wake. He said that only I remember certain things about his life, things that even he has forgotten. He's completely mad. He even wanted to bring over the group of violinists who played at our table in Paris, on our honeymoon, more than twenty years ago, so that they could play at the wake. They were old men then and have probably all died by now. It's absolutely mad. What have you got yourselves into, Daniel?"

"Does Dona Nina know about this?"

"Dona Nina has been completely out of it for years. She spends all day cleaning and disinfecting the bathrooms in Pedro's apartment. And now she's looking for the recorder."

"What recorder?"

"The recorder that Pedro used to play when he was a boy. He can't find it, and now she's hunting high and low for it, without the faintest idea why, but cleaning and disinfecting as she goes."

"What does he want with the recorder?"

"God knows. He wants to die with it. He said that Paulo died with a pair of trainers round his neck. I don't know what he's got in mind. You've got to put a stop to this, Daniel!"

Mara's voice in my ear. I had never heard her voice so close to my ear. The voice of the woman of our dreams; it was marvellous, even when angry, even when repeating what everyone else kept saying to us over and over, that we must put a stop to this madness. But it wasn't madness. I knew now that it wasn't. I couldn't say this to Mara, but I understood Pedro. On death row, everything became definite, everything became ritualized. Not even the violinists from Paris playing at his wake seemed such a bad idea to me. On death row, you have gone beyond a sense of the ridiculous, all you want is meaning.

The Chocolate Kid and Lucídio arranged to meet at my apartment in order to plan the August supper. Tiago arrived first; he had news. Gisela was discussing with her lawyers the possibility of bringing charges against me, personally, as the owner of the killer kitchen, since, although the Beef Stew Club had statutes and a coat of arms, created by Ramos, it was not a legal entity. And Tiago's investigations were beginning to reveal things which we already vaguely knew or suspected, but into which we had preferred not to probe.

"Samuel was brought up by Ramos from when he was a boy. Ramos paid for his education and, up until a certain age, Samuel lived with him. When we met Samuel, in Alberi's bar, he was still living with Ramos."

Four Eggs Samuel, our hero. A rogue and a sage.

Insatiable satyr and scrawny saint. The one who most loved us and most scorned us, the one who had convinced us that we would possess the whole world and who was now punishing us for our failure to conquer it. He had educated us through our appetite and now he was killing us through our appetite, very gently. We had never known anything about him. Perhaps because we preferred him to be a mystery. Whenever anyone asked Samuel about his parents, he would tell them that they had died of the Spanish flu. And if someone commented that this was quite impossible, since the Spanish flu epidemic had reached Brazil at the beginning of the twentieth century, he would respond: "Well, maybe it was Asian flu; I didn't ask it for its passport."

"So he and Lucídio did already know each other?"

"I don't know," said the Kid. "I don't know if your theory is right or not."

My theory was that Samuel was killing us with Lucídio's help. Samuel was methodically practising euthanasia on the members of the Beef Stew Club. Dispatching the angels one by one, liberating them from the bothersome company of their body and from their insignificant biography, definitively separating Zulmira from Zenaide.

"I don't know," said the Kid.

"Not that your investigations will get us anywhere. We're all going to die anyway."

Tiago reacted indignantly.

"Speak for yourself. I've no intention of dying just yet."

I was surprised by his reaction. I assumed that since he had gone along with the ritual this far, it was because he was prepared to go all the way. I had even started pondering my own death scene, once I had eaten my poisoned portion of *gigot d'agneau*. It would definitely include my set of flick football and my St-Estèphe wines. And perhaps a photograph of Mara. Yes, Verônica Roberta would have to be part of the allegorical tableau where they would find me dead. And alongside me a note, a treatise or perhaps a novel about suicide.

Lucídio arrived, his usual formal, elegant self. He said that he was thinking of making a selection of soufflés for Tiago's supper. Three soufflés one after the other, with no entrée, and nothing else. I said that Pedro adored soufflés. Lucídio said nothing. Having sorted out the details of the supper, Tiago took the opportunity to try to draw Lucídio out a little. Just to be friendly, nothing that might alarm him. Those meetings of the fugu brotherhood in Kushimoto, when were they held? At the end of the year, replied Lucídio.

"Does this mean that next year you might not be with us?" joked Tiago.

Lucídio remained utterly serious.

"By next year, I will have nothing more to do here," he said.

He will have killed us all, I thought. And once they had killed us all, what would he and Samuel do? Would they walk into the sunrise holding hands, given that they were both brothers of the order of the scale of the hermaphrodite fish? Or had Samuel merely hired Lucídio to do the job? Or did the job include killing Samuel himself, who, in alphabetical order, would be the next to die after Pedro? It was perfectly possible that the whole tableau had been set up by Samuel for his own suicide. The rest of the group would die first. Before he killed himself, he would kill all those who would remember him. He would kill himself and his own posterity. A total suicide.

Pedro's preparation for being a perfect executive had included classes in art history and music, and before finding perdition with us in Alberi's bar, he had been a gifted player of medieval recorder music. Pedro brought a recorder with him to Tiago's supper. Not the one he had played as a boy, for Dona Nina had failed to find that, but a new one which he had bought two days before and then spent those two days trying to re-learn. Yes, he would give a recorder recital before supper, before the soufflés. Playing the recorder was the last thing he had done well in his life. He had destroyed the companies left to him by his father, he had destroyed his marriage to Mara, but he prided himself on two things: his soufflés and his recorder. He said all this to me when I opened the door to him, and he grabbed me by my shirtfront.

He was wearing a suit, the jacket of which was covered in all kinds of phoney decorations. Electioneering badges and the badges of football teams, medals awarded to his father for services to industry, even bottle tops stuck to his lapel. And he was more perfumed than ever.

"The touch of an angel, you know. The touch of an angel. That's what my recorder teacher used to say: 'You've got the touch of an angel.' And that was the very first time I ever played a recorder. I can still remember it today."

I tried to wrench my shirt from his grasp.

"Come in, Pedro."

But he wouldn't let me go.

"I had to sneak out. They didn't want me to come. Mara may even turn up. To rescue me. Yes, Mara, she's come back, Daniel. My Mara has come back."

"Look, come inside, Pedro."

"Daniel, I want you to speak at my funeral, all right? It has to be you. I've sorted everything out. Mara knows what to do. I want you to be there, Daniel!"

"All right, all right, but let's go in now. Everyone else has arrived."

I could get the whole group in my study now. Samuel, Tiago, Pedro and myself. The Beef Stew Club had become mincemeat. There were more people to toast than people to make the toasts. Fortunately, Pedro forgot about his recorder, and we were spared the recital. He had calmed down a little. But when we went to the supper table, summoned by Lucídio, he made a point of saying a few formal words before the meal. He said that we might not know this, but for a long time he had given money to Paulo and his causes. He had even given money to the armed guerrilla movement. It was a shame Paulo wasn't here to confirm this. Paulo used to call him a bloody reactionary, but that was just a cover. And he had been the one to give Paulo a job when Paulo failed to be re-elected.

"Do you know what?" said Pedro, as if the idea had just occurred to him. "I reckon our companies collapsed because of all that money I gave to left-wing causes."

We all knew that Pedro had been an active supporter of government repression and had only taken Paulo on because Paulo's brother, a member of the secret police, had asked him to. But this, for Pedro, was the moment of truth, so why spoil it with the real truth? The Beef Stew Club looks after its own. On with the soufflés.

Lucídio did not need to ask who wanted the small amount of soufflé – just enough for one – left over in the kitchen. Pedro – who had eaten all the soufflés in turn with growing enthusiasm, exclaiming: "They're even better than mine!" – did not wait for the ritual offer of the final portion. He said: "I want more, I want more!" And: "Man is man because he wants more!" And Lucídio brought in the last serving, which Pedro demolished almost in one forkful.

After the cognac, while Pedro was surveying his happiest memories and concluding that his best moments had been those spent with his dogs, well, first his dogs, and then Mara, Samuel looked fixedly at Lucídio and said:

"The art of our necessities is strange, that can make vile things precious."

Act III, Scene 2.

But if Samuel and Lucídio were accomplices in that ceremonial massacre, how could one explain the look of hatred in Samuel's eye?

9 The Club of Flies

"PHILOCTETES," SAID SAMUEL. WE HAD BEEN barred from entering the chapel where Pedro's body was being guarded by Paulo's brother, the ex-secret policeman, now a beaming retiree, who begged us to respect the family's grief. "Oh, no," he said, smiling, "not you." Through the open door of the chapel we could see Dona Nina beside the open coffin, shooing away imaginary flies from her son's body and, now and again, adjusting a lock of hair or straightening the dead man's tie. Samuel, Tiago and myself were like Philoctetes, the wounded warrior whom no one wanted around because his wound stank. We smelt of mortality. We had gone from being peculiar to being grotesque, and we belonged in exile with Philoctetes on his island, far away from normal people. Then Mara entered the chapel, without even a glance at us. None of Pedro's wishes regarding his own wake were being respected, and a graveside address by me had been unanimously and vigorously vetoed by the family, mainly by Dona Nina, who remembered me as an insalubrious little boy whose proximity to the coffin would doubtless constitute a threat to the dead man. Daniel? Certainly not! The night before, Pedro had arrived back late from supper, but had not gone into the house. He had headed for the kennel at the bottom of the garden. He had decided to die with his dogs. He had been found dead, with his arms around a boxer called Champion and being licked by another called Jackson.

Samuel, Tiago and I set off to the cemetery on foot. Samuel was even more hunched and sombre than usual; he seemed to age several years with each wake. The previous night we had concluded that we were in a dilemma: it was early August and all the members of the Beef Stew Club who were still due to host a supper were dead. Tiago had even suggested that we declare the year over and the Beef Stew Club extinct, but Samuel and I did not agree. Pedro had already considered himself a dead man and he had gone without a murmur. No one said as much, but it did not seem right to end it, whatever "it" was, in that way. It wasn't fair to the dead. That was when Lucídio suggested hosting his own supper. He would make crêpes. A supper consisting entirely of crêpes. He would pay, it was a gift, a present. And so we agreed that September's supper, to be held once more in my apartment, would be Lucídio's homage to the Beef Stew Club, to its dead and to its survivors, and it would be a simple supper of crêpes.

"If the deaths are in alphabetical order, then you're next, Samuel," said Tiago in the cemetery.

"I'm not that keen on crêpes," said Samuel.

"Nor am I," I said.

"Nor am I," said Tiago.

None of us would ask for more crêpes. There would be a supper in September, but no one would ask for more, which would mean there would be little likelihood of another wake in September.

On that late afternoon, while Pedro's wake was being held in the chapel, Samuel, Tiago and myself, the orphans, wandered the cemetery paths, dragging behind us a silence that was becoming heavier and heavier. I usually find it impossible not to talk, but even I said nothing, and Tiago was making a real effort not to ask all the questions he was burning to ask Samuel. He drew breath to speak a dozen times, but lacked the courage. In the end, it was Samuel who spoke, stopping by the statue of a sword-wielding angel that adorned one of the mausoleums.

As we walked back, Samuel began, in the tone of someone arguing with himself: "Certain cultures speak of a Sacred Executioner. He is the necessary murderer, who plays his part in a necessary ritual, and who is not always understood. He is almost always banished and is only understood later on, when he has become a myth. Cain, for example, who is a villain in the Bible, becomes, with the passing of time, a perfectly respectable figure – Cain the patriarch, the founder of cities ... "

I thought he was constructing his own defence and so I took a chance and asked:

"Does this Sacred Executioner choose his role or is he chosen by someone else?"

"No one chooses him. History chooses him. Necessity chooses him."

"But who decides that the ritual is necessary? In our case, for example?"

"What do you mean 'in our case'?"

We had stopped walking.

"I mean in our case, Samuel."

Tiago could contain himself no longer. The Chocolate Kid, the obsessive, needed facts.

"You and Lucídio knew each other already, didn't you, Samuel?"

Samuel said nothing. Then he nodded and added:

"Slightly."

"He's the Sacred Executioner, so what does that make you?"

The question was mine. He shook his head sadly. He began walking again, and we followed. Without turning round, he said:

"You simply don't understand."

*

We arrived back at the chapel as the cortège was leaving. We walked behind the cortège, keeping our distance as exiles. I saw Gisela, who looked away, and Mr Spector, who again sent me semaphore signals, which I understood to announce an imminent visit. We were standing some distance away as Pedro was placed in the family vault, beside his father, unaccompanied by any speech. Mara had her arm around Dona Nina, who seemed quite calm. Her Pedro was finally free of all contagion. Only when the small crowd began to disperse did Samuel, who was next to me, speak again.

"In our case, I'm the person to be executed."

We had gone to the wake in Tiago's car. I don't have a car. I've never been allowed to drive. Ever since I was a child I have shown a natural talent for accidents. It is my only apparent talent. On the way back from the cemetery, Tiago said:

"I don't know about you, but I think it's time we put an end to this little game."

Samuel and I said nothing. Tiago went on:

"All right, then. We'll have our last supper, eat our crêpes, and then call a halt, right?"

We continued in silence. Samuel was sitting in the passenger seat next to Tiago, and I was in the back.

"I think we should denounce Lucídio before someone else does. Gisela is making moves to do just that. She says she's going to investigate Abel's death, that she's going to bring charges. Any day now, they'll arrest Lucídio and us along with him as, oh, I don't know, as accomplices I suppose. And another thing . . . "

"'Wanton boys'," I said.

Samuel turned his head.

"What?"

"'Wanton boys'. Where does that come from?"

"*King Lear.*"

"You're not even listening to me, damn it!" said Tiago angrily.

Here's the full quotation. I bought a paperback copy of *King Lear* in the shopping mall the following day. My English is even worse than my memory, and it wasn't easy tracking down all the quotations I had heard from the lips of Lucídio and Samuel during the past few months. But "wanton boys" is there. Act IV, Scene 1. "As flies to wanton boys are we to the gods; they kill us for their sport." Ramos had told me about his "wanton boys", one in Brazil, the other in Paris. The one in Brazil was Samuel, a "wanton boy" *par excellence*. The one in Paris was Lucídio. Ramos had perhaps paid for Lucídio's cookery course. He had probably passed on to both of them his taste for "Shakespeare and sauces". He had doubtless made them both learn the whole of *King Lear* by heart. And that, judging by what I had seen, was not exactly a proof of love. In the version I bought in

116

the shopping mall, the footnotes explaining the incomprensible words take up a good part of each page. The explanations are longer than the actual text. During the last few months, Lucídio and Samuel had been duelling with quotations from *King Lear*. Whatever was going on, it was something that concerned Lucídio and Samuel. It wasn't about us, about our punishment or our redemption. "I'm the one to be executed," Samuel had said. We were just the flies. We were dying like flies.

My father carried out his threat to stop my allowance. Nothing is going into my bank account. Lívia won't let me die of hunger, but I need to find a way of earning enough money to buy some nuts. I don't know how to do anything. Once I thought of writing specialized cookery books. A guide to aphrodisiac meals, another to meals that were entirely red or white or brown. A book of exotic meals from around the world, with ingredients like dog, monkey, ants, grasshoppers. A compilation of meals made or consumed in strange situations, like eggs fried on asphalt, three-yard-wide pizzas, jelly being licked from somebody's navel. There wouldn't be a market for my stories of the lesbian Siamese twins, especially now that they have entered their final phase of terminal terror, with Zenaide forced to remain eternally awake in order not to be bitten by her vampire sister, and Zulmira distracted by endless ramblings about the human condition, about appetite, obsession and death. Lívia thinks that, since I've never grown up, I should write for children. And I've been trying to think of ways of adapting the stories of the lesbian Siamese twins to make them suitable for children.

Tiago was in a good mood when he arrived at my apartment for the crêpe supper. He said:

"So we agree, do we, that tonight no one is going to poison anyone? Is that right?"

Lucídio was in the kitchen. Samuel was sunk in one of the leather armchairs in my study. After opening the door to Tiago, I returned to the armchair facing Samuel, from which, for the last fifteen minutes, I had been observing his sinister silence. We paid no attention to Tiago, who cancelled his smile, slumped down in another leather armchair and resigned himself to the prevailing quiet. Samuel hadn't said a word since he arrived. After another five minutes of silence, I spoke.

"So, you're the one about to be executed."

"That's right."

"By Lucídio."

"That's right."

"Why?"

"Revenge."

We sat waiting for Samuel to continue, but he wasn't prepared to make our interrogation easy.

"What has Lucídio got to avenge?" asked Tiago.

"Ramos' death."

Tiago and I glanced at each other. It was my turn:

"What did you have to do with Ramos' death?"

"I was the executioner."

I thought he meant AIDS. Samuel had been Ramos' lover and felt responsible for Ramos' illness. But Tiago thought differently. He had no time for metaphors. He preferred his detective stories to be simple and direct.

"Ramos died of AIDS."

"No, he was poisoned. I poisoned him."

I still thought he was talking in metaphors.

"You mean you poisoned him with the virus."

"No, I poisoned him with the mint sauce."

Lucídio came into the study to say that there were two types of caviar to serve with the first course of crêpes, black and red. Would we like both or did we have some preference? We unanimously voted to have both. Lucídio returned to the kitchen.

The Sacred Executioner, then, was Samuel. He had killed Ramos in order to hasten Ramos' death. He wasn't thinking of Lucídio when he mentioned the Sacred Executioner in the cemetery. He was the necessary murderer. Lucídio was retribution. And we were the flies.

"Now, hang on a moment, hang on . . ."

Tiago was completely lost. He asked for clarification.

"You poisoned Ramos, Lucídio found out . . ."

I broke in:

"How did Lucídio find out?"

"Ramos told him. He wrote to him from the hospital, on his last day."

"Did Ramos know you had poisoned him?"

"He asked me to poison him."

"Now, hang on a moment, hang on . . ."

"You put poison in the mint sauce at Ramos' last supper because you knew that only he would put mint sauce on the lamb. Because you loved him and wanted to ease his suffering. Because he asked you to."

Samuel was sitting with his eyes closed, supporting his head with his fingertips resting on his temples. He opened his eyes and stared at me for a long time before speaking.

"I loved you all, Daniel."

Tiago was growing impatient.

"Now, hang on a moment, let's just go over . . ."

"What exactly did you want from us, Samuel? You must have known, right from the start, that none of us would ever amount to much. From the days at Alberi's bar, you knew that no one there would ever be anyone. You wanted to save us, you experimented with all the vices for us, you fought for us, you almost killed yourself for us, you even screwed Mara for us, and we never knew what it was you wanted from us."

"And now it's too late," said Samuel, smiling and revealing his blackened teeth.

Tiago wanted to get back to the part of the story that interested him. If Lucídio wanted to have revenge on Samuel for killing Ramos, why did he not poison him first? Why kill everyone else and leave Samuel to last? Samuel gestured with both hands in my direction, still smiling, indicating that he was giving me the right to reply for him. The floor was mine.

"Because they are both bad little boys, Tiago. Because Lucídio wanted to prove to Samuel that he could be even crueller than him. Because the best revenge Lucídio could take was to kill not only Samuel, but to kill everyone he loved first. We were just the flies."

"And because he," added Samuel, indicating Lucídio, who had just come into the study to announce that supper was served, "is an utter bastard."

And he added, getting up from the armchair:

"In the worst sense of the word."

We drank iced vodka toasts to hunger, to Ramos, to Abel, João, Marcos, Saulo, Paulo and Pedro. Lucídio remained standing by the table as we ate the first course of crêpes, with red and black caviar. He took no part in the conversation.

"And you just kept quiet," said Tiago. "You let him kill us one by one . . ."

"I wanted to see how far he would go," said Samuel, squeezing lemon juice over the black caviar. "Call it morbid curiosity."

"But, but . . ."

Tiago was so indignant he almost forgot about the caviar. He certainly wasn't going to choke to death on caviar.

"And what are *we* doing here, Tiago?" I asked. "Why are we allowing ourselves to be poisoned? No one wanted to miss a single one of Lucídio's suppers. Apart from those who had already died, of course."

"I came for the food, not for the poison."

"But you came."

Samuel had finished his crêpes and caviar. He always ate more quickly than the rest of us. He said:

"You knew, right from the start, that this was some form of retribution, and that Lucídio was the executioner. It's just that you all thought the ritual had to do with you, that the retribution was aimed at you, that you were the sinners. Everyone died convinced that they deserved to die."

"Apart from André," I said, correcting him.

"Who?"

"André."

We had left André out of the toasts. André, sacrificed by accident. The only innocent party in the whole affair.

"But anyway, it's over now," said Tiago.

"No, it isn't," said Samuel.

"It's over, it's over. Gisela is taking legal action. She's going to bring charges. I'm going to take steps too. This madness is over. Sacred Executioner, retribution . . . my eye! This is murder, my friends, pure and simple."

Tiago looked at Lucídio, who was collecting up the empty plates, and felt obliged to add:

"Nothing personal, you understand."

After the first course of crêpes came more crêpes with various toppings, which Lucídio placed around the table. Tiago insisted that Lucídio sit down at the table with us, just to show that there were no hard feelings. After all, setting everything else aside, Lucídio was a great chef who deserved our admiration and respect. And Tiago saw with satisfaction that Lucídio ate the food he himself had prepared.

We picked at the crêpes. None of us was particularly keen on them. Lucídio offered to make a few more, but we all declined. For Tiago, the important thing was not to let Lucídio out of our sight for a second, especially in the kitchen.

"Are you sure you don't want more?" Lucídio asked Tiago.

"No, thank you."

"Dessert?"

Tiago hesitated.

"Is it more crêpes?"

"No, it's chocolate marquise."

Tiago swallowed hard.

"Chocolate marquise?"

"That's right. But there's just one problem . . . "

"What's that?"

"There's only enough for one. I didn't have time and . . . "

The Chocolate Kid gave us a look of terrible sadness. What were we doing to him?

"You have it Kid," I said.

"Yes, you eat it Tiago," said Samuel. "I don't want it."

"But I don't want it either!" screamed Tiago.

"Then I'll eat it," said Lucídio, going back into the kitchen.

"Wait!"

Lucídio turned round. Tiago asked him how he had made the chocolate marquise. Lucídio told him in detail. As Lucídio spoke, Tiago seemed slowly to collapse, like someone imploding in slow motion. When Lucídio had finished his description, Tiago was slumped over the table, his arms hanging by his side, his head resting on the cloth. He remained in that position as he said:

"I'll have it."

Lucídio stood by the table while the Chocolate Kid devoured the marquise with tears pouring down his cheeks.

"'Dost thou know the difference between a bitter fool and a sweet fool?'"

I've found it already. Act I, Scene 4.

Samuel got up from his chair and went over to Lucídio. Samuel:

"We have to arrange the October supper."

Lucídio:

"The fifteenth."

Samuel:

"Here."

Lucídio:

"I'll cook."

Samuel:

"My favourite dish is beef stew with egg *farofa* and fried banana."

Lucídio:

"Your favourite dish is *cassoulet.*"

Samuel:

"I've changed."

10 Mr Spector's Visit

"THINGS THAT LOVE NIGHT LOVE NOT SUCH
nights as these." *King Lear*, you can ask me anything
you like about it now. "In such a night . . . " It was a night
of Shakespearian storms, with artificial lightning and
thunder from a thunder sheet, when Samuel and Lucídio
met for the final scene of their story, in my apartment, in
my empty rooms. At the Chocolate Kid's funeral, which we
witnessed from afar because they would not let us into the
cemetery, Samuel had said:

"Of course I'll go to the supper. I owe it to the group."

"In the name of the group, I release you from that debt."

"It's too late now."

"In such a night . . . " It was pouring with rain, the wind
was shaking the windows, and, when Lucídio came into
the large salon bearing the tray with the beef stew, the
egg *farofa* and fried bananas, the lights all went out. For

a considerable time, only flashes of lightning lit the scene: Samuel and I eating the beef stew, filling our mouths with beef stew, egg *farofa* and fried bananas and grunting like pigs, and Lucídio standing stiffly by the table in his long white apron, with the table cloth and the walls turning blue with every lightning flash, and us washing down the food with Coca-Cola just as we used to do at Alberi's bar. By the time the lights came on again, we had finished. Lucídio asked Samuel if he wanted more. Samuel said no.

"No?"

"Look, don't take this the wrong way, but Alberi's beef stew was much better. Beef stew just isn't your forte."

"Are you sure you don't want any more?"

Samuel took a few moments to respond. Outside in the street, there were cataracts and hurricanoes and winds cracking their cheeks.

"All right," said Samuel. "Bring me another fried banana."

If Samuel had prepared some final words, he did not have time to say them. He died eight minutes after eating the banana, contorted with pain. He was the only one whom I actually saw die. I watched his death agony paralysed, gripping the edge of the table, unable to take my eyes off that body in convulsions on my parquet floor. Seeing Samuel die cured me of any idea of allowing myself to be poisoned too, of carrying the ritual to its logical conclusion. That particular story was over. I don't know why I was saved. Perhaps simply to be the one who survived to tell the tale. The spasms shaking Samuel's body finally ceased. I was just about to stand up when Lucídio stopped me with a gesture. He dragged the corpse over to one of my sofas. Then, as he began clearing the table, he said:

"Call an ambulance."

"An ambulance?"

"They'll assume it was a heart attack."

"But what about his family . . ."

"He hasn't got any family. He hasn't got anyone."

"But they'll be suspicious . . ."

"Why?"

"Yet another death."

"So?"

Lucídio was heading back to the kitchen. I sat down again, stunned. Then I jumped. The ambulance. The phone. Where was the phone? I was in my own apartment, but I didn't know where the phone was. I only found it when it began to ring. I followed the sound. It was Lívia, wanting to know if I had eaten.

"Yes, I've eaten."

"What?"

"What do you mean 'what'?"

"What did you eat, Zi?"

"Beef stew. *Farofa*. Banana."

Lívia was surprised. That wasn't amongst the frozen meals with which she had stocked up my freezer for the week. Beef stew? *Farofa?* Banana?

"I'm coming over, Zi. You sound odd."

"No don't, you can't come out in this storm."

"What storm?"

I looked out of the window. There was no storm.

"I'm fine. I'm going to bed now. We'll talk tomorrow."

"Did you hear about Gisela?"

"No, what happened?"

"She's dead."

"What? But how?"

"Apparently her heart gave out."

"Her heart? At eighteen?"

"That's right."

Lucídio volunteered to tell the ambulance crew what had happened. I was in no state to speak. We had been eating, when Samuel had suddenly stood up, clutching his chest, and the next thing we knew he was under the table. We had tried to revive him, but without success. No, we didn't know his family. He lived alone. Who should be informed of his death? We had no idea. Who would pay for the funeral? Lucídio glanced at me. I nodded. And I began calculating what I could sell in my apartment in order to get hold of some money.

The only people present at the October wake, Samuel's wake, were myself and Mr Spector. Lívia wouldn't come with me. She isn't talking to me, not since she found out about Samuel dying in my apartment. She wasn't convinced when I told her that it really had been a heart attack, that it had nothing to do with the suppers, the group, the madness. Mr Spector approached discreetly and asked: "Cancer?" I replied: "Heart" and he shook his head and said something which, at the time, I didn't understand:

"I'm sure he won't regret it."

I arranged for Mr Spector to visit me two days later, to talk. He realized that this wasn't the moment. After burying Samuel, I caught a taxi and asked to be taken to the district where we used to live. I hadn't been there for years. Where Alberi's bar had been, there was now a video shop. I stood on the pavement staring at the new building and trying to remember how the old one used to look. I caught another taxi and returned to my tree house. If I had been saved in order to remember, then I would do a pretty terrible job. That is why I started to write.

Mr Spector began by saying that he had heard of our "organization" through a friend, and that he was interested in what we were doing because it chimed in with an idea of his own, or rather, it wasn't just his idea, but that of a group of people he represented. A group.

"Interested in what we're doing?"

"That's right. I don't know quite how I'd describe it . . . Mercy killings, perhaps?"

"Mercy killings?"

"Easeful deaths?"

"Easeful deaths?"

"Terminal pleasures?"

"Terminal pleasures?"

"What would you call it, sir?"

"What would I call what?"

"What you do, killing people with an excess of what they most like."

He interpreted my silence as wariness and hastened to reassure me that I could trust him, that any agreement we reached would be strictly confidential.

"Right, hm. Yes. This friend of yours . . . Could you tell me what exactly he told you?"

"He's more than a friend, really, he's my cousin. A doctor. He was treating a patient with terminal cancer who decided, shall we say, to take advantage of the services your organization offers and to allow you to kill him. This friend of mine, this cousin, didn't approve, obviously, although he's not entirely against the concept."

"What concept?"

"Of . . . euthanasia with joy."

"Euthanasia with joy?"

"Orgiastic release."

"Orgiastic release?"

"Going out with a bang."

"Going out with a bang?"

"Sympathetic apotheosis?"

"Sympathetic apoth . . . Listen, what exactly did this patient tell the doctor?"

"That you killed terminal patients in the manner of their choosing. With an excess of good food, with an excess of sex, with an excess of whatever gave them pleasure."

João always was a liar.

"And what exactly are you proposing?"

"I represent a group of people interested in taking part in this initiative."

"You represent a group of people interested in investing in our, erm, organization?"

"No, no. They're interested in using your services, they're interested in dying in your hands."

I must have pulled a face, because Mr Spector added quickly:

"And prepared to pay good money for it. In advance, of course."

"Of course."

I asked for time to think about it. I needed to consult the other members of the, erm, organization. We had never considered expanding our services like that. We normally only helped out friends. We were a sort of club of death in a way. We manufactured angels, but only angels we knew, always assuming that anyone who died in our hands, begging for more, more, more, could properly be called an angel. As I'm sure you will understand, we need to consider the practical details, the moral connotations, the possible legal implications, it's not easy. Mr Spector said that he understood. We agreed that he would come back tomorrow to find out our response. As he was leaving, I asked if Mr Spector was himself ill with a terminal disease and he, with a modest air, said no, he was merely an intermediary. But he confessed that he had often thought of the happiness it must bring to be able to plan one's own end. It would be a little like looking at the last page of a mystery story before you read it. That way you would read it more intelligently.

I phoned Lucídio, fearing that he might have left town. But he was still in the same apartment. He did not have the slightest intention of leaving. Which meant that he was not in the least concerned that I would reveal everything I knew about his terrible revenge. Since he had also eliminated Gisela, though how I don't know, and since I could not possibly denounce him without admitting my own complicity in the affair, all he needed to do was to allow time to pass and for people to forget about the sad demise of the Beef Stew Club. He could then open a restaurant with the money left over from his inheritance from Ramos. I told him about Mr Spector's visit and his proposal, expecting Lucídio to burst out laughing. But Lucídio never laughs. He asked if I was sure that Mr Spector really was who he said he was. He might be a police inspector, perhaps he was carrying out an investigation, perhaps he had invented that whole story about a group who wanted to die of pleasure because he knew of my taste for unlikely stories. He suggested that we invite Mr Spector to supper in order to talk over his proposal, tomorrow. And he said:

"After all, I still haven't made your *gigot d'agneau.*"

Today, when Mr Spector arrives, I'm going to invite him to supper. I hope he likes *gigot d'agneau* too. The more I think about his idea, the more I like it. If Lucídio agrees, we could earn a lot of money, and I need money. St-Estèphe wines are getting dearer and dearer, and I've sold everything in my apartment, apart from Marcos' paintings, which nobody wants to buy. With Mr Spector as our agent, supplying us with clients eager to experience our sympathetic apotheoses, we might even consider expanding the business and making it more like the lie that João invented for his doctor, more like the bizarre tale told by our teller of jokes. I can see us not only killing the terminally ill at grand suppers in my empty rooms, but also organizing Caribbean cruises for the dying, millionaires' tours of Europe's capitals, of Asia's dens of iniquity, of all the world's definitive pleasures, providing mortal adventures, ultimate ecstasies, fatal extremes, supreme orgasms, monumental erections to whoever wants more, always more, and more, more, more, more, more, more, more, more, more, more, more, more . . . Daniel, stop it!